# CRASH & CARNAGE

Tarnished Angels Motorcycle Club Book 2

## EMMA SLATE

Tabula Rasa Publishing

This book is a work of fiction. Names, characters, places, and incidents
are the product of the author's imagination or are used fictitiously. Any
resemblance to actual events, locales, or persons, living or dead, is
coincidental.

## Crash & Carnage
### (TARNISHED ANGELS MOTORCYCLE CLUB BOOK 2)

Adderly "Boxer" Ford is nothing like the men of my past.

He's an outlaw.

A criminal.

My opposite in every way.

I save lives.

He takes them.

I'm makeup and mink.

He's leather and ink.

I'm a fan of monogamy.

I'm not sure Boxer knows the definition of the word.

It's a bad idea to get mixed up with him and his motor-cycle club.

But when his lips meet mine, and his fingers plow through my hair, my desire for an orderly, safe life goes out the window.

In his bed, I discover passion.

With his club, I find a family.

In his arms, I am safe.

I don't belong in Boxer's world.

But when you fall for a Tarnished Angel, you get a lot more than you bargain for.

## Prologue

*NOW OR NEVER.*

I lurched forward, slid my zip-tied wrists over Paul's head, and yanked them against his neck. I pressed my knees to the back of the seat and used leverage to choke him. I pulled with all my might.

"What the fuck!" Cletus shouted from the passenger side.

Paul reared back, his foot slamming down on the gas as he tried to relieve the tension on his neck. The car shot forward and the engine screamed, sounding like it was going to explode. Paul gasped and lifted his hands up and clawed at my arms. His knee jerked the wheel, causing the vehicle to veer out of the lane and onto the shoulder of the highway.

Cletus grabbed on to the passenger door to brace himself as the car continued to swerve.

Anger and adrenaline coursed through me.

I was out for blood.

I tightened my hold on Paul's windpipe as he

attempted to regain control of the car, which kept diverging on and off the road. His foot refused to release the gas.

Cletus reached into his pants and pulled out a pocketknife. He flicked it open and stabbed me deep in the meaty part of my upper arm near my shoulder.

I yelled in pain, but I still wouldn't let go. It only enraged me further, and I yanked my fists into Paul's Adam's apple as hard as I could.

"Let off the fucking gas!" Cletus bellowed.

A gurgle escaped Paul's lips, and I looked in the rearview mirror. His face was red. Blood vessels and capillaries burst in his eyes making him look like a deep-sea diver who'd come to the surface too fast.

My strength was waning, but if I could just hold on a little longer…

Cletus grabbed my hand and then slid the knife through the zip ties holding my wrists together. I lost my clasp on Paul's neck and fell backward.

A horn blared from the oncoming lane.

"Fuck!" Cletus yelled, dropping the knife and wrenching the wheel so we didn't collide with the approaching truck.

Cletus overestimated the torque, and combined with our demonic speed, the small car screeched and skidded across the asphalt, tilting up on its side as we veered to the right.

My body catapulted into the door, and my head smacked against the glass. Stars danced before my eyes, clouding my vision.

I prayed the vehicle would right itself.

But God didn't hear my prayer.

The car flipped, and the world stilled.

For a heartbeat, we were suspended in midair...and then the vehicle turned upside down.

Screeching metal across asphalt was the last sound I heard before I passed out.

# Chapter 1

*A couple of months earlier…*

"I'm stupid jealous of you right now," Emily said with a shake of her head.

"You're jealous of me?" I demanded. "Why?"

"Why? Because you get to examine that hottie over yonder."

"Over yonder?" I asked in amusement. "You cute little Texan, you."

"Shut up. And check him out." Emily tilted her head toward the examination area. A man with dirty blond hair sat on a hospital bed, his left hand pressed against the lower right-hand side of his body. His face was pinched in obvious pain.

He had scruff for days and hair that was mussed just enough to look like a woman had been running her fingers through it. He wore a black leather vest and leather boots with thick soles.

"When did he come in?" I asked.

"About fifteen minutes ago. Justine checked him in."

"That means his information is already in the system," I said, reaching for my tablet with his medical files. "Justine is a powerhouse of organization and efficiency."

"She missed her calling as a Marine general."

I grinned, turned my attention back to the patient's chart, and reviewed his symptoms. "Appendicitis."

"You sure?"

"Can't be completely sure without examining him first, but yeah, I feel pretty confident."

"Wanna bet?" she asked.

"What did you have in mind?"

"If you're right, you have to come out to happy hour with me and the other nurses."

"And if I'm wrong?"

"How often are you wrong?" she asked. "You've been here a month, and you've already got the best diagnostic statistics of any doctor in the ER. I'm literally betting you're right to ensure that I win."

"Now you're just trying to flatter me."

"Is it working?"

I smiled. "Kinda, yeah." I raised the tablet again and looked at the man's chart for his name.

"Adderly Ford," I said. "What kind of name is *Adderly Ford?*"

"The hot kind."

"You're boy crazy."

"Boy crazy is for teenagers. I'm man crazy—and totally proud of it. You could do with being a little man crazy."

I rolled my eyes.

"I bet he smells like woodsmoke and whisky," she said dreamily.

*He probably smells like cheap perfume and sex.* A man who looked like him—dressed like him—yeah, he screamed skirt chaser.

I looked in his direction. He was staring at the ground, wincing with each breath.

"Please sniff him and report back," Emily said.

"Emily," Justine barked from a few feet away.

I saluted Emily and left her to go toe-to-toe with Justine. With the tablet in one hand, I approached the man.

"Mr. Ford," I greeted. "I'm Dr. Ward. I'll be examining you today."

He slowly raised his head and stared at me with glassy, gray eyes. Dove gray. Beautiful. Fringed with long blond lashes.

"Call me Boxer."

"Boxer," I said with a nod.

"You're my doctor?"

"Yes."

He attempted a grin, but it came out as a grimace.

"What?"

Boxer grunted. "Nothing, I just—wow, okay."

I pulled the curtain closed around the cot to give us privacy. After setting down the tablet on a stainless-steel tray next to the bed, I reached for a pair of Nitrile gloves.

"I looked at your chart, and I need to examine you. Will you please unbutton your pants and lift your shirt?"

"Your wish is my command," he joked, but his smile was strained. His complexion was ashen and the blond hair at his temples was dark with sweat.

He lowered his jeans a couple of inches and raised his black shirt so I could see his belly. I ignored the six-pack, the light dusting of blond fuzz, and the swirls of ink marking his skin. I gently palpated his tender abdomen.

A hiss of air left his mouth.

"How long have you been in pain?" I asked.

"A few days. I took some ibuprofen, which seemed to help a bit, but today it got a lot worse. It's not going away, Doc."

"You can button your pants now. I'm ordering some scans to confirm what I believe is appendicitis, but I'd like to get you in surgery as soon as—"

Boxer leaned over and vomited on my sneakers.

"Possible," I finished with a sigh.

"His pressure is dropping, Dr. Ward," Jackie said.

"Dr. Maxwell," I called out to the anesthesiologist, my eyes still on Boxer, who was draped and unconscious on the table. "Talk to me."

Dr. Maxwell had jumped off his stool at the beep.

I dropped the suture clamp onto the operating tray. The nurses rolled over the defibrillator setup in case I needed to jump start Boxer's heart.

"Looks like he's having an allergic reaction to the anesthesia," Dr. Maxwell pronounced. "I'm administering epinephrine. Everybody take a deep breath and give it sixty seconds."

Dr. Maxwell quickly prepared a syringe of epinephrine from the tray in front of his station and administered it to Boxer's IV. After a few moments, the beeping stopped and Dr. Maxwell said, "His pressure's stabilizing. I think we're good."

There was a collective sigh of relief in the room, and then Jackie rolled the defibrillator back to its position in the corner.

"Excellent," I said. "Let's finish flushing out the cavity,

and then we can close."

The operating room was my sanctuary. My haven.

I was good at this. Sometimes, I felt like it was the *only* thing I was good at.

"He was lucky," Jackie said.

I looked up at her. Her brown eyes were crinkled at the corners, and I knew she was smiling behind her mask.

"Lucky, how?" I demanded.

"His appendix only just burst—it could've been a lot worse."

"Nearly slipping into anaphylactic shock from an allergic reaction to the anesthesia for a routine surgery doesn't sound very lucky to me." I sighed in frustration.

An hour later, I strode into the waiting room and looked around. A group of swarthy tattooed men wearing leather sat in the corner, and for just a moment I found myself observing them before I said, "I'm looking for Adderly Ford's—Boxer's—family."

"That's us." A dark-haired, hulking, broody giant rose. He gestured to several other men with him. "We're Boxer's family. I'm Colt."

He held out his massive paw toward me. I shook it firmly and tried not to be intimidated.

"Nice to meet you, Colt." My eyes swept over his leather vest pocket with a patch that read, *President.*

It all made sense now. Boxer's nickname. The leather vest. The boots and tattoos.

Boxer was a biker.

The few people in the waiting room had given Boxer's friends a wide berth. The men in leather saturated the space, their collective aura radiating a back-the-hell-off energy that was both mesmerizing and titillating.

Another man with dark brown hair and a jaw that

looked like it could cut marble peered at me as he asked, "How is he, Doc?"

I had to tilt my head back so I could meet his eyes and then my gaze wandered from him to the others.

"His appendix ruptured," I announced.

There was a smattering of rumbled curses, but when I raised my hand to get their attention, they surprised me by quieting down almost immediately.

"He'll be on heavy antibiotics for a couple of weeks, just to ensure there's no infection. We cleaned his abdominal cavity, and we'll monitor him closely the next couple of days while he's here."

"Whew." The blond blue-eyed devil shook his head. "I knew the fucker was sicker than he said he was."

"You were the one passing him the bottle of bourbon," Colt said dryly. "To help him self-medicate."

"When can we see him?" the blond asked me, ignoring Colt completely.

"Tomorrow during visiting hours. Right now, he needs to rest."

"Tomorrow it is then. Come on, boys," Colt called to the other men in leather. To me, he said, "Thanks, Doc."

The men trekked to the elevator. Their vests all had the same emblem on the backs: a skull flanked with angel's wings. I hadn't expected them to be genuinely concerned about their friend's well-being; I knew very little about bikers or biker clubs, only what I had seen in pop culture.

I also couldn't believe how insanely attractive they all were. They were all so virile and...earthy.

"Um, was that a fleet of hot bikers I just saw?" Peyton asked.

"I prefer the term convoy," I joked. "But yes."

"Wow. Just wow," she said, as we headed toward the lounge.

"Yeah, I didn't think bikers could look like that. I expected… I don't know. Something else."

"I get it." She chuckled.

"What's so funny?" I asked.

"You were staring up at them, and your eyes were ping-ponging from one to the next."

"Oh, shut up," I said with a laugh as I followed her into the staff lounge.

She went to the refrigerator and pulled out two bottles of water and handed me one. "It's okay, you know."

"What is?"

"To admit you want to scratch your itch with a biker."

"*Me?*" I raised my brows. "What about you?"

"What about me," she averred.

"Yeah, okay. You're not ready to scratch your itch and neither am I."

# Chapter 2

"How are you feeling this morning?" I asked, as I stepped into Boxer's recovery room.

"Like roadkill."

"I'm sorry to hear that."

"Don't be. It's a step up from how I was feeling yesterday."

He smiled at me, and I couldn't help but smile back. Boxer seemed to have a natural good cheer that was hard to shake.

I took a moment to discreetly study him. His jaw was covered in stubble a shade darker than the dirty blond hair on his head that was askew. Ink snaked up his muscled arms to disappear beneath the hospital gown. I'd seen some of his tattoos the night before when I'd removed his appendix, but I hadn't studied them, my mind clearly on other concerns at the time. But I was innately curious about them now.

*Interested in his body—his hot body.*

"Well, Doc? Am I gonna live?" he drawled.

"You'll live, but there were some complications we didn't expect."

His expression instantly changed from good humor to attention. "What kind of complications?"

"Your appendix ruptured on your way to surgery. You're on heavy antibiotics to ensure you don't get an infection."

When I paused, he nodded.

"During surgery, your blood pressure dropped substantially. We deduced that you have an allergy to the anesthesia you were given. There was no way to know until you were already under. I've made a note in your chart, but that's something you need to be aware of in case you have to undergo any other surgeries. It's very serious. We could have lost you last night."

"I almost died?"

"Yes."

"Fuck," he murmured. "That's—I don't even—okay then. That was not how I expected to go out."

"Go out?"

"Die," he stated. "Dying on an operating table? In a hospital gown? Fucking pathetic."

I wasn't sure what to say to comfort him. It was like he was taking it as a personal insult. But death was death and none of us got to choose how our time came to an end. Luckily, this wasn't Boxer's end.

I cleared my throat, wanting to move the conversation forward. "I'm keeping you here for a few days to monitor you and make sure the antibiotics are doing their job and that there are no further complications of any kind."

"You've got to be kidding me," he muttered. "First I almost die like some frail old man and now I've got to laze around here? I'm gonna go crazy."

"Which is a nice segue into what's going to happen when I release you into the wild, I presume."

"I'm not gonna like this, am I?"

"Probably not." I smiled. "Rule number one: no alcohol. Not until you're back on your regular diet, which will be in a few weeks."

"How many rules are there? Should I be writing these down?"

I glowered at him. "I mean it, Boxer. Do not put any undue stress on your body. Do you hear me?"

"Yeah, Doc, I hear you." It was his turn to scowl.

"Rule number two: no strenuous activity for a few weeks. You can walk around, climb the stairs, but no lifting anything over twenty pounds. And no sex or masturbation."

"Doc, come on. You're taking away my two favorite hobbies," Boxer complained. "What the hell am I supposed to do for the next few weeks?"

"Hydrate and rest. Perhaps read a book or two," I suggested. "I hear it expands the mind."

"Does a dirty magazine count?" he threw back.

"Let me guess, you read them for the articles, right?"

He smiled.

"You could learn to knit," I suggested. "I hear it's all the rage again."

"Kill me. Kill me now."

I ignored his snark. "I want to stress something else. The next time you're in that kind of pain with a fever of over 102 °F, I suggest seeing a physician, not the bottom of a bourbon bottle."

"How'd you know it was bourbon?"

"I smelled it when you vomited all over my shoes," I said dryly.

"Oh, yeah. Sorry about that."

"You aren't the first man to throw up on me, and sadly, I doubt you'll be the last. You should get some rest." I headed for the door.

"Doc?"

"Yeah?" I looked at him over my shoulder.

His grin was lopsided, sincere. "Thanks for saving my life."

I paused for a moment and then met him smile for smile. "It was my pleasure."

As a general surgeon, most of my surgeries were scheduled and I'd performed two procedures that morning already. I worked the ER on rotation. After checking on a few of my patients, I caught a couple hours of sleep in an on-call room. By noon, I was eating lunch in the lounge and making follow-up notes in a patient's chart about her gallbladder removal.

"Hey, Linden," Peyton greeted.

"Hey," I replied. "You done for the day?"

"Yup. Heading out now. What about you?"

"I have a few more notes to write up, and then I'm done."

"Emily wanted me to tell you that you owe her a drink. What's that about, anyway?"

"Last night when Boxer came into the ER, we had a bet about his diagnosis. She said if I was correct, I had to go to happy hour with the girls and buy her a drink."

"She's doing anything and everything to try and get you to socialize," Peyton said.

"I made the mistake once of going out with you guys when I first moved here. I've never been so hungover in my entire life."

"A rite of passage when you hang with the nurses." She winked. "You know it's just because we adore you, right? You're not like the other doctors here."

Her words warmed my heart. "I appreciate that. I really do."

"But you're still not going to risk your liver's future by drinking with us at happy hour?"

"Right you are," I said with a laugh.

"See you tomorrow then."

"Bye."

I finished my lunch and quickly moved through the rest of my charts. As I chucked the plastic silverware in the trash along with the container that once had macaroni salad, my pager buzzed. I immediately headed to the nurses' station.

"I got a page."

"Hey." Amanda smiled. "Boxer's refusing morphine."

I blinked. "Refusing morphine? Don't be silly. There's no way he's refusing morphine a day after surgery."

"Sure as I'm standing here in front of you," Amanda stated. "It's kind of hot."

"What is?" I demanded. "The fact that he's choosing to be in pain when he could be comfortable?"

"Well, yeah." Amanda raised her brows. "Do you have lipstick in your pocket?"

"Lipstick? Why would I—" I frowned. "Amanda? What's going on?"

"I just thought it would make your full lips even fuller."

I narrowed my gaze.

"You're single. He's single. And freakin' adorable and charming."

"Adorable? No. Kittens are adorable. Men with biker tattoos aren't adorable," I negated.

"You're right. They're manly. And he's *super* manly. But he's also really cute and really nice. And all the nurses on the floor adore him."

"He's been here one day," I said in exasperation. "How can all the nurses adore him?"

"It's a thing called charisma," Amanda said. "And if you could get your grandma knickers out of their twist, you might notice that he's charismatic."

"I don't wear grandma knickers," I protested.

"You're missing the point. Entirely."

"Has he been buzzing you guys a lot?"

"No, actually. He hasn't buzzed us at all. Babs went and checked in on him to monitor his pain. It took her half an hour to come back to the nurses' desk, and when she did, she had a dreamy smile on her face." Amanda scratched the bridge of her nose. "So, naturally, Lizzie was curious to find out who made grumpy Babs' day."

I bit my lip to stop my smile at Amanda's description of Babs. I tried not to gossip, but the doctors called Babs Nurse Ratched behind her back.

Apparently, Boxer had a way with women.

"And you? What do you think of Boxer?" I asked her.

"I think if I wasn't happily married with a two-year-old, I'd have sex with him in a public bathroom."

"Amanda!"

She shrugged. "What? You asked. He's that kind of guy that *you know* would get down and dirty with you in a public bathroom."

"That's unsanitary. And not at all sexy."

She pinched her nose and then said in a nasally feigned intercom voice, "Paging Grandma Knickers."

"It's Dr. Grandma Knickers. At least give me my medical title that I spent so many years acquiring."

"Fine, Dr. Grandma Knickers, stop dawdling. Now go find out why he's refusing morphine. And seriously consider putting on some lipstick…and blush. You look pale. And take your hair out of that braid. It makes you look like a nun. If I had your blonde hair, I'd go around swinging my head like I was in a shampoo commercial."

"What's gotten into you?"

"My husband—last night. Boom!" She mimed an invisible mic drop.

"Boom, what?" Babs asked as she approached the desk, pushing a strand of silver hair behind her ear as she walked. Her chin length bob made her look severe. Her tone was naturally brusque, but she had a kind heart and I saw past the gruffness.

"I'm just giving Dr. Ward a hard time about not making up her face before she goes to see the patient in 317," Amanda said.

"If only I were younger…" Babs muttered under her breath and then trailed off. She rested her elbows on the ledge and looked at me. "You should really do something about that."

"Do something about what?" I asked. "Why would I do *anything* about that? He's my patient."

Babs and Amanda exchanged a look.

"What? What does that look mean?"

"He's been asking about you," Babs said.

"So what?"

Amanda sighed. "You're dense."

"I'm not dense. I just—it doesn't matter. He's my patient, and it's against the rules."

"Aha!" Amanda grinned. "I knew it! I knew you were thinking about him."

"I'm not—give me a piece of chocolate," I muttered, diving my hand into the glass jar on the counter.

"Chocolate is not a substitute for sex," Babs said.

"Chocolate and sex, my two favorite things. They go well together actually," Amanda said.

"My husband ordered chocolate body paint for our

anniversary," Babs said, "and let me tell you, it spiced up everything…"

Amanda stared in shock at Babs. "I never knew you had it in you!"

Babs shrugged and didn't appear at all embarrassed. "When you've been married as long as I have, you have to do things to keep it interesting. Last week, I got a bikini wax in the shape of a heart. It drove my husband crazy!"

"I'm so proud to know you, Babs. I really am," Amanda said with an amazed grin.

*That's my cue.*

I walked away, their laughter echoing in my ears. Why did I need to go to happy hour with the nurses when it was clear they had their own version of water cooler talk in the middle of the day?

When I entered Boxer's room, his gaze was directed toward the TV in the corner, but when he saw me, he shut it off.

"Doc," he greeted with a genuine smile. "I didn't think I'd be seeing you today."

I arched a brow. "Boxer."

"Uh-oh."

"Uh-oh what?"

"I'm in trouble, aren't I?"

I let out a huff of a laugh. "What makes you say that?"

"You brought your stern voice with you."

"Seems you've gotten yourself a little fan club," I stated. "The nurses are gaga over you."

"I'm flattered." He shot me a grin. "You know the thing about fan clubs? They need a club president. You look like you're up for the job."

"I'll pass, thanks," I said, my expression sobering. "What's this about you not taking morphine?"

"That's right."

"You don't have to play tough guy in here. You just had major surgery. No one will think less of you for taking pain meds."

He frowned. "It's not about being tough."

"No? Then what's it about?"

Boxer rubbed the blond stubble along his jaw and paused a moment before looking at me and saying, "Addiction runs in my family."

His response wasn't one I'd been anticipating, and it shut me up immediately.

"Hmm. Rendered you speechless, did I?"

"I'm sorry, I didn't expect that. I just thought…"

"You thought I was trying to get your attention."

"What?" A slight blush stained my cheeks. "No, I didn't."

"It's okay, Dr. Ward. I know you've been thinking about me."

"Are you in cahoots with the nurses?" I demanded.

"Cahoots about what?"

"Never mind. Why didn't you tell the nurses about addiction running in your family?"

He ran his fingers through his blond hair. "I don't know."

"We have other options for controlling pain. We can make you comfortable without narcotics."

"I'd rather not, if it's all the same to you." His gray eyes were clear when they looked at me. I had the sudden feeling that I was seeing something more beneath the flirty biker exterior he portrayed, and it had me intrigued.

I had no business being intrigued.

I was his doctor. He was my patient. Nothing more.

"I'll tell them not to bother asking you about morphine again. Okay?" I said.

"I appreciate it."

"How's the pain, though? On a scale of one to ten."

"About a seven."

"Boxer."

"I'm fine, Doc. Really. I've wiped out on my bike before. Been in plenty of fights. Pain I can deal with, okay?"

"Is that how you got your nickname?"

The question was out of my mouth before I had a chance to stop it.

"No, that's not how I got my nickname." He smiled in amusement. "And it's not a nickname, it's a road name."

*Darn my curious nature.*

"Oh. Road name. Right." I sighed. "If you change your mind—"

"I won't," he assured me.

Nodding, I headed for the door. "Have a good rest of your day."

"Is your shift over?" he asked.

"Yes."

"Perfect." He grinned and held up two low-fat yogurt cups that rested on his food tray. "Which one do you want?"

"Neither. You enjoy them."

"Come on, Doc. It's not a marriage proposal. It's not even a date. It's yogurt."

I wasn't hungry, but he was irresistible. I understood why the nurses liked Boxer. There was an ease to him, like he didn't take himself too seriously. I was being pulled toward him by some giant invisible magnet. Against my better judgement, I sat in the chair next to his bedside.

He ripped open both yogurt cups, put the spoons in them, and then handed me one.

Our fingers brushed when I took the plastic cup from

him. I attempted to ignore the pulse of electricity that shot through my arm.

It felt like a hit of dopamine fit for a junkie. It went straight to my head, making me feel light and airy.

"Thanks."

*Did my voice sound breathy?* I hoped he didn't notice.

"You're not from here," Boxer said. "Texas, I mean."

I shook my head. "Watch Hill, Rhode Island."

"Amanda said you moved here recently."

"That Amanda." I shook my head. "What did you do? Offer her yogurt and ply her with questions?"

"Nah. I only save the yogurt for cute doctors." He winked. "Besides, she's the one who offered that piece of information freely. Where'd you move from? Watch Hill?"

I paused, unsure of how I felt about Amanda discussing anything about my personal life with Boxer. But then I figured, what was the harm? It wasn't like he'd asked anything truly intimate.

"I was in Durham—at Duke University Hospital."

"Duke's fucking prestigious, Doc. You must be at the top of your field. And you can't be more than…thirty, I'm guessing."

"It's not polite to guess a woman's age," I joked, trying to keep the conversation light when it was venturing into a topic I didn't want to discuss.

"Do you play tennis?"

"Yes, I play tennis."

"I knew it."

"Knew what?"

"You're a blue blood."

I stopped stirring my yogurt and looked at him.

His grin widened. "Don't worry. I don't hold that against you."

I set the untouched yogurt down on the tray and stood. "Thanks for the yogurt."

He frowned. "What'd I say?"

"Nothing," I lied. "I just shouldn't be fraternizing with a patient."

Boxer was just about to speak when the door to his room opened.

A young guy with brown hair and scruff entered. He hadn't been in the hospital waiting room the previous night with the others, so I didn't recognize him. Two other young men trailed behind him. The three of them were wearing leather vests labeled *Prospect*.

"Prospects, meet the doc who saved my life," Boxer introduced.

"Hi," I said awkwardly.

"Hey, Doc," the brown-haired young man said. The other two gave me chin nods in greeting. He pulled out a pack of cards from his back pocket. "Colt told us to come entertain you."

"You guys bring money?" Boxer asked.

"Yeah, we brought money," the blond prospect said. "And a deck of cards."

"Perfect. Sit down and I'll show you how to cheat at cards and make it look believable." Boxer's eyes found mine. "Bye, Doc."

"Bye," I murmured as I headed for the door.

Just before it closed, one of the young men said, "That's the doctor that saved your life? You're so damn lucky."

# Chapter 3

I TRUDGED through the lobby of my condo building and immediately went to check my mailbox. *Nothing.* Not even a bill.

"Linden," the middle-aged security guard greeted, coming out from around the desk.

"Hi, Jerry," I said with a genuine smile. "What did your wife bring you for lunch today?"

"Eggplant Parmesan."

I raised my brows. "No chance of any leftovers, are there?"

"Nope. Sorry." He grinned. "When are you going to settle down with a nice man who knows how to cook and take care of you?"

"You're starting to sound like the Italian mother I don't have," I warned.

"Eggplant Parmesan. Homemade," he reminded me. "I've got a nephew actually. Recently divorced…"

"Oh wow, look at the time," I drawled and booked it to the elevator. I quickly punched the button. "See you tomorrow. I'm in for the night."

"It's not night yet," he said.

"It is by my body clock. I've been up since four."

First the nurses, now my well-meaning but nosy security guard? I'd only broken up with my boyfriend a few months ago. Did I have a sign painted on my forehead that read *lonely doctor in need of a good boning?*

I snorted, wondering if that was how my personal ad would read in five years.

The elevator arrived and after the chime, the steel doors opened, and I got in. They closed behind me, and I turned to press the button for the top floor. When I got out, I padded down the long white hallway with slate gray carpet and came to a light wood door.

The condo was everything I needed. The woman who owned it had gone to London for a job, so the place had been rented to me completely furnished. It had made moving from Durham a breeze. I'd been able to leave my old life behind and start fresh.

The apartment had an open floor plan with a modern kitchen and stainless-steel appliances, yet the living room was inviting and airy. Light gray walls matched the accent pillows on the white couch and high-end white trim carpentry highlighted the room. The walls were bare, but there were small holes from where photos or paintings had hung.

I hadn't added any personal touches to the place yet. Even though my life and time revolved around the hospital, I could've taken a few days and really made the apartment feel like mine, but I just didn't have the inclination. I liked the décor that had come with the condo, and it was comfortable and clean.

I plucked my phone from my clutch. I had a few missed texts and two voicemails. I played my mother's message first as I kicked off my sneakers.

"Linden, it's your mother." Her cultured and deeply condescending voice came through the speaker. "If you would deign to call me, I'd appreciate it. We haven't heard from you in days, and I assume it's because you're working and not because you're lying in a ditch somewhere."

I rolled my eyes. Guilt and obligation had been my mother's one and only strategy to exert her rule over me. It had worked until I'd told her I was going to medical school. She hadn't been happy with my decision. Not even a little bit proud of me. My mother was a brittle socialite who spent her days going from martini lunches to charity balls. When I refused to follow in her footsteps, she'd taken it personally. She thought I'd done it to slight her, when all I'd been doing was pursuing my own path. Then again, she thought my dreams were my father's dreams and that wasn't a box I was interested in unpacking.

Her message ended. I didn't bother listening to my father's voicemail—I just deleted it.

I stripped out of my clothes as I headed to the bathroom. I turned on the shower, and as I waited for the temperature to adjust, I undid my wheat blonde braid and ran my fingers through the waves in my hair.

As I stepped underneath the steaming spray, my mind inevitably drifted to Boxer. He'd caught me completely off guard when he pegged me as a blue blood. I hadn't expected him to be insightful, but clearly, he saw that I was East Coast, and there was nothing I could do to hide it.

He wasn't what I expected from a biker. I wondered why I even cared.

There was an endless revolving door of patients from the hospital that had allowed me to meet all types of people from all walks of life. I considered myself a good judge of character, but Boxer had thrown me for a loop.

I turned off the shower after cleaning up and reached for the blue towel on the heated rack. I quickly dried off and slathered my body in lotion. I left my wet hair down to air dry.

The espresso I'd downed a few hours ago had long since lost its potency, and I felt the crash coming. I changed into a pair of leggings and a slouchy sweater and then opened a bottle of red wine. My stomach rumbled in hunger, and I ordered my usual from the Thai restaurant around the corner.

Dinner and wine for one.

*Pathetic.*

The next afternoon, I walked into the waiting room and looked for the Taylor family. They sat in the corner, occupying three chairs. Mrs. Taylor had an open magazine on her lap, but she was staring out the window. One of her adult sons reached over to grasp her hand and gave it a hearty squeeze. She smiled absently but didn't turn to look at him. Her other adult son returned to her side, carrying three small cups of hospital coffee that had no business being called *coffee*.

"Mom," her son said.

"Thanks." She took a cup from him, blew on it for a second, and then set it aside on a wooden table.

I observed them for a moment with the trained eye of someone that had cultivated the skill to perceive, calculate, and act accordingly based on the information at hand. Time was of the utmost importance in my profession, but it was a delicate balance. Move too quickly and you could make an irreconcilable mistake. Don't move fast enough and the same fate could occur.

"Mrs. Taylor," I greeted with a smile as I strode toward the middle-aged woman who'd kept her trim figure.

She rose, her face carefully blank, as if she refused to allow herself hope. "Dr. Ward."

Her sons also stood and instinctively moved closer to her, seemingly preparing for bad news.

I smiled. "The surgery went well."

There was an audible sigh of relief from the three of them.

"I'm optimistic the colectomy was a success, but it'll be a few weeks before he's made a full recovery."

Tears of relief rolled down Mrs. Taylor's cheeks, and then her sons were embracing her. Their emotion was on display, so great that they couldn't hide it.

"Charlie is being taken to recovery. He's going to be groggy for a while, but you can see him in a bit. I'll send one of the nurses out to get you when it's okay to go in."

Mrs. Taylor broke away from her children and flung herself into my arms, gripping me in a strong embrace. "Thank you," she whispered.

I patted her back.

She pulled away, her blue eyes watery with tears. "I'm so relieved. Thank you."

"It's a beautiful day, Mrs. Taylor. Let's all enjoy it." With a smile, I gently extracted myself from the presence of the Taylor family and left the waiting room.

My heart felt light. Today, medicine had been on my side.

"You look happy," Amanda said, as I approached the nurses' station.

"I am happy." I smiled. "It's a good day, Amanda. Charlie Taylor's surgery went well."

"Oh, that's great. Truly. I'm about to make your day even better."

"Yeah?"

"You got a flower delivery." She gestured to a bouquet of red roses resting on the counter of the administrative desk. "I wonder who they could be from?"

"Judging by your tone, I would say you already peeked at the card," I remarked drolly, holding out my hand for it.

"Just the signature." She handed me the card. I took a few moments to read it but didn't have a feeling one way or the other.

"Well," she pressed. "What did Parker have to say?"

"He said he had a good time on our date last week and would love to go out again."

"That's great!" she said.

"It is?"

"Well, yeah, isn't it?" She paused, and then she grinned. "Oh, I see. You're no longer interested in the suit-wearing lawyer type. Not after meeting Mr. Down and Dirty."

"Mr. Down and Dirty?" I raised my brows.

"Come on, Boxer's got *down and dirty* written all over him. Slathered in ink. Yum."

"You're ridiculous. And Boxer has nothing to do with why I'm not going out with Parker again,"

"Yeah, right."

"Will you stop, please? I don't have a thing for Boxer."

"Then go out with Parker again," she taunted.

"No."

"Why not?" she demanded.

"Because, as nice as he is, he reminds me too much of my ex." I placed my hand on her arm. "I know you mean well. I know all the nurses mean well, but can we stop this pushing me toward every single guy? I'm happy with my life the way it is. Okay?"

"Okay," she said, not looking at all like she believed me.

An hour later, I was strolling past Boxer's room when I saw a pregnant brunette sitting by his bedside.

"Doc!" Boxer called out with a smile. "Come in here! I want you to meet someone."

"Don't talk to the doctor that way," the pretty woman said, lightly smacking his arm.

Bile rose in my throat.

*Of course.*

I'd fallen for his easy charm and reluctantly been impressed that he'd refused opiates. He'd been intriguing, different. And I'd noticed.

I felt lower than low, but there was no way I could get out of meeting Boxer's wife. But then I realized it wasn't my fault. Boxer had led me to believe... He never mentioned anyone or wore a ring. I never would've sat and had yogurt with him if I'd known.

I mentally braced myself and smiled at the woman who was married to a dog, and I wondered if she knew it. "Hi, I'm Dr. Linden Ward." I held out my hand to her, and she gave it a hearty shake.

"I'm so glad I got to see you so I could give you these in person." She held a plastic container of cookies out to me. "I made these for you. My way of saying thanks for... well, being Boxer's guardian angel."

"Oh," I murmured. "It was my pleasure. Really." My eyes drifted to her belly. "When are you due?"

"In about eight weeks. Each day I keep getting bigger and bigger." She laughed, her face radiant.

"Congratulations." It was impossible not to smile at her genuine warmth. Too bad her husband was a complete and utter jerk. "I'm sorry, I didn't catch your name."

"Ugh. Preggo brain." She smacked her forehead. "I'm Mia Weston."

"Weston," I repeated, my gaze darting to Boxer.

*Not Ford.*

"This is *Colt's* wife," Boxer said slowly, his smile deepening as if he knew what had been going through my mind. "They're in love and committed and everything."

Mia frowned in confusion as she looked at Boxer. But then she turned her attention back to me, seemingly unaware of the internal battle I'd been waging. "You met my husband the other night. He's the big burly one."

"You forgot grumpy," Boxer added.

Mia wrinkled her nose at Boxer. "He's not that grumpy anymore. I make him happy."

"Sometimes," Boxer teased.

"Hush, you." She tweaked his nose, and I couldn't help but smile at their sibling-like interaction.

"I would've been here," Mia went on, "but we've got a twelve-year-old son and I was home with him."

She didn't look old enough to have a twelve-year-old son, but I kept that thought to myself. I also kept the thought to myself that she was a very lucky woman to be married to Colt, because *wow.*

"Here," she said, insisting I take the cookies.

I grasped the container. "Thank you for this, but it really wasn't necessary."

"If you don't want them, I'll take them. Mia bakes the best cookies," Boxer said.

I clutched them tighter. "You're on a restricted diet and sugar won't help you heal."

"Damn," Boxer muttered. "And here I thought you were gonna take pity on me."

"You don't need pity," I said. "You get enough of that from the nurses."

"That's our Boxer." Mia rubbed her lower back. "I've got to get going. It was nice meeting you, Dr. Ward."

"Call me Linden," I insisted.

Her smiled widened and she nodded. "Linden."

"Thanks for making the drive, Mia," Boxer said.

"Drive? What drive?" I asked.

"From Waco." She frowned. "That's where we live. The club, I mean."

"Oh. I thought for sure you were all from Dallas. I just assumed because Boxer—"

"I was hanging out with a buddy in Dallas when the pain in my side got to be too bad," Boxer explained. "I wasn't going to be able to make the long drive home. So I came here."

"Ah," I said. "Got it."

"The boys are still handling stuff in the city, so they'll be by in a bit. Don't climb the walls." Mia grinned and then waddled out of the room.

My eyes followed her, and then I looked back at my patient, lying there, appearing too smug for his own good.

"Jealousy looks good on you, Doc."

I marched to the end of his bed and set the cookies down. "I wasn't jealous."

"No? Didn't look that way to me," he teased.

"I thought I'd pegged you wrong," I stated. "And that you were the kind of guy that was two-timing his wife. A pregnant wife."

He laughed. "You should've seen the look on your face. Man, I wish I'd had a camera."

It hadn't been jealousy—it had been regret that I'd read him wrong when I deemed myself a good judge of character. And if I was being honest with myself, it was disappointment in Boxer.

"Did she really drive all the way from Waco just to visit you?" I asked. "That's a bit of a trek."

"She's been wanting to go to this fancy schmancy baby boutique in Dallas. She made a day of it here." Boxer examined me for a moment. "So, are we gonna talk about why you went all weird yesterday?"

"Weird about what?" I evaded.

"You know what. Don't play dumb. That's not who you are."

"Who am I, Boxer?" I demanded.

"Come on, you're a surgeon," he pointed out, not at all taken aback by my tone. "You're clearly not an idiot."

I paused, weighing my words before I spoke. "People assume things about you, when they know you come from a privileged background."

"Just like people assume they know things about you because you wear a leather cut and ride a motorcycle."

"Touché," I said with a wry grin.

"Posture."

"Huh?"

"It's your posture. The way you carry yourself, Doc. You never slouch or shuffle. Asking you about tennis was just a confirmation of what I already knew."

"You noticed how I walk?"

"Yeah." He smiled. "It stands out. *You* stand out."

"I spent years at cotillions and having manners drilled into me."

"Sounds like a nightmare."

"It was," I admitted.

"Yogurt?" Boxer reached for one of the plastic cups on his meal tray.

"Excuse me?"

"I was hoping you'd stop by so we could eat yogurt together. It'll be the highlight of my day."

"Are you always full of wind?" I demanded. "Speaking of wind…have you passed gas yet today?"

He stopped mid-pull while opening the foil on one of the yogurt containers. "You're kidding, right?"

"I'm your doctor. I have to know if things are working."

"Like hell I'm gonna tell you that." He finished ripping off the foil and set it aside. "I'm trying to impress you. If I tell you I've farted—"

"So, you *have* passed gas then?"

"*If.* Jesus, I said if—you know what? Let's not talk about that anymore."

"How's your pain today?"

"Six and a half."

"Yesterday it was a seven," I pointed out. "So, you're feeling a bit better. That's good."

"I always feel better when I fleece the prospects out of a few bucks. But they don't really offer me that much of a challenge, you know? I like a challenge."

"Yeah, I bet you do," I mocked.

He raised his brows. "What's that supposed to mean?"

"Nothing."

"Not *nothing.* Say it like it is, Doc."

I sighed. "I'm sorry. I was doing that thing again."

"What thing?"

"Assuming I know who you are because you flirt with everything that walks."

"Um. Ouch. And I don't flirt with everything that walks. There are a few male nurses here you know, and as nice as they are, they're not really my type."

"What's your type?" I blurted out before I could stop myself.

His grin was slow, appreciative.

"Yeah, walked right into that one," I muttered. "I blame the sleep deprivation that goes with the job."

"Really? I think you should blame your overwhelming attraction to me. Just admit you don't know how to handle it."

"I'll pay you five dollars to change the subject," I said, feeling testy and antsy, and wondering why I didn't have the willpower to get up and leave.

"Okay, Doc. Let's talk about when I can get out of here."

"One more day," I said. "You're responding well to the antibiotics, but I want to make sure there's no infection before I discharge you."

"Gas, infection, and you just said discharge." He shook his head. "There's no way in hell you're ever gonna give me a chance once I get out of here, are you?"

"Give you a chance?" I arched a brow. "Give you a chance to do what, exactly?"

"Buy you an ice cream soda and ask you to wear my letterman jacket, of course. And if you're really nice to me, I'll even take you to the sock hop."

"You know just how to treat a girl from the '50s." I chuckled. "I think you're swell, but I don't want the complication. Plus, you're my patient, and that's against the rules. Actually, I shouldn't even be sitting here with you—"

"You think I'm swell?" he asked.

I rolled my eyes.

"Let's get back to this idea that you think I'm a complication."

"Men usually are."

He raised his brows. "Maybe the kind you normally date. The ones who wear bowties and talk about stock portfolios."

*Totally nailed.*

"You're my patient," I said. "I don't date my patients."

"After you discharge me, I won't be your patient anymore."

He had a point.

"So that just leaves your issue with thinking I'm a complication. I'm the least complicated guy you'll ever meet. You clearly need a man you can blow off steam with. So how about it, Doc?"

"How about what?"

"How about we get together and—"

My pager vibrated against my hip, effectively ending the conversation that was rapidly spinning out of control. Because as much as I tried to ignore his banter and flirting, I was enjoying it immensely.

I stood up and set the half-eaten yogurt on the tray before checking the page. "I've got to go."

"Damn. It was just getting interesting."

I headed for the door.

"Doc?"

I looked behind me.

"Think about it."

"Think about what?"

He grinned. "Me. Naked. I've got tattoos you haven't even seen yet."

"You're incorrigible."

He reached for my yogurt. "You're already thinking about it. I know it."

# Chapter 4

THE DOOR to the on-call room opened and a bright shaft of fluorescent light poured in. I winced, propping one eye open.

"Sorry to wake you, but we've got a problem," Lizzie said from the doorway.

I shielded my eyes from the glaring lights of the hallway. "How big of a problem? Like, someone's limb is ripped off type of problem or a kid swallowed a Monopoly house problem?"

"Neither. It seems there's a party going on in room 317. I've tried breaking it up, but they won't listen to me. They just smirk and keep drinking."

"They're drinking?"

"Yes. They're a raucous bunch. And I'm…"

"Intimidated?"

"Um, yeah. They're *bikers*. Should I call security?"

I swung my legs over the side of the bed and sat up, careful not to hit my head on the top bunk. "No, no. I'll take care of it. Where's Babs? She's a hard ass. Why didn't she handle this?"

"I can't find her. And I doubt she'd school Boxer. She's all but worshiping at his leather altar."

I found a piece of gum in my scrub pocket, popped it into my mouth, and went to break up the party. I heard the bikers' laughter before I'd even gotten through the door of Boxer's room.

Two bikers leaned against the far wall while another sat in the chair by Boxer's bedside, chowing down on the cookies Mia had brought me. I'd forgotten to take them when I'd been paged earlier.

Boxer looked at Lizzie who stood in the doorway behind me. "Thanks, Lizzie."

"Sure thing," Lizzie said, her tone breathy.

I glanced at her over my shoulder. She looked flushed and giddy, like a schoolgirl with her first crush.

"Lizzie," I warned.

"I'm gone, I'm gone." She hastily closed the door, leaving me in a room with three bikers I recognized from the night I removed Boxer's appendix. Aside from the flask I saw being passed around, I was surprised to find the get-together was the antithesis of rowdy. There was no loud music, no strippers, no bags of white powder on the nightstand.

As far as what I knew about bikers, this wasn't the kind of get-together I'd expected to walk into.

A plastic bag rested next to Boxer, and I wondered if they'd brought him junk food and other contraband that wouldn't aid in his healing.

"Hey, Doc," Colt greeted. "Zip." He held out his hand to the man whose patch read Vice President. "Whisky."

Zip handed over a flask, and Colt took a long sip from it.

"You can't have alcohol in here," I stated.

"Says who," Zip asked with a grin.

"It's hospital policy. There are sick people here trying to recover. We can't have visitors getting unruly," I stated lamely.

"Who said anything about getting unruly?" the biker with the cut jaw and dark hair asked. "This shit is tame. If you want unruly, we can show you unruly."

"I'd prefer it if you didn't." I whirled and glared at Boxer. "You better not be drinking."

"I'm not."

"*Boxer*," I warned.

"Seriously, Doc. You can smell my breath if you don't believe me." His dove gray eyes were guileless and sincere.

I peered at him for a moment. "I believe you." To the rest of the men in the room, I asked, "How much whisky have you guys had?"

Zip's blue eyes twinkled with humor. "Not enough to be a menace on the road. We'll make it back to Waco in one piece. Promise."

"I drank Boxer's share." The dark-haired man grinned. "Sucks to be you, brother. We brought the good shit."

"Don't rub it in, Reap," Boxer stated.

Reap shrugged.

"Visiting hours are over," I informed them in my no-nonsense tone.

"No fun," Reap muttered, swiping the flask from Zip as they trekked from the room.

"Thanks for looking out for him, Doc," Colt said, as he sauntered to the door. "He needs it."

"I heard that," Boxer muttered.

Colt shot his friend a smile but didn't reply. When I was alone with Boxer, I crossed my arms over my chest and raised a brow.

"What?" he demanded.

I sighed. "Nothing."

"Not nothing. What is it?"

"I don't like being manipulated," I said finally.

"Who manipulated you?"

I raised my brows to my hairline. "Lizzie made it sound like there was trouble going on in this room. Clearly, that wasn't the case."

"So, you really didn't care that they were drinking?"

I shrugged. "I wasn't a fan of it, but I was more concerned that you might have been drinking."

"I took to heart what you said, Doc. You talk; I listen."

"Well, good," I said, feeling ridiculous.

"Are you busy right now?" he asked.

I paused and then replied, "No…"

"Good." He reached into the plastic bag and pulled out a candle. He then set it down on the swiveling wooden table in front of him.

"Candles aren't allowed in hospital rooms either. Fire hazard," I explained.

"How are we supposed to have any ambience if I can't light the thing?"

"*We're* not supposed to have any ambiance at all."

He rolled his eyes. "Apple juice or cranberry?" He dug around in the plastic bag and held up two kids' juice boxes with attached straws.

"Where did you get all this?" I asked.

"Where do you think?"

"Lizzie," I said with a sigh. "Lizzie helped you with this, didn't she?"

"Yup. She likes you, Doc. All the nurses do."

"Hmm," I murmured noncommittally. The nurses were like the sisters I didn't have. Meddlesome and obsessed with whether or not there was any romance in my world. It was like they'd all collectively banded together to fix my love life.

"So, which juice do you want?"

"I don't think I should encourage bad behavior," I stated.

"You look like you're in desperate need of some bad behavior, Doc. Come on, live a little."

"Apple, please." I walked to him, and he placed the juice box in my hand. I sat in the chair that Reap had vacated. "This goes against all my better judgement."

"You think too much."

"Probably," I agreed.

"Cheers," he said.

We bumped our juice boxes together, and then I took a sip. "I haven't had apple juice in years. It's surprisingly delicious."

"Glad you're enjoying it."

He took a drink of his cranberry juice. "So, Doc, what do you do in your spare time?"

"I don't have a lot of spare time. I work eighty-hour weeks."

"That's insane."

"Maybe," I agreed. "But someone's got to do it. I enjoy it, actually. I'm more comfortable in a hospital than I am anywhere else."

"Your home away from home?" he joked.

"Something like that."

"But when you are home, what do you do?"

"Laundry."

"Laundry?" he repeated like he didn't believe me.

I nodded. "And I go grocery shopping."

"Come on. You're not that boring."

"I really am," I assured him.

"Don't you have hobbies? Interests?"

"It's hard to have hobbies and interests when you work as much as I do."

"So, you don't spend your spare time with your boyfriend?"

"I don't have a boyfriend," I said before I could stop myself.

His smile was slow. Boxer took a drink of his cranberry juice and then asked, "Why don't you?"

"Because I don't."

"I'm not trying to ruffle feathers here, Doc. I'm just asking a simple question."

"Why?"

"Because I'm curious."

"Why?"

Before Boxer could utter an explanation, the door to his room opened, and my superior strode inside. Dr. Sawyer quickly took in the scene: me sitting with a patient, the unlit candle, the juice boxes. It didn't look good. Not at all.

"Dr. Ward, may I see you outside for a moment?" His tone was clipped and formal.

I set my juice box down and rose, trying to appear like I hadn't been doing anything wrong. Boxer saluted me on my way out, and I glared at him.

Thankfully, Dr. Sawyer wasn't paying attention because he was already waiting for me in the hallway.

He was about a decade older than me and very sure of his position at the hospital. "What are you doing?" Dr. Sawyer demanded the moment the door to Boxer's room closed. "You know that fraternizing with patients is against the rules."

"I wasn't fraternizing."

"It didn't look that way to me." He stared me down. "I need my overnight shift in the ER covered on Saturday. You're going to work it for me. Hope you didn't have any plans."

He turned and marched away without saying another word.

I glared at his back, biting back a waspish retort.

"Well, Boxer," I said late the next morning. "It seems our time together has come to an end. I'm discharging you. You can go home. I'm releasing you back into the wild."

"Is that how you see me, Doc? As a wild animal?"

"Don't get distracted. Do me a favor and attempt to heed my rules."

"Which rules would those be?" he drawled with a mischievous glint in his eye.

"You know which ones, but if it will give you a kick to hear me say sex and masturbation, then I'll oblige. No sex and no masturbation for a couple of weeks."

He chuckled. "It did give me a kick. Thanks."

"You should be up and moving freely, no heavy lifting, no exercising. I wish you'd take something for the pain, but you're a grown man who knows his limits. I'm asking you to observe them."

"Anything else?" he asked in amusement.

I handed him a sheet of paper. "If you have any of these symptoms, you need to go to the hospital immediately. No dawdling."

He took the blue paper and glanced at it for a moment before folding it in half and placing it on the bedside table.

The humor in his eyes remained, but his smile dimmed. "I got you in trouble, didn't I? With Dr. Prick."

My lips twitched at Boxer's apropos nickname of Dr. Sawyer. "You didn't get me into trouble. I got myself into trouble. I should never have been spending time with you."

"Is that why you've been avoiding me this morning?"

"I haven't been avoiding you. I had an emergency bowel obstruction I had to deal with."

"Hopefully not yours," he quipped.

"A patient's." I mock glared at him, which made his teasing grin widen. "Please take care of yourself. Your recovery is important, okay?"

"Okay."

"Seriously, Boxer."

"I heard you. You've got my word that I'll take it easy."

"Good."

"It was nice meeting you, Doc," he said.

"Take care, Boxer."

I left his room, feeling a twinge in my chest. I didn't understand it any more than I understood the sudden bout of melancholy that washed over me.

An hour later, I was at the nurses' station watching Boxer leave his room with a prospect by his side. He was taller than I realized. His blue and black flannel shirt was rolled up at the sleeves, showing off his inked forearms. Boxer wore a leather vest, which proudly sported the Tarnished Angels logo on his back.

Even though he was moving slowly, I detected a hint of natural swagger, like an eighteenth-century pirate hell-bent on destruction and damnation.

"Be still my ovaries," Lizzie murmured.

"Right?" Amanda added.

"Stop it you two," I demanded.

"If your ovaries aren't doing cartwheels right now, then you need to get your hormone levels checked," Lizzie said.

Boxer sauntered to the elevators, and when he saw me noticing him, he waved and then pretended to doff the rim of an invisible hat.

The prospect stood near him, ready to lend a hand, but Boxer didn't need it. The young man pushed the button, and the elevator came almost immediately. The two of them got in, and Boxer called out, "You'll miss me when I'm gone, Dr. Ward! Admit it."

The doors closed but not before I saw his cheeky grin.

"Please tell me you're about to make a bad decision with him," Amanda demanded.

I shook my head slowly. "Nope."

"What?" Lizzie gasped. "Why not?"

"Because he's a patient."

"Not any more he's not," Lizzie said. "What other excuses do you have?"

"He's a biker," I said.

"Uh, yeah. That's *exactly* why you should go for it," Amanda said, with Lizzie nodding along.

"How do you figure?" I demanded.

"He's a leather-wearing, incredibly hot alpha male who's charming as hell," Amanda went on. "He'd be fun to run around with for a little while."

"And then you can release him back into his natural habitat," Lizzie added. "No muss. No fuss."

"All guys are a fuss," I said. "I doubt Boxer is any different."

"You're really not going to even consider it?" Lizzie asked. "After I helped him set up the adorable juice box cocktails date?"

"It wasn't *that* adorable," I protested.

"Yeah, Linden, it was," Lizzie said.

"It was a manipulation tactic, and I didn't like it," I admonished.

"You lie," Amanda teased. "You *so* liked it."

"I would totally be all over that," Lizzie said. "Maybe I should run after him and give him my number?"

"You could try," Amanda said. "It wouldn't matter, though, because Boxer is all about Team Linden."

"Oh, I see," Lizzie said slowly. "I get it now."

"Get what now?" I asked, my brow furrowing.

"You're a snob. Amanda? Will you hand me that pen—"

"Hold on a second," I interrupted. "I'm *not* a snob."

"You are," Lizzie stated with a nod. "It's okay. Don't hide from it."

"You think I'm a snob because I won't date a biker?"

"No, I think you're a snob because you won't even give him a chance," Lizzie countered. "You need to shake things up."

"I've shaken things up plenty," I insisted. "I just broke up with someone a few months ago. I took a job across the country and moved my entire life here. I'm more shaken up than a dry martini, okay?"

Amanda sighed. "You went on a date with that lawyer guy, Parker, remember?"

"Yeah? So? What does that have to do with anything?" I demanded.

"It means you might've moved across the country and taken a new job, but you're not really into taking risks," Amanda said. "You went on a date with your usual type, didn't you? So how much have you *really* shaken things up?"

"I never should've gone to happy hour with you guys that first week I moved here." I shook my head. "You guys seemed too innocent and sweet."

"We got you drunk on purpose," Amanda said with a grin. "We wanted you to spill your guts."

"You're one of us now, Linden," Lizzie added. "Which means we look out for you and tell you like it is. And, you need to have some fun with Boxer."

"I'll think about it," I lied.

"No, you won't," Amanda said with a feigned sad face.

"No, I won't," I agreed. "Can I get back to work now, please?"

~

"Time of death, 11:57," I said, my eyes on the clock. I removed my gloves and threw them down on the instrument tray and ripped the surgical mask off.

I didn't meet anyone's gaze as I stalked from the operating room, anger pumping through my veins.

I took death personally.

Every time I failed to save a life, I imagined the Grim Reaper laughing in my face.

It was a mockery of my craft, sadness, and failure all rolled into one, and it didn't matter how much schooling or training I had. But, inevitably, there were times when the circumstances were beyond my control and no amount of training or modern medicine could fix them.

Losing a patient never got easier, no matter how many times it happened. A loss was a loss. And for some reason I couldn't quite pin down, the deaths seemed to outweigh the lives I'd saved.

I walked by the nurses' station and met Amanda's eyes. She knew in an instant that I'd lost my patient.

Her gaze was somber, and she nodded.

I turned in the direction of the waiting room, walked a few feet and paused, and then pushed through the doors.

"I'm looking for the Martinez family," I called out.

"*Sí*—yes." A young woman rose from her chair, her blonde hair tied up into a messy bun, her face devoid of any makeup. Her eyes searched mine and before I'd even gotten a word out about the fate of her husband, she broke down into tears.

Even though I was the messenger, the one who'd come

to tell her that her husband was dead, she grasped me to her and held on tightly, as if in that moment I was the last living connection to him that she would ever have.

"I'm sorry," I said softly, switching from English to Spanish.

She cried harder, sobbing with the entire force of her body. Amanda came into the waiting room and approached me.

I shook my head, silently telling her that I didn't need her to take over. I wanted to comfort the Martinez widow. I'd let her cry out her anguish in my arms while she mourned for her husband and began to taste the cruelty and unfairness of life.

Amanda discreetly headed back to the nurses' station, and my arms around Mrs. Martinez tightened.

When her storm of emotions passed, she ripped herself from my embrace and dragged her hand down her cheeks, clearing away the proof that death was hardest on those left behind.

"I'm so sorry for your loss," I said to her.

She nodded, but it was instinctual, not like she'd actually heard me.

"His injuries were substantial. There was too much internal bleeding…"

"I should've forced him to go to the hospital, but he was stubborn," she murmured, still speaking in her native tongue. She looked away from me to stare out the window. Sun beams painted the sidewalk. It was a perfect, sunny day on the saddest day of her life.

Fate had a cruel, twisted sense of humor.

"Are you sure you're okay to drive?" I asked her.

She nodded, a lone tear streaking down her cheek. She hastily swiped it away.

When I was sure she was in control of her own

emotions and it was safe for her to drive, I left the waiting room and went to the nurses' station.

Without saying a word, Amanda set down a chocolate peanut butter cup in front of me.

"I'm gonna need a lot more than that," I said, swiping it off the counter and unwrapping it.

"I have a whole bag."

"That's a start," I said with a sigh. "Do you want to go out tonight?"

She blinked. "Really? You never want to go out."

I nodded. "If I go home, I'll sit and drink a bottle of wine and think about how I couldn't save Mr. Martinez. And I *really* don't want to sit and stew. So, how about it?"

"Sure. Where do you want to go? Tony's?"

I shook my head. "Something not hospital related."

Tony's was the hospital's watering hole and the bar the nurses had taken me to when I'd first moved to town. Normally, I would have been fine with it, but I wanted something different tonight.

"I haven't had a chance to really explore the city that much," I said. "You've lived in Dallas a while. Where's a good spot?"

"You want something different. Something unusual?"

I nodded.

She paused, tapping a manicured finger to her lip. "How about The Rex Hotel?"

I frowned. "The Rex Hotel?"

"Yeah. They have a Whisky Room. It's the top floor of the hotel, and it looks like an English smoking den. They have killer cocktails and after dinner drinks. It's also got the most amazing view of the Dallas skyline. I think a snazzy East Coaster like yourself will appreciate it."

"Dress code?"

"Yep," she said with a grin. "Wear something fancy."

# Chapter 5

"HOLY COW, YOU WEREN'T LYING," I said to Amanda, as I looked out at the Dallas skyline from my spot at the bar. "This place is incredible."

"Right? Cheers."

I clinked my vodka gimlet against her chocolate martini and then took a sip. It was the perfect blend of tart and sweet.

Her cell phone trilled in her beaded black clutch. A shadow of annoyance passed over her face as she reached for it. "Sorry. It's probably Martin."

Smiling, I took another drink of my cocktail.

"Unbelievable," she muttered. "The one night I want to get dressed up and go out for a fancy girls' night, Martin says Daphne feels warm. I need to call him real quick. Do you mind?"

"Not at all," I said. "I'll be here."

With a roll of her eyes, she hopped off the stool, grabbed her clutch, and stalked away. I noticed a few men in suits watching her. Amanda was a petite brunette with curves, and the green dress she wore had a flouncy skirt that showed off a lot of leg.

As I waited for her to return, I scanned the room. There were clusters of people sitting on couches, and the gas fireplaces roared with cheer and warmth. I sipped on my cocktail, my eyes resting on the two men at a table in the corner by the window.

The lighting in the room was dim, but there was something familiar about one of the men. And then he turned his head ever so slightly, revealing a strong jaw covered in scruff and mussed dirty blond hair.

"You've got to be kidding me," I muttered.

I heard the click of Amanda's heels, and then she appeared next to me. I glared at her.

"What's that look for?" she demanded. "I wasn't even gone five minutes."

"Not that." I gestured with my chin in the direction of Boxer. "*That.*"

Amanda's expression was quizzical. "What's he doing here?"

"Don't play dumb."

"Play dumb? Why would I—oh my God! You think I did this on purpose, that I knew he'd be here. No, Linden, I swear I didn't know."

"Why the hell is he here? What's he doing at The Rex?"

"No idea." She pitched her voice lower. "He's looking over here."

"Nuh-uh."

"Yeah, huh," she said with a nod. "And…he just got up."

My eyes widened.

"He's coming over." She flashed a grin and urged the cocktail toward me. "Take a hearty swallow and stop looking terrified. You have no reason to be terrified. You look fucking hot, and he noticed."

I downed a hefty swallow of my gimlet, and then I rotated on my stool to watch him as he approached. He was moving slowly, no doubt from the pain of his recent appendectomy, but his natural swagger made my heart flutter.

He was wearing his leather cut, but also a white button-down shirt underneath. It looked out of place—just like he did. He didn't belong in The Rex. He was too earthy, too primal and no amount of feigned dressing up was going to change that.

Boxer sauntered toward me, an affable grin on his face. "Doc."

"Boxer."

His dove gray eyes raked over me in appreciation, but his gaze wasn't lewd. It caused my skin to erupt in tingly pinpricks.

Boxer looked at Amanda, and his smile widened. "Hey. Are you having a girls' night?"

"We were supposed to," Amanda said blithely. "But I left my husband at home with a two-year-old, who decided to get sick on my one night off this week. Sorry, Linden, I've got to bail."

My head swiveled to hers, and my gaze narrowed. I had no idea if she was telling the truth or if she was using her child as a convenient excuse to push me into Boxer's vicinity.

"I hope Daphne feels better," I said.

"I'm sure it's just a twenty-four-hour bug," Amanda said, all but admitting her crafty nature. "I'm sure you can find someone else to entertain you." She looked pointedly at Boxer.

"I just finished up my shit," Boxer said, taking the

empty stool next to mine. "I'm free as a bird, with nowhere to be."

"Lucky how that worked out." Amanda grinned and then quickly hugged me. "Cheer her up, Boxer. She needs it. See ya later, Linden."

With a wave and toss of her brown hair, she strode toward the elevator.

"So," Boxer said, reluctantly pulling my attention back to him.

I sighed. "So."

"Could she have been more obvious?" Boxer grinned.

"I don't think so." I shook my head.

"Why do you need cheering up?"

"What are you doing here?" I fired back, ignoring his line of questioning.

"Here? You mean at The Rex?"

"Yeah. It doesn't really seem like your scene."

The bartender approached and asked Boxer what he wanted to drink. "Club soda, thanks." He shot me a wink. "I'm following your orders, Doc."

"Glad to hear it."

"I'm here because I'm buddies with the man who runs The Dallas Rex."

I raised my brows and looked in the direction of the table where Boxer had been sitting. His friend was no longer there. "You're *buddies* with the man who runs the hotel? Do you always drive an hour and half to hang out with your buddies?"

"Sure, why not? It's not that big of a deal. I make the drive a couple of times a week. Now, why do you need cheering up?"

I skimmed the rim of my martini glass as I replied, "Tough day at work."

"Yeah? Tell me about it," he invited.

I frowned. "You want to hear about it?"

"Yeah. I'll listen, if you want to talk."

Did I want to? Or did I want to forget and drown my sorrows in another expensive cocktail?

I gestured to the bartender and said, "May I have another vodka gimlet, please? Thanks." I finished the rest of my drink and pushed the empty glass across the bar.

"I lost a patient," I said finally. "Early thirties. He left behind a wife and a couple of young kids."

"Fuck," he said. "That's gotta be rough."

"Yeah," I said with a sigh. "Today was not a day I enjoyed being a doctor. Today I felt like I failed."

"Could you do anything about it?" he asked. "I mean, you did everything you could, right?"

"Of course, I did everything I could, but it didn't matter. I lost him anyway."

The bartender set my fresh cocktail in front of me.

"Thank you."

"So, you went out with Amanda tonight, looking for a little bit of a distraction?" Boxer asked, pulling my attention back to him.

"Something like that."

"I can distract you."

I raised my brows. "Oh, can you?"

He leaned forward, close enough that I could smell the scent of his skin and feel the warmth emanating from him. "Yeah, Doc. I can distract the fuck out of you."

My pulse pounded in my ears and desire coasted along my nerve endings to settle deep in my belly. Temptation coiled through me, and I turned my face up to his, silently begging for him to kiss me.

"Linden?" he whispered.

"Yeah?"

"How are you at playing jacks?"

I blinked. "Excuse me?"

"Jacks," he repeated. "Johnny, can we have a bag of jacks?"

The bartender grabbed a small brown leather pouch and set it down in front of Boxer. "Anything else?"

"Keep the drinks coming."

I was going to kill Amanda. I was going to kill her slowly, and I was going to make it hurt.

This was all her fault.

She'd used her child as an excuse to ditch me and now I was drinking, laughing, and spending time with a biker.

I wanted Boxer to kiss me.

I hoped for it.

But Boxer hadn't obliged. In fact, he was being obtuse —and for a man who'd charmed the entire nursing staff, I wondered what the hell was wrong with me.

Why didn't he want to kiss me?

Why didn't he brush my hair away from my shoulder?

Why didn't his eyes linger on my lips?

"You're up, Doc," he said, reaching for his glass of club soda.

"What number are we on?" I scooped up the pile of jacks into my hand and grabbed the ball with the other.

"Sevensies."

I scattered the jacks and then dropped the ball, letting it bounce once. But in my haste to grab seven jacks in one hand, I knocked over my half empty martini glass, spilling vodka gimlet across the bar.

"Whoa there," Boxer said, sliding back on his stool to miss being covered in a sticky mess. "Are you sure you're the same woman who took out my appendix?"

Cheeks flaming, I hastily reached for the cocktail napkins that had *WR* stamped in red on them. "To be fair, I hadn't had any alcohol before your surgery."

Johnny came to our rescue with a rag and cleaned up the spill with a smile and an air of professionalism. "Another drink?"

"God no," I muttered. "I'm fine. Thanks." I peered at the ornate clock behind the bar. "Is that the time? Crap, I need to get home."

"Did you drive?" Boxer asked.

"I—yes. Dang. I can't drive home." I glared at him. "This is your fault."

"My fault? How'd you figure?" He looked amused.

"You're the one that told Johnny to keep the drinks coming."

"You didn't have to guzzle that last one."

I gasped. "I do *not* guzzle."

"You're a guzzler. Face it, Linden, you're no better than a frat guy doing keg stands."

"I'm offended."

"No, you're not."

"No, I'm not." I sighed. "But I still can't drive home. This is bad. I guess I can take a cab."

He held out his hand. "I'll drive you."

"What?"

"I'll drive you," he repeated.

"You're not supposed to drive."

"Says who?"

"Says me, remember?"

"I'm not on any painkillers, and I haven't been drinking. My pain is at a five today. How far away do you live?"

I blinked at his rapid change of discussion. "I'm only about a ten-minute drive, actually."

He flashed a grin. "I promise to get you home in one piece. Okay?"

"Okay," I said on a sigh.

He held out his hand to me.

I took it.

Boxer chuckled. "I meant for you to give me your keys."

"Oh." Embarrassment washed through me, and I hastily dropped his hand. "The valet has them." I grabbed my clutch and hastened toward the elevator, wobbling on my heels as I went.

*What other stupid things was I going to do by the time he dropped me off at my condo?*

We were silent during the ride down to the lobby. I chanced a peek at Boxer who was facing forward, all but ignoring me. It didn't make any sense. Where was the guy who'd asked the nurses about me?

I couldn't figure him out.

The doors opened. In my haste to leave, I lost my footing, and my ankle gave out. I would've gone down, but Boxer was suddenly there, catching me before I fell.

He grunted.

"Boxer!" I hissed. "Your stitches!"

"I'm fine." He grimaced.

"You're not fine. If you start bleeding because—"

"I'd rather start bleeding than ever let a beautiful woman fall to the ground. Besides, you're a menace to yourself," he teased, as he wrapped his arm around my shoulder. "You need me."

I tried not to notice the strength in the lines of his body that I was nestled up against, or the excitement I felt when his hand slid down to claim my waist.

"I'm okay," I said, hating that I sounded breathless. "You can let me go."

"Hmmm. And let you face plant? Nah."

My skin was alive with want. I could've blamed the alcohol. It would've been safer to blame the alcohol. But there was something about Boxer. Maybe it was his ease. His charm. His confidence. Maybe it was a combination of all those things.

We walked across the lobby, with Boxer's arm still around me. The doorman opened the door, and we stepped out into the valet area. Two attendants snapped to attention when they saw us. I reached into my clutch and pulled out a ticket and handed it off. Before I could tip, Boxer had let me go and was pulling a twenty out of his pocket and handing it over.

"You didn't have to do that," I protested. "Let me pay you back."

"Don't worry about it, Linden." When I was about to insist, he looked at me and said, "Seriously. I got it."

"Thanks," I said, wondering if this was more than just about tipping a valet. "Oh, no."

"What?"

"I forgot to pay my tab in the Whisky Room." I turned around to head back inside when Boxer's hand grasping my wrist stopped me. Amanda had gotten the first round of drinks and I'd never given Johnny my credit card.

"I took care of it."

"How? I didn't see you pay."

"Buddies with The Rex manager, remember? Johnny knows me."

"Well, still," I protested lamely. "You shouldn't have."

He shrugged and then let me go.

I was just about to ask why he'd paid my bill when the valet returned with my black Mercedes AMG edition SUV. The waiting attendant held open the passenger door for me.

"Thank you," I murmured, setting my clutch on my lap. He closed the door, and then I buckled up.

Boxer eased himself into the driver's side. I couldn't help the snigger that escaped. He was too tall for my seat adjustment, and he looked completely wrong in my car.

He peered at me and grinned, and then he maneuvered the seat settings as he got comfortable.

I plugged my address into the GPS, and then he was pulling away from The Rex Hotel.

"How are you getting home?" I asked, needing—wanting—to fill the silence that had descended between us.

"A prospect will come get me."

"So, you didn't drive yourself to The Rex? Or ride your motorcycle?"

"At ease, Dr. Ward." He winked. "I have a chauffeur."

I leaned my head back against the seat, letting my eyes slowly close. Lights of the city melded into patches of gold behind my lids, and I sighed.

The GPS announced her directions and Boxer turned down my street and into the parking garage.

"Code?" Boxer asked.

I gave it to him. The security arm lifted, and we drove through. He found a spot near the elevator and parked.

"Thank you," I said. "For driving me home."

He plopped the keys into my hand. "It's the least I could do for the woman who saved my life."

I rolled my eyes but couldn't stop the smile from spreading across my face. "Thanks for tonight, too. I mean, for making this day a lot less horrible."

Boxer raised his brows. "I think that was a compliment."

"It was," I assured him. I got out of the vehicle, and he did the same, though he moved slowly. After the doors were shut, I hit the clicker and the car locked.

I headed for the elevator, and he followed. I pressed the button, and the doors opened immediately. "Well, thanks again, Boxer. Have a good night."

I stepped into the carriage and turned.

He was staring at me with a blank expression, but something moved in his eyes. Something I couldn't decipher.

The doors began to shut but just as they were about to close all the way, his hand shot through the gap. They opened, and then he was stepping into the elevator and one of his arms went around me, while the other cradled the back of my head.

He stared into my eyes for just a moment, and then his lips covered mine. His tongue thrust into my mouth, and I heard someone moan.

It was me.

And then I was kissing him back, and I dropped my clutch so I could grab the lapels of his leather vest and pull him toward me.

Boxer's mouth was a match, and I was a rope doused in kerosene. I twined around him, wanting to get closer.

Just as I was about to sink deeper into our kiss, he pulled away. He looked down at me, and his thumb skimmed across my cheekbone.

"Have a good night, Linden."

He released me and stepped out of the elevator.

His intense silver gaze was the last thing I saw before the doors closed.

# Chapter 6

"Mom, I already told you," I said calmly. "I can't come home for Christmas."

"But why?" she demanded. "I don't understand. You need time off as much as anyone."

"I'm the new hire, remember? Just because I'm a surgeon doesn't mean I run the hospital and can take off whenever I want."

"Last year it was because you were finishing your fellowship, and you didn't want to take time off. The year before that you were spending it with Jeff in Chapel Hill. Before that it was—"

"I'm not doing this with you." I pulled out my leftovers from the hospital lounge fridge and brought them to the counter.

"I guess I should be glad you called at all." She sniffed, threatening to unleash the crocodile tears.

"Mom, I've got to go. I'm working."

"When are you *not* working?"

"Love you too," I said. "Give my best to George." I

hung up and shoved the phone into the pocket of my scrubs.

"Mommy dearest?" Peyton asked as she came into the staff room.

"Yup." I rubbed the spot above my left brow. I hadn't needed that conversation after the week I'd just had. I hadn't slept well in days. Even though I'd climb into bed exhausted, my mind didn't play by the same rules as my body. Instead, I lay awake, my head full of thoughts of Boxer, churning like the drum of a washing machine.

He'd kissed me and then ghosted me.

And I was stupid enough to admit that it annoyed me.

More than annoyed me.

I sat down on a couch in the lounge and opened my plastic container. "Dang, I forgot a fork. Will you hand me one, please?"

Peyton went to the drawer and pulled out plastic silverware. She came over and plopped down next to me to peer into my container. "What did you bring?"

"Italian."

"Yum." She looked me up and down. "When was the last time you had a home-cooked meal?"

I paused with the fork halfway to my mouth.

"If you have to think about it, it's been too long. Come over to my house. I'll cook for you."

"You don't have to do that," I said, eating a bite of cold lasagna.

"You didn't even bother heatin' it up," she said with a rueful shake of her head. "It's also much more fun to cook for two, so you'd be doing me a favor."

I swallowed and then nodded. "Then I'd be glad to accept your invitation. Can I bring the wine at least?"

Peyton smiled. "Absolutely."

I looked down at the food in the plastic container. It

was cheap. Disposable. I'd throw it away after a few uses because it would inevitably stain from oils in sauces and stews.

Why did I feel a kinship with a dumb plastic container?

"Linden?" Peyton asked.

"Huh?" I looked up at her.

"Are you okay? You tuned out for a second."

"Do you ever reevaluate your life?" I asked.

She looked at me. "Reevaluate how?"

"Nothing. Never mind." I forced a grin and went back to eating.

"It's not *nothing, never mind.*"

My pager vibrated against my hip, and I looked at it. "I've got a consult in the ER. Gotta go." I shoved my lasagna at her. "You finish it. You're practically drooling over it anyway."

She grinned. "I'll eat it, but we're not done with this conversation."

"After a bottle of wine, I'll spill my guts," I assured her.

I took the stairs down a few floors to the ER. Some of the beds had patients waiting to be seen by doctors on call, but it wasn't pandemonium. There was a lull, which was good for humanity, but bad for doctors. Doctors had a hard time being idle.

"I got a page," I said to the nurse on duty.

She gestured in the direction of a hospital cot, and I turned to see what she was pointing at.

Boxer was sitting on the bed, legs stretched out, a roguish grin on his face. I immediately rushed toward him in concern.

"Hey, darlin'," he drawled. "Miss me?"

My heart jumped into my throat, but I forced myself to remain calm. "Miss you? I've forgotten what you looked like."

He raised his brows. "Thinking about me nonstop?"

I sighed. "Are you in pain? Is that why you're here? I knew it, you have an abscess full of pus. It'll have to be drained, and it'll be gross—you should've gone to a hospital in Waco—"

"Is this your version of foreplay?"

"Foreplay?" I blinked. "Who said anything about foreplay?"

He got up off the bed and crowded my space, but only so he could reach over me, grab the curtain, and shut it, concealing us from prying eyes.

"What are you doing here, if you're not in pain?"

"I came to ask you out."

"Ask me out? Why?"

"Because when a boy likes a girl, he often wants to spend time with her."

"You spent time with me the other night," I pointed out. "And then you…"

"I what?"

"Kissed me, didn't ask for my number, and ghosted me."

His smile widened into a devilish grin.

"What's that grin for?" I demanded.

"You wanted me to get your number."

"I wanted…" I sighed. "Darn it. You confuse me."

"You're not my type, Doc."

His pronouncement stung, so I did what I always did to cover my hurt feelings: I tossed my hair over my shoulder and leveled him with a haughty stare. "Good. You're not my type either."

"Hmm. Judging by how you clung to me in the elevator, I beg to differ."

I glared at him. "I can still want to kiss someone who's not my type. Hormones are hormones."

"Oh good, I'm about to get a biology lesson, aren't I?"

"Why are you here?" I demanded. "You didn't have to show up at the hospital just to tell me I'm not your type."

"I had fun the other night."

"You did?" I asked in surprise.

"Yeah. And not just when I had my tongue in your mouth. The other stuff too."

"The other stuff. You mean the talking part of the evening?"

He smirked. "Yeah. That's unusual for me."

"You don't talk to women?"

"Not if I can help it."

"You're really selling yourself, here. I don't even know what you're here for."

"You."

"Me?"

"I want to take you out. For real. I want to pick you up, hold your hand, and buy you some food."

"Why?"

"Why what?"

"Why do you want to take me out? You literally just told me I'm not your type. What gives?"

"I just told you."

"You're gonna have to tell me again," I gritted out. "And explain it better this time." My ego was more than a little bit bruised.

"I haven't been able to stop thinking about you," he said.

His gaze was intense like liquid silver.

"It's been a week. You could've contacted me long before now," I said. "So why didn't you?"

"I was talking myself out of it. Or trying to. It didn't work." He stepped closer and towered over me, but not in an authoritative way.

I tilted my head back to look at him. "Boxer, I don't think—"

He covered my lips with his. He tasted like mint, and the scent of his cologne wrapped around me, heady and potent like a summer night with a touch of spice. Boxer spliced his fingers through the loose part of my braid at the nape of my neck, urging me closer, urging me to live in the feeling of his hot mouth on mine.

I set my hand on his shoulder to steady myself and then I sank into his touch, sank into the need I couldn't deny now that I was faced with it.

"Say yes," he said against my lips.

"To what?"

"To going on a date with me."

His lips settled against mine again, and then his tongue was in my mouth. He wasn't playing around, clearly. When he lifted his lips from mine, I was sure I was staring at him with a bemused expression splayed across my face.

Boxer was raw sexual appeal and excitement. He was everything I'd shied away from my entire life. And my body softened into him. I placed my palm against his chest and felt the steady pulse of his heart.

"When's your next day off?" he asked.

"Tomorrow."

"Unless you want a prospect to be our third wheel, you better clear me to drive. Officially, that is."

"Are you blackmailing me?" I asked with a slight curve of my lips.

He grasped the end of my blonde braid and tugged me toward him again. "Linden."

"Boxer."

"I like the sass, Doc. I really do." He released my hair, and then dipped his hand into my scrub pants pocket and pulled out my cell phone. "Unlock this so I can give you my number."

I took my phone and unlocked it and then handed it back to him. His fingers flew across the screen and a few moments later I heard a buzz. Boxer reached into his pocket and extracted his cell.

"Now you've got my number," he said. "I'll pick you up at five." He gently grasped my chin and slid his lips across mine. It was quick, a tease of what he could do with his mouth.

"See you tomorrow, Doc." He winked and then pulled the curtain back and left.

I stared after him for a good long moment only to realize I'd never officially cleared him to drive.

"Labs for Alice Whitcomb," Peyton said, handing me a tablet.

"Thanks." I took it, and without leaving the nurses' station, I scrolled through them to read the results.

After a few moments, I let out a long sigh.

"Bad news?" she asked, pitching her voice low.

"Biopsy came back positive. Stomach cancer," I said quietly.

"Damn, really?" Peyton asked, her eyes concerned.

I nodded. "It's spread too. Lymph nodes."

"Damn," Peyton repeated.

"I really hate this part of the job." I took the tablet and headed to Alice's room.

The sixty-three-year-old grandmother of four was lying in a hospital bed, crocheting scarves for family members. I hoped like hell she would be able to finish them.

I entered. The TV was on low, mostly for background

noise. She was setting aside her crochet needles and the current project she was working on.

"Dr. Ward," she said with a warm smile.

"Hi, Alice."

Her smile trembled, and her brown eyes rested on me. "It's bad, isn't it?"

"Stomach cancer," I said, not beating around the bush. "It looks like it's spread to your lymph nodes, so we need to talk about the next steps."

She leaned back against the pillows and closed her eyes. "I was having stomach pain weeks ago. I didn't think anything of it. I didn't think it was serious." She opened her eyes and stared at me.

Alice fiddled with the wedding ring she wore on a chain around her neck. It had belonged to her husband who'd passed away at fifty-five.

I knew my patients. I got invested in their lives. I asked about their children, grandchildren, and vacations.

I had made up my mind a long time ago that if they were going to come into my life—whether it was for a day or a week or longer—I wanted to know about theirs. Treatment became personal. It was much harder, but the caring made it real for me. These weren't just patients; they were people.

And right now, I was the person who'd just blown apart Alice's entire world, all because of my diagnosis.

"I'm going to have my staff set up a meeting between you and Dr. Lowell, the hospital's senior-most oncologist," I said. "She can go over your options and treatment plans. She's very good, Alice."

Alice nodded and then grabbed the crochet needles like they were a lifeline. "I'd appreciate that. Thanks."

She buried her attention in the yellow yarn as her fingers worked diligently and efficiently.

I didn't know what else to say to her, so I quietly left the room, the sounds of someone winning a game show and the cheers of the crowd filtering to my ears.

I didn't return to the nurses' station right away. Instead, I took the detour to the stairwell and went down a floor and found the janitor's closet.

Among the cleaning supplies, I let out all my feelings, crying as I wished I could save them.

Save them all.

It was late afternoon when my shift ended. Though the autumn sun was warm on my back as I made my way across the parking lot, my heart and head were heavy. Imparting bad news to patients was part of the job, but it got inside me, infected my soul. Watching the truth wash over Alice's expression had gutted me.

My phone buzzed, and when I saw that it was Boxer, a reluctant smile spread across my lips and a deep exhale left my lungs.

> **BOXER**
>
> Do you want to know where I'm taking you tomorrow?

I stopped walking to text a reply.

> **ME**
>
> Surprise me.

> **BOXER**
>
> You trust me that much?

> **ME**
>
> No sex dungeons. That's all I ask.

BOXER

Damn. You read my mind. I guess it'll have to be plan b.

The drive home was long and slow. Traffic was a bitch. Finally, I turned into the underground garage of the condo building and found a spot near the elevator. I gathered my belongings and climbed out of the car. The carriage came almost immediately. I trudged across the floor to my apartment and then accidentally dropped my keys. Leaning over, I scooped them up, and for a moment, I pressed my forehead to the wood.

Once inside, I released my stuff where I stood, shut the door, and locked up for the night. I sank to the floor, and didn't move for a long, long while.

# Chapter 7

THE INTERCOM BUZZED. I went to answer it, my heart pounding in my ears. I pressed a button. "Hello?"

"Linden, it's Jerry. I have a…Boxer here to see you."

I swallowed my nerves. "Yes, I've been expecting him. Send him up. Thanks."

I released the button and then rushed to the bedroom. I quickly slid into a pair of tight dark jeans and a loose weave emerald–green sweater. I'd fishtail braided my hair, letting it fall across my shoulder and then added dainty diamond studs to my ears.

When there was a knock on my front door, I went to let Boxer in.

He was leaning against the door jamb, dressed casually in jeans, a flannel shirt rolled up to the elbows, and his leather vest. Ink snaked up his arms to disappear beneath his shirt, and he wore a devastating grin.

My heart surged into my throat, and I was suddenly aware that I had no idea what I was doing with a man like him. A man like him couldn't be contained or brushed off. He was nothing like Jeff or any other man I'd dated.

It was intimidating as hell.

He marched through the door and crowded my space as he forced me to take a few steps back. Boxer reached up to gently cradle my face in his hands, tilting my head back so I stared him in the eyes.

"What's wrong?" he demanded.

"Nothing's wrong," I lied.

"Something changed."

I glared at him and wrenched out of his grasp. "Nothing has changed."

He sighed. "Damn it, you've been thinking and now you're having doubts."

"I haven't been thinking," I protested.

"You're a doctor. When do you ever *stop* thinking?"

"Good point."

"Tell me what's going on in your head."

I nibbled my lip. "You're a biker."

"Yeah."

"We live in two different cities."

"So?"

"Who can afford the commute time? How is that going to work?"

"You think too much. Did you have fun the other night?" he asked.

"Yeah."

"Do you want to get to know me better?"

I sighed and then reluctantly nodded.

"Then come out with me and have some food and don't worry about the other stuff."

"Says the guy who ignored me for a week because he was trying to talk himself out of asking me on a date."

"I had to weigh the pros and cons," he said with a casual shrug.

"The pros and cons of what?"

"Getting involved with a woman who's high maintenance, darlin'. I just had to decide if I wanted to put up with that shit."

"High maintenance? I'm not high maintenance."

He raised his brows and looked me up and down, smirking. "Yeah, okay."

"I'm *not*!" I insisted.

"So, a part of you isn't worried about the fact that you're slumming it?"

"Slumming it? Is that what you think I'm doing?"

Boxer shrugged. "Can't say one way or the other, but it seems to me like you're a little rich girl slumming it with a biker as a sort of test drive for rebellion."

I glared at him. "For the record, if I was going to rebel, I would've done it in my teens like a normal person. Furthermore, I never once thought of you and *slumming it* in the same thought. I want to go out with you because you make me laugh, and you kiss like a prisoner on death row."

He shot me a lopsided grin. "Fine, you don't have to beg me, Doc. I'll date you."

"Shut up, Boxer."

With a laugh, he dipped his head. His lips brushed mine as if saying hello. I opened to him and let his taste and smell overwhelm me.

I'd never met a man like him. He had such confidence and assurance, and I knew he was toying with me, but I wanted him to.

When he pulled back, he looked down at me and smiled. "You want to get out of here?"

I nodded. "Let me just get my boots. Come in for a minute."

He came farther into the condo and closed the door. Boxer looked around. "Nice place you got here."

"Rental," I explained.

73

Boxer nodded but didn't seem inclined to ask questions.

"I need a pair of socks. I'll be right back."

"I'll be here," he assured me.

I went to my bedroom and grabbed my black leather ankle boots and returned to the living room. Boxer was wandering around the open floor condo, his expression showing curiosity. He trekked into the kitchen and pointed to the Italian espresso machine. "What the ever-loving fuck is that?"

I laughed and slipped on my other boot. "An espresso maker."

"Whatever happened to good old Mr. Coffee?"

I stood up. "I get enough of the dishwater-flavored coffee at the hospital. But at home, I only drink the good stuff."

"It looks like it could fly us to the moon." Boxer shook his head. "You ready?"

"Yeah, I'm ready." I went to the counter to gather my belongings. I checked my brown shoulder bag to make sure I had my keys, cell phone, and wallet. "Where are we going?"

He flashed a grin. "I'm not telling you."

"No sex dungeon, though, right?"

"Uh, sure."

I rolled my eyes. We headed to the door and Boxer got there first, opening it for me. I looked at him in surprise, which only made his grin deepen. "Just because I have tattoos and wear a leather cut doesn't mean I don't have manners."

"A leather cut?" I asked, brushing past him, close enough to smell his cologne. I suddenly wanted to bury my nose in his chest and inhale deeply, taking all of him in.

"The vest. It's called a cut."

I quickly locked the condo and after I stuck my keys in my purse, Boxer grasped my hand.

"How are you feeling?" I asked him.

"Pretty damn good." He looked at me and winked.

"Would you even bother telling me if you were in any pain?" I asked him.

"So you can poke and prod me and think of me as your patient again instead of the hot guy you're going out with?" He shook his head. "No way in hell. But you don't need to worry. I'm not on any painkillers. Not even Tylenol. I'm clearheaded to drive."

"I believe you," I said.

"Yeah?"

I nodded.

"The pain is nothing more than a dull throb. Inconvenient."

"So, no pus or oozing—"

Boxer's crack of laughter echoed across the hallway. "For the love of all that is holy, please stop."

I chuckled and let my question go. I breathed in the moment, enjoying the feel of my hand in his.

When we got to the elevator, Boxer pushed the button and the doors opened immediately. He tugged me inside and pressed the lobby button. And when we had privacy, he gently maneuvered me against a wall.

"What are you doing?" I asked.

"Kissing you in an elevator." He flashed an arrogant grin, and then his lips found mine. His hand was at my waist, and his tongue slid into my mouth.

My hands wandered up his body to slip beneath the fabric of his flannel shirt. His skin was warm. I wanted to strip him down and examine every single piece of his body art.

The doors opened.

Boxer ended our kiss—far sooner than I was ready for him to—and stared down at me. He didn't say anything, he just quirked his lips into a knowing smile and brushed a thumb across my cheek.

I was sure my face was beet red as we walked hand in hand across the lobby. Jerry's eyes darted between us.

"Have a good night, Jerry," I called to him.

"You too," he murmured.

We stepped out into the brisk evening and walked through the waning sunlight a few feet to Boxer's truck. He opened the passenger door for me.

"Thank you," I said, climbing into the seat.

He shut the door and then went around to the driver's side.

"So, Adderly McLintock Ford," I began. "That's an unusual name."

"You're one to talk."

I laughed. "Fair enough. Where did Adderly come from? Family name?"

He turned on the truck. "You like jazz?"

"I don't listen to it much."

Boxer looked at me and grinned. He pressed a button on his steering wheel, and the warbling notes of jazz began to filter through the speakers. After a few moments of getting situated, he put the truck into gear, and we were on our way.

"My pops was a bass player in a jazz band. Loved Count Basie, Charles Mingus, and some other greats of their time. But he was really into this saxophone player from the '60s named Cannonball Adderly."

"Is that who we're listening to now?"

"Yeah," he said with a roguish grin.

"Ah, and it all becomes clear." I smiled. "Your mom went along with it."

He smirked. "Yeah, she went along with it. She was the one who saddled me with the middle name McLintock. John Wayne fan. They humored each other that way."

"Sweet."

"Sweet," he repeated. "Yeah."

I looked at him in confusion. His expression was suddenly closed off. I wondered if I'd accidentally unearthed something that he had wished to remain buried.

"When did you get your first tattoo?" I asked, wanting to lighten the conversation.

"Sixteen. I was trying to impress a girl."

"Did it work?"

"Fuck yeah, it worked. I don't kiss and tell, but let me just say, I was a rock star my junior year of high school."

I laughed. "I wouldn't have known what to do with a guy like you back in high school."

"Darlin'," he drawled. "You don't know what to do with a man like me now."

No truer statement had been uttered between us.

"Are you still not going to tell me where we're going?" I asked.

"Slow your roll. You're gonna enjoy yourself, I promise."

We drove to the outskirts of town and passed a lot of abandoned brick buildings and old storefronts that were empty.

Boxer turned down a side street that looked like an alleyway of sorts. A bright neon sign flashed the name "Pinky's."

"It's not a biker bar, is it? I'm not really dressed for a biker bar."

"It's not a biker bar," he said with a chuckle.

"What? What did I say?"

"Nothing. I just had this vision of you walking into a biker bar and your eyes bugging out of your head."

"Why would my eyes bug out of my head?"

Boxer paused for a moment and then rubbed a thumb across his chin stubble. "I don't know, maybe all the leather, women with teased hair and tats, and a bunch of people who give no fucks might be a shock to someone used to boat shoes and bow ties. What do you really know about bikers, Linden?" His tone was serious, and he'd used my name. He wanted me to pay attention.

"I don't know a lot really. Just what I learned from pop culture."

Boxer nodded thoughtfully. "We're not like normal people."

"Bikers?"

"Yeah, but in particular the Tarnished Angels," he corrected. "We live by our own rules. We value loyalty, family, and our community. We choose to make our own reality in a world that would rather put us in a box. We prefer the open road under blue skies. We live free, Linden."

"I don't understand," I said.

"Not everything we do is lawful."

*And there it is.*

"So, you're an outlaw?"

"Yeah." He stared at me. "Darlin'?"

"Why are you bringing this up now?" I asked in annoyance. I didn't want to be confronted with the truth. I wanted fun and light, and this was anything but fun and light.

"So there's no confusion about who I am or what I do. I am who I am. I'm a biker with a high school diploma. You're a doctor. We live very different lives."

"I know that."

"Do you? Because women have this habit of saying they understand and then when their bodies get involved, so do their emotions. Don't think you can change me."

"Change you?" I repeated. "Why would I try and change you?"

"Because that's what women do."

"Not me," I assured him.

"If you say so."

"I *do* say so," I insisted. "Don't you go trying to change me."

"What? How would I do that?" he demanded.

"I work eighty-hour weeks. I love my career, and I'm incredibly good at what I do. I'm not giving it up to sit on the sidelines of life waiting for a man to pay attention to me."

He frowned. "What the hell are you talking about?"

I took a deep breath. "I ended a relationship a few months ago. Before I moved out here. He had this idea of what he thought I should be. He wasn't happy when he discovered that reality and his expectations didn't match."

"Well, here we are," he muttered. "Look, let's just agree that I won't try and change you, and you won't try and change me. We'll have fun and good times. We'll have some laughs, and we won't put any pressure on each other, and we'll keep this easy. Deal?"

"Deal," I said quickly.

I unlatched my seat belt and was out of the truck before Boxer was able to come around and help me. He draped an arm across my shoulder and pulled me into his side. I liked his casual, relaxed affection, and I liked that we'd set our expectations. This thing with Boxer had no future. It wouldn't go anywhere. There was no danger of falling in love with each other because we were both clear on what we wanted.

*Easy and light.*

We walked down the alley to a thick, heavy wood door that he pulled open. There were red vinyl booths and a counter with red vinyl covered stools. Retro diner signs covered almost every inch of the walls. It was like stepping back in time.

"Are those pinball machines?" I asked in excitement.

"Yup. They're vintage and they've been restored."

I looked up at him and smiled. "You brought me here to play pinball?"

"Partly. Pinky's also serves the best chili dogs I've ever had."

"I can't remember the last time I had a good chili dog," I admitted.

"Well, tonight we fix that."

I didn't give him any grief about his after-surgery diet. It had been a couple of weeks. Boxer was moving around with relative ease and at some point, he had to get back to normal life. And that included his regular diet. I was just glad he'd laid off the booze the night I hung out with him at The Rex.

Pinky's was nearly empty, but I had a feeling it would get busy later on. Boxer still had his arm around me as he guided me to a table.

"Shouldn't we wait to be seated?" I asked, shooting a glance at the buxom, platinum blonde behind the counter who was wiping down liquor bottles and not paying any attention to us.

"Nah, it's fine." He gestured to the booth.

I slid into one side and Boxer took the other.

"How did you find this place?" I asked.

"It's a secret." He winked and then removed a red vinyl menu from between the vintage mustard and ketchup squeeze bottles.

"Why is it a secret?" I asked.

"You haven't earned the truth yet, darlin'."

"The truth about Pinky's?" I leaned forward. "Is this a place that houses your nefarious activities? Is there some secret door in the back or something?"

He let out a laugh. "You're cute when you're curious." He shoved the menu in front of me. "Decide what you want."

"I thought we were getting chili dogs."

"You want onion rings, fries, or tots?"

"Fries."

"Shoestring, wedge, or waffle?"

"Shoestring."

"Spicy, savory, or salty?"

"Salty." I smiled. "Any other questions?"

He leaned forward. "What color is your underwear?"

"Nice try but no dice," I said in mock admonishment. "You haven't earned the privilege of knowing."

"Damn. This is what I get for trying to seduce a smart dame."

The platinum blonde came out from around the counter and approached our table. She wore a pair of tight jeans and a white tank top that showed off the cherry blossom tattoo winding up her right arm.

"Hi, Boxer," she greeted.

"Hey, Freddy." He reached across the table and took my hand, linking his fingers through mine. "Meet Dr. Linden Ward, the woman who saved my life."

Freddy's blue eyes lit up and she smiled, and before I knew it, she was leaning down and enveloping me in a side embrace. "Thank you so much."

I shot Boxer a confused look, but said to Freddy, "Oh, yeah. Sure thing."

Freddy pulled back and hastily turned her head, but

she couldn't completely hide that she was swiping a hand across her eyes.

A moment later, she faced us again. Her lashes sparkled with tears she'd failed to rein in.

*What the heck?*

"We'll have three chili dogs, one order of salty shoe-string fries, and two grape sodas," Boxer said.

"Grape soda?" I asked.

"Trust me. It's the best."

"Nah, orange is the best," Freddy countered.

"One of each," Boxer relented. "Then Linden can choose."

"You got it." Freddy left to put in our order.

"You know her," I said to him when we were alone. "You come here a lot, then?"

He skimmed the back of my hand with his thumb, causing tingles to erupt along my skin.

"I got her a job here," he said. "About three months ago. I pop in every now and again to make sure she's doing okay. She's a nice kid. A good kid."

Freddy returned with two glass bottles of soda and two straws. She set them down in front of us, then reached into the short green apron tied around her waist and pulled out a small plastic cup and placed it on the table.

"Food should be up shortly," Freddy said. "Holler if you need anything." She left again and then went to check on the only other occupied table in the place.

"You called her a kid," I said, picking up our thread of conversation.

"She *is* a kid. She's twenty-two."

*She doesn't look like a kid to me.*

Boxer's eyes didn't stray from my face. "What are you really trying to ask me, darlin'?"

"I don't know."

"You do," he insisted. "So, own it and ask, or stop pussy-footing around."

"Have you slept with her?"

He looked amused. "No."

"Do you want to sleep with her?"

"No."

His gray eyes darkened with emotion, and his hand tightened on mine.

Freddy appeared at our table with a red tray. "Here we go," she said. "Can I get you anything else?"

"I'm good, thanks," I said, forcing a smile.

She looked down at me and grinned. "Which soda did you choose?"

"I haven't yet." I reached for the grape soda and took a healthy swallow. It was like a fizzy grape popsicle. "Sold. I don't even need to try the orange."

Boxer grinned at Freddy. "Told ya."

Freddy glanced at Boxer. "Need anything else?"

"I'm good. Thanks, darlin'."

She smiled and then left our table.

He grabbed a dog, and a glob of chili landed on his plate.

I gingerly lifted mine and brought it to my mouth. I hesitated for a moment and then went for it. The chili was the perfect blend of spice and heat and I chomped away, not looking up until it was halfway gone, to find Boxer staring at me.

A slow smile of appreciation crossed his lips, and then he went back to eating.

All conversation was put on hold while we devoured our chili dogs. When I had one bite left, Boxer nudged the plate of shoestring fries toward me. "Try one."

I snatched a fry and stuck it into my mouth, moaning

at the salty potato taste on my tongue. "That's one of the best things I've ever had."

"Glad you're enjoying it," he said with amusement, eyes flashing with heat.

I polished off the last of my chili dog and then reached for another fry. Boxer grabbed for the same one, and our fingers collided.

"Fight you for it," I teased.

"Nah, you have it, babe. I like watching you enjoy yourself."

The underlying sensual connotation was unmistakable, and my nipples hardened against my sweater.

"You got any more questions for me?" he asked.

"The questions can keep," I stated. "Let's play pinball."

"You ready for me to whip your ass at pinball?"

"Whip my ass? I play a mean pinball."

"Like you play jacks?" he teased. He grabbed the container on the table and shook it. Coins rattled against plastic. "Loser buys a slice of banana cream pie."

"You're on."

There were three vintage pinball machines in the back corner of the room, all lit up, and waiting to be played.

"Lady's choice," Boxer said.

"This one," I said immediately, placing my hands on the glass.

He held out the container of coins to me. I moved into position. "What do you say? Best two out of three wins?"

Boxer grinned. "Yup."

I slipped the token into the slot, and the machine flashed in expectation. I grasped the plunger to pull it back and then released it. A silver ball shot up, hit a bunch of bumpers on the way down, and then zoomed past the flippers before I could even attempt to save it.

"Rotten luck," Boxer drawled.

I glared at him.

"You've got a competitive streak, don't you, Doc?"

I slid the sleeves of my sweater up to my elbows. "Stand back. I need room to work."

Laughing, he moved.

I released the plunger again—but this time I was ready. I played for a good three minutes before I lost the ball. One more chance to score some points, and then it would be Boxer's turn. When I lost my final ball, I stepped to the side.

Boxer sauntered up with an arrogant swagger to the machine and then handed me the container of coins. He took one and slid it into the slot.

"Ready to be impressed?" he asked.

"Ready," I said in amusement.

He pulled back the plunger. The steel ball pinged and ponged, lighting up the machine. I watched in astonishment as his score kept going up. Finally, the ball dropped down and he flung it up again. It took him ten minutes to lose the first ball.

"You really are a pinball wizard," I said in amazement. "How did you get so good?"

"When I was a kid, I spent most of my free time in the mall arcade. Had to learn how to make a dollar last." His smile was wry.

We'd had such different childhoods, I realized. Mine had been spent learning how to ride horses, sailing on yachts, tennis lessons, and dinners at fancy restaurants. His had been full of mall arcades and who knew what else?

"Come here," he said, stepping back. "I'll show you how it's done."

"What about our bet?" I asked.

He laughed. "I'll buy you a slice of pie no matter who

wins." He took my hand and gently tugged me toward him, positioning me at the machine. Boxer stood at my back and pressed even closer.

He was a wall of heat, and then I ever so slightly brushed against him to feel his erection.

Boxer sucked in a breath. "You don't fight fair, darlin'."

"No, I don't. Do you?" I said, turning my head to look up at him over my shoulder.

He gazed down at me, his steely gray eyes like liquid mercury. "Not even a little bit."

Our eyes locked, and I drowned in the moment. He looked at my lips before he closed the space between us. Boxer kissed me. He kissed me with feeling and purpose. He made my head spin, taking me to some other time and place. Only when he pulled back and smiled at me—that charming, knowing smile—did I come back to the present.

I turned around fully so my butt was pressed against the pinball machine. My hands went to his belt loops so I could pull him toward me.

"Boxer?"

"Yeah, darlin'?"

"Earlier, you asked what color underwear I was wearing."

"I remember."

I leaned toward him so I could gently nip the side of his chin. "I'm not wearing any underwear."

His hand came up to grasp my neck so he could tilt my head back. "Yeah, babe. You *definitely* don't fight fair."

Just when he was about to kiss me again, his cell phone rang. With an aggrieved sigh, he let me go and reached into his jeans pocket to retrieve it.

"I've got to take this."

I nodded, and then Boxer answered the phone and strode toward the exit. He took his warmth and my attention with him. As I watched him walk away, I studied his body for signs that he was in pain from his appendectomy, but there were none. He moved with a fluid grace, a man confident in his own skin.

He disappeared through the door, and I was alone in the restaurant. The other couple had paid and left sometime during our pinball playoff, but no one else had come in yet.

I waited a few minutes to see if Boxer would return, but when it was clear his phone call would take a little more time, I quickly played the last two balls, not putting that much effort into it. When I lost, I grabbed the container of tokens and went back to the table.

Freddy was clearing away our plates and had replaced our two sodas with fresh ones.

"How was the food?" she asked.

"Perfect comfort food. Loved it."

"I'll pass along your compliments to the chef."

"You want to sit for a minute?" I asked.

Her eyes lit up. "Sure." She plopped down in Boxer's side of the booth across from me.

"Are you from Texas?" I asked.

"Yeah. From Fort Worth. I went to college at A&M."

"What did you study?"

"Engineering. I dropped out last semester." She paused. "Life stuff."

"Life stuff. Yeah, I get that."

*I so get that.*

She looked at the door, but it remained shut. Freddy's gaze darted back to mine. "Okay, listen. Boxer would kill me if he knew I told you this, but I want to say it anyway. He's a good guy. A *great* guy. Don't take him at face value."

"Face value?" I repeated.

She nodded. "He got me this job. He went out on a

limb for me when he didn't have to. He might come across…like he's only out for a good time, but that's just not true."

"It's not?"

Freddy shook her head. "Like I said, I haven't worked here long, but he comes in every now and then and he's never, not once, brought a woman."

"You care about him," I said with a genuine smile.

She nodded. "Like a brother."

I chuckled. "You must've heard us talking about you."

"I *might* have." Her blue eyes twinkled. "He's a flirt. I'm sure you've noticed that by now?"

"Uh, little bit."

She chuckled but then sobered. "There's much more to him than that. Women just see a hot face, a guy willing to have a good time, a guy who's in a biker club so he's got that dangerous thing going on, and they never get to know him. They never stick around."

"How do you know so much about him?" I asked, my curiosity spiking to new levels.

"I've gone to a few of the Tarnished Angels' parties… at the clubhouse in Waco. I've seen him with other women. I see how they are with him."

I wasn't about to tell her that I wasn't going to stick around. Even if what she said was true, I wasn't the woman for Boxer. We were from two different worlds. I wasn't slumming it, no matter what he thought, but neither did I expect to be picking out china patterns with him.

"You go all the way to Waco to party?" I asked in surprise.

She grinned. "Some parties are worth the drive."

The door to Pinky's opened and an elderly couple walked in, Boxer trailing behind them. Boxer said something to the older man who wore a navy–blue baseball hat with yellow writing that I couldn't read from where I was sitting.

The couple went to a table on the other side of the room, and Freddy hopped up. "I gotta get back to work."

"Thanks, Freddy," I said. "For your insight."

She beamed.

"We'll take a slice of the banana cream pie," I said to her. "Two forks."

"You got it."

Boxer was at the table talking to the older couple when Freddy joined him. A few moments later, Boxer had the elderly woman giggling like a teenager and the older gentleman shaking his hand.

I watched him interact with them and realized that he had a gift for making people feel comfortable.

He came back to the table and slid into the booth. "Sorry about that."

I waved my hand in dismissal. "Not a problem."

"You lost interest in pinball?"

"I wanted pie more. I ordered us a slice."

"Thanks," he said. My hand rested on the table in front of me, and he took it.

"What was that about?" I asked, gesturing with my chin to the couple. "Do you know them?"

Boxer shook his head. "Nah. Met them just now when I was holding the door open for them. Nice couple."

Freddy arrived with our banana cream pie, and she set it down between us, along with another plate. "Lemon icebox," she explained. "This one's on the house. You're gonna love it. Anything else?"

"Put Jed and Sylvie's dinner on my tab," Boxer said.

"Will do." She swept away and headed back to the bar.

"That's kind of you," I said to Boxer. "Buying total strangers dinner."

"Jed served in Vietnam," he said. "It's the least I can do."

"Face value," I murmured.

"Hmm?" He took the fork resting on the lemon icebox pie plate and cut a bite.

"Nothing," I said with a small smile. "Nothing at all."

# Chapter 8

WE FINISHED OUR PIES—THE banana cream was the winner in my book. Pinky's had begun to fill up, and another bartender hopped onto the floor to help Freddy.

I looked at my watch. "Holy hell. It's nine p.m."

"Still early," Boxer said with a grin.

"Not for someone who gets up every day at four in the morning," I quipped. "Whether or not I have to work."

"You get up at four in the morning. I don't even go to bed until then."

"You must work odd hours."

"I don't work."

I blinked.

"I'm just kidding," he said with a laugh. "I work at Charlie's Motorcycle Repair shop."

"So, you're a mechanic?"

"Nah, I work in the office. I'm the spreadsheet and parts guy. It's a sweet gig. Not too challenging. Flexible. Allows me to drive to Dallas every now and again to seduce a hot doctor." He winked.

"Maybe you need to be challenged."

"Why? I like that I can do my job on autopilot. We're not all driven to become doctors."

"No, of course not. I didn't mean to imply—"

"Yes, you did." He pushed the empty pie plate toward the center of the table and placed his crumpled paper napkin on top of it. "I'm a biker, Linden. Not everything I do is on the books. You get me?"

I nodded slowly. It was one thing to *know* he was a biker. It was another to have him admit to the darker part of his life.

He pulled out his wallet and laid more than enough to cover our meal, Jed and Sylvie's, and a large tip left over for Freddy.

"You love being a doctor, don't you?" he asked.

"Most of the time, yeah. The medicine and helping people. It gives me—"

"Purpose?"

"Yeah." I paused. "Purpose."

"You must be good at hitting the books." He grinned. "Bet you love libraries."

"How did you know?" I teased.

"You sniff books, don't you?"

"I might."

He slid out of the booth and then put out a hand toward me. I grabbed my purse and took it. He pulled me into his arms and wrapped an arm around my shoulder.

"Freddy!" he called. "We're out!"

She looked up from behind the bar, shot us a smile and a wave, and then grasped the cocktail shaker.

Boxer and I stepped out into the night. It was cooler now, and I shamelessly used it as an excuse to nuzzle closer. I enjoyed the casual ease of being with him.

He unlocked the truck and helped me with the passenger door. Before he shut it, he stared at me for a moment. We drove in relative silence with jazz playing through the speakers. Boxer reached over the center console, searching for my hand. I gave it, linking my fingers through his. It was comfortable, easy. There was no need to fill the void with mindless chitchat.

When we got to my condo, there was a parking space right in front on the street. Boxer easily maneuvered the truck into the spot and turned off the ignition.

"I'll walk you up," he said, unlatching his seat belt.

"You don't have to," I said with a smile.

"Yes, darlin'. I do. I want to make sure you get into your place safe and sound."

I frowned. "My building has a security guard."

"Humor me."

With a shrug, I grabbed my purse and hopped out of the truck. Boxer took my hand and linked his fingers through mine, as if he wasn't ready to say goodbye or stop touching me.

We entered the building. I waved to Jerry, and we continued toward the elevator. I pressed the up button, and a few moments later the doors opened. Boxer and I stepped inside.

"So, I'm gonna go out on a limb here and say this was your best date ever," Boxer stated.

A bubble of laughter escaped my lips. "Careful out there on that limb. It might snap."

He let go of my hand and then draped his arm around my shoulders. Boxer pressed his lips to my forehead.

The doors of the elevator opened, and we stepped out.

His hand slid down my arm to rest on my hip, his finger teasing the denim at my waist. "I'm dying to know if you were yanking my chain, telling me you're not wearing underwear. Is that true?"

I batted his hand away. "If I tell you, you might get ideas and overexert yourself. I haven't cleared you for your favorite hobby yet, remember?"

"Give a man a reason to dream."

"You don't want to dream. You want spank bank material."

"You've got a dirty mouth, Doc." His grin was wicked. "I never would've guessed…but I like it. I like it *a lot*."

I chuckled and placed my hand on his chest, not to force him away but because I wanted to feel his heartbeat. It raced with strength, and I shivered with want.

Boxer saw it.

His eyes darkened, and he stepped closer. "You're killing me slowly, Doc."

He gently pushed me against the door, angling his pelvis against me so I could feel how much he wanted me. His hands tore through my braid, loosening the strands and plowing his fingers through my hair.

"Linden," he growled, right before his mouth covered mine.

I grasped the lapels of his leather cut and pulled him into me. My eyes closed, and my heartbeat fluttered in my neck.

He pillaged my mouth, mimicking with his tongue what I was sure he wanted to do to my body.

My skin erupted with warmth, and I suddenly felt like I had too many clothes on. One of his hands snaked beneath my sweater, his breath catching when he realized I wasn't wearing a bra. His thumb grazed my nipple, causing it to harden.

He pulled back and stared into my eyes. "I want to see your skin flush with pleasure. I want to see your beautiful blue eyes roll back into your head when I bury my face between your thighs and lick you until you come. And then I want you to beg me to slide deep inside you."

His vision flashed in my mind, and my legs trembled. I wanted to pull him into the condo, strip him down, and demand he make good on his promises.

Boxer smiled, his hand cradling my cheek. And then he kissed me soft, gentle, like he hadn't just told me he wanted to screw me into oblivion.

"Good night, Doc."

He kissed me one last time and then he left, taking his heat and promises with him.

"Linden? Earth to Linden," Peyton said, waving her hand in front of my face.

I absentmindedly stirred creamer into my third coffee of the day as I looked at her. "Sorry? Did you say something?"

Peyton grinned. "What's with you?"

"What do you mean?" I took my cup of coffee to the staff couch, glad to have a few minutes between patients.

"I mean, you don't even look like you're on this planet." Peyton quickly made herself a cup of coffee and took the seat next to me. "Are you going to tell me what's gotten into you?"

I debated confiding in Peyton. I didn't want my personal business to spread throughout the entire hospital. I'd sworn Amanda to secrecy about running into Boxer at The Rex and so far, she'd kept her mouth shut. Not that I thought Peyton would blab on purpose, but there was always chatter between nurses.

"Does it have anything to do with that hot, yogurt-loving biker?" Peyton asked in delight.

My cheeks flamed. "How did you know it was him?"

"Because I know for a fact it wasn't that stuffy lawyer you pretended to give a chance a while back."

"He wasn't stuffy," I protested, but then immediately recanted. "Yes, yes he was."

"So, I'm right then? About Boxer?"

"You might be right about him. We went out the other night."

"Did you, now? Well, well, well, the plot thickens. Did it turn into something dirty?"

I snorted. "No."

"Will it?"

"Eventually."

"When?" she demanded.

"My love life is not a create your own adventure book," I said with amusement. "If you're so hard up for it, find yourself a hot guy. I hear home improvement stores are great places to find men with tools."

"Thanks. I'll think about it," she said, her tone dry. "But seriously. Is it going to get physical?"

I paused and then nodded.

"Are you seeing him again?"

"Yes."

"When?"

"Don't know," I admitted. "He kissed me outside my condo door and then left. He has a habit of kissing me and walking away without making any plans."

"You mean he's done this before?"

*Whoops.*

"Yeah," I admitted slowly. "I kind of accidently bumped into him at The Rex—the night I went out with Amanda."

"You've been holding out on me! We need a bottle of wine and girl talk immediately!"

Dr. Sawyer strode into the lounge, saw Peyton and me talking, and shot us a look that was both condescending and full of arrogance at the same time.

Peyton quickly hopped up like she'd been caught doing something illegal and skittered out of the lounge.

"Dr. Ward," he drawled. "When you find the time after enjoying yet another leisurely cup of coffee, please discharge my patients in rooms 302 and 327."

"Right away," I said.

Nodding, he strode out of the lounge.

"Right away, Dr. Prick," I muttered under my breath.

My phone buzzed in my lab coat pocket, and I grabbed it. A smile bloomed across my face.

BOXER

You owe me another date.

ME

I owe you? For what?

BOXER

I had to settle for my hand instead of you.

I pressed a button and put the phone to my ear. It rang for a moment, and then Boxer picked up the line and I said, "You lay it on thick, don't you?"

"Yup. Are you gonna punish me for disobeying your orders? You told me not to touch myself, and I didn't listen. Punish me, Doc. Punish me real hard."

I laughed. "I knew you weren't going to be able to keep from jerking it. Why do you think I told you weeks? I knew you'd only be able to hold out for a little while."

"Did you manipulate me?"

"Yup."

He chuckled. "So, when do I get to see you again?"

"I'm working the next forty-eight hours."

"Forty-eight hours is too long."

"It's my schedule, Boxer. I'm free the two nights after. You can have your pick."

"Wednesday."

"Dr. Ward," Dr. Sawyer barked as he appeared in the doorway of the lounge. "Are you incapable of following my request for some reason I should know about?"

"Sorry, I'll be right there." I turned away from him again, and then into the phone I said, "Sorry, I have to go."

"Who's yelling at you?" he demanded.

"No one. Don't worry about it. I'll talk to you later." I quickly hung up with Boxer and shoved my phone back in my pocket. It vibrated immediately.

Dr. Sawyer glared at me. He was in a fine snit today, and I just hoped it didn't get worse.

It got worse. Way worse.

Dr. Sawyer became my shadow, and every moment I tried to sit down to have a quiet moment, he found something else for me to do. He made me run labs and draw blood, remedial tasks that normally only interns and nurses did. Any consult in the ER that was needed, particularly when it was something vile, he sent me. Just to prove he could.

I'd worked with people like him before, those that were intimidated by others who showed promise and skill. Instead of cultivating it, they resented it.

After eighteen hours on the go, I finally managed to drag myself into an on-call room. I kicked off my shoes and all but collapsed face first onto the mattress. I was asleep within minutes.

An hour later, my pager went off. Groaning, I rolled over and flung my legs over the side of the bed. I quickly slid into my tennis shoes and was out the door.

I popped a small mint into my mouth and made my way to the nurses' station.

"I was paged," I said to Lizzie.

"I didn't page you," Lizzie said.

I frowned and grabbed the pager at my waist, which had no missed notifications. I felt another vibration in my pocket and checked my cell phone.

BOXER

Turn around.

I turned—and saw him rising from a chair in the hallway waiting area.

I strolled toward him, my traitorous heart fluttering like a caged butterfly. "What are you doing here?"

"I wanted to make sure you had some decent food instead of having to eat that shit in the hospital cafeteria." His hand touched my cheek. "Damn, you were asleep."

"How did you know?"

He leaned forward and whispered, "You have a pillow crease on your face."

My hand flew to my cheek, and I groaned. "This is what I get for rolling out of bed and not bothering to check my appearance.

"This is how you look just waking up?" He shook his head as if he couldn't believe it.

"Yeah."

"Fuck," he muttered.

"What?" I asked.

"Never mind." He held up the brown bag. "You have time for some food?"

I nodded. "Let's go to the cafeteria."

"Sorry I woke you up, darlin'."

"Don't apologize," I said. "You brought me food. That was—you didn't have to do that."

"I was at The Rex when I thought about you not having a decent meal, and then I remembered the restaurant has killer steak and mashed potatoes."

"You didn't." I opened the brown bag and peered into it, the smell of meat wafting to my nose. "You *so* did."

"Careful, you're drooling." He winked.

I pushed the down elevator button on the wall and stood back. The doors opened, and I stepped in with Boxer next to me. Once the carriage closed, he wrapped his arm around me and dragged me toward him. His lips covered mine in a hungry, demanding kiss. I curled my hand into his shirt, desire zinging through my blood.

He pulled back and looked down at me with a lopsided grin. "Three birds, one stone. That was the first bird."

I laughed and pressed the button for the cafeteria.

"I wanted to bring you food, which I've now done, so that's the second bird."

The elevator opened, and we stepped out. It was quiet this time of night, but there were a few people sitting on the other side of the room.

I gestured to a table near a large plant, and Boxer nodded. He set the bag down and removed containers of food.

My stomach turned to marshmallow fluff. "So, the third bird?" I dug into the steak and only my ingrained manners prevented me from eating like a hyena. It was that good.

"I wanted to show my face to the asshole who yelled at

you while I was on the phone," Boxer said, leaning back in his chair. "Though I have a pretty good idea of who it is."

I stopped chewing and peered at him. His expression gave nothing away and even though he looked relaxed, there was something in his body, an alertness, a readiness to spring.

"Why?"

"I'm curious."

"About?" I asked in confusion.

"How's the steak?"

"Perfection. And don't change the subject."

"I want to meet the guy that's riding your ass hard at work, okay?" His gray eyes glittered with challenge. "I'm not gonna cause trouble, if that's what you're thinkin'."

I looked at his hands that rested on the table. They were large. And his fists could do serious injury.

"I wasn't thinking that," I admitted.

"Liar," he said on a laugh.

I blushed in shame.

"Hey," he said, reaching across the table. I gave him my free hand, and he threaded his fingers with mine. "If someone treats you bad, I'm gonna want to punch the shit out of them. That's just my nature. But I know that kind of crap won't fly here. This is your terrain, not mine, and it'll just cause you more trouble. But I'd be lyin' if I said I didn't want to meet the asshole and give him something to think about."

I looked Boxer up and down, from his tattoos, to his leather cut, to the overall dangerous vibe he put out. Boxer made women's heads turn and men sit up and take notice.

A natural predator.

"You remind me of a lion," I said to him. "Sitting the way you are. Like you're happy to laze in the sun but ready to pounce at a moment's notice."

A smile spread across his face.

"What?" I asked in amusement.

"You. That's all." He gestured with his chin to the remainder of the potatoes. "Eat up, and then I'll walk you back upstairs."

We got up to the floor, and the nurses on night duty watched us with fascinated gazes. I thought about being embarrassed—embarrassed because Boxer kept a possessive hand clasped to mine. But then something truly marvelous happened.

I realized that I didn't have to care what other people thought of us.

"Thanks for bringing me dinner," I said, turning my back to the nurses' station.

"Happy to do it."

I stood on my toes and pressed my lips to his. "I'll see you soon."

"Yeah, dame, I'll see you soon."

"Dame?" I repeated.

His grin was impish, boyish. "Yeah. You're a dame, through and through." He grasped the tail end of my braid and used it to tug me forward. "Now, kiss me again. Only this time, use your tongue."

"But they're watching," I murmured.

"Even better. Give them something good to talk about."

Laughing, I kissed him again and my tongue slid into his mouth to tangle with his.

When he pulled back, his eyes were heated with promise. "Don't start what you can't finish."

"Oh, I plan to finish," I teased. "You'll just have to wait for it, but trust me, it'll be worth it."

"I don't doubt that for a second."

With one final tug on my braid, Boxer let me go, and

then he sauntered to the elevator. Only when the doors shut, did I finally come back to the present.

"You were totally staring at his butt, weren't you?" Lizzie called out.

I turned to look at her. "Yeah. I totally was. No shame."

Boxer's impromptu visit stayed with me the rest of my shift, leaving me warm and buzzy, like I'd consumed too much caffeine. Every part of me tingled with energy. Not even Dr. Prick's incessant demands and throwing me each nasty case that came through the ER dampened my spirits.

Texts from Boxer every now and again emboldened my spirit and kept me going. I didn't spend any time dwelling on why the charming playboy biker was using his time to randomly text me. I was a sure thing once I deemed him healed. In fact, I was more than ready for it. My brain was no longer protesting, and my body was primed and eager.

By the time my shift was over, and I was back in my own clothes, I was dragging hard. I stopped by the nurses' station on my way out. Peyton was gathering her belongings and jacket.

"I'll walk with you to the parking lot," she said.

"Great."

We headed to the elevators as she asked, "Do you want to come over this week for dinner?"

"Sure, that sounds good. I have the next two nights off, but I already have plans for tomorrow night."

"Do you, now?" Her smile was slow, and she raised her brows. "I can't wait to hear all about it."

The late afternoon sun bathed the parking lot, glinting

off the rainbow of cars. I got my keys out and unlocked my Mercedes with the clicker just as my phone buzzed.

I quickly removed my cell, a smile already making its way across my face. It died when I realized it wasn't Boxer but my mother. I didn't even bother to read her text.

I opened the car door and tossed my phone and bag onto the passenger seat. After climbing in, I shut and locked the door, and just sat for a moment, getting my head together.

My phone vibrated again. I eyed it warily, and then with a sigh, I grabbed it.

This time my smile came fast and furious.

BOXER

Do you like carnivals?

I turned on the car and then pressed a button on my steering wheel. His phone rang once, and then he answered.

"Hey," I said. "I can't text. I'm about to pull out of the parking lot and drive home. And no, I don't like carnivals."

"Why not? You don't like Ferris wheels or funnel cakes?"

"I can get behind the funnel cake, but I'm afraid of heights and carnivals make me sad."

"Why?"

"I don't know. They're—never mind."

"Tell me why they make you sad."

"Because they're seasonal and transient. And when they pack up and leave, there's a big open space and left-over trash and forgotten stuffed animals, and the fun is gone. It's sad."

He didn't say anything for a long moment and then he said, "No carnivals then."

"No carnivals," I agreed. I put on my seatbelt and then

slowly backed out of my spot. "Though I do appreciate a good merry-go-round."

"Yeah?"

"Yeah. It reminds me of that scene in Mary Poppins when they jump into a chalk painting."

Boxer chuckled. "I never know what you're gonna say. I like that about you."

"You do?"

"Yeah. Hold on a second. Silas! You and Brock need to get in the truck! Linden? You still there?"

"Yeah, I'm here. Who are Silas and Brock?"

"Silas is Mia's kid. Brock's his best friend. I'm at the park with them. Silas decided he wanted to try out for the soccer team because the most popular girl in his class said she liked soccer players."

"You're not supposed to be doing anything too strenuous!" I admonished.

"I'm not. It's cute though, how you worry about me."

"I'm not worried."

He snorted. "Yeah, okay."

"Silas is twelve and already into girls?" I asked.

"How did you know he was twelve?"

"Mia said so when I met her."

"Huh."

"Huh what?"

"You listen. When people talk."

"Well, sure. I'm a doctor. I'm supposed to listen so I can make things better."

"Do you know how many people don't give a shit about that?"

"Language, Boxer, you're around children."

"Yeah, Doc. School me. I like it."

I let out a laugh. "So is Silas any good at soccer?"

"The kid's got two left feet," Boxer said with a chuckle.

"But what he lacks in coordination, he more than makes up for with enthusiasm."

"Boxer!" a young boy yelled. "Stop talking to your girlfriend!"

"Hold your horses, kid. When a pretty girl wants to talk to you, you take your time."

"You better get going."

"Yeah, I better." He sighed. "They're making asinine kissy faces at me. I've got to have a sit-down talk with them about women."

"Silas is practicing his soccer skills to impress a girl. I'm pretty sure he's already clued in."

"Still. It's my job as his uncle to level with him about how to really impress women."

I grinned at the idea of a young boy mimicking Boxer. "How should I dress for our date tomorrow? Jeans?"

"No. Wear a dress. A fancy, sexy one that shows a lot of leg."

"Where are you taking me?"

"Somewhere special."

"The Rex Hotel?"

"Nope, somewhere else. Somewhere else that's gonna wow the fuck out of you."

"You don't have to," I said.

"Yeah, I do."

"Okay, but let the record show, I didn't ask to be wined and dined."

"Trying to prove you're not high maintenance?"

"Yeah. Is it working?"

"Nope. It's okay, though. It's keeping me on my toes."

My heart lifted in my chest like a birthday balloon. "Any color you've got in mind?"

"Nah. I'll leave that up to you."

"Anything else, Boxer?" I demanded.

"No underwear. I want to be able to slide my hand up your leg and—"

"Boxer! The kids!"

"They're already in the truck. They can't hear me."

A horn blared in the background.

"Okay, now I really do have to go. See you tomorrow. Seven."

# Chapter 9

"I'm sorry, folks," Jerry said. "The water's out for the next few hours."

"What happened?" I asked as I strode across the lobby, trying not to drip sweat from my recent morning workout onto the polished floors.

Three other tenants—an older woman wearing pearls at her neck with a miniature poodle under one arm, a guy wearing a suit who looked like he was ready to head off to the office, and a young woman near my age—stood at Jerry's security desk.

Jerry looked at me. "A pipe burst, so we've shut off the water."

The hair at my temples was damp, and I was sure my face was red. My heart rate hadn't yet stabilized from my three-mile run. All I wanted was a shower, but when I'd gotten back to my condo and turned on the water, nothing had happened.

"Why didn't you call everyone in the building to tell us what was going on?" the uppity poodle owner asked.

"Maybe it's because it's a weekday and most people are at work," I stated, instinctively coming to Jerry's defense.

She looked at me, her gaze raking over me in disdain. "And why aren't *you* at work then?"

"I'm a surgeon, and I just worked a forty-eight-hour shift. It's my weekend."

"Hmmpf." She strolled out of the lobby with her nose in the air. Literally.

"I'm supposed to cook dinner for my girlfriend tonight," the young corporate guy said. "It's kind of a big deal. Will the water be back on by then?"

"I don't know for sure," Jerry said. "But I'm doing everything I can."

Young corporate guy raked a hand through his hair. "I'm proposing tonight. I've had this planned for weeks."

The young woman next to him piped up. "Hi, sorry to interrupt, but I manage the Bar & Restaurant at The Rex Hotel. Let me see what I can do for you."

"That would be incredible," the young suit said.

"Do you have a few minutes before you have to be at work?" she asked with a smile. "Let's talk about what your plans are, and I'll see if I can help."

The two of them wandered toward the exit, chattering to one another.

"Sorry about this, Linden," Jerry said.

"It's not your fault," I said. "I can shower at the hospital."

I didn't want to go there on my day off, but I didn't really have a choice. The idea of sitting in workout clothes for hours hoping the water came back on was not an option.

I went back upstairs to my condo and gathered a change of clothes. I had toiletries in my locker at work, so I didn't bother packing any of that. As I was locking up, my phone hummed.

I frowned as I saw my father's name across the screen. I silenced his call. He didn't leave a voicemail, but a few minutes later, he called again.

He'd been trying to get ahold of me for weeks, but I refused to talk to him.

When he called the third time, I answered it. Before he could utter a greeting, I stated, "I'm blocking your number. Stop calling me."

I hung up, the bitter taste of anger sharp on my tongue.

～

"What are you doing here?" Amanda asked, looking me up and down as I walked across the floor past the nurses' station.

"Water is shut off in my building," I replied. "I'm showering here and then heading home."

"You okay?" she asked.

"Yeah. Why?"

"I don't know. You look…pinched."

"Pinched?"

She scrunched up her face. "Annoyed. Like your bowels are blocked."

I let out a laugh. "My bowels are fine. It's the water thing. It's just inconvenient."

"Ah, yeah." She held up a plastic container toward me. "Cookie?"

"Thanks." I filched one and took a bite.

"Mia Weston sent them," she said. "She paid for overnight shipping and wrote this beautiful handwritten note thanking the nurses for taking care of Boxer."

I found my first smile in an hour. "Super thoughtful of her. She's a good egg. I like her."

"Yes. And she makes wicked good cookies."

"You deserve all the cookies," I said to her. "You guys are the heart of the hospital. Not us doctors."

She raised her brows. "You guys are the ones that perform the surgeries."

"You're the ones who care for the patients and comfort their loved ones. What you, Amanda, Peyton, Lizzie, and all the other amazing nurses do is special. You're special people. I just wanted you to know that. I wanted you to know that I love working with you."

"Linden," she said quietly.

I waved my hand at her. "Let's not get emotional. I just—"

My phone pinged, and I riffled through my bag to find it at the bottom. It was an email notification about the following month's hospital schedule.

I scrolled through it, my annoyance morphing into anger. "You've got to be kidding me."

"What's wrong?" Amanda inquired.

"My schedule next month is an absolute nightmare. I have several shifts in a row followed by one day off. Or four days off followed by one shift."

"That's obnoxious," Amanda said.

"Way obnoxious. But that's the way the cookie crumbles, I guess." I rubbed my face. I shoved my phone back in my bag. "I better go shower." I waved and then headed toward the locker room, munching on my cookie as I went.

Dr. Sawyer was waiting in the hallway when I stepped outside the locker room. "Hi," he greeted. "Amanda said you were here because the water's out at your condo?"

"Yeah." I forced a placid expression. "What's up?"

He fell in step beside me. "I just wanted to discuss your

schedule next month. I know it's chaotic. I'm really sorry about that."

My gaze narrowed at his tone. Normally he yelled or berated me. And he never apologized.

"Donaldson had a family emergency and has to fly to Kansas tomorrow. Carter has a conference. And Weaver's private practice is open now, so he's only in rotation once a month. I did schedule Chambers and Brenner, but you're a natural in the ER. I've watched you. You never lose your cool, and you don't get flustered."

"Oh. Thanks," I said, wishing he hadn't noticed.

"I just wanted to let you know that I'll be working alongside you. It wasn't fair to ask you to work and not work those shifts too."

Not only was Dr. Sawyer being pleasant, but he was also being complimentary. It felt unnatural since he was usually barking orders and criticizing me for not moving quickly enough.

"Thanks for explaining," I said hastily. "Have a good rest of your day."

I booked it to the elevator, wondering why it felt like he lived by the mantra *keep your friends close, and your enemies closer*.

# Chapter 10

By MIDAFTERNOON, the water was back on in my condo. The annoyance of the day melted away, and I was left with buzzy anticipation at the thought of seeing Boxer. My skin heated and my stomach flipped when I remembered how it felt to have his lips on mine, to be pressed against his strong, muscular form.

The promise of pleasure blasted through my veins, and I wanted his sweaty, naked body writhing over mine as we both erupted in pleasure. I knew it would be explosive when we were finally able to be together.

I slipped into a ruby–red satin dress that hit above the knee. It was sleeveless with an open back, and I couldn't wear a bra with it. It was the perfect dress to seduce. It gave away just enough to entice, but also left enough of a mystery to create desire. It would tantalize and drive Boxer mad.

I twirled up my wheat blonde hair to get it out of my way while I did my makeup, something smoky and dramatic with a red lip that would inevitably draw his attention. We were playing a game of cat and mouse, but I was ready to be caught. I wanted him in my bed tonight. He'd been out of the hospital for a few weeks. He was running around with kids, so clearly he was feeling well enough for aerobic activity.

My cell phone rang as I slid the mascara wand through my lashes. Without taking my eyes off my reflection, I pressed a button and put Boxer on speaker.

"Are you on your way?" I asked in flirtatious purr.

"Linden, it's your mother."

*Crap.*

Her voice was frosty, and I swore I could feel the proverbial ice shards she was throwing at me through the phone.

"Ah. Hi, Mom."

"You must be going out," she said. "Do you have a date?"

"No. I'm going out with a friend," I lied.

"That's how you talk to your friends?"

"What can I do for you? I'm kind of on a time crunch here."

"Who is this friend?" she pressed.

"Peyton. She's a nurse I work with."

She paused. "So, you're not going on a date with that tattooed heathen?"

I lowered the mascara wand. "Tattooed heathen? Who are you talking about?"

"Don't play dumb. It's beneath you. Seriously, Linden. What are you doing with that man?"

"It's none of your business," I seethed. "How do you know about him? Hmm? Who did you pay to spy on me?"

"You forced me to pay someone to spy on you," she stated, not even denying that she'd done it.

"You're psychotic. You need psychological help."

"Do not diagnose me, Linden Evelyn Ward."

"Do not ignore societal boundaries, Charlotte Rushford Ward Exeter."

Rage stormed through my blood, and I gripped the counter as she verbally marched on, "You tell me nothing of your life. You gave up your position at Duke, dumped Jeff for no good reason, and then moved across the country. If I hadn't called while you were packing up your things, would you have even bothered to tell me?"

"Yes," I stated. "I would've told you."

*Probably. Maybe.*

"You are my daughter, and yet we're complete strangers."

"You made it this way."

"That's not fair."

"It *is* fair," I insisted. "When I told you I got accepted to med school and I was going to be a doctor, you didn't talk to me for six months. That was all you, Mom. You've never understood me. You've never tried to understand me. After Dad left—"

"Do *not* bring him into this!"

"He called me today. He's been calling me every day this week. I haven't heard from him in years, and he's trying to get in touch now? Why?"

"How should I know?" She suddenly sounded tired.

A part of me considered telling her the truth about why I'd left Duke. About why I'd left an entire life behind. But my mother was mercenary. She'd used my weaknesses and vulnerabilities against me throughout my entire life. I didn't trust her not to hurt me.

"Who do you have feeding you information, Mom?" My voice was soft but threaded with steel.

She paused for a long moment and then she said, "Jerry."

My screen flashed, alerting me to the fact that she'd hung up on me.

I set my phone aside and placed my palms on the counter of the bathroom. My face was red and blotchy.

I'd never liked my mother, but in that moment, I truly loathed her.

My vision blurred with rage.

I stalked barefoot into the kitchen. I looked around at the stainless-steel appliances and the custom designed counter tops and cabinets. I suddenly hated the clean lines and spartan appeal.

This wasn't a design aesthetic that appealed to me—it was just familiar. This was my mother's style, through and through. I'd accepted it for so long I'd thought it was mine. I wasn't original. I knew nothing about what I truly wanted or even liked.

I opened the cabinet that had a complete set of glazed white dishware. I picked up a plate. It was heavy in my hand, and I held it for just a moment before throwing it to the ground.

It shattered.

I picked up a salad plate and chucked it against the far wall. It put a massive dent in the drywall and then fell to the floor with a resounding crash.

Each broken dish fed my fury, until all the cabinet doors were open and empty, the remains of china littered across the wooden floors.

My heart thumped in my ears, savagely clawing at my insides with sharp talons, demanding to be let out. Demanding to destroy everything. Only in the aftermath of the destruction would it be calm.

I didn't feel better. There weren't enough plates in the homeware department of Harrods to make me feel better.

My wrath was years deep, and it had blown like a volcano that had been dormant for generations.

A knock resounded on the condo door. I froze. My mind was static.

"Linden?" Boxer called through the door. He knocked again.

I surveyed the room and realized that I was so consumed with my meltdown, I'd forgotten he was on his way. I stepped over a pile of glass, mindful that I was still barefoot.

When I opened the door, I was greeted with Boxer's warm smile. Without a word of hello, I grasped him by the lapel of his leather cut and pulled him inside.

"What the hell happened in here?" he demanded as he quickly surveyed the room and all the broken glass that I hadn't had time to clean up.

"I don't want to talk about it," I said, my hands climbing up his chest, demanding, silently begging for him to ignore the room.

Boxer looked down at me, his expression blank. "What do you need, Linden?"

"Oblivion."

He pushed the door closed with one hand, staring at me with steely eyes. Then he was on me. His lips against mine, his tongue in my mouth, his hands underneath my skirt.

"Turn around," he growled.

I did as he commanded, not questioning his edict. He pressed me to the door and my palms flattened against the wood so I could keep my balance.

His hand snaked underneath my skirt as he delved for the place between my legs. His breath hitched when he realized I wasn't wearing underwear.

I sucked in air when he slipped his finger into me from

behind. I took it easily, welcomed it. I was more than ready. I was primed for sex. Anger was a powerful aphrodisiac that clouded my brain but ignited my body. I clamped around him in sweet agony.

Boxer removed his finger, and I moaned at the loss of him. His chuckle was dark, husky. It made my blood turn to liquid heat.

He fumbled with his belt, and then metal clanked against the wooden floor. I looked over my shoulder. His jeans were down by his ankles, and he was rolling a condom down his impressive length. His gaze met mine as he slowly lifted the skirt of my dress to bare my backside to him. He took himself in one hand and positioned himself at my entrance.

He slipped into me, filling me completely.

My breath hitched, and then I hissed in pain. One of my hands curled into a fist, and I beat the door with it. "More," I demanded. "Give me more."

Boxer thrust into me, his hands grasping my hips. I was wet, slippery, and he drove deeper.

He screwed me with abandon. I lost myself in him, in the feel of him between my legs.

I was so deliciously full. His scent engulfed me, mingling with mine. We made something new, a unique perfume of lust and sweat.

Closing my eyes, I pressed my flushed cheek to the door and drowned in desire.

His fingers reached around to the seam of my body, searching and playing, demanding I come for him. He was relentless, pounding into me from behind as he stroked me.

My skin tingled and for one moment, I froze, and then I clenched around him and rode out my pleasure.

He grasped my hips and speared into me a few more times before stilling. His chest covered my back and pushed me against the door. He dropped his forehead to my shoulder, his breathing labored.

My skin was flushed with pleasure and sweat. Warm from the inside out. The anger inside me had been a wildfire, but it had burned itself to ashes.

Boxer pulled away from me. I winced at his departure. I was sore between my legs.

He moved behind me and I glanced at him over my shoulder. He was removing the condom, his head bent. He was still half erect, and even diminished, he was bigger than all the other men I'd been with. There hadn't been many, but there had been enough to know how impressive Boxer was.

And he knew how to use it.

It was no wonder he was a savant when it came to women. It was no wonder they wanted him in bed.

Boxer tied off the condom and looked up to find me watching him. His gray eyes were clear, his expression blank.

He reached down to pull up his pants, which he'd left bunched around his ankles, but he didn't button them. Without a word, he turned and walked out of the living room, clearly searching for the bathroom.

I looked around at the carnage I'd created. A part of me was ashamed that I'd let my emotions get the better of me. The other part of me, the larger, more vocal part of me, realized it had been necessary.

After a few minutes, Boxer came back into the living room with his pants buttoned and his belt buckled. He stared at me for a long moment. "What the hell happened?"

I raised my brows. "I thought that was obvious."

"Linden."

"Boxer."

His gaze narrowed. "Something happened to you. What was it?"

"Why does it matter?" I demanded.

He didn't reply.

My gaze dropped to his belly, and my breath hitched. "Did I hurt you?"

His smile was calculated to look amused, but I could still see the tension beneath it. "Nah, darlin'. I'm fine."

"Show me your incision."

"No."

"No?"

"You're not my doctor anymore. You're fired."

"You can't fire me," I commanded.

"Sure, I can," he said. "What's it called? Conflict of interest?"

I glared at him.

"You stopped being my doctor the moment my tongue was in your mouth."

"Stop it."

"Stop what?"

I walked to the door and opened it.

He raised his brows. "You holding that door open for a reason?"

"You were just leaving."

"You used me for sex and now you're kicking me out?"

"Isn't that the way this is supposed to go?"

"If this was the way it was supposed to go, I wouldn't have bothered putting on a button-down shirt and wearing my best pair of jeans. I wouldn't have asked you to wear something fancy. You look dynamite, by the way."

My expression didn't change, and I didn't move away from the door.

"Broom?" he asked.

"Hall closet," I said before I could stop myself.

He walked to the closet and pulled out the broom and dustpan. And then he began to sweep up the mess I'd made.

I slowly closed the door.

He wasn't showing any signs of pain, but I was instantly ashamed of myself. He was still healing, and I'd used him as my own physical playground. I'd unleashed my rage and demanded escape from my anger. His body had been a balm to my battered emotions. I'd never escaped my feelings using sex before.

He swept broken dishware into a few piles. I grabbed the dustpan and squatted down so he could sweep the rubble into it. It felt strange, what we were doing. Like all the boundaries and rules we'd erected had been shattered like the china the moment he'd stepped into my apartment.

I wasn't the Linden he was expecting tonight.

"Sorry I ruined your plans," I said.

"What plans?" he asked as he began to sweep again.

I walked over to the trash can and dumped the broken glass into it. "Your plans to wine and dine me."

He shrugged. It looked deceptively casual. But something about his posture told me he felt anything but. "Don't worry about it, Doc. You gave up the goods before I had to shell out a small fortune. I guess I won, in the end."

The lightness of his words belied the truth.

"Boxer," I said softly.

He kept sweeping even though there was no longer even a speck of china dust on the ground.

"Will you look at me?" I pleaded.

After a few seconds, he paused and met my gaze.

"I'm sorry." My voice sounded small. "I'm sorry I used you the way I did. I'm sorry you walked in and I…"

"Couldn't keep your greedy hands to yourself?" he asked with a forced grin. "It's fine, Linden. Really."

It wasn't fine.

I was suddenly deeply ashamed of myself. Not because I just had mind-numbing sex with him, but because I had used him for my own personal needs.

Never in my life had I been so selfish.

He looked at me. "Do you want to talk about what happened now?"

"No."

He handed me the broom, and I took it.

"Well then, I guess there's not much else to say." He headed for the door. "See ya around, Doc."

# Chapter 11

THE CONDO WAS SUDDENLY bereft and cold now that I was alone.

I should've called out to him. I should've asked him to stay. I should've told him about my mother.

Only...

Only telling him anything about my family wasn't keeping things casual. I'd told Jeff after six months of dating, but I had never been truly comfortable with him knowing about our family's skeletons in the closet.

Boxer was a biker. We belonged in different worlds. There was no point in explaining to him anything serious because what we were doing was supposed to be finite from the get-go.

And yet, the loss of Boxer's presence carved deeper than I expected.

I looked around. There were no longer any physical remains of the mess I had made.

No, the mess was inside of me.

My emotions were like a hodgepodge of childhood toys thrown haphazardly into a chest.

I was a grown woman, and yet I had behaved like an irrational teenager. I always seemed to go back to that place whenever my mother was involved. It was like a Pavlovian response. I'd never mastered the art of not caring when it came to her. I'd never grown enough emotional scar tissue to protect myself where she was concerned.

And without realizing what I'd been doing, I'd treated the man with all the casual indifference of a stranger.

But he didn't feel like a stranger.

I walked to the bedroom and stared at my big, empty bed. Tonight was supposed to have gone differently. My mother never should've called; I was meant to be out sharing a meal with Boxer, laughing and touching each other with the sensual, teasing pleasures that would lead him to coming home with me.

I'd have invited him in, and he would've stared at me with dove gray eyes that darkened with lust. He'd march me into my condo, heading for the bedroom, where he'd lay me down on my bed…

But I'd blown it all to hell because I was an emotional hand grenade, and my pin had been pulled.

I changed out of my dress, throwing it in the laundry basket. I'd never wear it again. Every time I looked at it, I'd remember this night, this shame.

I pulled on a fuzzy lavender sweatshirt and black yoga pants, and then I went into the bathroom to wash my face. The mascara was smudged beneath my blue eyes, and my red lipstick had been smeared from my mouth. I looked like a broken circus clown.

I gently removed the makeup, tossing the soiled cleansing pads into the garbage.

Without my face painted, I looked young.

*Vulnerable.*

I went out into the kitchen, wanting to make myself a cup of tea, only I hadn't spared any of the mugs.

I was too tired to be angry at myself. I grabbed my cell phone and searched through my contacts list for the management company that took care of the building. I called and left a voice message, asking to speak to the owner.

When that had been dealt with, I made sure the condo was locked up for the night, and then I turned off the light.

I sat on the couch and pulled the blanket onto my lap, and then I stared into the darkness and cried.

I fell asleep, my cheeks wet with tears.

My trumpeting phone jarred me awake the next morning. I winced at the bright sunlight coming through the living room windows as I reached for my cell.

"Hello?" I croaked.

"Oh, crap. Did I wake you?" Amanda asked.

I ran a hand across my face. "No."

"I was just calling to find out how your date went. Did you boink the biker?"

"Boink? Really?"

"Not a fan of the word boink? Okay. Did you boff Boxer?"

"Did she do it?" came Lizzie's voice in the background.

"I better not be on speaker phone," I stated.

She paused.

"Amanda!" I hissed.

"Chill out! It's just me and Lizzie in the lounge. And if someone comes in, I'll hang up on you. Your secrets are protected."

"I'm not telling you."

"Oh my God, you totally did it!" Amanda crowed. "I knew you had it in you! Or should I say I knew you had *him* in you?"

"Yippee!" Lizzie cried. "Hallelujah! I'm so happy for your vagina."

*Eff my life.*

"On that note, I've got to go," I said.

"Wait, wait, wait!" Amanda cried out. "I want details! And diagrams. And did you take any photos of his penis? I mean tattoos. Yeah. Tattoos."

"Goodbye, guys," I said. "See you later."

I hung up on them and let out a long, drawn-out sigh. Under normal circumstances, I would have been excited to gush about Boxer. I was the new doc on the block, and they could've ignored me, been cold and unwelcoming. Instead, they'd invited me out with them and then had taken me into their fold.

It might have come from them being overly involved in my social life, but that's what you got when you let people in.

I rose from the couch and stretched my arms over my head, feeling the vertebrae of my back pop. I trudged to the espresso maker and got as far as frothing milk for a cappuccino in the silver container before realizing I had no mugs to pour the espresso or milk foam into.

I winced, remembering my behavior from the previous evening.

With a sigh, I stopped frothing the milk and then set it aside and went to take a shower. Twenty minutes later, I was out the door.

I made sure not to go through the lobby, that way I wouldn't have to see Jerry. Jerry, who I had been speaking with almost every single day as though he were a friend, and who'd betrayed me by feeding information to my mother.

Just as I was climbing into my car, my phone rang. It was an unknown number, but the area code wasn't one from the East Coast, so I answered it.

"Hello?" I answered.

"Hello," came a pleasant and rumbly voice, tinged with a Scottish accent. "Is this Linden Ward?"

"It is."

"I'm Ramsey Buchanan. I own the condo building. The management company passed along your message, and I'm returning your phone call."

"Thanks for getting back to me," I said.

"What can I do for you, Ms. Ward?"

"You have a problem with one of your security guards. Jerry, at the front desk."

"What do you mean?"

"He hasn't done anything illegal, but my mother paid him to spy on me. He's not trustworthy, and he's making me extremely uncomfortable being here."

Ramsey paused on the other end of the phone and then finally said, "I'm sorry at the invasion of your privacy, and I'll take care of this. Have a great day."

He hung up on me, and I stared at the phone for a moment and then set it aside.

I left the apartment and drove to Folson's, a luxury department store that rivaled Neiman Marcus. I walked into the building, breathing the crisp, circulated air. I wandered through the women's department and found the escalator that would take me to the housewares section.

A stunning blonde greeted me the moment I stepped off the escalator. "May I help you find something?"

"Yes, actually," I said. "I need an entire set of dishware.

And while I'm at it, can you point me in the direction of sheets and linens?"

Thirty minutes later, I'd found several things I couldn't live without. "Great choice on those bed linens," Debbie, the saleswoman, said. "Let me see if I have a new set in the stock room for you, otherwise we might have to special order them."

"Thanks," I said with a genuine smile.

Debbie left me in the bedroom furniture showroom as she went to the back.

I took a seat on the four-poster bed and took my phone out of my purse. I dialed one of my closest friends, who still lived on the East Coast.

"Help," I said the moment she answered the phone. "I'm about to buy the entire housewares department at Folson's if you don't stop me."

"Why should I stop you? Folson's is great," Quinn said. "Crap. Helena just threw up on me. Yup, it went down my shirt. Hold on."

I snorted.

"Okay, I'm back," she said after a few moments. "Why are you at Folson's anyway? Did you finally decide to decorate your condo? You really should consider buying, if you're planning on staying in Dallas long term."

"I don't know if I plan on staying in Dallas," I admitted.

"No? How are you liking the change of scenery?"

"I'm liking it."

"So, no regrets about leaving Durham?"

"No. It was time."

"Hmmm. So, let's get back to why you're at Folson's and buying the entire store."

"I broke every single dish in the condo."

Quinn paused and then asked, "Did you?"

"Yes."

"Why?"

"My mother called—and let it slip that she paid the security guard in my building to feed her information about me."

"Major violation. *Not* okay."

"Not okay at all." I sighed. "She's never respected boundaries. I know that, but this time it was different."

"Different how?"

I looked around, wanting some measure of privacy. Luckily, it was late morning and there were no other customers in the section of the store I was in.

"I met someone," I admitted.

"You did? When?" she demanded.

"A few weeks ago. It's complicated. Well, I made it complicated."

"You're being super vague. Who is this guy?"

"He was my patient," I admitted. "Which breaks so many rules."

"Did you start dating when he was still your patient?"

"No."

"Then you didn't really break any rules," she pointed out.

"Yeah, I guess."

"Go on. I'm dying to know what's going on. This is so exciting!"

I chuckled. "You sound like the nurses I work with. They're all very determined to see me matched up. Anyway, he came over to pick me up for our date—" Debbie approached, appearing as if from nowhere. "Gimme a second," I said to Quinn and held the phone away from my ear.

"Sorry, Linden," Debbie said. "I couldn't find the

sheets for a king-sized mattress. Would you like me to order them for you?"

"That would be great, thanks."

"I can have the dishware, comforter, and everything else sent to you."

"Is express delivery an option?"

"Absolutely."

"Perfect." I flashed a grateful grin and then dug through my purse for my wallet and pulled out a credit card. She rang me up on her touch-screen tablet, and I gave her my address. "Thanks for all your help, Debbie."

"Come back anytime." She smiled and then with a wave, she left.

I put the phone to my ear. "You there?"

"Yeah, I'm still here. I'm dying for the rest of this story."

As I walked through Folson's toward the exit, I told Quinn everything. I got through the parking lot and climbed into my car, setting my purse on the passenger side.

"I'm so proud of you," she said.

"Proud of me? Why?"

"Because you're getting out there. I was worried that you were moving to Dallas to bury yourself in your job."

"I tried to bury myself in my job, but it didn't work out so well." I sighed. "I screwed this up. Whatever *this* was. My mother railed at me for getting involved with what she referred to as a tattooed heathen, and it threw me for such a loop that I reverted to destructive behavior and broke things. Pretty things."

"Wait a second," she said. "Let's go back to this tattooed heathen thing. I need a visual."

I sighed. "Dirty blond hair, scruff for days, tattoos, leather cut, and swagger. So much freakin' swagger."

"Leather cut?" she repeated.

"Yeah." I paused. "He's in an MC."

"He's not."

"He is."

"Wow," she said.

"Wow *what*?"

"That's so not your normal type."

"I know."

"You like him, don't you?"

I sighed and finally decided to admit it out loud. "Yeah, I like him. And I treated him, well, not good, Quinn. I kicked him out after having sex with him because I didn't want to get into my family drama."

"And you are feeling badly because…"

"The moment he left, I thought about going after him and explaining."

"Huh."

"I know."

"You have feelings for a biker…"

"It's looking that way, yeah. He's—God, Quinn. I don't even know. He's just different."

"Well, sure. He's a biker."

"I don't mean about that. Yeah, I guess it's part of it, but it's more. Boxer's funny and insightful, and he doesn't care what people think of him. It's refreshing. And he keeps me on my toes."

After a long pause, she said, "Boxer?"

"Yeah."

"What MC is he in?"

"What does that have to do with anything?" I asked in confusion.

"Humor me."

"The Tarnished Angels."

She laughed like it was the funniest thing she'd ever heard.

"Quinn," I demanded. "What the hell?"

"The world is so damn small I can't even believe it sometimes."

"What do you mean?"

She sighed. "Sasha is friends with Flynn Campbell. Flynn Campbell owns The Rex Hotel empire. Flynn is also old friends with Colt Weston, president of the Tarnished Angels. So, yeah, that's the club your new plaything is in. They're all involved in business together."

My mouth dropped open as her words digested. "Business? Your fiancé is in business with Flynn Campbell? And an MC club?"

"Business," she repeated. "You just had the best sex of your life with a man who's deep in the criminal underworld."

"I never said he was the best sex of my life," I protested.

She laughed. "Honey, you didn't have to."

# Chapter 12

Cool evening air teased my temples as I stood on Peyton's doorstep. I rang the doorbell and a moment later she opened the door, looking fresh and casual in a pair of dark slacks, a cream sweater, and bare feet.

"You didn't have to bring flowers," Peyton said, waving me in across the threshold of her townhouse.

"Yes, I did." I handed over the bouquet of white lilies and the bottle of cabernet and then removed my boots. "You offered to feed me. The least I could do was bring flowers. The wine was a given."

Peyton beamed. "The flowers are lovely. And thoughtful. Thank you."

The living room and the kitchen were one large room. The kitchen itself wasn't overly spacious, but it had decent counter space and new appliances. Peyton had made her home warm and vibrant. Bright red and turquoise pillows accented the gray couch. A matching gray ottoman rested in front of the gas fireplace that was currently on, blazing with heat. Photographs graced the walls and leafy plants brought the entire space together.

I set my purse aside and was unable to stop myself from reaching for my cell phone. No missed calls or texts. I held in a sigh. Reason told me not to expect to hear from Boxer. Hope was telling Reason to shut the hell up. But after the way I treated him, I couldn't blame him for not calling. And I was too chicken to call him.

*So here we are.*

"Bad news?" Peyton asked.

"Hmm?"

"Bad news," she repeated. "You're frowning."

"Oh." I hastily stuffed the phone back into my purse and stood up straight. "Not bad news. Just hoping to hear from someone."

"Someone." Her grin widened. "Yes! I finally get the details! Let's open this bottle of wine. The chicken and rice are already in the oven; I just need to make a salad. And while I do that, you're going to tell me everything that's happened."

I was talked out after having spent an hour on the phone with Quinn. My mind was a whirl.

"Do we have to?" I asked in exasperation. "Didn't you get the details from Amanda and Lizzie?"

Peyton's blue eyes twinkled. "I want the play-by-play from the source. You promised me."

Peyton's rescue cat slid out from underneath the couch and came to greet me. He walked through my legs, his tail curling around my calf. I reached down to pet him.

"Hello, Magic."

He turned his head into my palm and purred as I scratched behind one jagged, scarred ear.

She opened a kitchen drawer and pulled out the wine opener. In a few deft moves, she had the bottle open and poured the wine into two glasses.

I took one of the glasses.

"Did you sleep with him?" she asked.

I nodded.

"And?"

"It was amazing."

*And I felt him all the way down to the part of me that was hiding.*

I flushed with heat, remembering his hands on my body, remembering him inside me.

Peyton let out a light chuckle. "Ah, I see."

"What do you see?" I demanded.

"It scared you. Whatever you felt when you were with him."

I blew out a breath. "It was everything I needed it to be."

"Then what's the problem? Unless you immediately wanted something more with him?"

I shook my head. "*He* wanted more of me than I was willing to give."

She set her glass of wine aside and then went to the refrigerator. Peyton pulled out all the ingredients for a salad.

"Do you have a vase?" I asked.

"Top of the fridge." She pointed. "What do you mean he wanted more of you?"

"I wasn't myself when he came over. I was—there were…" I sighed. "I'd gotten into a fight with my mother." Peyton knew about my mom. I tended not to talk about my family life and childhood if I could help it, but one day while I was on break, she'd caught me in the throes of a conversation with my mother. Inevitably, curiosity and questions arose. I'd just moved to Dallas, I was feeling vulnerable, and she was willing to lend an ear. We'd waited until the end of our shift and gone out for a drink. I'd spilled about my mother, and she spilled about losing her husband.

"Boxer came over to take me out on a date, and I sort of took out my aggression on him. Sexually."

Confusion marred her expression. "And he was upset about that?"

"No. He let me. But after, he started to dig into what was going on. I didn't want him to dig."

"Huh."

"Scissors?"

She opened a drawer and handed the scissors to me. I talked while I snipped the stems of the flowers. "I don't understand why he cared. This was supposed to be easy and light. Easy and light doesn't mean you talk about your family dynamics."

"Didn't he show up at the hospital with food from The Rex?"

"The gossip wheel is greased and working I see," I said with a rueful grin. "Yeah, he did show up with food."

"And the night you had sex with him, you were supposed to go out again, right?"

"He told me to wear a nice dress. He was dressed up, too. Well, nicer than normal for a biker, I guess."

Peyton grabbed a tomato from the fruit bowl and rinsed it off. When she hadn't said anything for a few moments, I prodded, "What? What are you thinking?"

"I'm thinking actions speak louder than words."

"I had sex with him and then kicked him to the curb."

"Not *your* actions. His. From everything you've told me, it doesn't sound like a man who wants something easy and light. If all he wanted was fun, he wouldn't drive all the way to Dallas just to see you."

"He's not driving all the way to Dallas just to see me," I protested. "He says the club has business in Dallas, so he makes the trek a few times a week."

"Fine. But he's still thinking about you, bringing you food and wanting to take you out on dates. That's effort. Serious effort."

"Yeah," I admitted. "You make a very valid case for him."

"The man's got charm. You can admit that, right?"

"He has it in spades," I agreed with a disgruntled frown.

Peyton smiled. "He flirts with women. He teased and joked with all the nurses on the floor. Hell, he even got Babs to smile and dare I say it, look *soft*. For just a moment, mind you, but he achieved the unachievable."

"So?"

"So, there's something about you that made him take a closer look."

"He doesn't want for female companionship," I muttered.

"Companionship and a true partnership are not the same thing. If he was out to just have sex with you, do you think he'd be going through all this effort?"

I moved the vase of lilies to the end of the counter and out of the way so it wouldn't get knocked over.

"Does the biker thing bother you?" she asked suddenly. "And by biker, I mean criminal thing?"

"How do you know he's a criminal?" I hedged.

"Please," she said with a laugh. "There are some men who pretend to be dangerous, and then there are men who are actually dangerous."

"Does the criminal thing bother me," I repeated. "It didn't. Because I wasn't thinking of a future with him."

"But if you were?" she prodded.

"But I'm not." My tone was emphatic.

"Sounds like unfinished business to me," she said.

"It's finished. Done."

"Why? Because of your baggage? Because one night you booted him out? We all have baggage."

"Yes, but showing him my baggage might scare him away."

"So, you're rejecting him before he has a chance to reject you."

"I'm…crap," I muttered. "That's exactly what I did."

"You don't think he has the chops to stick around after you get deep with him? Don't judge Boxer by the same standards you've judged the other men in your life. Boxer might surprise you."

"What makes you say that?" I was fascinated by Peyton's read on the situation. I was too close in on it and Quinn, as much as I loved her, was engaged to a criminal. Her judgement was clouded.

"The way he watched you. Like he couldn't take his eyes off you. Like he was hungry, starving."

I rolled my eyes. "Lust, you mean."

She shook her head. "No. Hungry for something he couldn't name."

My traitor of a heart fluttered with longing in my chest. "We barely know each other."

"Fine. Don't listen to me. You're going to choose what you want to do regardless of what I say." She looked up from chopping vegetables to stare at me. "But let me say one thing: There are times in life when nothing makes sense. When you can't make sense of the reality you're living in and you're angry all the time." She smiled sadly. "I know what it's like. Don't let the anger rule you. It doesn't just incinerate everything around you—it takes you with it. Ask me how I know."

I flinched. "Peyton."

She shook her head, sending her bright red hair spilling across her shoulders. "When Tom died, I lost myself for a long time. You're a young, brilliant surgeon at the top of your field, and you were working at one of the most renowned hospitals in the country. You were on the path to being chief of surgery —that's what they were grooming you for, wasn't it?"

I nodded.

"And yet, you gave all that up to start over in a different city where you have to prove yourself all over again to new colleagues that no longer respect you for how smart you are because you walked out on a sure thing, and they don't trust that you'll stick around."

I opened my mouth to reply, only to realize I had nothing to say. I'd told the nurses that I'd left Duke behind because of a breakup and wanting a fresh start. It was partly the truth, but there was more. There was always more.

I grabbed my glass of wine and wandered back over to the couch. A glossy magazine rested on the coffee table. A handsome man with dark brown curls falling rakishly over his forehead and emerald-green eyes smirked at me from the cover. His three-piece gray bespoke suit fit him perfectly.

I leaned down and picked up the magazine. "Most Eligible Bachelors of Dallas." My eyes widened in surprise when my gaze scanned the name in small text next to the photo. Ramsey Buchanan also ran The Dallas Rex.

His connections to Boxer went far deeper than just a normal friendship.

"Holy crap," I stated.

"What?"

I held up the magazine and showed it to Peyton. "Ramsey Buchanan owns my condo building."

"Really? Wild. He's sexy as sin, don't you think?" Peyton asked, picking up a plate.

"Sexy as sin," I agreed, but the man with dashing curls falling across his forehead and entrancing green eyes did nothing for me.

I had a thing for a leather-wearing, tattooed biker.

*Sigh.*

"Dinner's ready." She served hefty portions and then handed me the dish.

I took the plate of food Peyton gave me and sat down. Even after she joined me at the table, I stared at my plate but didn't dive in.

"Something wrong with the food?" she asked.

I shook my head.

"Then what is it?"

"How did you get over the anger?"

She reached for her glass of wine. Peyton took a sip and then held her glass, looking thoughtful. "Anger was a form of denial. Of blame. I blamed God. The universe. Myself."

"Why did you blame yourself?"

"I regretted all the times we'd fought over things that didn't matter. For all the times I didn't say *I love you*. For all the kisses I never got to give him. For all the hugs we missed. For all the trips we didn't get to take." Peyton shook her head and discreetly kept her eyes away from mine as she wiped a tear from her cheek.

"He was my favorite person. My best friend. He changed me. He made me better. And there's nothing I wouldn't do to have just one more day with him." She inhaled a shaky breath and continued on, "There's never enough time when you find the person you're supposed to be with. So, if you have a shot in hell of finding someone real, someone meaningful, someone that gets inside of you and lights you up, then embrace it. And who fucking cares how it looks. You get one life, Linden. Don't waste it."

Magic curled around my leg. I took a small piece of chicken and held it out to him. He devoured it and then settled down on top of my feet, purring loudly.

"We haven't known each other very long," I said. "How can you see right through me?"

"Because I've been where you are, working all the time, keeping busy on my days off. It's easy to see that in someone else once you've already lived it."

I shook my head. "I would really like to talk about you now." I reached for my glass and took a sip.

"I miss sex."

I choked on my wine, and it went up my nose. I hastily set my glass down and wiped my face with a blue cloth napkin.

Peyton grinned. "You said you wanted to talk about me, well, there it is."

"I did," I admitted with a laugh. "So, you miss sex, huh?"

"If you meet another rough and tough biker you're not interested in, send him my way."

My mouth dropped open. "You'd seriously sleep with a biker?"

"In a heartbeat."

"Why?"

"Because those are the kind of men who make a woman feel alive."

My skin remembered Boxer's calloused palms, the warmth of him at my back, the feeling of being completely at his mercy.

I sighed. "I'm a damn fool."

Peyton grasped the bottle of wine and topped off my wine glass. "Yeah, Linden. You are."

I hugged Peyton goodbye. "Thanks for dinner. It was… illuminating."

When I stepped back, she reached for the door. "Are you going to call him?"

"And say what? Sorry I kicked you out. Sorry I didn't want to talk about all my issues? Sorry, can you come back and rock my world all over again?"

"Yeah, any of that would work. As long as you mean it." Peyton smiled. "Life is messy, my dear. That's what makes it beautiful."

I hugged her one last time. "See you soon."

She stood in the doorway as I headed to my car. Peyton didn't go back inside until I pulled out of her driveway.

I used the drive back to my condo to process what she'd said. Why was I unable to let the idea of Boxer go? We'd only just started something. Something that was supposed to remain uncomplicated. I thought back to the night he took me to Pinky's and his easy, friendly way with Freddy and how he'd treated the older couple, talking to complete strangers and buying them dinner just because he wanted to.

"He's complicated," I said out loud to myself. "But he pretends not to be."

There was a depth to Boxer that he didn't show people. He portrayed a *what you see is what you get* kind of man.

What was it that Freddy had said to me? Women only expected a good time from Boxer, and he never promised anything else.

Did he want to?

"Crap," I muttered.

I was worse than those women who didn't see below his fun, flirty exterior. At least they were honest about what they wanted from Boxer. I'd seen underneath it, and I'd turned my back on it. I'd rejected him when maybe, just maybe, he'd been willing to show me something deeper of himself. He'd brought me food, he'd taken me on a date, and he'd let me kick him out of my condo without putting up a fight.

When I pulled into the underground parking garage of my condo building, I slid into my spot. I turned off the car but didn't get out right away.

A tidal wave of shame for how I treated Boxer washed over me.

Before I could think too much about my actions, I pulled out my phone and dialed his number.

My heart lifted, expecting to hear his voice, teasingly calling me out for not being able to stay away from him. When I got his voicemail, I frowned in disappointment.

It beeped, but I was suddenly tongue-tied.

"Boxer, hey," I stuttered. "It's Linden. Can we talk? Call me."

I hung up and then pressed my forehead to the steering wheel, feeling like an idiot. Feeling like I was in unchartered territory. Feeling like I'd lost the chance at something real.

$$\sim$$

Silence.

Four days of silence.

Boxer never returned my call, nor did he text.

I had my answer. He was done with me—us—whatever this was.

He'd realized I was more trouble than I was worth and that there were other women—less complicated women—he could spend his time with.

I only had myself to blame for getting my hopes up that he'd call back.

By not calling me, he was sending a clear message and I had to respect it.

Luckily, I had work to dive into. I performed a colon resection, repaired a hernia, biopsied a thyroid tumor, stitched up a forehead, and treated an adult who'd uncovered a wasp's nest in his garage and had been stung to the point of going into anaphylactic shock.

I was nearing the end of my forty-eighty-hour shift, my eyes bloodshot from too much caffeine and too little sleep. "You look like you could crash for days," Amanda remarked when I approached the nurses' station.

"I feel that way." I threw out an exhausted smile. "But I'm so keyed up, I doubt I'll be able to fall asleep right away."

"You know what helps with that? Sex. Raunchy, dirty, twisty sex." Amanda grinned. "You should call your hot biker and ask him to oblige."

He wasn't my biker anymore, and I was depressed.

I wanted Boxer in my bed, the sheet pulled up over his body, naked chest on display as his heavy-lidded eyes watched me strip and then crawl on top of him.

"Your jaw just went slack," Amanda said with a laugh.

I closed my mouth and shook my head. "You're rotten."

An hour later, I was home. I hadn't seen Jerry for days and there was a new guard on duty. I waited for the wave of guilt for getting Jerry fired, but then again, he'd been the one spying on me and feeding information to my mother. I had nothing to feel guilty over.

The late afternoon sun drenched the condo in a soft, warm glow, making me want to curl up in a patch of light and fall into a dreamless sleep.

I was so exhausted that I just stood in the living room, wondering what I wanted and in what order. The caffeine buzz was no longer in my system, and my limbs were shaky with fatigue.

Boxer not calling me back grated on me.

I groaned. This was stupid. I was being stupid.

Stupid, tired and irrational.

*Screw it. If I'm going to be irrational…*

There were things I wanted to say to Boxer, and I wanted to say them face to face. I wasn't sure why that idea took root, but it seemed imperative.

Nothing had been settled as far as I was concerned. It still felt unresolved, at least on my end, but I couldn't figure out why. I'd asked him to leave, and he left. That should have been the end of it.

I went to the fridge and pulled out the carton of orange juice. As I poured the last of it into one of the new glasses delivered from Folson's, I tried to silence my thoughts.

"Gasoline on a fire? Good idea or a bad idea?" I said aloud. This would've been a perfect moment to ask a pet for its advice, but I was a workaholic that would've forgotten to feed a goldfish, much less some furry living thing.

I opened a new browser on my phone and searched for the number to Pinky's. I pressed the number and waited.

Someone answered after two rings. "Pinky's," a woman greeted.

"Hello, may I speak to Freddy?"

"I'm Freddy."

"Freddy, hey. It's Linden."

"Linden," she repeated slowly.

"Boxer's friend."

"Yeah." She laughed. "I remember you."

"Right," I muttered.

"What can I do for you?"

I sighed. "Tell me about the Tarnished Angels' parties…"

# Chapter 13

It was official. I was off my rocker. Certifiable.

Even after a few hours of sleep, my ability to think rationally hadn't been restored. It had effectively left the building. It was MIA, and it was never coming back.

*I shouldn't be doing this,* I thought silently as I stared at my reflection.

But my reflection no longer looked like me.

I'd left my blonde hair down, and I'd curled it into big waves to brush across my shoulders and down my back. My makeup made my blue eyes pop, and my lips were bright red.

But it was the outfit that was truly out of my norm.

I was in a pair of black leather pants that fit me like a second skin, and I wore a black Harley Davidson tank top.

"You look perfect," Freddy said as she sat on the edge of my bed.

I glanced at her. Her platinum bob was pinned in perfect 1950s curls and her high-waisted jeans showed off her curves. She wore green espadrilles the same shade as her blouse.

"I look like I'm dressed up to go to a Halloween party," I stated. "I'm thirty years old. I'm too old to be doing this."

"Doing what, exactly?" she asked.

"Too old to be making a fool of myself," I scoffed. "Forget it. I'm not going."

"Oh, hell no. You're going." She grinned.

"I guess it was good fortune there was a party tonight," I muttered. "I'm suddenly terrified."

"Don't be. Boxer won't be able to resist you."

"Why are you helping me do this?" I asked her. "I mean, it's more than just your affinity for Boxer. It has to be."

She paused and then boldly met my gaze. "I told you he never brought a woman into Pinky's?" When I nodded, she went on, "I've seen him at parties. He laughs, he flirts, he sleeps around."

I winced.

"Sorry, I'm just trying to paint you a picture of who he is most of the time."

"You didn't have to be so honest," I mumbled, feeling stupid and girly, not wanting to hear about his escapades.

"I'm not finished," she said in amusement, a smile flashing across her red pouty lips. "Ever since he got out of the hospital, he's been different."

I frowned. "Different? Different how?"

"Different like not drinking, not partying, not being his normal unruly self."

"I told him to take it easy and let his body recover."

She shook her head. "It's more than that. He's changed."

"What am I supposed to do with that information?" I asked.

Freddy shrugged. "No idea. I just know the Boxer that

went into the hospital came out a very different man. He told me he almost died during surgery?"

I nodded.

"He said it casually. Like it was an afterthought, but he never seemed... I don't know. He's a biker. He lives hard and fast. But it was like this got inside him somehow. Shook him deep."

"I've witnessed countless patients who've looked death in the face and walked away with their lives. Facing death changes a person."

"It might've been facing death," she agreed. "Or it might've been you. You're the one that saved his life."

The hopeful side of me wanted to believe Freddy. Every woman, whether they admitted it or not, wanted to be someone's exception to the rule.

"Let's go," she said. "We have a bit of a drive. You can follow me. I know the way."

"Freddy? What if this doesn't go the way I hope?"

"Then I'll bail on Bishop and we'll stay the night at a shitty motel in Waco and drink ourselves silly."

"Who's Bishop?" I asked with a sudden smile.

"Bishop is vice president of the Coeur d'Alene Tarnished Angels. They're tight with the Waco Tarnished Angels, and they frequently visit each other and party. I met Bishop a few months ago when he was in town and he came into Pinky's with Boxer. We've got a thing, but only when he's in Waco. It's casual."

"Ah, now I know the real reason you're willing to drive all the way out there. This has nothing to do with helping me," I teased.

By the time we got to the clubhouse, it was after nine. Nerves danced in my stomach, and my palms were clammy.

Freddy drove up to the brightly lit gate, guarded by two

men in leather I didn't recognize. They waved her through and then did the same to me. I parked next to her on a gravel parking lot. She cut the engine and then immediately climbed out. I was slower to follow.

I was surprised by the number of cars that were parked, but more so the fact that none of them were busted or looked like they needed to be impounded. Motorcycles were angled along the grassy lawn but not in a haphazard manner. They'd been cared for and were clean, and some of them looked very expensive.

Freddy marched up toward the large brown house that resembled a lodge, not even waiting to see if I was behind her. Bright lights illuminated the exterior, and there were cameras up above the door.

The cool autumn air nipped at my skin, but my blood ran hot. I was about to come face to face with a man I'd screwed in the living room of my condo among the shattered remains of my kitchenware during an emotional storm.

With a deep breath, I steeled my spine, forced a bravado I didn't feel, and entered the clubhouse. The foyer immediately opened into an extra spacious kitchen and living room with a long couch and a few recliners. Counter space was congested with bottles of alcohol and mixers. There wasn't any food.

It was empty except for two women who were sitting in the loungers. Both wore heavy makeup and had teased hair. I heard the thumping base of speakers farther in the back.

"Freddy!" The brunette got off the couch and came toward us. She was tall, her smile friendly.

"Hey, Rachel." Freddy hugged the woman and then said, "This is Linden."

The woman blinked, and then her smile turned into a knowing grin. "Oh, so *this* is Linden."

She clearly knew who I was and yet didn't seem at all surprised to see me in the Tarnished Angels clubhouse.

"Nice to meet you," I said.

"You too." She took my arm and dragged me over toward the couch. She pointed to the diminutive bottle blonde who sat in one of the recliners with a baby blanket covering her front. "That's Allison nursing the newest Tarnished Angel."

Allison looked at me and smiled. "Hi."

I couldn't help but smile back.

"Do you want something to drink?" Freddy asked me.

"No, I'm good," I said.

"You sure?" Freddy raised her brows like she didn't believe me.

"Yep," I promised. I didn't want the addition of booze in my blood adding to my already emotional state.

Freddy moved to the counter of alcohol and mixers.

"Allison came inside to feed the tiny tot," Rachel explained. "I came inside because the woodsmoke from the bonfire is making me nauseous."

I frowned, and then understanding dawned. "Oh, are you pregnant?"

"Yeah." She smiled. "That's right, you're a *doctor*." She pulled her loose tank tighter across her belly showing a slight bump. "I miss the days of wearing tight as fuck pants. Now everything feels squashed down there." She scanned my legs. "You're rocking the Bad Sandy look. I approve."

"Thanks," I said in genuine appreciation. "I was nervous about it."

"Don't be. You look great," Allison added.

"This bunch doesn't lie," Freddy said. "You can trust their word."

"I'm glad to finally meet you for myself," Rachel said. "Boxer told us about what happened during his surgery—about his pressure dropping. Thank you for everything you did for him and for saving his life."

"I'm glad it turned out the way it did," I said truthfully.

"How'd you enjoy the steak and mashed potatoes?" Rachel asked with a wink.

"He's never brought a girl food," Allison added.

I looked at Freddy who was grinning. She shrugged. "Told ya. Different."

"So different," Rachel said. "Like, he became an adult overnight or something. Freakin' weird if you ask me."

"Are there any secrets among you guys?" I demanded, smiling in exasperation.

"No," Allison piped up. "We're family. We're in each other's business all the time."

"Hmm. You remind me of the nurses I work with," I said, my tone dry. "They've made it their mission to meddle."

"We don't meddle. We don't," Rachel insisted when Allison looked at her and raised her brows. "Boxer didn't tell us you were coming."

"He doesn't know," I said. "I wanted to surprise him."

"He's out back," Allison volunteered.

"Let's go," Freddy said, gesturing with her chin to the hallway.

I waved at them. "It was nice to meet you both."

"You too," Allison said, looking from me to the infant at her breast.

"Yeah, you're cool," Rachel said.

As I followed Freddy down the hallway past closed doors, I heard the unmistakable sounds of couples in rapture. None of them seemed to care that they only had the illusion of privacy, then again, judging by the noises, they were clearly enjoying themselves and I doubted they were thinking about what others thought of them.

The music grew louder the closer we got to the back-yard. Freddy pushed open the screen door and stepped out into the night. A large bonfire had been lit and flames danced toward the sky. Men and women stood in clusters holding drinks, laughing, and talking. Some were perched on logs and camp chairs in front of the fire.

I quickly scanned the area, searching for Boxer, but I didn't see him.

"He's at the picnic table by the fence," Freddy said.

I looked where she pointed and felt an emotional knife stab my chest. "He's...not alone." A woman was hanging on his arm, running her fingers through his hair.

And she was *hot*.

She sighed. "Sorry, I had no idea, I didn't think he'd—"

"It's not your fault. It's mine. I'm fine, Freddy. I swear."

"Yeah, you look fine. Might want to uncurl those fists, unless you're planning on punching him. Or her, if that's your thing…"

I released my clenched hands.

"I know you said no booze, but trust me, I think you need it." She handed me her red Solo Cup. I took a sip and nearly choked. "What the hell is that?"

She grinned. "Apple pie moonshine. You're welcome."

"You guys are nuts."

I watched another woman approach Boxer, her hands reaching out for him. When she got to his side, her fingers danced up and down his body. I expected to see his face light with excitement and good cheer, but he was ignoring both the women fawning all over him. He held a bottle of liquor but didn't make a move to drink from it.

He looked...lonely. And morose.

I handed Freddy her cup and then walked confidently toward the picnic table.

He didn't even turn to see who was approaching, like he didn't care.

*Yup. Definitely morose.*

This was not the Boxer I thought I knew.

"Hey," the insanely hot woman greeted as I approached.

"Love your pants," the other said.

"Thanks," I said, surprised that they were being nice to me. I'd expected cat claws to come out since I was about to interrupt their fun time with Boxer.

Boxer's head whipped around. Without taking his eyes off me, he said to the women, "Trish, Tanya, our Coeur D'Alene boys had a hard ride down here. Why don't you go keep them company?"

"Ohhh, look, Knight's alone," one of the women said.

They exchanged a look and then clasped hands and all but skipped toward a cluster of men in leather. They didn't seem at all upset about switching allegiances.

"They're...*friendly*," I said.

"The friendliest."

"Sorry I ruined a sure thing." I gestured with my chin.

He lifted the bottle of liquor to his lips but didn't reply.

"Guess you're no longer following my rules."

"What rules would those be?" he pressed.

"The drinking rules."

"Well, I had really vigorous sex a few days ago, so I figured that made all the other rules null and void. Plus, I fired you as my doctor, remember?"

"I remember," I repeated, flushing when I thought of our night together. "What are you drinking?"

"Bourbon."

"Ick."

"Not ick." He held it out to me. "Try it."

"After the moonshine Freddy gave me, I'm good."

He paused. "Why are you here, Linden?"

"I wanted to talk to you."

"You could've called. You didn't have to stalk me."

"I didn't *stalk* you," I said, voice angry. "And I did call you."

"No, you didn't," he insisted.

I reached into my purse and pulled out my phone. I scrolled through my recent call list and handed it to him.

He looked down at the screen. "You called me."

"Yup. You didn't call me back."

"Lost my phone somewhere on the ride up to Idaho." He looked at me and handed my phone back.

"You've been riding your motorcycle?"

"Of course," he drawled. "Why did you contact me?"

"I don't like how things ended that night."

"Told you not to feel guilty about it, Doc."

His expression was placid, but I knew there was something lurking beneath the surface.

Maybe it was the leather pants, maybe it was the fact that I didn't know who I was anymore, but I faced him and said, "I don't like that things ended at all."

# Chapter 14

BOXER STILLED, and then his chin dropped. "That was your choice."

"You were asking personal questions. My walls went up."

He laughed, but it didn't sound like he was truly amused. "Walls? Nah. You erected a fucking fortress."

"Yeah." I nodded. "You had seen too much. I was embarrassed."

He sipped from the bottle again and then patted the seat next to him. I came to the table, and he held out his hand to help me up.

"Christ, are you wearing leather pants?"

My skin warmed from his touch. "Yeah."

"I'm a dead man."

I laughed and with a shake of my head, I took the bottle of bourbon from him and drank. I wheezed and coughed.

He chuckled and took the bottle back. Boxer rested his elbows on his thighs and spread them apart so his knee grazed my pants. "You came here to talk. So, talk."

"Why are you depressed?" I asked instead.

"Who says I'm depressed?"

"Those girls were crawling all over you, and you barely even noticed them."

He climbed off the picnic table and turned to face me. Boxer held the bottle of liquor by the neck, and he let his hand fall to his side. He loomed over me, his face darkening with annoyance.

"You shouldn't have bothered coming. It was a waste of time. If you're not gonna be honest with me, then what the hell are you doing here?"

I swallowed, my mouth suddenly dry with nerves.

"Fuck this. I'm done." Boxer turned and started to walk away. He was leaving, and I wasn't doing anything to stop him.

"I miss you," I blurted out.

He halted but didn't turn to face me.

I'd hurt him, I realized.

"Boxer?"

"What?"

"Will you please turn around?"

He turned slowly.

I stepped down off the picnic table and walked toward him, my heart drumming in my ears. Instead of looking up and peering into his eyes, I moved closer—close enough to press my cheek to his chest.

I inhaled an apprehensive breath, smelling the woodsmoke of the fire on his clothes, the scent of cologne on his skin.

"You saw me. The real me," I said quietly. "And I didn't know how to handle it."

He dropped the bottle of bourbon, which splashed on the grass, and then his arms were around me, rough. "God, woman." Boxer grabbed a fistful of my hair and pulled my head back so he could look into my eyes. "You just…"

"What?"

Instead of finishing his thought, his lips took mine in a hungry kiss. He tasted of bourbon and sin, of want and remorse. Boxer dragged me closer, so I was flush against him. Just as his tongue thrust into my mouth, I heard a chorus of cheers, whistles, and claps.

Boxer pulled back, shot me a wink, and then wrapped his arm around my shoulder. "You're not cold?"

"A little."

He released me, but only so he could take my hand. And then he was dragging me toward the clubhouse.

The cheers and whistles resounded again, but I was too focused on Boxer to pay attention.

He all but hauled me up the stairs to the second floor. We walked down the hallway, and he pushed opened a door before flipping on the light. It was a small bedroom with just enough space for a queen-sized bed flush against one wall and a narrow three-drawer dresser on the other.

"You don't live here, do you? There's not even a bathroom."

"Bathroom is down the hall," he explained, shutting the door. "And no, I don't live here. It's my clubhouse room, where I crash if I don't want to ride my bike home. I used to have a room on the first floor, but I gave it to Rachel and Reap."

"Why?"

"It's bigger than the room they had at the clubhouse, and with Rach being knocked up, they're gonna need more space for a crib and other shit."

With a sigh, I leaned forward and rested my forehead against the warm column of his neck. "Why were you brooding out there?"

His hand worked its way up the back of my tank and walked his fingers up and down my spine before settling his palm at the small of my back. "I wasn't happy with how things ended between us, Doc. I wasn't sure what to do with that. And after five days on the road, I still didn't have you out of my head."

He pressed me closer. It wasn't nearly close enough.

"I wanted *you*, Linden, even when I thought you didn't want me back."

I lifted my head to stare into his eyes. "I do want you, Boxer."

He quirked a smile. "Yeah, darlin', I know."

"But it's even more than that."

"That's why you showed up here tonight?"

"I lied to myself about why I came here." I exhaled. "I told myself it was because I wanted to apologize. Clear the air."

"I forgive you for using me like a sex toy," he said. I shoved his shoulder, but then he captured my hand and brought it to his lips. "I'm glad you came."

We stared at one another. His quicksilver eyes were beautiful, soft, when they looked at me.

"This is insane," I whispered.

He nodded.

"We haven't known each other that long."

He nodded again.

"You're a criminal."

He shrugged.

"I'm a basket case."

He nodded vigorously.

I sighed, brushing my lips against his hand. "I'm a good doctor, Boxer. But that's all I'm good at."

"That's not *all* you're good at," he teased.

"There's more to a relationship than sex."

"Which is why I don't do relationships. Too hard. Too complicated. Too much talking when people could be doing something else with their mouths…"

I raised my brows.

"But damn, you might be a crazy enough broad to keep me entertained. In *and* out of bed." He grinned cheekily. "I haven't fucked anyone since I fucked you."

"Really?"

"You don't believe me?"

"What about Trish and Tanya? If I hadn't shown up, would you be in here with them right now? You know what, don't answer that. I don't want to know."

"You're gonna be in my bed. And while you're there, there won't be any others. Okay?"

"Okay," I said with a nod.

"The same goes for you," he commanded. "I won't fucking share you."

"You don't have to worry about that," I assured him.

"Like hell I don't," he groused. "You're gorgeous. I know you've got tons of guys sniffing after you."

"The only one who I'll allow to sniff me is you," I said with a laugh, my insides doing cartwheels at the thoughts of being with him.

"My schedule changes all the time," he stated. "I'm not a guy who punches a timecard."

"I'm a surgeon who sometimes works forty-eight-hour shifts straight," I pointed out. "Don't expect me to be waiting at home for you in an apron with a pot roast in the oven."

"Now that's a damn fine fantasy," he teased. "I've got to find a way to get you in nothing but an apron so I can fuck you from behind while you're bent over the kitchen table."

My eyes widened.

Boxer smirked. "You like that idea."

"I *might* like that idea."

"We'll have to make that happen," he said, his voice soft yet husky.

"Boxer?"

"Yeah, Doc?"

"Can we please stop talking now and get to the fun part?"

"Hell yeah," he stated.

I stepped back, only far enough so that I could lift the tank top over my head and toss it aside. His eyes seemed to turn even more liquid as he stared at me.

We hadn't gotten undressed the night we'd been together. Even though we'd slept together, tonight was the night we were going to be intimate.

He pushed away from the dresser and took a step toward me. He reached out to graze the curve of my breast.

I'd worn a demi cup black satin bra.

His fingers skimmed lightly across my flesh in an achingly slow manner. "I didn't get to see much of you that night. Damn shame. You're fucking gorgeous."

My skin continued to heat under his penetrating stare and sensuous touch.

He was going slow. Too slow.

I reached around to unclasp my bra and then let it fall off my body. But I didn't stop there. I bent over to get rid of my heavy, leather biker boots and then undid the leather pants so I could slither out of them.

My skin immediately cooled.

I stood before him in nothing but a black thong.

"You have too many clothes on," I admonished with an arch of my brow.

His lips curved into a grin. "Demanding, are you?"

"Yes."

He set his pistol on the nightstand, and then he slowly removed his leather cut to place it on the top of the dresser. Boxer lifted the hem of his T-shirt and then tossed it aside.

I couldn't stop the gasp from escaping my lips when I saw his defined and utterly lickable abs. His muscular chest was covered in a light blond fuzz that I wanted to drag my fingers across. His arms were a sculptor's dream.

Boxer went for his belt next and the button of his jeans.

My eyes tracked his every movement until he was standing in front of me wearing nothing but a pair of army green boxer briefs.

I reverently touched the Tarnished Angels tattoo that graced the left side of his rib cage. I continued to examine him, grasping one of his hands and tugging on it so he was forced to straighten his arm. I wanted to study the sleeve of ink winding up his appendage. Flames started along his forearm and moved toward his bicep, morphing into a lion with a flaming mane. It looked so real, almost like a photograph, and I was amazed at how intricate and colorful it was.

On his other arm was a crow resting on barbed wire, a dying rose clutched in its beak. I peered closer, noting a tear dripping from one eye. It was evocative and full of emotion.

He linked his fingers with mine and dragged me closer.

Boxer was done with slow.

So was I.

He plowed his fingers into my hair to pull me toward him. "This'll change everything," Boxer said. "You know that, right?"

I nodded, even though I had no idea what he was talking about. But it didn't matter because we were here, now, because both of us had chosen to be with each other.

His lips covered mine, and then I ceased to think at all. His tongue plunged into my mouth as Boxer urged me to the bed. The back of my knees hit the mattress, and then I flopped down. He quickly covered my body with his, propping himself up on his elbows. Boxer didn't give me any time to think. His tongue was back in my mouth and the scent of him wrapped around me, enveloping me in a haze of need.

He dragged his lips from mine to pay homage to the tender skin below my ear and neck. His stubble rasped against me, and I gloried in the whisker burn. I wanted a reminder of him tomorrow, when the sun rose, and I had put myself back in a box. But when I was with Boxer and his hands were on my body and his tongue was on my skin, I was reduced to a woman with no name. A woman who wanted only pleasure, only to live in the moment. A woman who didn't care about tomorrow.

"Were you sore?" he asked as his hand slid over a breast, rolling my nipple between his fingers.

I sucked in a breath of air as sparks of pleasure shot from my nipple to my core.

"Answer me," he stated, his voice low. "Every time you moved, every time you walked, did you remember what it felt like to have me inside you?"

"Yes," I hissed out as he pinched my nipple.

He lowered his head and captured the other with his lips. He sucked and drew it farther into his velvety hot mouth. A hearty zing between my legs made me arch and press into him.

"You were so fucking wet," he said around the nipple in his mouth. "Tell me you're wet now."

He let go of my breast and skated his hand down my belly, his fingers gliding into my thong. He rested his finger on the seam of my body and didn't move it for moment.

"Boxer," I demanded.

"What, Linden? Tell me what you want." He grazed the tip of his finger against my aching, swelling flesh.

I thrashed against him.

"You want this?" he asked, exerting more pressure. "No? What about this?" He slid his finger down and then slipped it into my body. Boxer curled his finger, grazing that hard-to-reach place that caused my back to bow and my eyes to roll into my head.

"Yeah, you like that," he chuckled, his breath coasting over my skin. He undulated his finger, and then gently added another, teasing me to the edge only to pull back again and again until I finally snapped.

"Enough."

"Enough what?" His gray eyes were bright. "Tell me what you want, Linden, and I'll give it to you."

"I want you inside me. Now."

"Not as graphic as I'd like, but I'll take it. We gotta work on your dirty talk, darlin'."

Boxer slid out of my body. With sharp eyes watching me, he stuck his fingers in his mouth and licked them clean.

"Fuck," he groaned. "I can't wait to bury my face between your thighs and make you scream."

My vision momentarily darkened as a hazy sensual picture formed in my mind. My hands in Boxer's hair, his tongue relentlessly teasing me until I came.

He leaned over me to the bedside drawer. He yanked it open and extracted a condom. He was in too much of a hurry to bother shutting the drawer.

Boxer tossed the foil packet onto the bed next to me and then moved so he could strip out of his briefs. He took himself in hand and tugged on his engorged shaft a few times before letting it go.

My mouth watered at the sight of him. He was close enough to me that I reached out to gently cup his testicles. The heavy weight of them rested in my hand, and I gave them a little squeeze.

Words stuck in my throat. Every filthy dirty word about what I wanted to do to him came to my mind, but I was too shy to say them.

"I can't wait to feel your hot wet tongue on my dick," he growled.

"I can't wait for that either," I said, breathless.

He gently batted my hand away and grabbed the condom. Boxer ripped the foil with his teeth and then rolled it on.

I slinked my thong down my legs and tossed it aside. And in a fit of pure boldness, I spread my legs, wanting him to see all of me.

"The things I'm gonna do to your body," he groaned. He grasped himself and then came toward me. The head of his member teased my swollen flesh, and then his crown slid into me.

He paused for just a moment and then thrust slowly but firmly to the hilt.

I gasped at the welcome invasion.

His hands were everywhere, stroking, playing. He lifted one of my legs and bent it back, so my knee nearly touched my chest and then somehow, he sank even deeper.

And then he began to move.

Every cell in my body came alive like they'd all been charged with electricity and were now spinning, buzzing free with frenetic energy.

My skin tingled and sweat coated my skin. Boxer let go of my leg, and I wrapped them both around him. I placed my hands on the curves of his backside, urging him faster, silently demanding more.

He fit me like no other. Every movement pushed me closer until I was finally shoved over the cliff of pleasure. I clenched and bucked; a scream trapped in my throat.

Boxer thrusted a few more times before clasping me to him, moaning out his release.

I clung to him, long after the ripples of pleasure ceased. My eyes were closed, and I let myself drown in the scent of us as serenity enveloped my soul.

He lifted himself off me and pulled out, but I still didn't open my eyes. I wanted to hold onto the moment and remember the feeling.

"Linden?"

I heard the concern in his voice and finally opened my eyes and smiled at him.

He stood next to the bed. Boxer had removed the condom and now loomed over me, looking like a naked, inked angel.

God, he was beautiful. Sleek rippling muscles, unconcerned about nudity, and confidence in every part of him.

I sat up. "I need to use the bathroom."

He padded to the dresser and opened the middle drawer. He took out a white T-shirt and brought it to me.

"Thanks," I said as I threw it over my head. I looked around, attempting to find my thong. It was hanging on the lampshade on the bedside table. Laughing, I reached for it and then quickly slid it on.

I went to the door of the bedroom and opened it slightly, peering out into the hallway. I listened for a moment and heard nothing—no sounds of couples in the heat of passion or the heavy thud of footsteps coming up the stairs.

I slipped into the hallway, closing the door behind me, and then I went to find the bathroom. It was a half bath, and it was far cleaner than I expected the bathroom in a clubhouse of bikers to be.

As I washed my hands, I looked in the mirror. My red lipstick was smeared across my mouth and my hair looked like a wildcat had raked its claws through it.

I smiled.

The woman in the mirror smiled back. It was hard to believe that was me. I pulled my hair into a ponytail, tying it with the elastic band around my wrist. There was only bar soap, but I used it to wash off my makeup.

I didn't want to use the hand towel to dry my face, so I lifted the hem of the T-shirt I wore and dabbed my cheeks. It left a big wet spot at the belly. It didn't matter. I didn't plan on wearing his shirt long.

I stepped out into the hallway and halted. Zip, the Tarnished Angels vice president who I'd met at the hospital, was just coming up the stairs, a statuesque woman behind him.

Their hands were linked and when they both saw me, they stopped.

I was standing in the hallway in a thong and a white T-shirt that was thin enough to show my jutting nipples. At least the shirt covered my butt.

"Linden, right?" the woman asked.

I nodded.

She beamed. "Hi, I'm Joni. Colt's sister."

Zip wrapped an arm around her shoulder and hauled her into his side. "You should lead with *Zip's Old Lady*."

She pressed a hand to his chest and smiled up at him, but then quickly looked back to me. "We're having a housewarming party this week. I'd love it if you came."

"Oh," I said, a smile spreading across my face. "Thank you so much. I'd love to. Crazy doctor schedule permitting."

The door to Boxer's room opened, and he stepped out into the hallway—completely naked. "Shit!" he muttered, rushing back into the room and slamming the door shut.

Joni began to laugh, but when Zip looked at her, she pretended to cough instead.

"How much did you see?" Zip demanded.

"I didn't see a thing," Joni assured him. "Aren't we going to your room now?"

"Doc, good to see you." Zip sent me a chin nod and then grasped Joni's hand and pulled her down the hallway in the opposite direction of Boxer's room.

Joni looked over her shoulder at me and mouthed *wow.*

I hastily covered my mouth so I wouldn't laugh.

Their door closed, and I headed back to Boxer.

He was in bed, the covers pulled up to his waist, his tattooed arm nestled underneath his head. His eyes found me, and he grinned. "Well, that was fun."

"The peep show or the other thing?"

"The other thing. Get over here."

I went to him, stripping off the damp T-shirt as I went. He pulled the covers down, and I climbed in next to him. "I guess we're not going back to the party?"

"Party's over," he stated. "I mean, for the most part. Everyone's got a family. Gray and Darcy have to get home to their kids. Allison and Torque have a newborn, so they're out. Rachel's knocked up and needs rest, so Reap will take her home. Mia and Colt will get out of here too. Only the Idaho boys and the newly patched in Tarnished Angels will stay up late, and they'll be getting into all sorts of trouble with the girls downstairs."

"The Idaho boys are from Coeur d'Alene, right?" I asked, my eyes drifting closed as Boxer's fingers moved lightly down my arm.

"Yeah, how did you know?"

"Freddy mentioned it. Is that where you were these last few days? Up in Coeur d'Alene?"

"Yep."

"What were you doing there?"

"Club shit. I can't talk about it," he said evasively. "What happened that night? Before I came over?"

"Life shit. I can't talk about it."

"Ah, I see what you're doing there. But club shit is not the same as life shit. Come on, Doc. No one escapes the life shit."

I took a deep breath. "My mother paid the security guard at my condo building to feed her information about my life. Like, I was literally being spied on, and when I talked to her on the phone the night we were supposed to go out, she mentioned you."

When he didn't say anything, I met his gaze. "You're not what she would call...*suitable*."

"Damn right, I'm not suitable. Not for a broad like you."

"Don't talk about yourself that way," I snapped. "That's not even the point. The point is that she shouldn't have known anything about my life except what I chose to share with her. And I share nothing with her for exactly this kind of reason. I talk about my job and the weather. I ask how my stepfather is doing. I make excuses about why I'm not flying home to Watch Hill for Christmas. Until now, we've both operated knowing this was how our relationship was always going to be. We lived within these parameters and mutually avoided discussing things on a deeper level. But now..."

"She changed it all by invading your privacy." He sighed. "Damn."

I nodded. "I just lost my cool. I was *so* angry, Boxer. It became its own living, breathing monster, and I wanted to smash and break things. The only reason I stopped was because I ran out of dishes." I sent him a wobbly smile.

He didn't smile back.

"And then you came over and I just—"

"Needed not to think."

"Yeah."

"Did it work?" he asked.

"It did."

"Good."

"Good?" I sighed. "How can you say that?"

"Yeah, good. You were hurting; I put a stop to it. I'm glad I could do that for you."

"Is it that black and white, Boxer?"

"Yeah, Doc. It is. You needed to release your anger by using someone. I was there." He smiled. "Do you see me complaining?"

"Don't."

"Don't what?"

"Don't pretend there's nothing more to you than a good time. Not now. Not while we're doing this and pulling off the Band-Aid."

"Can I give you a piece of advice?" he asked.

"Okay."

"The next time you want to let out all that aggression and anger, you let me know and I'll take you to the shooting range."

I blinked.

A smile crept across his lips.

"The shooting range?" I repeated.

"Yeah, Doc. The shooting range. It'll give you a feeling of control you've never experienced before. Trust me."

I did trust him, I realized.

We fell silent for a moment and then I said, "Joni invited me to her housewarming."

"Of course she did," Boxer muttered.

"What? You don't want me to go to the party?" I looked at him.

"Oh, I want you to go to the party, but you better be prepared for them to ask questions."

"Questions? What kind of questions?"

He rolled me so that I was flat on my back. He quickly draped his muscled, inked body on top of mine and stared into my eyes. "For starters, how good I am in bed. Be generous with your praise. I've got a reputation to protect."

I laughed and threw a leg over his hip, nestling myself against him. "If you want praise, you have to do something worthy of the praise."

His hand slid to my hip and then wandered between our bodies. "I better get to work, then."

I woke up on my belly, Boxer's heavy leg strewn across mine. I lifted my head ever so slightly, looking for an alarm clock to tell me the time. I didn't see one. Music no longer played outside. The party had gone on for hours without us while we'd been holed up in his room. Now, everything was quiet.

A hand stole across my back.

"You're awake," I whispered.

"So are you." He scooted closer, dragging me against him. "Your breathing changed, and it woke me up."

"You're a light sleeper," I said in surprise. "I would've expected you to be a hard sleeper."

"Why?"

"I don't know. Just seems like you'd crash hard." I wriggled in his embrace, and he let me go. I rolled over onto my back. He placed his cheek on my chest, and I felt his warm breath on my naked skin. My fingers sank into his hair, and I stroked his head.

"So, are you ready for a weird coincidence?" I asked him.

"Go for it."

"It seems your buddy who runs The Rex is also the owner of the condo building I live in."

"No shit. Ramsey owns your building? How'd you find that out?"

"I called the management company wanting to speak to the owner so I could report Jerry. Ramsey was the one who called me back."

"Small fucking world."

"Right?" My fingers drifted lower to trace swirls on his back. "Ramsey was on the cover of a magazine. 'Most Eligible Bachelors of Dallas.' I read the article, Boxer."

"Yeah. So?"

"So, I know you spend a lot of time in Dallas doing *business*—whatever that means."

"Don't fish, Linden. If you want to ask a question, ask it."

"Would you even tell me the truth?"

"Try it and see."

I sighed. "Does the name Quinn O'Malley ring a bell?"

He sat up and stared at me. "Yeah, it rings a bell. What about her?"

"We met when I was doing my residency at Boston General."

"No shit."

"Yeah," I said with a nod. "A few days ago, we were on the phone, and she told me all about her fiancé's business relationship with Flynn Campbell. And Flynn's relationship with Colt. Ramsey's wrapped up in all that, too, isn't he? That's why you're in Dallas a few times a week, right? Because you're doing business with Ramsey that isn't on the up and up?"

He ran a hand across his cheek and then scratched his chest. "Here's the thing, Doc. All this shit you're talking about is club business. And we don't involve our women in club business. What did Quinn tell you about us?"

"Nothing," I said. "She was vague."

"Good."

"Not good," I replied. "Why don't you tell the Old Ladies what goes on?"

"If they need to know anything, it's broad strokes only."

"You guys keep them completely in the dark?" I accused.

"It's for their own protection." He paused. "There's a code among clubs. No women, no children get caught in the crossfire. Usually."

"Crossfire? *Usually?*"

"Look darlin', you're into a whole can of worms here. Some bad shit happened about a year ago." He sighed. "Fuck. This is already getting complicated. This, right here, is why I stick to broads who know how the club operates. They know what they're getting into. They know the danger that surrounds us, and they don't ask questions. Yeah, there are times when life is normal and not much happens around here, but then there are times that shit goes south. You just never know when that's gonna be."

I sighed but didn't reply.

"What's that sigh mean?"

"I've never thought of this stuff," I admitted. "Maybe I should have dug a little deeper before coming here…"

"Why didn't you?"

I glared. "Why didn't I? I don't know. Maybe I was too

pissed off because you didn't call me back, and I'd thought you'd ghosted me. Again."

"I did ghost you," he said without a hint of apology. "Again."

"You bastard."

"Woman, I was trying to get you out of my head. We'd barely started this thing, and I was already fucked up over it. I tried to keep my distance, but then you had to show up at the clubhouse wearing leather pants—"

"Do you wish I hadn't come here?" I asked quietly. "Do you wish I'd just let things be and we'd gone separate ways?"

He reached out to cradle my cheek. "It might've been easier on both of us if you'd stayed away. But no, Doc. I'm glad you showed up. But this could really turn into something, yeah?"

I swallowed my fear and nodded.

"Things in my life are fine until they're not. You'd be crazy to stay, even though I want you to. Every girl wants a bad boy, until they actually get one."

"What about Mia? Or Joni? Or the other women who decided to be part of this world? They're here. Why am I different?"

"Joni grew up in it. Her old man was club president. Her brother is the current president. She gets it." He paused. "Mia was an outsider for sure. Knew nothing about club business or what it meant to be an Old Lady."

"She looks pretty happy," I said.

"She wasn't always. She was involved in the shit that went down last year…" he trailed off.

"How bad was it, Boxer?"

"Bad. She was knee-deep in it. You're not knee-deep in anything. You can still bounce."

"Does it have to be all or nothing?"

"Yeah, Linden. That's how we roll. You either fuck around with a Tarnished Angel and then move on with your life or you become his Old Lady. There's no in between. We live a different kind of life. We don't play by the same rules as the rest of society. We gotta know that our women have our backs, that they're in this fucking rollercoaster for the long haul. Otherwise, they're just party playthings. They know it, and we know it. No one gets hurt that way. I'm just trying to lay out for you what you're really getting into."

He exhaled. "This family is everything to me. I don't want to bring some woman around who's gonna disappear after people start getting attached. Stay or don't, but you have to make a decision."

"I didn't expect to like you," I admitted. "But Boxer, this is a lot to think about."

"I know." He leaned forward and pressed his lips to mine. "But I'm still pushing for it anyway because I'm wondering if you've got what it takes to be part of this life. My life."

Did I?

I hadn't been able to close the door on my unresolved feelings for Boxer. I hadn't liked how I handled the situation at my condo. But choosing to stay meant choosing a man and a world that was completely foreign to me.

Peyton's words came roaring back to me.

Was I really going to walk away from a man who made me feel alive?

# Chapter 15

A FEW DAYS LATER, I walked into the lounge and immediately went to the coffee maker. The coffee in the pot was old and cold so I dumped it. While I was filling the appliance with fresh water, Peyton came in.

"Hey," she greeted. She headed to the fridge, opened it, and set a Tupperware on the top shelf, and then closed the door.

"Hey, yourself," I replied.

She was wearing light blue scrubs with a pink starburst pattern, her shiny red hair was pulled into a high ponytail, and her cheeks were rosy.

"You look…" I trailed off, surveying her from head to toe. "Different."

A slow smile crept across her face. "Different how?"

My jaw dropped open. "You totally got laid!"

"I might have," she said.

"But—but *how*?"

"You want me to draw you a diagram?" she asked with a grin.

I rolled my eyes. "You know what I mean."

"Well, after you came over for dinner, my alter ego had an intervention with my normal everyday self. It was weird, because I was standing in my kitchen, arguing with myself. Out loud, mind you."

Laughing, I said, "Then what happened?"

"I called someone who's made it very clear he would be happy to, ah, scratch my future itches." A blush stained her cheeks, making her look young and joyful.

"Well, hot damn," I said with a chuckle. "Good for you."

She cocked her head to the side. "Now, is there anything *you* want to tell me?"

Even though I was worried about the things Boxer had explained to me about his life, I couldn't stop my own telling grin from spreading across my face.

"Oh my God," she squealed.

"Stop," I said, looking to the door. "We can swap stories later. Right now, I have to get down to the ER."

"With Dr. Sawyer?"

"Hmm. Yeah."

"Sounds super fun," she said with a grin.

"The funnest." I shook my head. "I wish he wasn't such an ass."

"Don't take it personally," she said. "He's an ass to pretty much everyone."

"That actually doesn't make me feel better. Why is he such an ass?"

"He wants Chief Nelson's job when Nelson eventually retires. I think Dr. Sawyer is trying to assert dominance. Like the biggest dog in the dog park."

"So, I shouldn't take it personally that he rags on me all the time?"

"Definitely not."

As if summoned by a spell, Dr. Sawyer entered the lounge. "Ah, Dr. Ward. Glad I found you."

He was tall, and I used to think tall men were imposing. But after being around Boxer, I realized that wasn't always the case. Boxer moved like he owned the space around him, swaggering with arrogance, but with the goods to back it up and not in a way that was ever forced. Dr. Sawyer reminded me of a deflated birthday balloon that was trying desperately to hold onto the last bit of helium, bobbing up and down, struggling to stay afloat.

"I was just coming down to the ER," I said, trying to fend off a reprimand before it started.

"I need the biopsy results for my patient with the kidney tumor and then meet me in the ER." Without waiting for a reply, he turned, and stalked out of the lounge.

I sighed and shook my head at Peyton. "The biggest dog at the dog park...and I've definitely become his bitch."

The young woman sat on a hospital cot, her brown hair falling over her face as she held her shoulder with one hand.

"Ms. Carrington?"

She didn't look up right away and when she did, I could see the dark smudge of a bruise at the corner of her right eye.

I pulled the curtain shut around us to give the illusion of privacy.

It was hard to tell her age. She looked like she could've been in her late teens or early twenties. The way she hunched over, along with her injuries, told me everything I needed to know.

"What happened?" I asked.

"I fell down the stairs. I hurt my shoulder."

*Classic excuse.*

I examined her as gently as I could, but she winced in pain and then began to cry. Her shoulder was dislocated and needed to be put back into its socket, but from her reaction I guessed there was ligament damage and there was a good chance she needed surgery.

"Give me just a second," I said, pushing the curtain aside.

I went to the admin desk and waited for the nurse to get off the phone. "Hey, Dr. Ward."

"Hi Shelia, will you page Dr. Stillwater? I need an ortho consult. A young woman with a dislocated shoulder. It doesn't look good."

"Sure thing," she said, picking up the phone.

I went back to Ms. Carrington who'd clearly been abused. I'd seen this so many times.

Scared. Alone. Wide eyes. No one to turn to.

I pulled the curtain shut again and took a seat in the chair next to the bed. "Betty, do you want to tell me what really happened?"

She didn't look surprised that I deduced the truth. Betty inhaled a shaky breath. "I burned his dinner…"

"Whose dinner?"

"Dominic's…"

"Is Dominic your boyfriend?" I asked gently.

"Dominic is my son. His father is the one who—"

It was bad enough when a woman was being abused, but when children were involved, it made everything worse.

"I can help you," I said quietly. "I can make a call—"

"And what?" she asked, her dark eyes finally showing some fire. "What good will that do? So someone can take away my son? So his father can kick me out of our apartment after he beats me again? I'm a waitress at a shitty highway diner. I don't have a lot of options here. Besides he hasn't done this in a while… I should have been more careful."

"This isn't your fault. You must know that. There are places you can go…shelters. We can get you safe."

She snorted. "Those places are worse than what I've already got. Don't do me any favors. Just fix my shoulder so I can get back to my life."

I knew better than to push. If I pushed, she'd leave before even receiving treatment. And she needed her shoulder fixed.

The curtain around the cot was pulled aside. "Dr. Ward," Dr. Stillwater greeted. She was an attractive middle-aged woman who wore her brown hair in a neat chignon. "You asked for a consult?"

I nodded and introduced her to the patient.

Dr. Stillwater kept me posted on Ms. Carrington's surgery. Her shoulder was back in its socket, and she would be discharged the next day.

Eighteen hours later, I walked into my condo and dropped my purse onto the floor. I hadn't bothered showering at the hospital. I'd wanted to leave as soon as possible and had driven home like the devil was on my tail, haunted by the memory of the young woman I couldn't save. A young woman who had been dealt such a bad hand in life that she wasn't capable of saving herself, even when help was offered to her.

It was midnight, I was still in scrubs, and the residue of impotence clung to my soul.

Sometimes people came into the ER who were beyond saving. They either died on the operating table or found out later, after the surgery, that they were terminal. Other times, there were patients who I called husk people. The hope had gone out of them long ago. Their bodies still functioned, and they talked, walked, and moved normally. Their hearts still pumped blood, their kidneys filtered out toxins, but nothing could fix the true problems within. Life had beaten them down so much that they never bothered to get up off the grungy floor. They stayed down, just hoping to survive another day.

The husk people were the hardest ones to face.

How did you save people who wouldn't—couldn't—save themselves?

My phone buzzed in my pants pocket. I fished it out and looked at the screen.

BOXER

Hey, darlin'.

I could hear his drawl in my head, but it still didn't bring a smile to my face.

*Hey,* I texted back.

A moment later, my cell rang.

"Hi," I answered.

"What's wrong?" he asked immediately.

"Nothing's wrong. I just walked through the door. I'm exhausted."

He paused. "You can talk to me about it. I'm a good listener."

My ex had pretended he wanted to hear about my days, but he was never able to hide the glazed look on his face when I talked about my patients.

Boxer wasn't Jeff.

I stood in the living room, gathering my thoughts and then decided to level with him. "This young woman came in," I began. "Dislocated shoulder. Bruises on her neck and cheek. A black eye."

"Fuck."

"Yeah. Her X-rays showed so many healed breaks. I gave her my cell phone number to call me if she wanted help." I paused. "She'll never call, Boxer. None of them ever call."

I fell silent, and he didn't reply.

"You asked," I accused.

"I did," he agreed.

"I became a doctor because I wanted to help people. I wanted to fix things that were broken. Surgery can do that. But how do you repair someone's soul?"

I'd been trying for years to fix my own issues, but I was starting to believe they'd never be resolved. Were we all doomed to being imperfect people patched together, concealing the rot beneath?

"It makes you a good doctor," Boxer said.

"What does?"

"Feeling the losses. You let them cut deep. It means you care. It means you want to make a difference."

"Adderly Ford," I murmured. "You are a constant surprise."

"The name is Boxer."

"No," I said emphatically. "Not right now it isn't. Right now, you're not the charming playboy biker. Right now, you're…"

"I'm what?" he asked gruffly.

I sighed. "Exactly what I need."

"Linden!" Amanda called. "Over here!"

I grabbed my lunch tray, stalked across the cafeteria, and plunked it down at the table. Emily smiled around the juice box she was drinking from, and Peyton scooted the empty chair out next to her.

"Hey," I said. "What are we talking about?"

"Emily's birthday next month," Peyton said.

"I usually keep it low key," Emily said. "Have friends over, grill, drink some beers."

"That sounds fun."

My phone vibrated across the table. I caught the flash of Boxer's name, and I instantly scooped up my cell and set it in my lap. I discreetly opened my phone to read the text.

BOXER

How long has it been since I've been inside you?

I squeaked and dropped my phone into my lap.

Peyton look at me and frowned. "Are you okay?"

"Fine," I said.

"You're blushing," she noted.

I touched my cheek as my phone buzzed again.

BOXER

I'm waiting.

My fingers flew across the screen to answer him.

ME

Three days.

BOXER

Jerking off isn't cutting it. I need to see you.

"Oh my God," Amanda exclaimed. "You're totally sexting!"

Doctors eating their lunches a few tables away looked over in our direction. Including Dr. Sawyer. I didn't need to give him any more of a reason to lord his authority over me.

"Shut up," I hissed.

Amanda sighed. "I miss the days of sexting."

"You and your husband don't sext anymore?" Peyton asked.

She sighed. "No."

"Why not?" Emily demanded. "I knew you and Martin when you guys were dating. What happened?"

"We had a kid," Amanda said bluntly. "Nothing has been the same since Daphne was born. I keep hoping things will get back to normal, but they never do."

I watched Peyton's eyes dim as Amanda talked about her husband and child. Peyton had neither. I knew Peyton and her husband had wanted a family. My heart ached for her.

Another text came through my phone.

"Relentless," Emily said with a grin. "Admit you like it."

"I like it," I said easily.

But this text wasn't Boxer. It was from an unknown number, yet the words on the screen were familiar.

And I knew the sender.

"Linden? Are you okay?" Amanda asked.

"Fine," I said, my tone clipped. "I've got to go." I hastily stood up, grabbed my tray still full of food and dumped it into the trash, my appetite completely gone.

I set the tray on the top of the trash receptacle and left the cafeteria. Blood pounded in my ears, and I wondered why, no matter how far I fled, I could never escape my past.

~

Hours later, just as the sun was beginning to set, I walked out of the hospital and came to a halt.

Boxer was leaning against his parked motorcycle, a pair of silver aviators concealing his eyes. He wore his leather cut, a pair of dark jeans, and a green and black flannel shirt.

A smirk flitted across his face as he perused me up and down. When Boxer looked at me that way, my insides quivered.

"Hey, Doc," he drawled.

"What are you doing here?"

"I was in the neighborhood."

"Yeah," I drawled. "I bet you were."

"Came to say hi."

"Hi." I waved.

"That's not how I say hi. Come here."

"I think I'll stay over here," I said with a wry grin, enjoying the teasing and the banter. "I read your texts. I'm afraid of what's going to happen if I'm in your clutches."

"You want to get over here so I can whisper it in your ear, otherwise I'll say it out loud. What if your co-workers overheard me?"

"I was having lunch with the nurses when your dirty texts came through. They were very aware of your dirty texts."

"Oh yeah?"

"Yeah. They approve, by the way."

"Linden, get your ass over here."

With a laugh, I stalked toward him, stopping when I was close enough to see the stubble along his jaw. I wanted to rake my fingers through his messy, dirty blond hair and then drag him close and press my lips to his.

There was something so incredibly freeing about being

with Boxer. He wasn't ashamed to admit what he wanted. There was no embarrassment about his desires.

Boxer reached his hands out to grasp my jacket and pull me toward him. I collapsed against the wall of his chest.

His lips met mine in a ferocious kiss. Three days apart had ignited his hunger, and I felt the same way.

My hand slid into the hair at his nape. Closing my eyes, I sank into the feel of him, the smell, the drugging sensation of being in his arms.

The sound of a car beeping reminded me that we were in public, and I was all but being mauled by a biker.

I'd been doing a fair bit of mauling myself.

When I opened my eyes, I saw Dr. Sawyer standing at the driver's side door of a black BMW, but he was staring at me.

"Crap," I muttered.

"What?" Boxer asked, his hands coming up to cradle my cheeks. "You're cold."

"I'm fine." I sighed. "My boss just saw us kissing."

"Who cares?" Boxer asked. "It's none of his damn business."

"Yeah. I know. I just like to keep my private life private."

He cocked his head to the side. "Why do you care what others think about you?"

"How do you *not* care?"

He shrugged. "I just don't."

"Not helpful, but thanks."

I looked over Boxer's shoulder to stare at Dr. Sawyer. I waved.

He opened the driver's side door with force and climbed in.

Boxer chuckled. "That's the start of not giving a fuck."

His attention slid from me to stare at my boss. "Who is that? Wait, I recognize him. That's the douche that yelled at you for having juice boxes with me. That's Dr. Prick."

"Yup." I nibbled on my lower lip.

"Christ, woman, don't do that." He thumbed my lip. "It's all I can do to pay attention and keep it decent."

I smiled, but I was distracted. I didn't like that Dr. Sawyer had seen me kissing Boxer. It had nothing to do with embarrassment, and everything to do with not wanting Dr. Sawyer to find another reason to give me hell.

Boxer's hands went to my collar, and he flipped it up. "You look tired," he noted.

"Thanks," I remarked dryly.

"You know what the cure for exhaustion is?" he asked. "A massage, takeout, and a bath. But only after a good fucking."

"Let's go," I said eagerly.

# Chapter 16

No sooner had the door to my condo closed than Boxer pounced. I dropped my purse, not at all caring if my phone shattered.

In between bouts of kissing, we stripped off our clothes on our way to the bedroom. Somehow, we managed not to bash into the walls as we went.

My back hit the bed and Boxer stared down at me, his gaze raking me from head to toe. His hands went to my thighs, and he spread them. Suddenly, he was leaning over me, peeling me back, his tongue gliding over my flesh.

I sucked in a harsh breath, and my hands fisted at my sides.

"You like that, don't you?"

It was clearly a rhetorical question, but I was lost in sensation and nodded so he wouldn't stop.

He went back to licking me, flicking his tongue against the core of my body. "If I had any self-control, I would drag this out."

"If you drag this out, I will kill you."

He lifted his head and grinned, his lips glistening with

my desire. His fingers teased the trimmed blonde curls at the apex of my thighs before sliding in deep. I arched my back and moaned out my pleasure.

I was mindless with it, my brain melting as my body overruled everything. Sensation after sensation coursed through me. There was nothing but this moment. I wasn't even myself, a conscious being. I was an animal, guided by instinct.

Boxer slipped his fingers out of me. I managed to open my eyes, watching him from beneath heavy lids, as he stalked from the room. He was back almost instantly with a condom in his hand. Boxer ripped the foil with his teeth and then quickly sheathed himself.

He crawled onto the bed and hovered over me. Taking himself in hand, he guided himself to the entrance of my body. The head of him teased and tormented for a moment and then he pushed into me.

We both groaned, and then we were moving, meeting each other thrust for thrust. I scored his back with my nails, which only spurred him on. He was ruthless and determined, angling his pelvis and driving into me with one intent.

I bucked and cried out, clenching around him, gripping him, trying to get him deeper.

"Fuck, Linden," he growled.

We were sweaty and slick, and my brain was scrambled. Boxer was the perfect escape.

I didn't last long. My orgasm screamed through my entire body, lighting up every nerve.

And then he gripped my hips, speared into me again and came with his own shout. He pressed his forehead to the crook of my neck for a moment, and then he gently eased out of me. Boxer removed the condom, tied it off, and then headed for the bathroom.

I stretched, my muscles slack, as if I'd just had an intense workout. The late afternoon light floated through the window. I had no desire to move as I let the sweat dry from my body.

Boxer came back and stood naked in the doorway of the bathroom. "Bath? Massage? Take out?"

I stared for a moment, studying his sleek muscles, the ink on his skin, wishing I had enough energy for another round.

"Rain check on the bath and massage," I said, slowly sitting up. "I want food."

"What are you in the mood for?" he asked, pushing away from the doorframe.

"Greasy pizza."

"My perfect woman."

I rolled out of bed and went to the bathroom. After I cleaned up, instead of walking into the living room to pick up my clothes, I went to the dresser and pulled on an old, navy–blue sweatshirt that hung off my shoulder and a pair of black yoga pants.

"What do you want on your pizza?" Boxer called.

"Pepperoni."

"Yes!" he cheered.

I laughed and headed into the living room.

He hung up the phone and set it down on the coffee table. He was wearing his jeans, but no shirt. Without a thought, I trailed my fingers down his back and spine. He turned his head to look at me and smirked.

"Pizza should be here in about half an hour."

"I don't have beer," I said. "I only have wine."

"I'll run out and grab some." He leaned down and scooped up his shirt, hastily throwing it on. He moved toward me, grasped me to him, and kissed me quickly. "Joni and Zip's party is this Thursday. Can you make it?"

"Yeah, that works with my schedule. Is Freddy going?"

"No, why?"

"I need to give her back her clothes," I stated. "She was the one who dressed me."

"Remind me to send her a fruit basket," Boxer said with a grin, as he finally released me.

"Why won't she be there?"

He leaned down to grab his boots and socks and then sat down in the chair. "Because she's not family."

"I don't get it. She's sleeping with Bishop. I mean, I know he's not a Waco Tarnished Angel, but—"

"Yeah, she's sleeping with him. That doesn't mean anything. She's a free agent. No one has made her an Old Lady yet, and she's not asking to be one. She could fuck Acid and then tell Bishop all about it, and he wouldn't care."

"I haven't met Acid yet."

"He patched in just last year."

"So strange. You Tarnished Angels seem pretty possessive of your women. It really wouldn't bug Bishop if Freddy slept with another brother?"

"If you want a woman, you gotta claim her. The fact that he hasn't?" He shrugged and stood. "Do you have a beer preference?"

"Nothing light. If you're going to drink beer, drink *real* beer."

"Just when I think you can't be more perfect," he teased. He came over and leaned down to kiss me before sauntering to the door. It closed behind him as he left. And almost immediately, there was knock against it.

I went to answer it. Boxer stood on the threshold.

"Forget something?" I asked in confusion.

Boxer dragged me into his arms and kissed me deep

and hot, with a lot of tongue. He didn't say a word as he released me. With a wink and a salute, he was gone.

"Do you work the day after Joni and Zip's party?" Boxer asked, filching the crust from my plate.

"Hey, I was going to eat that."

"No, you weren't," he said, taking the bottle of sriracha and dousing the doughy bread.

"Yeah, I definitely wasn't. Knee jerk reaction." Full of pizza and two beers, I was relaxed and happy. "No, I'm not working the day after the party. Why?"

He chewed and then swallowed before answering. "Stay the night with me. At my place."

"Your place?"

"Not the clubhouse," he clarified.

I paused. "You sure?"

He nodded.

"Rachel, Allison, and Freddy…they all said you're not the same person. That you went into the hospital one man and came out another. What do they mean by that?"

He took a drink of his beer before he answered. "You might've noticed that the Tarnished Angels are paired off. Most of the Waco boys, I mean."

I nodded.

"I didn't get it. I didn't understand what made men like Colt, Reap, and Zip wanna settle down with one woman. I thought they were insane." He paused and looked down at the beer bottle in his hands. "I almost died. That's not the way I thought I'd go, Doc. I thought I'd be out on the streets, dying protecting those I love from bad shit, or worst case I'd die on the bike. It never occurred to me I could die in a fucking hospital bed like an old man. It made me think about things. Really think about them. What I wanted. What I was missing. And more than anything, it showed me that none of us are really in control of how it all ends."

"So, you only want me because I saved your life?"

"Woman," he sighed, "I want you because for the first time in my godforsaken life, you made me realize what the hell I was missing. I've never invited a woman to my home. I've never wanted one in *my* bed."

I'd never planned on meeting a man like Boxer. I'd never planned on this turning into something more than a casual, physical thing.

But I couldn't walk away.

I'd lived a safe and boring life, scripted by society. A life that was recognized as virtuous and worthy. But to whom, and for what?

Boxer was raw. Real. And he was offering me something I'd never experienced before: a life full of adventure and excitement. And I knew he would do anything to protect me.

Sometimes, there weren't enough words to express how I was feeling, so I settled for what was in my heart.

I smiled softly. "Yeah, Boxer. I'd love to stay the night with you."

# Chapter 17

"LINDEN," Boxer whispered, nudging me.

"Hmm?" I muttered into the pillow. I cracked an eye open, but it was night, and I couldn't see in front of me.

"I've got to go," he said. "Club business."

"What time is it?"

"Three in the morning."

"I'll walk you out." I searched in the dark for a T-shirt and found one on the floor. I padded to the living room, covering my yawning mouth with my hand. Boxer was already dressed and ready to go.

"I'll call you later," he said, taking me into his arms and kissing me. Then he was gone.

I locked up after him and then trudged my way back to bed. I flopped down and pulled the covers over me, but I couldn't seem to get comfortable. The scent of him was on my sheets; I grabbed his pillow and brought it to my nose.

I inhaled deeply, hugged the pillow to my chest, and fell back to sleep.

The next time I woke, it was past dawn. I stumbled

into the shower to wake myself up, and then I made myself a cappuccino.

Leftover pizza in the box rested on the kitchen counter. I ate a piece without bothering to heat it up and thought about what was happening in my life.

I was in a relationship with a biker. A playboy. A criminal.

There was no other way to slice it.

And feelings were developing.

For a man who claimed not to be the relationship type, he seemed to be a natural when it came to handling a woman's feelings.

I would have to tell him about my past eventually. He knew about my mother, but there was so much more that he didn't know.

I didn't want to sit around all day, but I had no chores to do, no errands to run.

Freddy had given me her cell number after I'd called her at Pinky's.

I needed to return her clothes, but I also wanted more insight into the Tarnished Angels, and what I was getting myself into.

I walked into the restaurant and lifted my sunglasses to the top of my head. I surveyed the tables and found Freddy sitting in the corner booth, a cup of coffee in front of her. She was dressed in costume pearls and a white blouse with navy piping. I couldn't see her pants or shoes, but I was sure she matched perfectly. She dressed like a 1950s pinup girl, and I loved that she went for it, no holds barred.

"Hey," I greeted with a smile.

"Hey," she said, her smile just as welcoming. "This was

a great idea. Meeting for breakfast. I so didn't want to cook."

I laughed and set the plastic bag on the table. "I brought your clothes back. Thanks for lending them to me."

"Keep them. I have a ton."

"You sure?"

"Yeah."

"Thanks," I said with a grin. I removed the plastic bag from the table and set it on top of my purse. "I really like them."

"Next time we're in Waco, I'll take you to Leather and Ink. You'll love Laura and her store."

The waitress arrived, and I quickly asked for a cup of coffee. Freddy ordered French toast while I took a moment to look at the menu.

"I'll have the muesli," I said to the waitress. "Thanks."

She scooped up our menus and dashed away.

"Muesli?" Freddy made a face. "When they have chocolate chip pancakes on the menu? I bet you like kale, too."

I arched a brow. "I love kale."

"Yeah, I knew it."

"So, this store…Leather and Ink. Is it a biker store?"

"Kind of. The Tarnished Angels gave Laura the money to open her store. She used to run around with them, but she kind of quit the biker chick lifestyle."

The waitress returned with my cup of coffee and then ran off again. I reached for the creamer and a few packets of sugar.

"Full disclosure, I invited you to breakfast to squeeze you for information."

She leaned back and grinned. "I'll tell what I can. But you have to tell me something in return."

"What?"

"How was the makeup sex with Boxer?"

I just smiled.

Freddy laughed. "Yeah, thought so. So, what's your actual relationship status?"

"We haven't technically labeled anything," I began, "but he told me that you're either in or out with the club. Either you become an Old Lady or you…"

"You do what I'm doing and screw around, and then go on your merry way."

I grimaced.

"I'm just being honest."

"Honestly crass," I pointed out with a chuckle.

"Whatever. You hang with bikers long enough and you no longer watch what you say. I heard you were invited to Joni and Zip's housewarming."

"Who told—"

"Bishop. He likes pillow talk."

"You and Bishop…is that a good thing?"

"For now."

"You really don't have any desire for more with him?"

"Nope." She arched a brow. "You know you guys were the talk of the party, right?"

"We were?"

"Uh, *yeah*. The two of you disappeared for the rest of the night. Of course everyone was talking about you. They're good people. Loyal. Protective of their own." She paused, looking like she wanted to say more, but took a moment to gather her thoughts. "You remember what I told you, when Boxer brought you to Pinky's?"

"About how women never stick around?"

She nodded. "They want to know if you have what it takes to stick around."

I nibbled on my lip and then admitted, "He asked me

to stay the night at his place after the party. He says he's never had a woman stay over in his home before."

"Did he now? This just got interesting."

The waitress came back and set our food down in front of us. We dove in and our conversation was put on hold, but my head swirled with tumultuous thoughts.

"What does one bring to a biker's house-warming?" I asked her.

"Normally, I'd say a nice bottle of liquor, but most of the Old Ladies are pregnant, so that seems like bad form."

"Yeah, just a bit," I said with a laugh. "Perhaps a succulent. I've heard plants really liven up a space."

"Yeah, I've heard that too. If you can keep them alive."

By the time I got home that afternoon, I still hadn't heard from Boxer. I was concerned. Nothing good came from calls in the early morning hours, and I was sure it was the same with club business and whatever nefarious activities they were up to.

Working in a hospital emergency room, I was also acutely aware of the fact that people often died at night. I'd treated my fair share of gunshot wounds and drug overdoses, and most of them had been at night.

I set my purse onto the counter and then headed to the bedroom to change into workout clothes. A good run on the treadmill would help quiet my mind.

I worked out hard, running five miles at a brisk pace. When I climbed off the treadmill, I was dripping sweat, and my legs felt like jelly. I grabbed my water bottle and threw the towel I'd brought with me to the condo's gym around my neck.

The afternoon passed without a word from Boxer, and my concern grew into fear. He said he'd call, but he hadn't. By ten, I finally picked up my phone and sent him a text asking if he was okay.

I went to bed without a reply.

A thump woke me out of a sound sleep. I sat up—heart in my throat—listening for a moment. I flung off the covers and got out of bed. The alarm clock read 3:12.

I flipped on the hallway light and made my way into the living room. I heard another whomp on the other side of the condo door, followed by a curse.

I glanced through the peephole, but I couldn't see anything. And then there was a heavy rap on the door. I unlocked and opened it, poking my head out into the hallway.

Boxer was slumped against the wall, his legs spread out in front of him. He looked up at me with glassy gray eyes. "Hey, Doc."

I crouched down next to him. "Hi." I ran my hand across his forehead. He didn't have a fever. When he exhaled, fumes of liquor hit me square in the face. "Well, I think I know your problem. How'd you get past the security guard?"

"I came in through the underground garage. I woke you up," he slurred.

"It's okay," I said. "Can you stand?"

He paused. "I'm not standing?"

I wedged my shoulder into his armpit. "Put your arm around me."

Boxer threw a heavy arm around me and nuzzled into my neck. "You smell good."

"I smell better than you," I said lightly. "Come on. Up you go."

Boxer managed to stand, and I held on to him tightly

as I got him into the condo. I kicked the door shut and then led him toward the bedroom.

"How did you get here? Please tell me you didn't ride your motorcycle."

"Nah, I made a sober prospect drive me."

"Shoddy deal for him," I said, wondering why a prospect was at his beck and call.

I guided him to the bed and moved out from underneath his arm. He plopped down onto the edge of the mattress and reached into his leather cut and pulled out a pistol, which he set on the nightstand. And then he fell back against the pillows.

I paused for a moment, looking at the firearm, and then unlaced his boots and slid them off him. Then I went to work trying to get him out of his leather cut and jeans, so he'd be more comfortable.

"Boxer, what's going on? Are you okay?"

"Better. Now that I'm here." He stretched out onto the bed and then rolled over, sliding his inked arms underneath my pillow and pressing his cheek into it.

He muttered something beneath his breath that I couldn't decipher.

"What was that?" I prodded.

"Save people. You."

A moment later, he was snoring softly. I looked down at him, wondering what had happened that was so bad that he'd had to drink himself stupid.

I smoothed his dirty blond hair off his forehead and then touched his whiskered cheek. I hoped he explained when he woke up.

I didn't go back to bed. Instead, I curled up on the couch and watched a movie on TV, keeping an ear cocked for any noise coming from my bedroom. Boxer slept on. Around dawn, I crept to the bed and peered at him, but he was still fast asleep. I'd left water and four aspirin on the nightstand, so when he woke up, he could pop them immediately.

Hunger forced me to the kitchen. I was cooking fried eggs on toast when I heard the bedroom door open. It was slow, like the door itself was in pain.

Boxer slinked into the room, his face ashen. He collapsed onto a bar stool at the counter and then placed his head in his hands.

"Coffee?" I asked him.

"Please," he rasped.

I grabbed a new mug from the cabinet and poured him a cup. I served it to him black. "Are you hungry?"

"God, no."

"Not even toast?" I prodded.

He shook his head.

I took my plate of food and stood at the counter to eat it. It was silent in the kitchen while I ate, and Boxer downed coffee.

When I was finished, I poured myself a second cup, made it light and sweet, and then took the stool next to him. "So," I began.

"So," he said, looking wary.

"You got really drunk and then came here."

He winced. "Yeah."

"Are you okay?"

Boxer rubbed the back of his neck but didn't reply.

"I was worried about you," I said quietly. "You said you were going to call me, and you never did."

"Yeah, sorry about that."

"This is the kind of stuff you were alluding to, wasn't it? About being part of the club and what it means to be an Old Lady? The waiting around…the not knowing?"

"Yeah. This is the kind of shit you'd have to put up with." He took another sip of his coffee. "I can't tell you anything about club business, but you need to know something. There are times when life is so fucking tragic and bleak. Innocent people get hurt sometimes, and it weighs on me. I'm sorry I came here. I'm sorry I brought this to your door."

He got up off the stool, but before he was able to move away, I put my hand on his arm. "Don't go. I'm not trying to make you feel guilty. I know what it's like, needing an escape. Even if you can't tell me what's going on, I'm glad you came here."

Boxer stared at me. "You sure?"

I nodded.

He let out a long exhale. "Can we forget about this?"

"No, I can't forget about this."

"Shit, this fucked it all up for you. I knew it. I knew something like this would scare you off."

"I'm not scared off," I protested. "But I am trying to figure out how to live in your world, Boxer. This is all new. Just…give me some time to process, okay?"

"Yeah," he said morosely. "All right."

"I'm not bailing."

"Right," he muttered.

"I'm *not*," I insisted. "You laid it all out there for me, and I'm glad you did but hearing it and seeing it are two different things. Just give me some time, okay?"

"Sure. Take as much time as you need."

His tone did not match his words.

I swallowed, not liking the tension that stretched between us.

Boxer's gaze dropped from mine as he reached for his phone. He shot off a text, and a few seconds later his cell beeped.

"South Paw will be here in a bit to pick me up."

"He's the one who dropped you off last night?"

"Yeah."

"Where did he stay?" I asked. "Did he sleep in the truck?"

"Probably hung out at an all-night diner."

"Waiting for you to call?"

"Yup."

I took his empty coffee mug and rinsed it and set it in the top rack of the dishwasher. "You don't have to leave."

"I have shit to do," he said. "You mind if I use your shower before I go? I smell like a distillery."

"Go ahead."

"Thanks."

He got up off his stool and immediately went toward the bedroom...without kissing me. Without hugging me. Without touching me.

*What the hell was going on?*

I was more than confused, I was downright befuddled. I heard the faintest sounds of the shower turning on, and then I made a snap decision. As I headed for the bedroom, I stripped off my T-shirt. My pajama bottoms followed. And then I strolled naked into the bathroom and opened the glass door of the shower.

His blond hair looked even darker when it was wet, and he hung his head to hide his face from me, but not before I glimpsed the anguish in his eyes.

I wrapped my arms around him, and he clung to me like a lifeline. He lifted his head and met my gaze.

"Linden," he whispered as his lips took mine, seeking escape.

Like the escape he'd given me days ago.

Would I do any less for him now?

I didn't have time to think as his tongue swept into my mouth, and his hands wandered up and down my body. He turned me so I went under the hot spray. My skin was slick and warm, and then he was positioning my back against the glass wall of the shower. He lifted one of my legs and opened me up to him.

His fingers teased my entrance, stroking and playing, but he didn't spend time like he usually did. I sensed his barely controlled ferocity. He gave himself a few quick pumps, and then he was guiding his shaft into me.

My body swallowed him, greedy, and ready despite the lack of foreplay. He rammed into me, hard, filling me completely.

I gasped, and it mingled with his moan. He pressed his forearm to the wall behind me so he could leverage himself better. The glass was cool at my back, and he was warm at my front. I closed my eyes and relished the feel of him, hot and hard inside me.

I nearly lost my footing, but Boxer's strong body offered support. My fingers grasped the hair at his nape, and I drew his mouth closer to mine.

He slid in and out, slippery and feverish. When he hit the perfect spot between my legs, I clamped around him as I drowned in pleasure.

The back of my head hit glass, and I didn't care. Boxer's hand clenched my hip, and then he hastily pulled out, so he didn't come inside me. He painted my belly with his seed and the shower washed me clean of him.

He licked his lips and then stared at me. He opened his mouth to say something, but I quickly pressed my fingers to his lips.

"Don't. I understand."

His expression softened, and then he turned his head to kiss my palm. I grabbed the bar of soap and worked it into a foamy lather. I smoothed it over his skin, washing him, tending to him. I was surprised he let me.

While he was rinsing off, I hastily cleansed myself, and then set the soap aside.

"Let me wash your back," he said, his voice husky.

I turned. His hands were gentle, as if all the violence he'd felt earlier had disappeared.

"I'm sorry," he said finally.

"Why?" I asked. "I've needed you in the same way."

"I'm not apologizing for that." He paused. "I was inside you without protection."

"So you were," I murmured.

He stopped washing my back and then gripped my arms to turn me to face him. "You don't strike me as the forgetful type."

I took a deep breath but held his gaze. "I didn't forget. I trust you, Boxer."

His gaze narrowed as his thumbs rubbed circles on my arms as he continued to hold me. "What about pregnancy?"

"I'm on the shot."

He gently pulled me to his chest and held me there, letting the water and words rain down on us.

We finally separated, and Boxer turned off the water. I grasped a clean towel and climbed out of the shower first. Boxer took the other one and rubbed his head, which made his hair stick up. He looked incredibly boyish, and it made me smile.

His cell phone trilled in the living room. "Shit," he muttered. "I bet that's South Paw." He strode out of the bathroom, wrapping the towel around his waist as he went.

I heard him answer his phone. I went to the dresser

and pulled out a pair of panties. I was sliding them on when Boxer came back into the bedroom.

"South Paw's downstairs," Boxer said, dropping the towel.

I wanted to pounce on him, but I forced myself to look away. "Okay."

"What time do you have to be at the hospital?" he asked as I heard him begin to pull on his pants.

"I'm off," I said, finally turning to look at him again.

He belted his jeans and then glanced at me. "You are?"

I nodded. "You could stay. If you want."

He pulled his cell out of his pocket and hit a button. Boxer put the phone to his ear. "Change of plans. I'm spending the day at Linden's. You can bounce but keep your phone on you. If I need you, I'll call."

Boxer hung up and tossed his cell on the bed.

"Does he just sit around waiting for you to tell him what to do?" I asked.

"Pretty much. He's a prospect," he said, as if that explained everything.

"So, he's your bitch?"

He chuckled. "Something like that."

He reached for his shirt and made a move to yank it over his head but then hesitated. "I think I spilled an entire bottle of bourbon on myself last night."

"Give it here, I'll throw it in the wash. You might as well take off your pants and briefs. I'll wash them too."

"What am I supposed to do? Walk around your condo naked?" He grinned, and I knew the idea didn't upset him in the least as he immediately stripped again. "Isn't this domestic? We're doing laundry together."

I rolled my eyes. "Dry towels are in the hall closet. Or you can wear my robe. Might be a bit short on you, but it's your call."

He opted for a towel. It was a small one, covering just enough of him to entice my fantasies.

"After a hot shower and steamy shower sex you seem back to your old self," I pointed out.

"Same could be said for you. You've got some of your own fire back."

"I never lost my fire," I countered. "I just know when to bank it."

The vulnerability he'd shown when drunk had been nothing compared to his anguish while sober. I wasn't sure if he had let me see it on purpose, or if he'd just been unable to conceal it. Sometimes the burdens we carried weren't so easily stowed away.

After I put Boxer's clothes into the washing machine, I headed back to the living room. Boxer was on the couch, the remote already in his hand.

I was grateful he wanted to do something mundane that would occupy our time. I was already emotionally spent after our time in the shower. I didn't have more in me and wanted to take it easy. He patted the seat next to him, and I curled up on the couch and pulled a navy–blue blanket over me.

"Here," Boxer said. He took an accent pillow from the couch and placed it against his lap. "Lie down."

I didn't need to be told twice. I stretched out, made sure I was covered, and then placed my cheek onto the pillow. His fingers dragged through my hair. Lulled by his touch and comfort, I quickly fell asleep.

I stretched my arms over my head as my eyes flitted open. I sniffed the air, unable to derive what I was smelling.

A timer buzzed.

I sat up and saw Boxer removing a glass casserole dish from the oven with red oven mitts. He set the dish on the stove and pulled off the gloves.

"What's that?" I asked, my voice husky with sleep.

Boxer looked over his shoulder at me and smiled. "You're awake. Just in time. I made mac and cheese."

I blinked. "You cooked?"

"Yeah." He was wearing his clean T-shirt and briefs, looking relaxed and at home. "You passed out and didn't even wake up when I got up to put the clothes in the dryer. Figured I might as well use the time to make us dinner." He cocked his head to the side. "You look confused."

"No, I'm not confused. I'm just…thank you. That was sweet of you."

"Yeah, that was definitely sweet of me." He grinned. "Keep that in mind for later."

I let out a laugh. "Will cook for sex? Is that what this is?"

"Nah. Will cook for blow jobs."

"Good to know where we stand," I said dryly.

I got up off the couch and headed to the bathroom. After I splashed some cool water on my face, I came back into the kitchen. Boxer had already served us, the plates set at the bar.

"You seem to be feeling better," I commented.

"Yeah, I feel okay."

We took our seats on the bar stools. I picked up a fork and took a bite of the mac and cheese. It was creamy and delicious, and everything I wanted.

"How is it?" he asked.

"Perfect." I set my fork down and got up. "Water?"

"Sure," he said.

"You cook?" I asked as I went to the cabinet.

"Nope. But I can follow a recipe every now and again."

"How do you survive?" I teased.

"The Old Ladies usually feed me. I won't starve. They won't let me," he joked.

"So, should I be flattered that you whipped this up for me?"

"Very flattered."

I brought our glasses back to the bar. "What are you going to do to impress me in the future?"

He looked at me, his smile soft. "Damn fine question."

# Chapter 18

My ALARM WENT off at four the next morning. The loud, high-pitched beep instantly woke me, and my hand shot out to hit the off button.

Boxer groaned. "Alarm clocks are the devil. It's still dark out."

"I warned you," I said, searching for any part of him so I could brush a kiss across his skin. "I told you if you spent the night, I'd be up early."

"There's early, then there's haven't-gone-to-bed-yet in the morning."

"Poor Boxer," I crooned, rubbing my cheek against his whiskered one. "Not all of us can escape being a slave to time."

"Don't make fun of me, this is horrible."

I let out a rueful chuckle and then reluctantly moved out of his warm embrace. Boxer slept naked, which made it a challenge to leave him.

"Don't follow me into the shower. I can't be late."

I crawled out of bed and went slowly toward the bathroom, hoping I didn't trip over anything. I wasn't in the shower five minutes before Boxer joined me.

"Reverse psychology," Boxer said. "I know I was manipulated, but I don't give a shit. Now bend over. I want you to remember this morning all day at work."

Somehow, I made it out the door on time. Boxer slid his tall frame into the passenger side of my car, and then I drove us to the hospital where he'd arranged for South Paw to pick him up. I didn't know if the guy had hauled ass all the way from Waco or if he'd stayed in the Dallas area, just waiting for Boxer to call.

"You guys haze prospects like they're joining a fraternity," I commented, wanting to glean a little more about how the club hierarchy operated.

"That's exactly what we do. It's a rite of passage for them, and it's also a chance for us to teach prospects how the club works. It's not as simple as people think, but when South Paw patches in, he'll get to treat another prospect the exact same way at some point."

"Seems sort of antiquated," I stated.

"Maybe. But this proves that South Paw really has what it takes to be part of the Tarnished Angels. It's not an open club. We do reject people from time to time."

"I wouldn't jump through any of those kinds of hoops. That's why I never joined a sorority."

He looked at me. "You didn't join a sorority?"

"Nope."

"You seem the sorority girl type, Doc."

"I don't know if I should be insulted by that statement or not."

"No insult intended," he assured me.

"My mother wanted me to pledge," I admitted. "I didn't have time. I was already taking extra classes and focusing on premed. Even if I'd had the time, I wouldn't have gone that route."

"Why?"

"Because they want an obscene amount of control over your life. They want you to look a certain way, act a certain way, date certain people. I already grew up in that kind of life. I wasn't about to subject myself to that again just as I had my first taste of freedom."

"What was it like? How you grew up?" he asked.

"For someone who's not a morning person, you're pretty chatty," I joked.

"Who said I wasn't a morning person?"

"You."

"No. I said I don't like mornings. I'm pretty chipper in the mornings."

"Semantics."

"Linden."

"Boxer."

He fell silent for a moment and looked out the window. "My old man was a jazz musician. I told you that." Boxer looked at me for confirmation.

I nodded, remembering our first date.

"He spent most of his time on the road. When he was home, he'd be fine for a few days. Happy. Excited. A regular family man. And then he'd start to get short tempered. Bickering with Mom. Picking fights. He blamed us for why he had to come home at all." Boxer smiled, but it was bitter. "He resented us as much as he loved us. Resentment always won, and he showed us just how much he resented us with his fists."

"Boxer," I whispered, my heart breaking for him.

He shrugged. "It is what it is. When he was home, I learned to spend a lot of time out of the house. I spent a lot of time at the arcade. Learned how to make my time there last."

"Pinball," I said in realization. "That's why you're so good."

"Yup."

I thought for a moment. "Our childhoods shape us, more than we care to admit. It's not so easy to let our pasts go, is it?"

"What parts of your past are you still holding onto, Doc?"

My hands clenched the wheel. "My mom, mostly."

"Yeah?"

"She was always challenging. I mean, she's not an easy woman to love. Hypercritical. Controlling." I swallowed. "It got worse after my dad left. She couldn't stop him from leaving so she became even more rigid and focused all her energy on me. Nothing I did was ever good enough for her. I realized I could never live up to her expectations, so I stopped trying."

"But you're a surgeon."

"Yeah? So?"

"No, I just mean—you're a *surgeon*, who's spent years in school, studying, probably not having a life just so you could excel. Isn't she proud of you for that?"

"My father's a surgeon," I reminded him. "To my mother, it felt like a slap in the face when I chose a similar career path."

"Enough said." He shook his head. "Let me guess, she can't be proud of you because you're more like him than you are like her, and everything you do reminds her of him."

"Spot on." I smiled wryly. "She thinks I did it to spite her. She thinks I did it because I wanted my father's attention."

"Did you? Want his attention?"

"I haven't spoken to him since I was ten. I don't want or need his attention."

"Why?"

"Why what?"

"Why haven't you spoken to him? Divorces happen. That's pretty normal."

I didn't say anything, and then I exhaled a long slow breath. "He didn't just leave my mother and me. He had another family in secret. I have two half-brothers I've never even met."

"Jesus. Are you serious?"

"Yeah. As soon as the ink was dry on his divorce papers to my mom, he married Callie."

He reached over to touch my thigh and gave it a little squeeze.

"He's been calling me recently, trying to get in touch," I admitted. "I've ignored his calls."

"What do you think he wants?"

"No idea. Don't care, really." I pulled into the near empty parking lot of the hospital. "What about your mom? Are you close with her?"

"Yeah, we were close."

I didn't miss the past tense. "Did she…"

"Die? Yeah. A few years after I patched in."

I turned off the engine. "I'm sorry."

"Don't be. She was in a lot of pain. It was better for her."

I leaned across the car, and he met me halfway. Our lips met, our breaths minty. For the first time, our need for one another wasn't fueled by lust. It was acceptance and solace. Understanding.

He pulled back and shot me a somber grin. "We know

how to have fun, don't we? Talking about heavy shit before the sun even comes up."

I sighed and leaned my head back against the seat rest. "That's new for me. Talking about my parents and family life."

"Same."

We got out of the car, and I hit the clicker to lock the doors. As we were heading toward the hospital, I heard the rumble of an engine. Boxer's truck pulled up to the curb and then idled for a moment.

"What service," I teased.

Boxer grinned. "You're gonna be thinking about me all day while you're at work."

"Am I?"

Boxer leaned in close to whisper in my ear. "Oh, yeah, you're gonna miss my mac and cheese and most off all, my great big—"

"Hey, Linden," Peyton greeted.

I jumped back from Boxer, embarrassed that I'd been so wrapped up in him that I hadn't heard her approach.

"Hey," I said, wondering if there was enough light coming from the hospital for her to see my flaming cheeks.

"Nurse Redhead," Boxer greeted with a flirtatious grin.

"I see you've fully recovered. An appendectomy didn't slow you down at all," Peyton remarked with a happy smile. "Linden, I'll see you inside."

I buried my head against the lapel of Boxer's leather cut and let out a low laugh. He gently eased my head back so he could press his mouth to mine. It was in no way chaste, but over far sooner than I would've liked. He kissed me one more time for final measure and then sauntered toward his truck.

The driver's side door opened, and South Paw got out. I waved to him and then headed inside the lobby. Peyton was waiting for me, an amused grin on her face. "So, you guys are doing sleepovers."

"Yeah, I guess we are," I admitted.

"How did you ever get out of bed this morning?" she demanded.

"Sheer force of will."

# Chapter 19

"Joey has something he wants to tell you," Mrs. Fosco said with a smile at her ten-year-old son.

I looked at the adorable boy with brown hair and freckles splattered across his cheeks who was leaning back against his hospital bed, looking embarrassed.

"I'm sorry I threw up on you." His tone was contrite.

It took all my effort not to laugh at his sincerity. "Thank you for your apology, but I understand why you did. In fact, you are not the first boy to throw up on me because of his appendix."

His eyes widened. "Really?"

I nodded.

"Who else threw up on you?" Joey asked in excitement.

"My boyfriend," I said before I could stop myself. I didn't even stutter over the word.

"You have a boyfriend?" Joey asked.

"I do," I admitted.

Joey flashed a toothy grin. "He's really lucky."

"Why," I asked with a smile.

"Because you're really pretty and smart."

I looked at his mother. "You're going to have your hands full."

She snorted. "Tell me about it."

"Did you save my appendix?" Joey asked, switching easily from one topic to another. "I want to take it to school and show all my friends."

Kids were fascinated with the most gruesome things. I looked at his mother for help.

Mrs. Fosco instantly jumped to my aid. "That's not appropriate, honey."

"What about my scar?" Joey pressed. "Can I show them my scar?"

I threw Mrs. Fosco a sympathetic smile and then hastily retreated.

I checked in on a few more patients and wrapped up my long shift. When I went into the locker room, Peyton was shrugging into her sweater. "Drink?" she asked.

"Yes, please. Like right now. I need it. I got puked on again today. It was this really cute kid, but puke is puke."

"I heard," she said in amusement. "I'll buy the first round."

"I'm so glad I'm off the next few days." I slid into my clothes and grabbed my purse, and then we headed to the elevators.

"Careful, it sounds like you're starting to enjoy your free time."

"Am I a fan of the erratic scheduling? No. But I'm digging the idea of several days off. It's almost like a mini vacation."

"We need those every now and again," Peyton assured me. "Emily's meeting us over there in a bit. She said to order her a vodka soda."

"She wants it ready and waiting," I said with a laugh.

The elevator doors opened into the lobby, and we

stepped out. I dug around in my purse, looking for a piece of gum.

"Linden," Peyton said.

"Hmm?"

"Linden," she said again.

"What?" I looked up at her and then glanced in the direction where she was staring.

Zip stood in the lobby, hands clenched by his sides. He was in a pair of dark jeans and a skin-tight black shirt that showed off his muscled arms and chest. His leather cut was boldly on display, and he caught more than a few stares. His blue eyes were stony, and there wasn't a trace of his usual good humor.

He appeared formidable, even more so when he stalked toward me. "I need to speak with you. Alone." Zip looked at Peyton.

"I'll see you at Tony's," Peyton said to me.

I nodded.

Zip watched her walk out of the lobby and when he was sure we were alone, he took my elbow and guided me to the corner.

"What is it?"

"Boxer," he said, pitching his voice low. "He's been shot."

All the blood froze in my body, and then my mind suddenly snapped into doctor mode.

"Where?"

"Arm. Bullet's still in there."

"Why didn't you take him to a hospital?" I demanded.

"Gun shots have to be reported. And it wasn't bad enough for the ER. The bleeding's under control."

Boxer and the Tarnished Angels were criminals. It would've invited questions.

"Clubhouse?" I asked.

Zip nodded.

"I'll meet you there." I turned to head back to the elevators.

Zip's hand on my arm stopped me. "Where the hell do you think you're going?"

"He's injured," I hissed. "I need supplies to tend to him. Things I don't just have on hand."

"We've got all that covered. Let's go. I'm driving."

"What? No, I need—"

"Linden, this isn't our first rodeo. We have everything you'll need to patch him up. Now, let's go."

"Okay, but drive fast."

"Woman," Zip stated, "fast is my middle name."

The prospects saw us coming and opened the gates to the clubhouse. Zip parked the SUV in the gravel lot, but before he'd even cut the engine, I was out of the car, my purse in my hand.

Reap and a familiar-looking man were standing on the front porch. The stranger with rakish curls falling across his forehead leaned against the railing and took a swig from the liquor bottle he was holding. He was dressed all in black, but he didn't wear a leather cut and I saw no ink on his skin. He didn't look to be a Tarnished Angel.

A flash of recognition kindled in my brain.

Ramsey Buchanan.

Reap placed a cigarette between his lips and lit it with a classic flip-top Zippo lighter.

"Smoking can kill you," I said in way of greeting.

"If something else doesn't kill me first," he said. He threw an arm around my shoulder and gave me a brief hug. "Thanks for coming."

"Where is he?"

"Inside with Colt and Gray," Reap replied.

I walked into the clubhouse, steeling myself for what I was about to see.

Boxer sat on a stool, looking woozy. Gray had his hand on Boxer's shoulder to steady him. Colt stood on the other side pressing gauze to Boxer's arm.

Torque and a few others sat quietly in the living room, watching me with somber gazes.

I set my purse on the counter and then went to Boxer. Not caring that we had an audience, I stroked a hand down his stubbly cheek to his jaw. "What did you do to yourself?" I asked.

"He tried to be a hero," Colt replied gruffly. "He's lucky this was in his arm... I got most of the bleeding under control, but you're gonna need to take a look."

"You're here," Boxer said, his eyes glazed with pain as they met mine. He exhaled, and I smelled the liquor fumes on his breath.

I smiled gently. "Yeah, I'm here."

"Took you long enough. I've been drinking for the better part of two hours."

"Yeah, well, maybe next time you should date a doctor a little bit closer to you so she can patch you up in no time," I said, trying to keep my tone light.

"Don't want another doctor," he muttered.

The bikers had pulled a table next to the stool, and it was littered with all the supplies I could possibly need to repair a gunshot or knife wound. "Where the hell did you guys get all this?"

"It's better that you don't know," Colt said.

"All right then," I said. "Okay. I need better light in here. Get me some lamps."

"Got it, Doc," a biker said, jumping up off the couch.

I turned my attention back to Boxer.

"What the hell am I going to do with you?" I whispered.

"Kiss me. And then sew me up."

I assessed the damage. The bullet wasn't deep, but I would've liked an X-ray to tell me if it had hit bone—and I wished I had a sterile environment, but this would have to do.

"Liquor is not advisable under the circumstances," I said.

His reply was to lift the bottle and drink.

I sighed. "Fine. Do you want to hear about the kid who puked on me tonight?" Without waiting for a reply, I launched into the story about Joey while I dug the bullet out of Boxer's body.

He grimaced but didn't complain. "Another contender? Why am I not surprised? Fuck, woman, hurry up and grab the damn thing."

I extracted the bullet and dumped it into a small metal bowl. I cleaned the wound. "Joey was pretty charming," I continued on, "and he had adorable freckles."

Ramsey came in from the porch, carrying a bottle of liquor. He sat down on the couch and drank.

I grabbed the thread and needle and sewed Boxer's flesh back together.

He swayed slightly on the stool when the needle pierced his skin. Colt had remained on the other side, and his hand shot out to steady him.

I finished the last stitch and then snipped the end of the thread. "The stitches are done. I need to give you a tetanus shot and some antibiotics, and then I'm putting you to bed."

He lifted the bottle of bourbon to his lips and took

another sip. I wanted to pull the booze away from him, but I wouldn't embarrass him in front of his brothers.

"Thanks for your help, Colt," I said.

"My pleasure, Doc. Thanks for coming. It means...it means a lot."

His brown eyes delved into mine and held my stare.

Something unspoken moved between us.

I quickly injected Boxer with antibiotics and a tetanus shot, and then removed my gloves, tossing them onto the table. "Okay, champ. Let's get you upstairs."

We got to the second floor, and then I opened the door to his room. I flipped on the main light and then stepped aside. He walked in and plopped down onto the bed. I knelt to help him with his boots; they were heavy and hit the wooden floor with a thud. I went for his belt next and eased off his jeans. He laid down on his back, and I tugged the covers up over him.

Boxer stared at the ceiling for a moment before looking at me. "You came."

"Of course, I came."

I swallowed. The terror of hearing that he'd been shot still lived in my throat. I needed something strong to wash it down.

"We don't involve our women in club business."

"So you've already told me." I went to leave. "Rest, Boxer. I'll be back later to check on you."

"Wait," he said. "Just wait. We don't involve our women in club business, but you're different, Linden. I talked to the club. For various reasons, they're okay if I let you in."

I stopped with my hand on the doorknob. "Why? Because I'm a doctor?"

"Yeah." He looked back up to the ceiling. "It isn't fair to ask you to come here like this and put your entire career on the line without telling you what's going on, and we're probably gonna need you again. Now, will you sit here and listen to me?"

After a brief pause, I let go of the handle and headed back to the bed to sit on the end of it.

"I still can't tell you everything. Not because I don't think you can handle it. Actually, I'm starting to think you can handle anything I throw at you." He smiled, but it wasn't in humor. "There are still some things you're better off not knowing. Certain details that might not sit well with you…emotionally."

"I get it, now spill."

He nodded. "We're not heroes. We're criminals." Boxer paused. "But even we have lines in the sand. Even we have hills we're willing to die on. People we're willing to die for."

My heart drummed in my ears, and my hands turned clammy. I wasn't sure I was ready to hear the truth. I wasn't sure I was ready not to.

"We had a tip off about a van heading for the Mexican border. The info was from a solid source, so we intercepted it. There were five women of various ages, bound and gagged in the back. While we were trying to untie them, the driver and passenger from the van fought their way free and ran into the brush. They circled back around, and I took a bullet."

He paused, gauging my reaction.

I exhaled slowly, trying to process everything he was saying. It was a lot, but he wasn't done yet.

After a moment, he went on. " We put them down, and then examined them. They were both marked with cartel ink. This is as serious as it gets. We just fucked up a shipment of human cargo for a cartel and nuked two of their guys. Do you understand, Linden?"

"Human trafficking," I murmured.

"Yeah."

I suddenly felt detached from my own body. My head and my heart severed from one another. "Where did they come from? The women?"

"We don't know exactly. This is as bad as you're imagining right now. They were abducted. If we hadn't gotten to them, then——"

"Where are the women now?" I asked, my voice soft.

"Acid dropped the van off at the ER entrance of Dallas Methodist and then had Crow pick him up a couple of blocks away. Gloves while driving the van, hooded masks, and sunglasses for the cameras and plate covers for the bikes, plus they took the back roads."

"Why didn't he stay with them?" I asked before I could stop myself.

"How the fuck would he explain that? Bikers rescuing kidnapped women and having a shootout with their abductors? We're supposed to stick around after we dropped them off at a hospital for the police to ask questions? Come on, you're smarter than that. The fact that we got to them before they crossed the border is a miracle. Their families, the hospital, and the police have to do the rest."

He fell silent, his eyes still on me, but they were struggling to remain open.

My curiosity hadn't abated. I wasn't done trying to piece it all together, and my mind raced with emotion and fear. "Why did you drop them off in Dallas? Why not Waco?"

"They were closer to Dallas. Besides, there's less of a chance they link us to this because we dropped them off in Dallas."

"And Zip was in Dallas already," I guessed. "Which is why he was able to pick me up quickly."

"Yeah."

"What happened the other night? Was it something like this?"

Boxer was quiet for so long I was sure he wouldn't answer, but he finally replied. "That night, we found children." His gray eyes met mine, bright with anger. "We rescued three, but we were too late to save one of them."

# Chapter 20

Boxer fell asleep soon after his pronouncement. I sat with him for a bit, listening to the sounds of his breathing.

I rose from the bed and went to turn off the light. I crept from the room, shutting the door behind me. As I leaned against the wall, I closed my eyes for a moment, trying to keep the bile in my belly. I breathed deeply a few times, trying to get my feelings under control.

There was a special place in hell for people who hurt the innocent, especially children.

Boxer and the Tarnished Angels saved women and children. I let out a snort.

*Oh, the irony of their club's name.*

I pushed away from the wall and trudged downstairs. The mood was somber, and no one was talking. Three Tarnished Angels lifted their bottles of booze toward me.

I took Colt's because he was the closest. Lifting the bottle to my nose, I then gave it a cautionary sniff. It made my eyes water.

"Moonshine," Colt supplied.

"Should've known." I took a massive drink and it

burned on the way down, but then a kernel of warmth spread through my belly. I took a seat on the arm of the couch, not sure of my place.

"He told you," Colt stated knowingly.

I nodded.

"Okay then. You should know we had church and discussed it," Colt said. "We all voted and agreed we were going to tell you."

"What's church?" I asked.

"It's how we discuss club matters," Zip explained. "It's all orderly and shit."

"Orderly and shit, right." I took another swallow, trying to scorch the horrors of what might have happened to the women and children from my imagination. "He had South Paw drive him to my place the night you found the kids."

Reap sucked in a breath, as if he was wishing for another cigarette.

"He didn't tell me anything," I hastened to say. "But he was drunk as a skunk, and he looked...haunted. Now I know why."

"You didn't press him, did you?" Colt asked. "About why he came to you in that state?"

I shook my head. "No."

"Why not?" Zip demanded.

"Because getting an answer from him wasn't the most important thing at that moment. He just needed me to be there for him."

The room fell silent for a moment and then Reap said, "Wow. You really get him."

I gave him a watery smile. "I think we get each other. I need some air, and then I'll hit the sack. Is the room next to Boxer's free?" There wasn't enough space to put a mattress on the floor and sleep near him, and I wouldn't share his bed. I wanted him to have as much room as possible.

"Yeah. It was cleaned after the Idaho boys left," Zip said.

"Thanks."

"If you're not going to keep drinking that moonshine, you mind giving it back?" Colt asked with a smile.

"Like hell I'm giving this back. I earned it," I said, causing the guys to chuckle. I got up and headed down the hallway to the back door. I pushed open the screen and stepped out into the night.

It was chillier than I expected, and I was just about to head inside to get my jacket, when the door opened. Ramsey strode outside, carrying my coat.

"Thanks," I said, letting him help me into it.

Blue and green camp chairs surrounded the fire ring where there had been a bonfire. I took a seat and leaned my head back to stare at the starry sky.

By unspoken invitation, Ramsey took the chair next to me.

We drank in silence for a while as the night wrapped around us.

"So, you're Linden," he said quietly, his Scottish burr husky and low pitched. "Nice to finally put a face to the name."

"So, you're Ramsey. You do more than just manage The Dallas Rex, don't you?"

He looked at me but said nothing.

"Right," I muttered. "Mysteries upon mysteries with you guys." I deduced he had been involved in rescuing the women, otherwise why would he be here?

"I'm impressed," he said.

I frowned. "With?"

"You. And I'm not easily impressed."

"Why are you impressed?"

"You didn't fall apart," he said.

"You expected me to fall apart?" I glanced at him. "You don't even know me. We've never met."

He shrugged. "Most people would have fallen apart."

"I'm a doctor."

"That's not what I'm referring to." He paused for a moment. "You were cool and efficient. Even though it was Boxer."

I thought about his words and nodded slowly. Objectivity had somehow reigned supreme, regardless of my relationship with the patient. "Emotion has no place in the operating room, regardless of who's on the table," I said finally.

He smiled slightly.

"What? What's that smile for?"

"You remind me of someone I'm very fond of."

"Who?"

"My sister-in-law."

"Your sister-in-law. The one related to you by marriage or Flynn's wife?"

Ramsey looked at me sharply.

I shrugged. "I read the article."

"That fucking article. I haven't had a moment of peace since. It was supposed to be a fluff publicity piece that would bring attention to The Rex. All it's done is complicate my life."

"With beautiful women throwing themselves at you?"

"Something like that." He sighed. "And I was referring to Barrett Campbell. That's who you remind me of."

"Flynn Campbell's wife." I nodded. "It seems you and I have some friends in common… Quinn O'Malley?"

"No shite," he said, a wry grin appearing on his very generous lips. "You're friends with Quinn?"

I nodded.

"She's a Boston girl. How do you know her? Are you from Boston too?"

*Crap.*

I hadn't been thinking. I'd just let my mouth get carried away by moonshine. "I did my residency at Boston General," I said. "Our paths...crossed."

Ramsey's eyes became somber, and he nodded. "Aye, Quinn. She's had a time of it."

"She has," I admitted. "But she's happy now. With Sasha."

He laughed softly. "I still can't believe you know Quinn. Sometimes, the world feels very small."

"The smallest," I agreed.

Ramsey took another drink from his bottle. "Did he tell you about what he saw?"

"Tonight, you mean? He told me about the women."

He paused. "Not the women."

"Oh," I said in understanding. "You mean the children."

"Aye."

I rubbed the bridge of my nose. "He didn't give me details, but I know... I know enough."

The man I was falling for was asleep, recovering from a gunshot because, despite what he had said about himself and the Tarnished Angels, they were saviors.

Protectors of the innocent.

Protectors of those too weak to defend themselves.

"Were you there?" I asked him. "The night they found the children?"

He nodded, his eyes glassy. With booze or emotion, I wasn't sure. "There are some horrors you can't ever unsee. Some horrors are there every time you close your eyes—nightmares that are burned onto your eyelids." He shuddered. "We were too late for one. I'll carry that guilt with me for the rest of my life. The others will too."

I exhaled a shaky breath and nodded. I carried my own guilt and realized that sometimes, there was no absolution for our failures.

But I didn't want to dwell on my past and the burdens fettered to my soul with iron shackles.

So, I left Ramsey with his own thoughts and went inside. And when I laid my head on a pillow in a clubhouse room, I thought about my future. For the first time in years, I thought there might be an added purpose to my life.

I woke up in the middle of the night to check on Boxer. His breathing was easy, and I stroked my hand across his forehead. He wasn't hot to the touch. No fever, which meant most likely no infection. I'd check his wound in the morning, and flush and change bandages as required. As I made my way to the door to leave, he whispered, "Stay."

"I didn't mean to wake you up," I whispered back.

"I was already half awake. Stay," he said again.

"I don't want to hurt you." But even as I said the words, I was stripping out of my jeans that I'd pulled on in case I encountered anyone in the hallway. But the clubhouse was quiet, and everyone was asleep.

I gingerly crawled into bed next to Boxer. I backed up until I hit the wall, wanting to give him as much room as possible.

We lay there in silence, and when his breathing didn't even out after a few minutes, I asked, "Are you still awake?"

"Yeah."

"Are you in pain?"

"Some," he admitted.

"Do you want—"

"No. No painkillers. I'll be fine."

"You sure?"

"I survived a hangover without aspirin and an appendectomy without morphine. I can handle a little bullet wound without painkillers."

I closed my eyes and reached out to gently set my hand on his chest, wanting, needing, to feel the rhythm of his breathing.

"I think the ones we couldn't save are in a better place," he said, his voice raspy in the dark. "This world is so fucking cruel sometimes."

"Yeah, that's the truth."

"Does it make me a bastard for saying it?"

"No. It doesn't make you a bastard."

It was on the tip of my tongue to ask about what he'd seen.

"I can't tell you the details, Linden," he voiced, as if reading my mind. "I'll never do it, and I don't want you to ask. Do you understand?"

I squeezed my eyes tight, but it didn't stop the tears from escaping from beneath my eyelids. I knew what he had seen was so bad he couldn't bring himself to relive it, and I wouldn't put him through it again.

"I won't ask," I whispered.

After a long moment of silence, he said, "I'm gonna find them, Linden. I'm gonna hunt down the sick fuckers that do this type of shit, and I'm gonna put a fucking bullet in their heads."

I slid my arm underneath his shoulders, trying not to jostle him. But then he rolled into my embrace, and I placed my cheek against his hair and silently wept for the things we couldn't control, the people we couldn't save, and the fragility of human life.

My dreams were messy, shadowed, and full of cobwebs. Talking to Boxer about what he was a part of had split my psyche open, and while I dreamed, my own demons found me.

When I awakened again, I was alone in bed and sunlight streamed through the half-mast blinds. I was sprawled out at a diagonal. No doubt I had pillow creases along my cheek.

I sat up and blinked, trying to get my mind to wake up. It was foggy, mushy, and unlike how I normally woke.

Melancholy weighed heavily on my heart, and not just because of my scattered nightmares. I was more than off kilter; I was raw, like my insides had been raked along coals and I was burning from the inside out.

The door to the bedroom opened, and Boxer ambled in. Aside from the bandage covering his wound, he didn't look any worse for wear. He had more than a few days of stubble along his jaw, but his eyes were clear, devoid of pain or meds.

I wasn't sure what to say to him before coffee and a good tooth scrubbing.

His gaze scanned my face and then my body. Despite the heaviness that weighed on me, my skin erupted in tingles with the promise of unleashing myself on him. But he was injured.

I wondered if our bodies should be leading our minds, or if we had it all backward. But what was more authentic than desire?

"Morning," I said.

"Afternoon, you mean."

My eyes widened. "It's the afternoon?"

He nodded.

"But how?" I gasped. "I never sleep this long."

"Guess you needed it."

"Guess I did," I said. "How are you feeling?"

"How are *you* feeling?"

"Boxer," I warned.

"Physically, I'm fine, Doc. Mentally... I might be taking your Basket Case title." His smile was tinged with solemn humor. "I won't be okay again until I'm deep inside you, and I forget all the shit in the world and just think about us."

I nodded in understanding. He'd put into words exactly what I needed and how.

"I want that too," I admitted, my voice raspy with desire.

"Yeah?"

"Yeah." I blew out a breath of air.

"I'm more than you bargained for, aren't I?"

"Definitely," I said with a winsome smile. I reached for my jeans. "I need a hot shower, clean underwear, and a cup of coffee."

"In that order?" he asked with a smile.

"Not necessarily."

I padded toward him and gently placed my hands on his chest. "I haven't brushed my teeth yet."

"I don't give a fuck," he growled, hauling me closer, his head dipping.

I sank into him and his touch, needing to feel our connection surge through me. When I was gasping for breath, I pulled away and pressed my cheek to his shirt and closed my eyes.

He moved his hand across my back and then wormed

it under the shirt that I'd borrowed from him the previous night. "I got you a clean towel, but you'll have to make do with Irish Spring and 2 in 1 shampoo and conditioner."

I smiled into him. "That works."

"As for the clean underwear situation... I suggest none."

I let out a laugh. "You would suggest that."

He stared down at me, grinning. "Coffee's waiting for you when you're done." Boxer kissed the end of my nose and then stepped away. "Thanks."

"For?"

"Sticking around," he said simply.

He left before I could muster a reply.

"I don't think I'm going anywhere," I murmured out loud to myself. "Not now."

# Chapter 21

My MIND WAS a swirl of thoughts. I hopped in the shower, hoping to clear it. While I was rinsing my hair, there was a quick knock on the bathroom door and then it opened.

"Linden?" Boxer called.

"Yeah?" I poked my head out from behind the shower curtain.

He leaned over and kissed me. It was quick, and then I ducked my head back into the steaming heat.

When I didn't hear the door open, I asked, "Are you still in here?"

"Yup." He paused. "I told you some dark shit last night."

"Yeah, you did."

"I wanted to make sure…fuck, I don't know. Are you okay?"

I scrubbed my arm with a lather of bubbles. "You mean am I going to go on a dish-smashing spree?"

"Are you?"

"The problem with falling apart is that there's always a

chance you can't scrape your feelings off the floor and stuff them back in the box where they belong."

"Maybe that's the problem. What if you let them out instead of getting to the point where they blow up the box you put them in?"

"Messy, either way."

"Life is messy."

I rinsed and then shut off the water. I grabbed the faded blue towel on the rack and quickly dried off before wrapping it around me and sliding back the shower curtain.

Boxer was leaning against the sink, looking deceptively casual. "I think you're doing a fair bit of deflecting, Doc."

"Ask what you really want to ask," I snapped.

His hands reached out to gently grasp my upper arms, and he rubbed his thumbs along my damp, warm skin. "Why can you be honest when it's the middle of the night and I can't see your eyes, but in broad fucking daylight, you can't be real with me? You didn't flinch, you didn't panic, you didn't break down. Why the hell not?"

"Did you and Ramsey talk or something?" I demanded. "Because he all but asked me the same thing last night after I put you to bed."

"And that's another thing. I won't be put to bed, woman, unless you're in it with me."

I rolled my eyes. "Stop. Just stop."

His grip tightened, and he hauled me toward him. Boxer's lips covered mine, and then his tongue was in my mouth.

I knew the real problem between us.

He ripped the towel from my body and flung it to the floor. And then his hands were between my legs, questing, seeking, needing. My hands went to his flannel shirt and with clumsy fingers, I managed to get the buttons open. I pressed a palm to his warm skin.

He undid his belt buckle and shoved his pants to the floor, including his underwear, and then he was backing me up against the sink. Boxer lifted my leg, opening me to his sensual, heated gaze.

With one quick thrust, he buried himself inside me to the hilt. He pounded into me like it was a punishment, like he was angry at me for something I couldn't name.

If anyone had any reason for anger, it was me. The Tarnished Angels had come to me. I'd put my career on the line. And Boxer was the one who'd taken a bullet.

He could've died.

I grabbed the back of his head, sinking my fingers into his hair. He wasn't going to break. I had no reason to be gentle. Even when he was injured, Boxer was stronger than most men.

He rammed into me harder, without mercy. "You shut me out."

We glared at one another as our mouths and words clashed. I bit his lip, tasting blood, tasting life.

"What is it you're still hiding from me? Because I know there's something."

I didn't want to talk. I didn't want him to see what I was truly feeling in that moment, so I closed my eyes and gave him everything I was feeling through touch instead of brutally honest words. My passion, my rage, my terror that we were all just one moment away from death and my fear that even though I was a doctor, I wasn't God, and I had no control over anything.

So I let him use my body as a battlefield, and did the same to his.

We collided against the bathroom mirror, and I heard a

crack. Boxer pulled me away and the mirror fell to the floor. Glass shattered and littered the ground.

Neither of us stopped to assess the damage.

I wanted it to be like this forever.

My heart beat with adrenaline and lust.

I knew what it truly meant to be alive in his arms, and for the first time in my life, I could finally admit what I'd been too damn scared to face.

I was in love with Boxer.

After my body shook and quaked and my orgasm nearly ripped me apart, I pressed my forehead to Boxer's shoulder while my breathing returned to normal.

His arms tightened, and he just held me.

It took me a moment to realize he hadn't slid out of me. He hadn't come yet, and he was still hard.

I squirmed against him, wanting him to move again. I was primed, ready for more.

"Linden, stop," he said, his voice low.

"No," I begged. "Please, Boxer."

His hands swept up my body to cradle my head, and he forced me to stare into his eyes. And when he began to move again, thrusting softly at first and then harder, he wouldn't let me go.

He wouldn't let me hide.

We stared into each other's eyes as I clenched around him, another wave of ecstasy pouring through my body. He slammed into me one final time and with a hearty groan, he came.

I placed a hand on his chest and felt the thundering of his heart.

While he'd been inside me, I'd had to stop myself from screaming the words. Saying them out loud to him would feel like a vow. Like a true commitment, one I wouldn't be able to walk away from. I was living on borrowed time before I told him.

He stared at me for a long moment, and then a veil went down over his eyes, shielding any vulnerability he might have been inclined to let me see.

I hurt him when I emotionally pulled away. But I wasn't ready to face it and all it would entail.

Boxer eased out of me. He grimaced when he reached down to pull up his pants. He didn't bother buttoning his shirt before leaving.

I looked at the shattered remains of the mirror on the bathroom floor, wondering why I destroyed, when all I wanted to do was heal.

Boxer wasn't in the living room when I came downstairs. I assumed that meant he was gone. Most of the Tarnished Angels were absent, too. A few remained—the young prospects and the newly patched in members.

"Hey, Doc, think fast," South Paw said. He lobbed a set of car keys at me which I caught in one hand.

I frowned. "These look like my keys. To my car."

South Paw grinned. "They are."

"But how did—these were in my purse last night." I blinked. "I don't get what's happening."

"I took your keys from your purse and drove with Crow to the hospital. We grabbed your car and brought it back for you."

"Was this part of the prospect hazing?" I demanded. "Because I don't know if I subscribe to that brand of torture."

"Happy to be tortured," South Paw said with a grin.

"Thanks, South Paw. I appreciate it. Have you seen Boxer?"

"He hitched a ride with Colt. They had shit to do."

I nodded, my heart heavy. He could've waited to see me off. He didn't, but I didn't blame him.

I waved to Acid, and he gave me a perfunctory chin nod. Reap was more effusive with his goodbye and gave me a quick yet strong hug.

"Glad to have you aboard, Doc," he said with a wink.

Was he letting me know that I was welcome in their lives as Boxer's woman, or was this because he expected me to patch them up in the future?

I decided not to ask.

The day was bright without a cloud in the sky, and I hardly noticed the chill.

My heart—and my mind—were with Boxer. I didn't like how we'd left things. Even as lovers, our last interaction had made me feel like we were adversaries.

Was I doomed forever, unable to open up?

I was just getting settled into my car when my phone rang.

*Peyton.*

Before I picked up, I took a deep breath. "Hello?"

"So…" Peyton began.

"So?"

"Why did a biker who wasn't your boyfriend show up where you worked last night?"

"You're going right for it, aren't you?"

Crow and South Paw were on the porch, watching me. I waved at them, and they waved back. I shoved the key into the ignition and turned on the engine.

"You never texted to tell me you weren't coming to Tony's, so I know something happened. So, what happened?"

"I can't tell you," I said quietly.

"You can't or won't?"

"Can't," I insisted. "I would if I could, I swear."

She paused and then sighed. "Just tell me if everyone is okay? That guy looked pretty intense."

"Zip," I said, supplying his name. "And yeah, everyone's fine."

"What about you?"

"What about me?"

"Are *you* fine?"

I leaned over and pressed my forehead to the steering wheel. "I'm fine. But I think I'm crazy."

"Why are you crazy?"

"For sticking around. I mean, Boxer's a *biker*. That's asking for trouble. I'm stupid. Aren't I?"

Her light chuckle came through the phone. "No. You're in love."

I sighed. "Same thing."

"You didn't even deny it."

"Who are we kidding at this point?"

"You know what I think?"

"What do you think?" I repeated.

"I think you should stop fighting what you *think* you should do, and instead you should follow your heart."

"Follow my heart." I sighed. "Yeah. If only I was good at that. Peyton?"

"Yeah?"

"When you and Tom would fight, and you were the instigator, how did you apologize? How did you make amends?"

She fell silent for a moment. "You guys had a fight?"

"Not a fight, per se. Just a sort of…I don't know. A disagreement, I guess."

"Whenever I felt I was at fault, and sometimes when I

wasn't, I always made him food. When you apologize, be sincere, then feed him. It works every time."

# Chapter 22

Boxer's front porch light was on, and I could see the glow of the living room lamps through the closed blinds.

He was home.

With a sigh, I cut the engine, and then sat for a moment in the parking spot on the street.

The front door to the house opened, and Boxer loomed in the doorway. Even though the sun had long since set, I could see him clearly, illuminated in porch light.

He was wearing a pair of jeans, a button-down red and black flannel shirt, and no shoes. His jaw was scruffy from not shaving, and his hair was messy. Boxer crossed his arms, leaned against the door jamb, and waited. He didn't appear to be in any substantial discomfort from his recent injury, and I seriously wondered about his pain tolerance.

Girding my loins, I grabbed the bag with the pie I'd bought at Pie in the Sky, my purse, and climbed out.

"How'd you get my address?" he asked.

"I asked Reap for it."

"You don't call?" Boxer drawled. "I could've been out."

"You don't call," I reminded him. "You just show up on my doorstep. I'm taking a play from your book."

I locked the car and then headed up the sidewalk, but before I got to the porch, I stopped.

"What'd you bring?" he asked with a nod at the bag.

"Pie." I held it up.

He didn't move, and I was worried he wasn't going to.

"What kind of pie?" he asked finally.

"Blueberry. From Pie in the Sky Bakery."

He pushed away from the door.

I came up the steps and before I swept past him, I stopped and looked up, meeting his gaze. I gauged his body for signs of fever. He wasn't flushed and his eyes were clear—and casually blank. In that moment, I realized it was his way of masking what he was feeling.

Boxer shut the door behind me and then took the bag from my grasp, careful not to touch me.

Sadness at his rejection enveloped me, and it was my instinct to continue pulling away, but he was always offering me honesty and openness. It was my turn to do the same.

"Sit," he commanded, pointing to the kitchen chair. He pulled out the pie and set it on the table.

"I don't like how we left things," I said.

"So you drove all the way back here to say that?"

"No. I drove around Waco all day to clear my head and to find the best comfort food that went nicely with an apology. If you don't want pie, I'll order chicken wings. Or barbecue. Or anything else you want. Just…hear me out. Okay?"

He sighed. "I'm listening."

"Everything feels very…*uneven* between us."

"What do you mean, uneven?"

"You talked about your childhood."

"You talked about yours, too," he pointed out.

"Yeah," I agreed with a nod. "I did. But it's not the only thing that I carry around inside me. There's something else I want to share with you." I paused, trying to summon the nerve. "I lost a kid on my table."

I heard the scraping of the chair next to me, and then Boxer sat. I felt this warmth, but he didn't reach out to touch me. I was glad he didn't. I was afraid that if he touched me in that moment I'd shatter like a crystal vase.

"It was my second to last year of residency. He was badly injured, and I had to make a call. It was a fifty-fifty shot, but it was the wrong one, and an eight-year-old boy died right in front of me." I exhaled slowly and forced myself to look at Boxer.

His eyes were full of sympathy but not forgiveness. No one could give me that. No one except me, and I'd spent years punishing myself for my mistake. I wasn't sure I was capable of ever forgiving myself at this point. I'd lived with it for so long. I understood the burden I carried, but it wasn't so easy to let it go.

"You don't know what it's like," I said. "Sitting across from hopeful parents when you're the one that has to tell them their child is gone. The light leaves their eyes, almost like they've died too." I turned my face away and closed my own eyes, but all that did was force me back in time to the worst moment of my life.

I inhaled a few breaths and then continued. "They made me take a few weeks leave after my breakdown. I saw a shrink and went to grief counseling." I opened my eyes. "That's where I met Quinn."

Shaking my head, I laughed softly. "We blew off grief group one day, got drunk, and talked. That did more for me than three weeks of counseling. I still don't know why."

I looked at Boxer, but still he said nothing.

"I came back to work, slapped a smile on my face, and pretended like each breath didn't feel like a razor shredding my heart. It was too much, so I left Boston and went to Duke. I met a guy down there. Jeff. We lived together. My mother liked him. I felt...lukewarm about him. I felt lukewarm about everything, really. A few months ago, he got promoted and took a job in San Francisco. He asked me to go with him and I said no and moved here."

I clasped my hands together and placed them in my lap. "I run from things. People. Myself. Something is broken inside me, Boxer. And it broke long before I..." I swallowed. "Before I killed that boy. I think it broke when my dad left. I stopped trusting. Stopped seeing the good in the world. I wanted to fix things in people that could be fixed. I want to help others because I can't help myself."

*I felt like a grandfather clock that chimed the wrong hours.*

"When I was nineteen," he said after long pause. "I walked into my childhood home and saw my father strangling my mother. He had his hands wrapped around her throat, and it was obvious he was really gonna do it."

His gaze was cold, steely. "I pulled him off her and while I was beating the shit out of him, she was sobbing next to me, begging for his life. The bastard was gonna kill her, and there she was pleading with me to let him live."

I couldn't imagine the horror of walking into the scene he described. I saw terrible things as a doctor, but to witness something that personal... God, he was stronger than I even realized.

"I beat his face until he went limp and pissed himself. I leaned down close to him, and he looked at me through swollen eyes when I told him if he ever touched her again, I'd kill him. I'll never forget how he smelled in that moment, like cheap gin and fear." He clenched his hands into fists, as if he was viscerally remembering the scene he'd witnessed.

"Something happens to men when they realize they're nothing more than mediocre has-beens who've never amounted to anything. They take it out on the people that love them."

He took a long, slow breath. "Later, when I walked into the clubhouse and told Colt and the others what I'd done. My knuckles were bloody and raw. And a few months later when they patched me in, they named me Boxer. It's the most honest thing that I am.

"I haven't seen my dad since that day. I doubt he's dead. Some men are too fucking mean to die." His smile was rancorous, and he looked straight at me. "Some people break and never recover from the things they've seen. They never figure out how to breathe deeply again. But you took the pain of your father leaving and turned it into something. You found a way to give back and do something good in this shithole of a world."

He finally reached out and touched me, cradling my cheeks in his strong hands. "People die all the time. You tried to save a life. That's more than what most people do. My old man was so miserable, he just wanted to spread it around. You spread good, Doc, because you *are* good."

"Boxer," I whispered, but he wasn't done.

"We're all broken in some way. If you're lucky, you might find someone whose broken pieces fit with yours."

I leaned into his touch. "You live a dangerous life."

"Yeah."

"I just dug a bullet out of you."

"It won't be the last time," he said with a rueful smile.

"You could've died."

"But I didn't."

"Boxer—"

"No, hear me out." He paused and exhaled a long sigh. "I almost died from my appendix bursting. I got shot but didn't die. I've been in fights with guys who've pulled knives and done shit on my bike you wouldn't believe. You have to live, Linden. You have to take risks, because if you don't, then you'll wake up at the end of your life full of regrets, and a head full of dreams never lived, and that's a lot worse than dying."

"I've never had a relationship that's lasted."

"Then they weren't the right ones."

"My dad left me," I said quietly. "That damage runs deep."

"It says nothing about you, and everything about *him*. My old man's shit isn't my shit. My dad's wounds aren't my wounds."

I bit my lip. "You'll get sick of me."

"Nah."

"I'll get sick of you."

"Like hell you will," he said with a grin.

"I'll drive you crazy."

"Without a doubt."

"What if I try to run?" I asked in exasperation.

"I won't let you."

"What if you try to run?" I pivoted.

"We need each other, Linden."

"What if—" His lips cut off what I'd been about to say by covering mine.

My mind was suddenly full of static, finally silenced, beaten into submission.

His hands dropped from my cheeks and then he stood. He grasped my hand and pulled me up. And then he kissed me like he'd never get another chance, like he needed me to be touching him so he could breathe.

My fingers tore through his hair and then he was hauling me toward the bedroom, his mouth fused to mine.

In our frenzied state, he bumped into the wall and then the doorway of the bedroom.

He flipped on the light and then let me go, but only so that he could quickly strip out of his clothes.

I did the same.

And then I was back in his arms, skin to skin. Warm. Alive.

He gently pushed me down onto the bed, and then he covered me with his body. Boxer spread my thighs and then he was deep inside me.

Our eyes locked.

Boxer thrust into me again and again, and the pleasure I felt between my legs spread through my body and up my spine.

I breathed in, smelling him, smelling us. His eyes were liquid silver, full of heat and want and something more.

It was the something more that made my breath shaky and my heart drum in rapid staccato.

And when I clenched around him, screaming out my pleasure, I cried, too.

Tears skated from the corners of my eyes to fall into the hair at my temples.

"I know," he whispered before taking my lips.

I clutched his shoulders and clasped him to me, feeling for the first time in my life, that I was where I was supposed to be.

Swaddled in Boxer's arms, I drifted off to sleep, my cheeks wet with tears. When I woke up, I expected to see sunlight streaming through the blinds of the bedroom, but it was dark, and he wasn't asleep next to me.

I sat up and listened for a moment. I heard Boxer moving around in the kitchen and wondered what time it was. The man didn't believe in clocks.

I turned on the bedside lamp and climbed out of bed. I found my underwear on the other side of the room, and then I put on Boxer's discarded flannel shirt. It was soft from many washings.

He was standing at the counter, bare chested. His white bandage was stark against his skin, reminding me of what he'd gone through.

My soft footsteps on the wooden floor made him turn around. He was in the process of finishing off the last of the pie.

"Could you be any cuter," I said with amusement. "Sneaking out of bed in the middle of the night to eat all the pie. You weren't going to share it, were you?"

"Nope." He grinned at me. Boxer held out the fork to me, his hand underneath it to catch anything that fell.

I went to him and let him feed me until the pie was gone.

His dark blond hair was mussed, and he wore a pair of green boxer briefs. I couldn't help but admire the expanse of skin and ink.

"Did you sleep?"

"Nope," he said. He grabbed the half-drunk glass of milk in one hand, took mine with the other, and led me into the living room.

I sat at the far end of the couch, my back pressed up against an arm. Boxer took the seat on the opposite side and then set down his glass of milk. He switched on the lamp and then dragged the blanket from the top of the couch to cover me. He then wormed his hands underneath the blanket.

"You're cold." He rubbed the top of my foot and then clamped it between his palms.

I leaned my head back and stared at the ceiling while his hands warmed my skin.

"What was wrong with him?" Boxer asked.

"What was wrong with who?"

"The guy you were dating. You lived with him?" He didn't sound jealous, merely curious.

"For a bit."

"Why'd it end?" he asked.

I paused and really took a moment to think about the answer. "There were a lot of factors. I guess the biggest and most important one was that I didn't love him." I shrugged. "We thought we were supposed to be together. On paper, we were a perfect match. In real life though, something was missing. Does that make sense?"

"No."

I snorted out a laugh. "Yeah, it didn't make much sense to me either. I worked all the time. He didn't like that, but it wasn't as if I was going to change it. This is my career, and I love it."

Boxer was quiet for a moment, and his hands moved to my other foot. "Did you tell him about what happened? Losing your patient?"

"No. I didn't tell him."

"Why did you tell me?"

"Because that's the ugliest part of me, Boxer." I stared him in the eyes. "And I wanted—no, I *needed* you to know me. Every part of me."

He let go of my foot and then lunged for me, pinning me beneath his body. "There's nothing ugly about you."

I looked down, trying to shield my emotions from him, but he was a battering ram to a castle wall.

"I'm a criminal, remember? You want to keep score on who's worse? I'll win. Easily."

"A criminal who rescues women and children," I said.

"I'm a sinner, not a saint," he quipped. "The good deeds don't outweigh the bad ones."

"Life isn't black or white, is it?"

He grinned. "You just proved my point."

I sighed.

"You deserve to be happy, Linden. You gotta let the guilt go."

"Easier said than done. Easier said than done."

"Get your ass out here, Boxer!" a female voice yelled. "I've got a bone to pick with you!"

I shot up in bed and looked around. Daylight streamed through the blinds, and Boxer was still in bed next to me.

His eyes were closed, but he scratched his chest. "Damn, that woman has a set of pipes."

I fell back onto the bed. "Who the hell is here at this hour?"

"Mia," Boxer groused.

"What is she mad about?"

"No fucking idea." He cracked one eyelid and peered at me. "You're not pissed she just walked in here like she owned the place? We could've been naked in the kitchen. Or naked in the living room. Or naked—"

"I got it," I said dryly. "You want us naked in all your rooms."

"Yup. It's gonna happen. I'll make sure of it." He flung the covers off him and then swung his legs over the side of the bed. Boxer ran a hand across his scruffy cheek and then got up. He went to his dresser and pulled out a pair of gray sweatpants and a black T-shirt.

"Don't leave me out there with her. She's in a fit, and she's full of hormones."

I snorted and rolled to the side of the bed, and grabbed the flannel he'd worn the night before. "Pregnant women scare you?"

I buttoned the shirt and then stared at him when he didn't reply.

He was still, looking thoughtful. "No. Pregnant women don't scare me."

Boxer stalked from the room. I quickly used the bathroom and then went to discover why Mia was here.

When I entered the kitchen, I smiled. Mia was looking up at Boxer, glaring at him.

He peered down at her, a goofy grin on his face.

"Hey, Mia," I greeted. "A little early for a visit, isn't it?"

"Sorry," she said. "Boxer's never had a woman here. I'll call next time. For the record, it's almost ten. Hardly early."

I inclined my head and accepted her apology and marveled that I'd slept so late. Then I remembered we'd woken up in the middle of the night for a chat…and other things. The other things made sleeping late easy.

The coffee was brewing but hadn't finished yet.

"Sit," I told her. "Get off those feet."

"How did you know?" she asked as she walked to a kitchen chair. She sank down into it and moaned softly.

"I guessed," I said in amusement.

"Good guess."

"So, what's this bone you have to pick with Boxer?" I asked.

"Jughead, here, taught Silas his ways with women."

255

She pinned him with another glare. "When I went to pick Silas up from school, not only did he have three girls buzzing around him, but they'd all baked him cookies. Cookies, Boxer!"

"What's wrong with cookies?" he asked with a raise of his brows. "You make cookies all the time."

The coffee maker was sputtering to the end of its brew cycle, and Boxer went to a cabinet and pulled out three mugs.

"None for me. I've already had my cup of caffeine for the day," Mia said.

"Was he disrespectful? To the girls, I mean? Because I'll tan his hide if that's the case," Boxer said lightly.

"No, he wasn't being disrespectful," Mia repeated. "He informed me he invited the three of them to dinner tomorrow night, and they all accepted."

"Three preteen girls all vying for attention of the same boy," I said. "That sounds like it could get a little catty."

"Don't worry, I taught Silas how to handle them," Boxer stated.

"*Handle* them?" Mia's face suffused with color.

"She's pregnant," I reminded Boxer. "Can you try not to raise her blood pressure?"

Boxer brought the two mugs of coffee to the table and then took a seat. He patted his knee, and I immediately went to him and perched on his lap.

"Are you really pissed that I taught Silas how to flirt? Or are you pissed that he's finally noticing the opposite sex?" Boxer asked.

Mia sniffed and quickly wiped her eyes. "He's only twelve."

"And you want him to stay a boy a while longer," Boxer said. "He came to me, Mia. I swear."

Mia nodded.

Boxer let out a soft laugh.

"What?" she demanded.

"He's killing it. Three girls hanging around him? Maybe he can give *me* some tips."

It was my turn to glare at him. He grinned cheekily at me. "For when you throw me overboard because you get sick of my shit." He wrapped an arm around me, and I sank back into him.

"I brought you a lasagna. It's in the fridge," Mia said.

I raised my brows at her. "You were pissed at Boxer, yet you brought him food?"

Mia sighed. "Yeah. Even when I'm mad at him, I feed him. No wonder Silas is doing great with the girls in his class."

I sipped my coffee and ran my fingers through the hair at Boxer's nape.

"Well, I better go. Sorry again about barging in here, Linden."

"You didn't offer me an apology," Boxer said.

"I promise not to abuse my key privileges," Mia drawled. "Okay?"

"Okay," he said. "The kid already knows about the birds and the bees. You know that, right?"

She sighed, her hand covering her swollen belly. "Inevitable, I guess. Bikers for uncles. I'm not ready for this. I'm not ready for this at all."

"That's life," Boxer said with a wry grin.

"Helpful. Thanks." She rolled her eyes. "See you guys tonight." The front door shut, and we were alone.

"Tonight," I repeated. "Ah, Joni and Zip's party. That's still happening?"

"Why wouldn't it?"

"Because you were shot?"

"And the world still turns, Doc."

I couldn't really argue with that.

"She brings you food even when she's mad at you," I said, changing the subject and getting up off his lap and going to the refrigerator. I opened the door and pulled out a carton of eggs.

"Does that bother you?" he inquired casually.

Far too casually.

"Was there anything between you guys?" I asked, not looking at him. "Mixing bowl?"

"Bottom cabinet in the corner," he said. "And no. There was never anything between me and Mia. It's not like that with us."

"She loves you," I said. I found the medium-sized bowl and set it on the counter.

"I love her. She's family."

I nodded and cracked an egg.

"You can say it you know," he said.

"Say what?"

"That *you* love me."

Shell fell into the bowl. With a curse, I picked it out and tossed it into the sink.

He chuckled, and then I felt him come up behind me. Boxer wrapped his arms around me and pressed his chin to my shoulder. "I should've warned you."

"About?"

"My lethal charm."

"It might've been helpful," I said dryly, turning to face him. "The nurses going gaga over you should've been warning enough."

He covered my lips with his and then his tongue was in my mouth, and I didn't care about eggs or breakfast.

I turned in his embrace, my back against the counter. I lifted my leg to rest it on his hip, opening myself up to him.

His hand delved between my legs, his fingers teasing the purple satin underwear I wore.

He found me wet and ready when he slipped his finger inside me. My back bowed as pleasure skated down my spine.

Boxer continued to torment me.

"Say it," he demanded. "Give me the words, Doc."

"Boxer…"

He pulled his finger from me and then he tugged down his sweats, freeing himself. Boxer pushed my underwear aside and tormented my entrance with the crown of his shaft.

I felt just the tip of him at first and then my body swallowed him, welcoming him inside me.

Our moans echoed off the kitchen walls. I tried to get my bearings by grasping for the counter, but all I did was knock the egg carton and bowl to the floor.

He rammed into me harder, his hand curling around my hip.

"Say it," he said, his silver eyes meeting mine.

I bit my lip hard enough to taste blood.

"Say it," he said, this time softer. He stilled inside of me, refusing to move.

"Blackmail," I snapped. "Not fair."

"All's fair in love and war, Doc. Say it and then I'll make you scream my name."

"Too charming and too arrogant," I said.

He rolled his hips, and I felt him everywhere inside me. My body was no longer my own, but his to worship and pleasure.

Boxer's hands left my hips to slide up my arms and then to cup my cheeks, so I was forced to stare into his unyielding gaze.

He swiped his thumbs at the corners of my eyes, waiting, seemingly eternally patient.

"I'm not ready," I whispered. "Please, I just need—"

His lips silenced my fears and ignited my body in pleasure.

My moans of desire reverberated off the walls as he began to thrust again and again. If anything, he used me harder, pleasured me deeper.

His hand slid to the nape of my neck as he came.

Our breathing was labored, and he was heavy, but I never wanted him to move.

I reached down and clasped his butt, dragging him even closer.

He shuddered with raw gratification. "I knew this kitchen had a better use than for cooking."

And then he eased out of me. He tucked himself back into his sweats as he looked around at the carnage. "Yeah, we'll be going out for breakfast."

I brushed a kiss along his stubbly jaw. "Shower first."

"Okay, but keep your hands to yourself, woman, or we'll never get out of here."

# Chapter 23

He took me to a café. The hostess showed us to a booth, and instead of sitting across from me, Boxer slid into the seat next to me. He wrapped his arm around my shoulder and tucked me into his side.

"This is going to make it hard to eat," I said.

"I'll feed you."

"Yeah, no," I said with a laugh.

Boxer grinned and winked at the waitress who handed us our menus. She blushed and mumbled, "Something to drink?"

"Linden?" Boxer prodded.

"Coffee, please."

"Same. Thanks, darlin'."

The young woman flushed even redder and scampered away.

"You're cruel," I said. "You embarrassed that poor girl."

"Didn't mean to." He leaned close to my ear. "You know the real reason I wanted to sit this close to you?"

While he was talking, his free hand that wasn't draped

around my shoulder wandered across my thigh toward the seam of my legs. When he grazed the fly of my jeans, it caused me to jump and bump my knee underneath the tabletop.

It rattled the creamer and salt and pepper shakers, and the noise caused heads to turn in our direction.

"Boxer," I hissed.

His grin was cheeky and full of trouble.

I was glaring at him when the waitress returned to the table with our coffees. I hadn't looked at the menu yet, but Boxer ordered while I scanned it.

A few minutes later, we were alone again.

"You can touch me, you know," he said. "I won't object."

"I didn't touch you enough this morning? Or last night? Or in the shower?"

He looked deep into my eyes and said, "It'll never be enough."

I sighed and then snuggled deeper into his embrace.

"Don't you guys look cozy," Zip said suddenly.

I jumped again, hitting my other knee. "Son of a…" I muttered, rubbing my stinging kneecap.

Joni elbowed Zip in the ribs, causing him to grunt. "Sorry," he apologized.

"It's okay. You guys want to join us?" I asked.

"We don't want to intrude," Joni said.

"Intrude, please." I grinned. "And maybe your presence will help keep Boxer in line."

"Yeah, right," Zip said. "I've never known anyone to keep him in line. I was hoping you'd be the woman for the job."

Something inside of me settled at his words. He was accepting me in his own way. I was humbled. And comfortable. Like just maybe, for the first time in my life I'd found people I could let my guard down around.

Joni and Zip took the seat across from us. Zip angled his body close to Joni and absently brushed a kiss to her hair.

I grinned to myself. I loved that the Tarnished Angels were not afraid to show affection to their women.

The waitress returned with our food and set our plates down in front of us.

She smiled at Joni and Zip. "Hey, guys. Do you want your usual?"

"Nah, I want to change it up," Joni said. "Grilled cheese and tomato soup, please."

"Zip?" the waitress asked.

"Usual for me, Suzie. Thanks."

"Right-o."

When she left, I looked at Joni. "You guys are regulars here?"

She nodded. "It's close to the garage."

"Garage? What garage?" I asked.

"Charlie's," Boxer said. "Where we work."

"Ah," I said. "Got it."

"I meet Zip here a few times a week. They've gotten to know us." Joni looked at Zip and beamed, her cheeks rosy. "I'm afraid we've gotten too predictable and comfortable in our routine."

"No shit," Zip muttered. "Every time I come home, the TV's on, and the woman is watching all that HGTV crap. It's like we've become sixty-five overnight."

"You were the one that wanted to renovate an old house," Joni reminded him. "So don't blame me for watching those shows so I have an idea of what the hell we've gotten ourselves into."

"You're renovating a house?" I asked. "That's really cool. I wish I had the time to do something like that."

"You're still coming over tonight, right?" Joni asked. "You don't have to work?"

"I'm free." I looked at Boxer. "My schedule the last few weeks has been wonky, but I'm using it to my advantage."

"Speaking of advantage...will you let me take advantage of you tonight when you crash at my place again?"

I stared into his eyes and grinned. "You can take advantage of me if you let me take advantage of you."

"I'm so here for that."

"I think they've forgotten about us," Joni said to Zip.

"Yup," Zip agreed. "They're practically shacking up. And another Tarnished Angel bites the dust."

"Dude, I can hear you," Boxer said.

Zip grinned. "How much shit did you give me over Joni?"

"Plenty."

"Turnabout is fair play, from where I'm sitting."

"So go sit at another table," Boxer said lightly. "And let me grope my woman in peace."

"Do I have any say in the matter on this groping in public?" I asked with an arch of my brow.

He winked. "You'll like it, trust me."

"Gag," Joni joked.

The server returned and plopped Joni and Zip's food down in front of them. Joni reached for the pepper shaker.

"Eat fast," she stage-whispered to Zip. "Then we can get out of here and let the love birds get back to their inappropriate groping."

She looked at me and shot me a wink and a grin.

I smiled back.

After the check was paid, Zip and Boxer went outside to discuss club business while Joni and I finished up our drinks. Joni glanced out the window, her brow wrinkling with displeasure.

"What's that look for?" I asked her.

"Zip's smoking again. He quit for a while and was doing really well, but he's clearly stressed out about something. It used to be me he needed a cigarette over." She grinned at me. "I drove him crazy while we were getting together."

I chuckled. "Of course you drove him crazy. Look at you. You're gorgeous."

"You're a doll." She brushed aside my compliment. "Has Boxer said anything to you?"

"About?"

"I don't know. Zip's been…on edge, I guess. For a couple of weeks now."

I tapped my fingers on the rim of my coffee mug, unsure of how to answer. It was clear to me that she didn't know that Boxer had been shot. He wore long sleeves, and his bandage was concealed. Boxer hadn't come out and said I wasn't allowed to say anything to the Old Ladies, but it didn't need to be addressed. They did not involve their women in club business, even if I was something of a novelty.

"Do you think it has to do with club business?" I asked evasively.

"Probably." She sighed.

"Do you wish you knew what went on? Boxer told me the club doesn't tell the Old Ladies what's what. Does that bother you?"

"Honestly? No. I think if I knew, I'd worry more. As it stands, I can somehow compartmentalize it. Almost pretend that Zip doesn't carry a pistol. And I can pretend I don't know that he's had to use it before…"

I swallowed.

She peered at me. "You know, this is not really the place for this discussion."

I instantly retreated, feeling foolish for asking.

She reached across the table and patted my hand. "I didn't mean that to sound the way it did—like I wouldn't talk about it. I'll talk about it, but maybe we talk about it tonight? When we're at my house?"

The knot of rejection uncurled inside of me. "That's a good idea."

Boxer and Zip came back inside and hovered by the table. Joni wrinkled her nose when Zip leaned down to press a kiss to her lips.

"You stink."

"Woman, don't start with me," Zip muttered.

"I'm a nurse," she said. "And Linden's a doctor. Do I really need to lecture you about smoking and your health?"

"Don't drag me into this," I said, hastily grabbing my purse. "This is between the two of you."

"Yeah, let's get out of here." Boxer reached for my hand. "Good luck, Zip."

We left the café and stepped out into the late autumn sunshine. Boxer removed his aviators from his leather cut pocket and put them on.

"I've got to stop by the garage."

"Fine."

He sighed. "You've got a tone. What's the tone for?"

"She's worried about him," I said to Boxer as we headed toward his truck.

"He's not a hard-core smoker. He'll go months without a cigarette." He opened the passenger door for me, and I climbed up into the seat.

"That's not her issue," I said. "She said he only smokes when he's stressed."

He shut the door and went over to the driver's side and

got in. "What do you want me to do, Linden? Zip's a grown man who can make his own decisions."

He jammed the key into the ignition.

"Yes, I'm aware. We can all make our own decisions," I told him. "She knows something's going on that has nothing to do with her or their relationship."

"He can't tell her about club business," he insisted.

"Maybe he should," I fired back. "I know about it. Why am I allowed to know about it, but she can't? Why can't the other Old Ladies know about it?"

"You know because you were the one to patch me up. And we've been clear that might happen again. No surprises with you."

"So, if I hadn't been a doctor, Zip would never have come to me."

"He wouldn't have had any reason to."

"So, I never would've known how you got injured, only that you *were* injured?"

I looked out the window.

"You don't get to be mad at me," he said.

"What am I mad at you about?" I demanded.

"I dunno. I'm just covering my bases."

"You're impossible."

"Impossible to stay mad at." He winked.

"I still think you should tell the Old Ladies what's what," I said.

"No."

I sighed. "I'm between a rock and a hard place. I know you've been shot. They don't know you've been shot. I'm hanging out with the Old Ladies tonight. Do you really expect me not to say anything to them about this?"

"Patient confidentiality, Doc. That's a thing. I thought you'd be used to it by now."

I stared straight ahead and fell silent.

"What, Doc? What's going through that big ol' brain of yours?"

I smiled absently at his teasing tone, but it quickly died. "I'm neither an Old Lady nor a Tarnished Angel. I'm just the doctor that got caught in the middle. Joni's offering me her friendship, Boxer. She's including me. It feels like I'm lying to them." I sighed. "Are you sure you're protecting them by keeping them in the dark?"

"Yes, Linden." He sighed, sounding tired. "Not only is it the way it's always been, it's critical that you understand it *has* to be this way. See what you're feeling right now? That pull to talk to them, tell them what's going on? Do you have any idea the risk we took telling you about any of this? It's insane, frankly, and I had to convince the club you were different. Doctor-patient confidentiality is the only reason they finally got on board with it. Imagine all the women in the club all talking about this shit, their minds going wild and calling family members and—oh fuck all that. It just can't happen."

"I get it, but how can Joni be there for Zip the way he needs if he won't confide in her?" I asked.

He pulled into Charlie's Motorcycle Repair Shop and parked.

"Linden, stop. Let me lay it out for you, okay? We love our women and children, and we protect them the best way we know how. If Joni or Mia or any of the other Old Ladies has problems with how we do shit, they shouldn't have stayed. They shouldn't have chosen this life. You're in our world now. There's gonna be shit you don't like, but that's just the way it is. So, make your peace with it or—"

"Or what?" I snapped.

"Or I'll help you make your peace with it." He leaned across the truck and settled his lips on mine.

I ripped my mouth from his. "You can't just—"

His hands grasped the back of my head, and he kissed me again.

Deep. With tongue.

So I stopped thinking—and collapsed against him, soft and needy.

He chuckled as he dragged his lips to my temple. "You already talk like you're one of us, Doc. I like that. I like that a lot."

Was it true? Why did I feel such loyalty to a group of people I'd just met?

I knew who I was when I'd come to Dallas. But after meeting Boxer and the Tarnished Angels, I wasn't sure I knew who I was at all.

He skimmed a thumb across the apple of my cheek. "Hey, Doc. You don't have to worry about a thing. Okay?"

"I'm not good at living in the moment, Boxer."

He grinned. "I'll help you."

# Chapter 24

IT WAS early evening when I rolled up to the Queen Anne Victorian house and parked behind a black SUV. Motorcycles and cars already littered the brick driveway.

I was dressed casually in a pair of jeans and a gray turtleneck sweater, my blonde hair in a loose braid down my back. I rang the doorbell. After a few moments and no one answered, I rang it again. Still no answer. I turned the knob on the heavy wooden door with a stained-glass window. It was unlocked, and I walked inside.

If Joni hadn't warned me about the fixer upper status, I would've been horrified. They had their work cut out for them.

I opened the sliding door and went out onto the back patio. Though it was still sunny, there was a nip to the air. Heating lamps had been placed all around the stone terrace.

An old gray u-shaped couch graced the edge of the patio with a matching wicker table that was covered in cups. The Old Ladies were sitting and talking, while a few children played cornhole on the lawn. The Tarnished Angels were nowhere to be found.

"Linden!" Joni greeted, hopping off the couch and coming toward me. She looked me up and down. "You weren't wearing that this morning. Did you go shopping? I know you didn't drive all the way back to Dallas just to change clothes."

"Good God, no," I said with a laugh. "I always have spare clothes in the back of my car. You never know when you're going to need them."

She smiled. "Can I get you a drink?"

"That sounds good." I handed her the orchid I'd picked up at a plant nursery in town.

"Thank you! I'll plant it this spring in the new garden—if it survives until then. I have a brown thumb, but I'm determined to get better. This is the perfect gift!"

"I'm glad you like it," I said, feeling my insides warm.

"Let's get you a drink." She headed to the makeshift bar, which was a few feet away from a gas grill. "Red wine, white, something stronger?"

"Oh, red, please."

She lifted a bottle of red and uncorked it, then poured me a serving in a plastic wine glass. "Have you been at Boxer's this whole time?"

I shook my head. "I left when he headed out for church. I wanted to buy you a plant and now here I am. This commuting for a relationship is kind of a pain in the butt."

"You could move here."

"It's a little too early to be talking about that," I protested.

"Is it?" She studied me for a moment and then smiled. "Come sit. The guys are in the garage. When they come back, we're grilling."

She looped her arm through mine and pulled me in the direction of the Old Ladies.

"Hey, Linden," Mia said with a smile.

"Hi," I said.

"Sit," Rachel said, getting up and pulling over a chair.

"Thanks." I sat and took a drink of my wine.

A woman I didn't recognize said, "Hi, I didn't get a chance to meet you the other night at the clubhouse party." Her hair was teased to high heaven, and she had a rocking body. "I'm Darcy."

"Nice to meet you."

"So," Joni began, taking the empty chair next to me. "What do you think of the house?"

I looked at her and then gazed at the other Old Ladies. All of their expressions were casually blank. "It's got great bones," I said diplomatically.

Peals of laughter echoed in the air.

"It's a fucking mess!" Joni said with a snort.

"You did tell me it was a fixer upper," I reminded her.

"About a month ago, Zip surprised me by handing me the keys. I just about strangled him when we walked in. But he said when he saw it, he knew it was perfect for us. We're going to breathe life back into the house."

"I love that so much," I said.

"Zip wanted a nest," Mia said with a grin.

"Took him long enough," Joni said dryly, fiddling with the simple, unadorned gold band on her ring finger. She looked at me. "We started with the patio and the upstairs because that's where we spend most of our time. The downstairs is a shitshow, and I wince every time I see it."

"You'll get it sorted, and it will be beautiful," I assured her.

"You guys have gotten a lot done in a short amount of time," Darcy said. "This patio is a work of art."

"That's what happens when you have prospects at your disposal." Joni shook her head. "I'm not above using young brawn to speed this process along."

Rachel laughed. "Young, shirtless, brawn, yes? Please tell me they walk around shirtless and wearing tool belts."

"Perhaps," Joni said with a devilish smile.

"I still haven't seen the upstairs," Rachel said.

"Later, after we eat, I'll give you the tour," Joni said.

I looked out across the lawn to stare at the kids and gestured at them with my chin. "Who's who?"

"The tall lanky one is Silas. He's mine," Mia said.

"The other two are mine. Cam and Lily," Darcy explained.

Allison adjusted the sleeping baby in her arms who was swaddled and protected from the chill. "This is Tank."

"Tank," I repeated.

She grinned. "His given name is Jones, but he was ten pounds when he was born, so…"

Rachel shuddered. "I just had the worst visual of what's going to happen to my vagina."

"You?" Mia demanded. "I have to go through it first." She rubbed a hand across her round belly. "Have you seen Colt? He's a beast. Kid's gonna be like Godzilla."

"Reap is not a small man either," Rachel pointed out.

"None of them are," Joni said.

The guys came around from the side of the house. Colt and Reap were carting a long folding table, and they set it up on the far edge of the patio. "Doc," Boxer greeted, wrapping me in a bear hug from behind. "How long have you been here?"

I looked up at him and smiled. "A few minutes."

He kissed me on the lips, and I thought for a moment about being embarrassed, but these people had already witnessed Boxer pulling me away from a party and disappearing for hours.

There was no point being self-conscious, and I chose to ignore the stares in our direction.

"Are you guys done doing manly things in the garage?" Joni asked Zip.

"Yeah, we're done," he said with a smirk. "Let's grill."

The guys wandered over to the barbecue and bar area, but Boxer remained. "Aren't you going to join your male brethren?" I asked him.

"Nah. I'd rather stay here and listen to girl talk. You were about to discuss me, weren't you?" Boxer flashed a teasing grin.

I looked up at him. "How am I supposed to exaggerate your manly attributes if you're sitting right here?"

"She's kidding about the exaggeration. I need no exaggeration. Joni can vouch for that, can't you?"

Boxer winked at Joni who then slugged him in his upper arm. "Ow."

"That didn't hurt," she said with a roll of her eyes.

"Yeah. You're right. It didn't hurt." His smile was strained, and I realized she'd punched him in his injured arm.

She didn't know he'd been shot.

A heaviness settled over my heart. I didn't like the secrecy, but it wasn't my choice about what to share with the Old Ladies.

Joni rose from her seat. "I need some help grabbing the burgers and hot dogs."

"I'll help," I volunteered immediately.

"Me too," Darcy said.

I hopped up, but before I could follow Darcy and Joni into the house, Boxer's arms went around me, and he pulled me flush to his chest. We met each other's gaze, and something passed between us in that moment. He raised his brows, and I shrugged. Now was not the time or the place to have it out about my feelings on how the Tarnished Angels ran their club or handled the flow of information to the Old Ladies. And more importantly, it wasn't the time to talk about how he'd steamrolled me and flat out told me I was going to have to live with it.

He ran a hand down the side of my face and pulled me closer for a quick kiss before releasing me.

On my way inside, I caught Mia's snarky grin. I stuck my tongue out at her, causing her to laugh.

Joni was taking out platters of hamburger patties and hot dogs from the refrigerator and handing them off to Darcy who proceeded to remove the cling wrap. There were different types of salads, platters of fruit, and trays of baked goods.

"How many people are you expecting?" I asked in amazement.

"The Idaho boys are coming over a bit later, but they're hanging with the younger Tarnished Angels—the ones that don't have wives or girlfriends," Joni explained. "The prospects aren't allowed to come. They're on club-house guard duty."

I frowned. "Guard duty?"

"It's not as sinister as it sounds," Darcy assured me. "But we have to keep an eye on things. Be alert."

"Right," I murmured. "Makes sense."

Only it didn't. Not to someone who'd never had to think about things like *guard duty*.

After Boxer getting shot, things like that shouldn't have surprised me, but I wasn't there yet.

"So…" Joni handed me a condiment caddy. "You and Boxer…"

"Me and Boxer what?" I prodded.

"You and Boxer were getting handsy in public, weren't you?" Joni asked.

"I—er—um—"

Darcy cackled. "Oh, I love this. I love this *so* much. But now is not the time for this. I want no interruptions from children or a man walking in on our girl talk. Plus, I want wine while I listen to all the juicy details."

My cheeks flamed. Though I was glad to be included in girl talk, and about to be subjected to their curiosity, I was in no way planning on kissing and telling.

"You're terrible, Darce," Joni said with a laugh.

"Me? You're the one that brought up the two of them getting handsy. I so need the dirt!"

"Why? It's not like you have to live vicariously," Joni pointed out. "Gray still looks at you like you're a steak dinner."

Darcy beamed. "He does, doesn't he? Still, it's fun to hear about the start of something when its new and exciting. Gray still excites me, but after years together and two children, it's just not the same."

Joni sighed dreamily. "I can't wait for all the phases I'll have with Zip. But right now, I'm enjoying the newly married phase."

We headed out back to the patio, carting platters and bowls and putting them onto the table. The grill was heating up and like most parties, the guys congregated in one area and the women in another.

A lanky boy sat next to Mia, and she absently brushed his dark hair away from his forehead. She looked at him with love and adoration. Because he was a kid, and a boy no less, he immediately ran his own hand through his hair to make it flop forward again.

"Can I have a cookie?" he asked.

"Just one," she said. "I don't want you spoiling your dinner."

"Mama!" A little blonde girl yelled as she dropped her bean bag and ran to Darcy, wrapping her arms around her mother's legs. "If Silas can have a cookie, can I have one?"

"Me too?" her brother asked, following at a slower pace.

"Sorry," Mia said to Darcy.

"You guys can split one," Darcy said to her children.

"That's not fair," Cam whined. "Silas gets his own cookie."

"Silas is not my child. You are. It's half a cookie or no cookie at all," Darcy said in a firm tone.

Silas shot up from the couch and raced to the table, Cam and Lily not far behind him.

"He's tall," I said to Mia.

She sighed with maternal pride. "And getting taller every day. Smart as a whip too."

Baby Tank started to cry, and Allison got up from her seat with a sigh. "I just got comfortable."

"I'll change him," Torque voiced, coming to his wife and son.

"No, he needs to be fed, too," Allison said. "I can change him."

"I'll come with you." Torque grabbed the diaper bag by Allison's feet, and they disappeared into the house.

"Did you ever think you'd see the day when Torque would volunteer to change the diapers and just sit there while his Old Lady breastfed his kid?" Rachel asked.

Mia shook her head. "You know him better than I do. Though he is finally warming to me."

"Having Tank softened him," Darcy said. "Don't let him hear me say that, but it's true."

Mia's brown eyes shined with happiness. "I can't wait to see Colt hold our daughter in his arms. There's something so beautiful about seeing a burly, tatted man cradling an infant."

Rachel sighed. "Yeah, I can't wait to see Reap do the same thing with ours."

"I need a refill," I said suddenly. "Does anyone need anything?"

"I'm good," Mia said.

"Me too," Rachel added.

I escaped the family and father talk, but their conversation hit me deep. They were all so happily settled down with wild and dangerous men, yet it was clear they wouldn't have chosen anything different. My childhood life had been nothing but fights between my parents, and then my father left. Listening to Mia and the other Old Ladies talk about their men made me realize how much I wanted the same thing. A loving partnership, a family, people I could count on. The insight walloped me hard and fast. I hadn't expected it.

"Hey, darlin'," Boxer crooned, sidling up next to me.

Startled, I jumped a bit and sloshed a few drops of wine over the side of the cup onto my hand.

"Sorry." Boxer took my fingers and brought them to his lips, and with his tongue, lapped up the wine.

My insides heated from the look of promise in his eyes.

"You okay?" he asked, not releasing my hand.

I nodded.

He stared at me for a moment and then he said, "I challenge you to a game of cornhole."

"You like your games."

"Some of them."

I knew we weren't talking about cornhole.

"You sure you want to challenge me to a lawn game? I'm from Watch Hill. Lawn games are a big deal where I'm from."

"I'll take my chances."

# Chapter 25

BOXER TOSSED a beanbag and it landed in the hole. He flashed me an arrogant grin. "Are you having a good time?"

I nodded and then stepped up to throw my beanbag. "Everyone's been wonderful."

"Have they squeezed you for information yet?"

"No, they're saving that for later. When the sun goes down, the kids are conked out, and the menfolk are elsewhere, I'm pretty sure that's when they're gonna grill me."

He tossed his second beanbag, sending it close, but it didn't fall in. "You sure you're okay?"

I swallowed, wishing I'd brought my glass of wine with me. "Yeah, it's just…"

"What?"

"The way they talk about their men and children. It's very… I've never been around a functional family. I didn't grow up in one. You—and the Tarnished Angels—are smashing everything I thought I knew about what families are supposed to look like."

He dropped his beanbag and then cradled my cheeks

in his hands. His eyes bored into mine, intense, unwavering. "Life is worth living. Grabbing it by the balls and owning it is all there is. Living the way we do…we all know we could die at any moment. So, when we find something good to hold onto, we don't let it go." He pressed his forehead to mine. "I know this is a lot, and I know it's fast. But, darlin', I've never met anyone who needs a family more than you. And if you let us, we can be your family.

"Your dad left you," he said quietly. "That fuckery is buried deep inside you. I get it, Doc. You're afraid I'm gonna bail." He leaned forward. "I'm gonna tell you a secret. I'm not going anywhere, Linden. You want to push me away, go ahead. Try. I'll still be here when you're done pushing."

I swallowed. "Why? Why would you want to put up with me and all my crap?"

He studied me for a long quiet moment. "Because, Linden Ward, you're worth it."

*You're worth it.*

His words swelled through the broken part of my psyche like ripples from a pebble in a pond.

I didn't know what to say to him because I didn't know what to say to myself. Normally, I would find a quiet place so I could sift through my thoughts, but I was at a party.

And I had no desire to leave.

We stared at each other, lost in the moment. I was unaware of everything around me, except for this man and in his own words, a declaration.

"Food's ready!" Zip yelled from the grill, shattering the intensity of the moment.

I dropped the bean bag. Boxer took my hand and led me back toward the patio where Zip was sliding cooked hamburger patties onto plates. Children buzzed around Darcy. They were hungry and very vocal about it. Once the kids were placated with food, the adults began to fix their own plates.

"Babe," Colt called to Mia. "What do you want?"

"One hot dog and one hamburger with the works," she shouted back.

I grinned at Colt's caring concern for his pregnant wife.

Boxer stayed close, one step behind me as I made myself a plate of food. I located my glass of wine and then went to join Mia and Colt. Boxer took a seat on the u-shaped couch right next to me.

Conversation was easy and flowed just like the wine and beer. I marveled at the way everyone interacted with one another. They were fascinating to observe. It was more than just camaraderie. It went deeper. Maybe it was because they weren't of the same blood, but a patched together unit, a chosen clan.

I saw Silas and Reap tease and joke with one another, and then Reap ruffled Silas's hair. It was at that moment that I realized this wasn't just a single family, but a village. If Darcy and Gray were occupied and unable to tend to the needs of their children, someone else stepped in. It went like this as long as I watched.

*And if you let us, we can be your family.*

Boxer's words resonated like a gong inside me.

The Tarnished Angels would embrace me as their own.

No reservations, no hesitation, because Boxer had chosen me.

"I've got to pee," Mia announced.

"Thanks for that," Zip stated with a grin, playing with the label on his beer bottle.

Colt helped his wife stand and then Joni hopped up. "Tour of the upstairs?"

The other women nodded and rose.

"Linden?" Joni looked at me. "Do you want to see the upstairs?"

I smiled at her. "Love to."

Boxer took my hand before I left and gave it a squeeze.

"Why don't you guys get the fire pit ready," Joni suggested.

"Woman, why are you always putting me to work?" Zip demanded.

"Because you like it when I tell you what to do," she sassed.

He gave her such a heated look that I didn't need to guess where their banter would lead.

"That's my sister," Colt remarked dryly.

"I put a ring on it," Zip stated. "I can do what I want."

"Let's get out of here before they pound on their chests like gorillas," Joni said to me.

"Excellent idea." I dropped Boxer's hand, but I couldn't stop myself from touching his shoulder before heading inside the house.

Mia was nowhere to be found. The other Old Ladies were in the kitchen, waiting to follow Joni.

A hallway door opened, and Mia stepped out of the bathroom, and then we all trekked to the second floor. The walls were in the middle of being stripped of paint. Joni pushed opened a bedroom door and waved us all inside.

"Ah, I get it now," Rachel said. "You really did start with the main bedroom."

"And bathroom," she said. "We didn't want to start on anything until we had the pipes and electricity inspected. Zip was ready to gut the place down the studs, but luckily it didn't have to come to that. And seriously, thank God for the prospects. There's no way any of this would've come together without their help."

A black and white photo of Joni and Zip hung over the

bed. She was in a wedding dress, and he was wearing his leather cut with a white shirt and black tie, and he was looking at her with love and naked adoration. Zip's expression stated that he was deeply devoted to Joni.

"I love that photo," Darcy commented.

Joni gently touched the dark frame. "Me too." She shook her head and grinned. "We couldn't agree on a wall color for our bedroom. I wanted blue; Zip wanted gray. We settled for a blue gray."

"You two are vile," Rachel teased with a grin.

Mia ran her hand across the darker blue gray coverlet on the king-sized bed. "I'm slowly phasing out the dude fortress decor in our house, but Colt is stubborn."

"That man gives you everything," Darcy said, laughing. "He really won't let you re-decorate?"

"He's really attached to the brown furniture." She sighed. "I'm hoping having a girl will eventually turn the tide."

"Gray swore when we had Lily that he wouldn't change. Guess who Lily asks to play princess tea party with? I'll give you a hint, it's not me." Darcy shook her head. "Tarnished Angels and their daughters."

"Babies melt that hard place inside you," Allison said. "I'd never call Torque squishy, but sometimes I see him watching Tank…"

A daydream flickered in my mind. A picture, a flash, of Boxer cradling his own infant.

I firmly rejected the vision.

"Soft and squishy with their children," Darcy said. "But not in the bedroom."

"True story," Mia said with a laugh.

"So, am I allowed to completely change the conversation?" Rachel asked.

"Yup," Joni said.

"Are your men acting different? Reap's been distant," Rachel announced. "It started a week ago, I think. Something's eating away at him. I thought he'd be over it by now, but…"

"I was going to ask you guys the same thing. Torque's been working out twice a day, hard. He keeps yelling while he's working out like he's trying to become Superman or something," Allison said. "He says he's fine, but he's clearly not. Whenever I ask him about it, he makes up some bullshit excuse and changes the subject."

"What about you?" Rachel asked Joni. "Has Zip been acting different?"

Joni frowned, and then nodded. "Kind of absent. Like I'll say something to him and then have to repeat myself. He's been smoking again."

Rachel looked at Mia. "What about Colt?"

Mia paused, a frown flashing across her forehead. "Definitely strange behavior. He was sitting in the nursery —in the rocking chair, holding a stuffed animal with this distant look on his face. Alone, with a bottle of bourbon…"

"Okay, that's odd," Rachel murmured. "Linden?"

"Hmm?"

"I know you just started dating Boxer, but you're close to him. Anything?" Rachel asked.

"Can you really ask that?" Darcy asked. "He hasn't really been the same since he got out of the hospital."

"I know," Mia agreed. "He doesn't look like he's being particularly distant where you are concerned, Linden."

I hesitated a moment and then said, "He's not."

"I'm sensing a *but*," Joni said.

"But even as light and carefree as Boxer comes across, he's been…" I paused, searching for the right word. "Serious."

"Serious?" Mia repeated.

I nodded.

"Serious how?" Rachel wondered aloud.

"Serious like, he wants something more from his life than he previously thought."

Joni grinned. "I never thought I'd see the day when Boxer wanted to settle down."

"Little Boxer babies!" Mia shrieked in excitement.

"Whoa there," I said, holding up my hand. "You guys are getting a little ahead of yourselves."

"You don't want little Boxer babies?" Darcy asked. "You've seen your new boyfriend, haven't you?"

"I haven't thought about it," I said.

"Seriously?" Joni demanded. "You're how old?"

I raised my brows. "Thirty. What does that have to do with anything?"

"Your biological clock isn't ticking?" Joni asked.

"Not everyone is like you, Joni. Hungry for biker seed," Mia drawled with a laugh.

Joni shrugged, and then grinned. "What can I say? I've been after Zip since we were teenagers." She pushed open a side door in the bedroom that didn't lead to the bathroom. It was a smaller room, and the walls were painted a sunny yellow. It was devoid of furniture, but a rug with a collage of animals graced the wooden floor.

"What are you going to do with this room?" Rachel asked.

When Joni didn't reply, all attention turned to her. Her eyes were shining, and her smile stretched across her entire face.

"Oh my God," Mia breathed. "Are you?"

Joni nodded.

Mia squealed and nearly jumped on Joni, embracing her.

"You're pregnant!" Rachel shrieked.

Tank, who'd been asleep in a sling across Allison's body, let out a wail. Allison shushed him while moving toward Joni and enveloping her in a one-armed hug.

Darcy was next and gave Joni a side hug. "When did you find out?"

"We confirmed it yesterday," she said.

"But the room…" I waved around the area. "It looks like this was started weeks ago."

Joni nodded. "As soon as we got the bedroom done, Zip started on this room. It's all I've wanted. To have a family with him."

The emotion swimming in her eyes made my mashed down feelings surge to the surface. "Congratulations," I said, but it sounded strangled to my own ears.

No one else noticed. They were too busy hugging and talking about Joni's good news.

"What are you doing?" Joni asked, staring at me from a few feet away.

"What do you mean?"

"Get in here. It's group hug time," she demanded.

Rachel grabbed my arm and hauled me toward them and before I knew it, I was one of them, celebrating a milestone moment in their lives.

Mia hastily brushed tears from her eyes. "I'm so happy for you. Like really, really happy."

"Me too," Rachel added. "Shit, Mia. You're making *me* cry."

We batted away our tears, laughing and crying in tandem. I'd never felt such acceptance.

"Come on," Joni said once she'd recovered. "Let's get back downstairs. I need chocolate."

"I need a wine refill," Darcy said.

Just as we made it to the patio, the guys erupted into

cheers. Zip beamed ear to ear as Gray slapped him on the back.

"I'm guessing Zip told them about your good news," I said.

"Looks that way," Joni agreed.

Colt swooped in and grabbed his sister, nearly crushing her in a bear hug. "I'm gonna be an uncle!"

Joni was swarmed by the Tarnished Angels. Boxer gave her a hug, said something in her ear that made her laugh, and then released her. He came over to me and put his arm around my shoulder, pulling me into his side.

The kids dropped their beanbags and ran up to the patio from the lawn, wondering about the commotion. When Darcy told them what was going on they rushed to Joni and clambered for her attention. They were just as excited and as happy as the adults.

As the sun set and those that could drink toasted to Joni and Zip's news, I felt something inside of me pry loose. There was such beauty here. Love and family. Happy children and laughter among friends. It sounded simple, easy. I'd been embraced as one of them. But now I knew what I'd been missing, and I never wanted to go back to a cold, empty life. My career lit me up, it challenged me, provided me the intellectual stimulation to grow my skills, but I couldn't go home to it. It didn't provide the nurturing warmth I so desperately craved but didn't realize I needed.

"The Idaho boys and the young'uns aren't coming," Zip said, putting his cell phone away. "They're having far too much fun where they are."

"You mean they don't want to hang out with a bunch of old married people?" Mia said. "Shocking."

"Who are you calling old?" Darcy asked.

"Not you, darling. You're forever young." Mia flashed a grin.

"Mia, will you braid my hair?" Lily asked, plopping down in front of Mia's lawn chair.

"Sure thing, Lily Burger."

"We're gonna get out of here," Torque said. "Allison is falling asleep."

"It's past my bedtime," Allison said as she stood.

One by one, couples started to leave, until it was just Boxer and me hanging out with Joni and Zip. He put another log on the fire.

"How did you find this place?" I asked.

"I talked to people in town," Zip said. "That's how you find all the best stuff. The owner lived out of state. I sent him a letter, and a few weeks later he called and sold it to me for what I offered."

"It reminds me of the house in *It's a Wonderful Life*," Joni said, brushing a kiss to Zip's cheek. "Full of possibilities. We get to make it our own, which I love. But it feels like… I don't know. It's a home, right? But this house was here before us. It'll be here after us. We're just caretakers for a period in its life."

Her poignant words struck my heart. I wasn't sure if it was the wine or the hours of spending time with Boxer and his Tarnished Angels family, but tears sprung to my eyes.

Joni leaned her head against Zip's shoulder and stared into the flames. He placed his cheek against her hair and suddenly, I felt like I was intruding.

"That's my cue," I said, making a move to stand. I stomped my feet and rubbed feeling back into my tailbone. "You guys look like you want to be alone."

Zip grinned. "You pay attention. I like that."

Boxer stood up and grasped my hand in his. "I'm out too."

Joni looked like she was about to get up, but I waved her down. "Stay. Enjoy the moment."

She snuggled against Zip. "You fit in well, Linden."

"Do I?" I glanced at Boxer and then back to Zip and Joni.

"Yeah, Doc. You're okay," Zip said.

Boxer and I walked hand in hand toward the house. "Did you have fun?"

"I did. A lot of fun. They're special. All of them."

"Yeah. They are."

I followed him home. After parking on the street, I cut the engine and then climbed out. I hit my clicker and walked toward the front porch steps.

"Bed?" he asked, as he closed the door and locked it. He dropped his keys into the bowl on the dark wood table.

I pushed him against the wall, and then my fingers went to his fly. "Floor."

We were on the carpet of the living room on a pile of blankets and pillows. The light of the hallway was still ablaze.

I propped up on one elbow so I could look down at him. I ran a hand across his scruff, enjoying the raspy feel of it against my fingertips. He turned his head and kissed my palm, but he didn't say anything more.

"Every time I'm with you, the Tarnished Angels, the Old Ladies, I feel…" I trailed off.

"What?"

"Like I belong."

He smiled. "You do belong."

"I didn't think I would." I paused. "It's not the clothes or the way of life. It's what's inside a person. They hugged me like I was one of them. Joni included me in her reveal of the nursery. That feels... I don't even know how to put it."

"It's called tribe, Doc. You've got a tribe."

"They hugged me. We were upstairs in the room that's going to be the nursery when Joni told everyone the news. They pulled me into their group, Boxer. Like I was one of them. Like I belonged." I snuggled back down. "They asked about you."

"Of course they did."

"No, not in a joking way. About the night you came to me. They said their men..."

"What?"

"Have been acting different. Like, across the board all the guys are bothered by something."

"What did you tell them?"

"I was evasive."

"You kept my confidence."

"I did," I agreed.

"Thank you," he said quietly.

I looked up at him. "You can trust me, Boxer. Like I trust you."

# Chapter 26

"I'll call when I can," Boxer said. "It'll probably be sporadic, though."

I nodded. "I get it. I work tomorrow afternoon."

"Feel free to text me any time. Pictures are great, too. Preferably dirty stuff. I like the dirty stuff."

Laughing, I wrapped my arms around his neck. "I'm well aware."

One of his hands grabbed my behind and the other snaked up my shirt and gently caressed my breast.

A zing of pleasure vibrated through my core. "Boxer, the boys are waiting for you."

He sighed and slowly removed his hands from my skin. "I've already got plans for you when I get back."

"Make a list," I teased. "And I'll make sure to stock your fridge with energy drinks."

Boxer let out a booming laugh. "Damn, woman. You sure do make it hard to walk away from you."

I stood on my toes so I could kiss him. Our relationship was new, and we were in the throes of pure obsession with one another. I hoped like hell it never waned. How did people stay together and not grow bored?

"Linden," he growled against my lips. "When my tongue is in your mouth, I'd appreciate it if your brain could get the damn memo and stop thinking."

"You and me both, boyo," I joked. I pushed against his chest.

He reached for my hand and turned over my palm, dropping a set of keys into it.

"What's this?" I asked in confusion.

"Keys to my place."

"Keys to your—"

"Don't get all weird on me," he warned.

I stared at the keys for a moment. "You sure you're ready for this?"

"I'm sure." He grinned. "The question is, are *you* ready for this. And will you actually use them?"

"I haven't decided yet," I said slowly.

"It's not that big of a deal."

"It's a *huge* deal—especially since you're the guy that hasn't had a woman spend the night ever, and now you're giving me keys."

"Linden?"

"Yeah?"

"Use the keys or don't. It's your choice. I just wanted you to know that I'm okay with you being here when I'm not."

I sighed and met his gaze. I wondered if I was looking all moony-eyed. "Safe travels."

With a grin and a wave, he picked up his bag, fit perfectly for a motorcycle, and left. A few moments later, his bike roared to life.

I quickly cleaned up the remains of our breakfast and

did the dishes. As I was sliding into my jeans, my phone rang. A stupid blast of hope shot through my chest, thinking it might've been Boxer already calling just to hear my voice.

It wasn't Boxer. It was Freddy.

"Hey, girl," she said. "Do you want to grab a drink tonight?"

"Ah, I'd love to," I said, "but I'm in Waco."

"You're in Waco? Well, well, well, that's interesting."

"It's not *that* interesting."

"Let me guess: You're deep in lust with Boxer and never want to leave his side."

"Would you think less of me if I said yes?"

She let out a laugh. "No, actually. I think it's adorable, and I want to hear all about it. And it just so happens I'm already in Waco."

"You are? Why?"

"The woman who owns Leather and Ink got in some new pieces and she asked me to model them for the website. I'm currently standing outside of a warehouse with a camera lens pointed at me."

"So let's definitely grab drinks when you're done. And then you can crash here at Boxer's tonight and not have to drive back to Dallas until tomorrow."

"He won't mind?"

"He's not here," I said. "He left this morning to head up to Idaho."

"And you're staying at his place without him?"

"Yeah."

"This just got serious."

I snorted. "Tell me about it."

"Shelly's. Seven o'clock."

Boxer's house was devoid of all adult food. And even though I had to head back to Dallas the next day, I thought it would be nice if he came home to a full fridge. Maybe then he'd stop relying on the Old Ladies to bring him food.

A few hours later, I returned from my shopping excursion. It was strange, walking into his place and not having him there. But it smelled like him. I wondered when it would smell like *us*. I smacked my forehead.

*Full speed ahead in the commitment and feelings department.*

He called when I was putting vegetables into the crisper.

"What are you doing?" he asked in way of greeting.

"Stocking your refrigerator. Have you ever heard of a vegetable?"

He paused for a second and then he said, "You're putting groceries in my refrigerator?"

I swore I could hear his grin in his tone.

"Yes."

"Domestic."

"I don't want you to die from lack of vitamins. The Old Ladies have been too soft on you. Casseroles and lasagnas are delicious, but you need some leafy greens in your life."

"Woman," he grumbled. "If you make me eat spinach, I will make your life a living hell."

"It's just because I want you to live a long time," I protested.

"Damn it," he muttered. "If you make it, I'll try it."

"Deal."

Excitement fluttered in my belly at our banter.

"So, do you miss me yet?" he teased. When I didn't reply fast enough for his liking, he pressed, "Linden?"

"Yeah," I croaked. "I miss you."

"Are we gonna talk about shit when I get home?"

"What kind of shit?" I evaded.

"The kind of shit that starts with L and ends with OVE."

"Oh look, the oven timer is dinging. Gotta go. Ride safe!" I quickly hung up with him and set my phone aside on the counter like it was a snake that wanted to lurch up and bite me.

A few hours later, with big curls, heavy lipstick, and tight jeans, I called a cab from Boxer's place. Shelly's was a brick building, with a large parking lot and a bright neon sign. When I entered the bar, the vintage jukebox was playing *The Waiting* by Tom Petty, and the women behind the bar were twirling bottles and lighting shots on fire.

I looked through the cluster of people and found Freddy at the pool table, nursing a bottle of beer and talking to a tall, broad, dark-haired man with heavily tatted arms that bulged with muscles beneath his army green T-shirt.

"Hey," I greeted as I approached.

Freddy turned to look at me and grinned, wrapping an arm around my shoulder. "Linden, meet Roman."

Roman held out his hand as his warm brown eyes swept over me. "So, this is Boxer's woman."

I rolled my eyes. "Does everyone in this town know Boxer?"

"Most of the women do," Roman said with a grin.

"Shut up, Roman," Freddy said with a laugh. "Linden is aware of Boxer's reputation, but they're committed now."

"How committed?" Roman inquired. "Committed like, I'll be seeing you in my chair and inking you?"

Frowning, I looked to Freddy for an explanation.

"Roman and his brothers own Three Kings—a tattoo parlor that does all the tats for the Tarnished Angels."

"Not a tattoo parlor, *the* tattoo parlor. You want the best art? You come to us."

"His brother Homer is going to do my back," Freddy said.

A man with the same shade of hair as Roman sidled up next to him and leaned against the pool table.

"This is my younger brother, Virgil," Roman introduced.

Virgil flashed a grin. "Nice to meet ya."

"Roman, Virgil, and Homer," I said. "Interesting names."

"Our dad's name is Horace," Virgil stated. "Has a thing for the classics. You guys want to play a game of pool?"

"Thanks," Freddy said, "but we're going to pass. Linden and I are having a girls' night."

We said our goodbyes to Roman and Virgil. "You grab us a booth," I said. "I'll get the first round."

I went up to the bar, maneuvering through the throng of people that seemed to grow thicker since I'd arrived. When I got to the bar, I waited patiently for the petite brunette to turn and grab my order. She swiveled, and I grinned in recognition.

"Linden!" she greeted in surprise.

"Mia." I laughed. "What are you doing here?"

"I work here. Well, I own the place."

"You *own* this place? Then what are you doing behind the bar?" I demanded. "You should be at home, resting those swollen ankles."

"Heard loud and clear, Doc." She chuckled. "One of my bartenders called in sick. Besides, Silas is over at a friend's house for dinner and homework, and I was lonely. I never thought I'd be the type that wanted to spend all my time with my husband, but there you have it. What are you doing here?"

"I'm here with Freddy. She was in Waco for the day and she suggested Shelly's."

"Freddy's here?" she asked. "Damn, I must've been in the office when she came in. I didn't see her." She quickly poured two shots of tequila, gave me a plate of limes and two saltshakers, and placed them on a tray. "These are on me."

"You don't have to do that."

"Sure I do. What do you want to drink?"

"A pint of something good."

"I got ya." She removed a glass from the fridge. "Old Ladies girls' night this week at my house."

"Great. Sounds fun," I said, reaching into my back pocket and pulling out some cash.

"On me," Mia said when I tried to pay her.

"No way," I said with a laugh.

"Family discount." She winked.

My heart warmed. "Thanks. Promise me you'll take it easy? Don't lift anything heavy? Sit when you're tired?"

"You sound like Colt," she said in amusement. "I promise."

I gave her my well-practiced doctor stare.

"I said I promise. Yeesh."

With a nod, I grabbed the tray of drinks and carted them back to the booth.

"What's this?" Freddy asked.

"Tequila. Courtesy of Mia."

"That was nice of her."

"I haven't done shots in years," I muttered.

"It's just one. Come on."

A few moments later, I was sucking on a lime, the tequila heating my belly. "Okay, that wasn't so bad."

"Right?" She smiled. "I knew you were a tequila girl."

"I'm trying all sorts of new things." I reached into my clutch and pulled out the keys Boxer had given me. I tossed them onto the table in front of Freddy. "He gave me keys."

"I knew it. I *so* knew it. I knew when he met a woman who turned his head, he'd be insta-mated."

My brow furrowed.

"You don't want him insta-mated?"

"It's not that," I said slowly, "it's just—well, I have feelings for him."

"Yeah."

"No, like, the *L* word type of feelings."

"Well, duh." She rolled her eyes. "Charming, flirty Boxer is one thing. Committed, attentive Boxer is like a battering ram to your heart. You didn't stand a chance."

"I definitely didn't stand a chance," I agreed. "I'm not sure I trust it."

"No? Why not?"

"It's not him. Just, my own stuff I'm trying to work through," I assured her. "How did you and Boxer meet? I'm curious."

"You know Allison, right? Torque's Old Lady?"

"Allison? Yeah, of course."

"I was college suitemates with her cousin, Sadie. We went to a party, and someone drugged my drink."

"Oh, Freddy," I said in sympathy.

"I had all of my clothes on," she hastened to assure me. "When I woke up the next morning, I mean. Sadie had called Torque, and Boxer came with him. Boxer had given me his number and said if I needed anything, to give him a call. A few weeks later, I did just that. He got me the job at Pinky's and I quit school."

"He never said a word to me about any of that," I said.

"No, he wouldn't have, would he? Aside from keeping confidences, he's not the kind of guy who wants accolades for being a good guy."

"The best guy."

She smiled. "The best guy."

Mia swept by our table, a hand across her belly. "Hi, Freddy."

"Hi," Freddy replied. "Thanks for the shots."

"Sure thing. Look, I'm in a bind. Silas is at a friend's house. Danny's mom just called and told me Silas has a fever and is throwing up. I have to pick him up, but we're short staffed."

Freddy sighed. "You want me to jump behind the bar, don't you?"

"Please?" Mia begged. "You weren't seriously thinking of making the drive back to Dallas tonight anyway, were you?"

"No. I was gonna crash at Boxer's with Linden," Freddy said.

"Boxer gave me keys," I explained to Mia.

She grinned. "Man, I wish I had time for that story, but I really do need to get going. There's an apartment slash storeroom over the bar. It's got all the necessities. You can totally sleep there so you don't have to drive when you get off. Please, Freddy? Tips should be really good tonight."

Freddy looked at me. "You mind?"

I shook my head. "No. I don't mind."

"Angel, darling, savior," Mia said, bending down to side hug Freddy. "Come with me and I'll introduce you to Danica, and she'll give you a run down."

"Dinner?" Freddy asked me as she slid out of the booth. "Soon?"

I smiled. "That sounds good."

"Come on," Mia said. "Let's get you sorted behind the bar so I can pick up my sick kid. See ya later, Linden."

I waved to them and watched them head to the bar. Since I had no one to hang out with anymore, and I didn't want to sit and drink alone, I pulled out my cell phone and requested an Uber.

The bar was getting busier and louder. I didn't want to be that person who took up a booth just for me, so I grabbed my nearly finished pint and purse and vacated my seat. I quickly downed the rest of the beer and then placed the empty glass on the end of the bar.

"Freddy!" I called. "Bye!"

She looked up from serving a customer just long enough to smile and nod.

I headed for the front door and stepped out into the night. I breathed in the cool air and wished I'd thought to wear a jacket, but it hadn't gone with my outfit.

My phone vibrated at the bottom of my purse, and I reached in and grabbed it. When I took it out, I saw Boxer's name flashing across the screen. I wandered around to the side of the building, farther back away from the front door so I could have some privacy.

I answered my phone, a smile on my face. "Hi."

"Hey, Doc. Whatcha doing? Are you at home sniffing my shirts?"

"Ha. You wish. I'm at Shelly's with Freddy, but I'm waiting for an Uber now."

"It's a little early to be calling it a night."

"Mia was working the bar, but Silas is sick, and she has to pick him up. Freddy's filling in, so I'm leaving and heading to your house."

"Are you now?"

"Don't make a thing of it," I warned. "I spook easy."

He chuckled. "Sorry your night got cut short."

"It's okay. I wouldn't mind taking off these tight jeans."

"Tight jeans? How tight are we talking?"

"Like a second skin."

"Woman, you must be trying to send me to an early grave. What else are you wearing?"

I told him.

"Yeah, it's official. I'm crazy about you."

I grinned even though he couldn't see me.

"Text me when you get home, okay?" he said.

"Okay."

I hung up but didn't put my cell back in my purse just yet. I leaned against the brick wall and sighed.

"You mind if I smoke?"

I was startled, not having heard someone approach. I hoped he hadn't been eavesdropping. The young man with lank brown hair, average in height, had a pack of cigarettes and a lighter in his hands. He was halfway in shadow, even with the lights from the parking lot.

"No, go ahead," I said, wanting to head back toward the street.

"Thanks." He grinned, showing crooked teeth. "I'm trying to quit. It's not working out."

I nodded absently, not really wanting to get drawn into a conversation with a stranger. My phone pinged with a text letting me know my Uber driver was just around the block.

He puffed on the cigarette and released a cloud of smoke. "Can I buy you a drink?"

"Thanks for the offer, but my Uber just got here. Have a good one," I said.

He moved like a jungle cat, swift and determined, clamping one of his hands around my wrist before I could even turn, and then using the other to punch me in the stomach so hard I thought I was going to pass out.

While I was gasping for breath, he grabbed me by the hair with both hands and yanked me toward the bushes. I couldn't scream for help because I couldn't get enough air into my lungs. He smashed an elbow into my jaw.

*Lights out.*

# Chapter 27

My body lurched, jostling me awake. I cracked open an eye to darkness. I blinked a few times, trying to clear my vision. Scratchy fabric covered my eyes, and the smell of heavy-duty tape filtered through my nose. I lifted my hands to remove the cloth shielding my gaze—only to find that I couldn't use my arms because they were bound behind my back.

I struggled to hoist myself up, the plastic ties digging into my wrists. My skin burned with pain. Panic swirled inside me like a tornado.

I couldn't see. I could barely breathe. And I had no control over my own body. My jaw throbbed from where I'd taken an elbow to the chin and my belly cramped from being punched.

*Who had kidnapped me? Why?*
*Did it matter?*
*No.*

I listened. It was quiet, except for the sound of rubber on asphalt. After a moment, I heard the crinkling of foil and the audible munch of food.

"Dude," a man barked. "Can you not treat my car like a dumping ground? Fuck."

"Where the fuck do you want me to put it? Not like there's a trash can around here," a second man said.

"I don't know. Stuff it in the door or something."

A man sighed and then I heard the crumpling of a bag. "How much fucking longer?"

"What are you? A six-year-old asking if we're there yet?"

"I gotta piss. Pull over," the passenger whined.

The driver cursed. "An hour ago, you needed a soda."

"Yeah, well, we needed gas."

Neither of them seemed to have noticed that I was awake and I was moving around in the backseat.

I felt the tilt of the vehicle to one side and the crunch of gravel under the tires. Before he'd even parked, I heard a door being flung open. The car dinged incessantly, signaling a door that remained ajar.

"Oh, hello, sweetheart."

My head swiveled in the direction of the voice.

The blindfold suddenly came off, gifting me with sight. It was dark outside, but the interior of the car was flooded with light due to the open door.

"Cletus," the driver called out to his companion. "She's awake."

"Great, what do you want me to do about it?" Cletus replied, zipping up his trousers.

"We've been on the road for hours. I'm sure the bitch has to piss."

"So? Fuck her."

"So, I don't want her pissing herself in the car. I'll never be able to get the smell out of the upholstery."

The back door opened, and before I could react, a

hand grasped my upper arm. I instantly recoiled in distress and slipped out of his grip.

"We don't have time for this," Cletus growled, clasping me tighter and hauling me out of the car like I was a stuffed animal.

His fingernails clawed into my skin, and I hissed through my nose in pain.

"*Easy*," the driver snapped. "He'll be pissed if she shows up damaged."

Cletus sniggered. "Maybe you shouldn't have elbowed her in the jaw, fucktard."

*Or punched me in the stomach.*

Cletus propped me up and let me go. My legs were wobbly, and I stumbled briefly, but with my sight returned, I managed to catch myself before falling onto the asphalt.

Cletus pulled a pocketknife from his pants and quickly released me from my binds. "Go." He gestured to the side of the road. He leaned against the vehicle and crossed his arms over his chest, smirking. "We don't have all night, darlin'. Time's a wastin'."

I shuddered at his use of *darlin'*, which only reminded me of Boxer. I held back a whimper. Breaking down while I was in the middle of some remote highway in the middle of nowhere without any clue about how far I was from civilization wouldn't help things. Maybe that was why they hadn't zip-tied my ankles: they knew I couldn't run away. Where would I run *to*?

My mouth was as dry as sawdust, the smell of duct tape in my nose.

Cletus sneered. "Bitch, lose the pants. You either piss here and now or get back in that car and I'll let you piss yourself and I don't give a fuck what Paul says about it."

I was about to burst and had no time for modesty. Whirling, I gave Cletus my back and fumbled with the button of my jeans and pulled them down. I couldn't hold in the moan of relief when I finally emptied my bladder.

"Paul," Cletus shouted to his friend. "You hear that moan? I bet this one is a screamer."

"Shut up," Paul snapped. "Get her back in the car, and let's get going. Someone's going to come by. Hurry the fuck up."

I stood upright again and after pulling up my pants, I hastily buttoned them, wanting to cover myself as quickly as possible. Cletus came for me and quickly zip-tied my wrists in front of my body. He then wrapped a hand around my arm and shoved me toward the blue Honda.

Because I wasn't completely in charge of my faculties, I crashed against the side of the vehicle.

"Easy," Paul stated. "You want to incur Dante's wrath?"

"I'm not afraid of Dante," Cletus blustered, but his grip on me lessened.

I wriggled into the backseat and Cletus shut the door.

Paul turned around again, reached over, and slowly removed the duct tape from my skin, and then he offered me a bottle of water.

I stared at it for a moment, wondering why he was giving it to me, and why they hadn't bothered to blindfold me again. His offer wasn't about caring if I was comfortable or not. It was because of the faceless Dante.

In that moment, I was terrified of a man I'd never met.

I took the water but didn't drink right away.

Paul noticed my hesitation. "It's not drugged."

"How do I know?" I asked, my voice raspy.

He shrugged. "You don't. Guess you'll just have to trust me."

My throat was parched, and I wanted to remove the sour taste of fear from my mouth. I unscrewed the bottle and drank. When I'd had my fill, I screwed on the cap and leaned my head back against the seat.

Cletus got into the car, buckled himself in, and we zoomed off into the night.

My mind was in overdrive. Terror of the unknown blasted through me like a wrecking ball. I was at the mercy of two men.

A phone vibrated somewhere in the front seat. Paul reached into his pocket and extracted his cell and put it to his ear. "Hello? Yeah. We're about five hours away." He looked at me in the rearview window. "Yeah, she's awake. No, no one saw us. We took her blindfold off to let her piss. We can put it back on if—Okay, sure. I gave her some water, and I'm making sure Cletus keeps his hands to himself."

Cletus made a noise in the back of his throat and shot Paul a glare.

"Right. See you in a few hours." Paul hung up and set his phone down in the center console.

"What the hell, man! You're going to get me in trouble with the boss."

"Cool it," Paul commanded. "And no more blindfolding her."

Cletus grumbled but then settled down. We drove for another few minutes before I heard a snore and knew Cletus had fallen asleep.

Goosebumps prickled along my arms as cold air circulated through the car. With each mile that Paul drove, my fear escalated, building slowly like the pressure beneath a volcano about to erupt.

His eyes met mine in the rearview mirror, lingering for a moment before looking back to the road.

"I have money," I pleaded. "Lots of money. Just let me go and I'll—"

He turned up the staticky music on the radio to drown out my voice. Cletus didn't stir.

Leaning my head against the window, I waited for dawn.

The sun was just starting to rise when we neared the Mexican border. As we sat in line to pass through the checkpoint, I noticed guards everywhere, standing at the ready, armed with machine guns and dressed in light tan and brown camouflage. Sniffer dogs were moved from car to car in the inbound United States side by large, mean-looking men. Suspect vehicles were being X-rayed by special machines off to the side after being separated.

We pulled to a stop, and I opened my mouth to scream, but before I could get out a sound, Cletus whirled in his seat and chopped me in the throat. I choked up immediately. My breath caught in my lungs, and my eyes brimmed with tears.

Paul rolled down the driver's side window. A guard wearing sunglasses left his booth and approached us. He looked more like a soldier and was built like a tank. He leaned down and peered into the car, and I knew it was all going to be over soon. He'd see me bound, fighting for air, tears in my eyes. He'd sound an alarm, and before I knew it, I'd be back home with Boxer, safe in his arms.

My eyes widened in supplication at him as I struggled to regain my breath, but all he did was smile at me. He held out his palm. Paul passed over two passports and the guard gave them a cursory glance before handing them back. He took a few steps away from the vehicle and waved us through the checkpoint.

The guys began to laugh.

Cletus looked at me, a sinister smirk across his face. "What? Did you think this was our first time doing this? These men are Alejandro Garcia's men—"

"*Shut the fuck up*," Paul snapped. "Jesus, you're a goddamn moron."

Cletus closed his mouth and stared out the window.

I had no idea who Alejandro Garcia was, but I could guess. It took a very powerful man to own guards at a federal checkpoint between two nations.

This was cartel business.

And I was in the middle of it.

# Chapter 28

ANOTHER FEW HOURS PASSED, and I slipped away to a place of cool detachment. Fear wouldn't help me now. Fear clouded judgement.

Thoughts of Boxer drifted into my mind. We'd just found one another. We were two wounded souls, and we'd been building something beautiful and special. Hope was a fragile thing. It bloomed like a bud in spring, nurtured into opening, until the harsh chill of winter killed it. I cursed my own stupidity for not telling him I loved him.

Now it was too late.

I was under no illusions that my life and my body were about to belong to someone other than me.

Undiluted rage poured through my veins, melting the icy calm inside me.

I was completely unable to hold on to my detachment.

It was fight or flight.

I squirmed in my seat, catching Cletus' attention.

"Stop that," he commanded.

"I can't," I gasped. "I have to go to the bathroom again."

My cinched wrists glided over to the seat belt latch, pressing down on it firmly in the hopes of discharging it without them hearing. "Come on, I see a town in the distance. Can't I use the bathroom at a gas station? I know how fond Paul is of his car."

"She's right, man," Paul said to Cletus. "We'll stop for a couple minutes. What's she gonna do?"

"Fine. But you're telling Dante why we're late," Cletus stated. "This shit isn't on me."

"I'll call him right now," Paul said, looking down for just a moment while reaching for his phone.

*Now or never.*

I lurched forward, slid my zip-tied wrists over Paul's head, and yanked them against his neck. I pressed my knees to the back of the seat and used leverage to choke him. I pulled with all my might.

"What the fuck!" Cletus shouted from the passenger side.

Paul reared back, his foot slamming down on the gas as he tried to relieve the tension on his neck. The car shot forward and the engine screamed, sounding like it was going to explode. Paul gasped and lifted his hands up and clawed at my arms. His knee jerked the wheel, causing the vehicle to veer out of the lane and onto the shoulder of the highway.

Cletus grabbed on to the passenger door to brace himself as the car continued to swerve.

Anger and adrenaline coursed through me.

I was out for blood.

I tightened my hold on Paul's windpipe as he attempted to regain control of the car, which kept diverging on and off the road. His foot refused to release the gas.

Cletus reached into his pants and pulled out a pocketknife. He flicked it open and stabbed me deep in the meaty part of my upper arm near my shoulder.

I yelled in pain, but I still wouldn't let go. It only enraged me further, and I yanked my fists into Paul's Adam's apple as hard as I could.

"Let off the fucking gas!" Cletus bellowed.

A gurgle escaped Paul's lips, and I looked in the rearview mirror. His face was red. Blood vessels and capillaries burst in his eyes making him look like a deep-sea diver who'd come up to the surface too fast.

My strength was waning, but if I could just hold on a little longer...

Cletus grabbed my hand and then slid the knife through the zip ties holding my wrists together. I lost my clasp on Paul's neck and fell backward.

A horn blared from the oncoming lane.

"Fuck!" Cletus yelled, dropping the knife and wrenching the wheel so we didn't collide with the approaching truck.

Cletus overestimated the torque, and combined with our demonic speed, the small car screeched and skidded across the asphalt, tilting up on its side as we veered to the right.

My body catapulted into the door, and my head smacked against the glass. Stars danced before my eyes, clouding my vision.

I prayed the vehicle would right itself.

But God didn't hear my prayer.

The car flipped, and the world stilled.

For a heartbeat, we were suspended in midair...and then the vehicle turned upside down.

Screeching metal across asphalt was the last sound I heard before I passed out.

Pain buzzed through my temples, and a hearty groan fled my lips. I took a deep breath. And then another.

I slowly opened my eyes and saw Paul's body suspended upside down, his neck slanted to one side. A piece of the windshield had severed his carotid artery and blood was pouring from his neck.

I moved my legs.

*Thank God.*

Cletus was not in the vehicle.

Had he been flung from it?

I slithered from my spot to the front seat. The scent of oil, burnt rubber, and other fluids from the car penetrated my nose. The passenger door was open, bent back at an odd angle. The rest of the vehicle was too crushed to escape from. The radiator hissed, and fluid leaked out onto the ground, splashing like a tub overflowing from a faucet left on too long.

I slid out onto the asphalt, my skin abraded by gravel and glass. I sliced my palms, but I kept going. My jeans had provided some protection to my legs.

When I was clear from the wreckage, I stood up and looked around.

The truck we'd almost plowed into had stopped on the opposite side of the road a few hundred yards away. Its hazard lights flashed in the weak morning light.

A man jogged toward me and across the street, calling out in Spanish, asking if I was hurt. He couldn't have been more than twenty years old, his brown eyes warm with concern as he looked me over. His gaze locked on my arm where Cletus had stabbed me. It was oozing, and I was about to tear off a piece of my shirt to wrap it when the young man spoke.

"I have a first aid kit in the truck," he said in Spanish. "Do you have any other injuries?"

"I don't think so," I replied in the same tongue.

He looked relieved that I spoke his language.

In the past twelve hours I'd been kidnapped, stabbed by an inept maniac, and in a violent car wreck after trying to kill one of my captors. Maybe my luck was turning, and this kind stranger would patch me up and help get me out of here.

The young man introduced himself as Roberto as we headed toward the truck. It was a large pickup, and the engine sounded like it was a diesel. The driver's side door was ajar, and he popped open another small door to the back, and then reached underneath the seat from behind to retrieve his first aid kit.

"I'm a doctor," I said.

The young man looked surprised but took my directions and helped me field dress and bandage my wound. It was a temporary fix, but it would stop the bleeding and prevent any other objects from entering the cavity.

Cletus had hit muscle when he stabbed me. I wouldn't know if he wounded something vital without an X-ray. I hoped there wasn't nerve or tissue damage.

*I can't worry about that now.*

"I need to make a phone call," I told Roberto. "Do you have a phone I can use?"

He nodded and pulled out his cell from his jeans pocket and backed away from the truck a foot or two to give me space.

I smiled in gratitude and took his phone. I struggled to get a signal and lifted the cell in the air.

Roberto's sharp inhale drew my attention.

Cletus stood behind Roberto and extracted a knife from between his ribs. Cletus then punched the blade in and out several more times in Roberto's kidney, like it was something he'd done before. The young man tried to scream, but the pain overwhelmed him, and he fell to his knees, his hand going to his back and sliding through blood that began to pool at his feet. He collapsed on the ground in front of me, eyes dimming.

Cletus folded his knife up as I stared in shock, and then he grasped my arm where I'd been injured. I cried out in pain. By the time I thought to wrench free and run, my body balked. It had been through enough trauma and refused.

He slapped me hard with his other hand straight across the face causing me to drop the cell phone. "*You fucking bitch!*"

My vision was spotty and I struggled to remain upright. The maniac reached over the driver's seat, turned off the truck, and pulled out the keys. He paused and then said, "Get in, sweetheart. We have some place to be. You're driving."

My fingers clenched the steering wheel of the diesel truck while Cletus sat next to me with his pocketknife in his hands, ready to use at a moment's notice.

"Keep your speed at eighty. No one's going to stop us around here," he snapped angrily.

"Okay."

"And don't even think about pulling any more shit." He sneered. "I'll slit your throat if you try another stunt like that and tell them you died in the crash."

His face was scratched from the car accident, but the idiot was more durable than Paul.

I'd once believed that every human life had value. That everyone deserved a chance to be saved.

How incredibly naive I'd been.

When people came to the hospital, it was my job to treat their injuries. It was supposed to end there, but I'd routinely gone above the physical repairing of human beings, wanting also to help battered women find new lives, new meaning.

But I couldn't fix people like Cletus.

What made someone aid in the kidnapping and human trafficking of another person?

There were sliding scales of criminality, clearly. I'd excused Boxer and his club's actions. Why? Was it because I loved Boxer? Because I'd been seduced by the idea of acceptance and family? Because even though they were criminals, they helped people?

Where was my own line?

What direction would my own moral compass point me in?

An innocent man had been murdered because he'd tried to help me. I'd carry that burden with me, just like I carried the death of my eight-year-old patient on my conscience.

"Turn up there at the sign," Cletus commanded.

I was still running on adrenaline. My head throbbed. I was thirsty, hungry, tired, and scared. I did as he said and turned off onto a side road off the barren highway.

Fifteen minutes later, I drove the truck up to a massive wrought iron gate built into a ten-foot wall that surrounded what looked like an old ghost town. Behind the gate, I could see pink adobe buildings, each decaying at their own rate but some still whole and appearing habitable.

I idled the truck at the gates and sat for a moment before Cletus made a phone call.

"Yeah, it's us," Cletus said.

No sooner had he clicked off did the gates begin to open on some electric chain mechanism, and I realized they were new despite the appearance of the small township behind them. I drove through and followed Cletus' directions and then parked the truck and turned the engine off before climbing out. My knees locked, and I bit down on my lip to stifle my moan of pain from my body's effort to move.

I took a moment to examine my surroundings. The edifices were dilapidated, and the doors were cracked and faded from the sun. Some were falling off their hinges and there was dirt and dust covering almost every surface. We had come to one of those forgotten towns in the middle of nowhere, and it had clearly been decades since any occupants had bothered to wash or paint the exteriors of the buildings. A few young women with wide eyes and gaunt faces hurried down the dusty streets, as if they didn't want to be out in the open. An old man with white hair and sunken cheeks from lack of teeth scooped beans from a wooden bowl into his mouth, muttering to himself in Spanish.

Cletus scrambled from his side of the truck and quickly came to me, grasping my bandaged arm.

I hissed in pain.

He released me instantly and then glared. "Don't open your mouth unless I tell you to. Got it?"

When I didn't reply, he leaned in close enough that I could smell the stale cigarette smoke and gingivitis on his breath and asked again, "Got it?"

"Got it," I snapped back.

The structure we'd parked in front of was larger than the rest. I wondered if it had been opulent in its heyday. It might've been gorgeous at some point but, it, too, had fallen into disrepair.

*Where am I?*

The heavy wooden front door opened, and a man loomed in the doorway. He was tall and lithe, with dark hair combed off his forehead. His gray silk shirt draped across his shoulders like it was a part of him, and contrasting black slacks topped expensive looking shoes that were polished to a perfect shine. He was urbane, and I didn't trust the veneer of his appearance at all.

He looked completely out of place in this poverty-stricken ghost town.

The man perused me up and down for a long moment, and then he turned his attention to Cletus.

"You're late," he said in heavily accented English. "And you're missing a partner."

"Paul's dead," Cletus said flatly. "Killed in a car accident."

The man's gaze came back to me, and my heart kicked up in terror.

He was the one to fear. I knew it in my bones.

"She's wounded," he said as he stalked toward me. I instinctively flinched away from him, but he captured my chin in his hand and turned my face from side to side for inspection.

"It's her fault," Cletus defended. "She caused the car accident trying to get away."

The man's jaw clenched, and he released me. I hastily scrubbed my skin as though I could somehow remove his touch.

"You were supposed to deliver her three hours ago, and in pristine condition," he said.

"But Paul—"

"Paul is dead, as you said," the man interrupted. "I don't like excuses."

I swallowed at the deadly calm in his voice.

Cletus' hands clenched by his side. "Look, I just want the money—"

"Money?" Dante repeated. "For a job not done to my satisfaction?"

"I nearly died bringing her here," Cletus argued. "And now you're not going to pay me? Fuck that, man!"

"Shh, easy now. I'll pay you," Dante crooned.

Cletus paused, looking befuddled. "You will?"

"Yes, of course."

A smile spread across Cletus' face, but he was either too stupid to recognize the coldness emanating from Dante, or he was too greedy to care.

Dante calmly but swiftly reached beneath his silk shirt and pulled out a golden pistol, engraved with ornate scroll work, and leveled it at Cletus' face. It happened so fast Cletus didn't have time to react. His smile had just started to fade when the gun went off and a bullet caught him between the eyes. The back of his head popped open as the shot rang out, and he collapsed to the ground, his blood and pink chunks of brain staining the dirt.

A gasp rose in my throat, but I clamped it down.

Dante lowered the gun slowly and looked at me. "Welcome to *Palacio de Sangre*."

*The Palace of Blood.*

*Fuck.*

# Chapter 29

DANTE's brown eyes raked over me, lingering on my face and then my arm with the bandage from my knife wound.

Without a word, he grabbed me by the hair and yanked me forward. I cried out in pain and reached up to try and pull his hands off, but it only made him tighten his grip as he hauled me down the road.

Even though tears leaked out the corners of my eyes, I was still able to look around and take in my surroundings. Faces peered through ratty curtains hanging on stained, dirty windows, but no one ventured outside. Their curiosity would not get in the way of their safety, and it became clear this was in fact still a ghost town.

People didn't live here, they survived here.

I tripped and almost fell, but Dante reached down and grabbed my wrist, relentlessly holding on to me to prevent me from crashing into the dirt. His fingers clamped around my slender bones, and I bit my lip to stifle my cry of agony.

When we came to the outskirts of the town, he stopped. We stood outside an old, faded pink adobe structure with iron bars rooted in the cement of the windows. He dragged me toward it, opening the cracked wooden front door, and then shoved me into the building.

*The town jail.*

I nearly choked on the scent of death that lingered in the air in the small front room. Piles of old rodent droppings in the corners mingled with the reek of decaying flesh and blood emanated from the building.

Dante pulled me down the hallway, revealing four rusted old jail cells, two on each side, and then he removed an iron skeleton key from his pocket and jostled it into the iron lock of the first cell on the right. The iron gate groaned in protest as he jerked it open against its will. He pushed me inside and I fell to the ground. He closed it, locking me in. The sound resonated with finality.

"Enjoy your accommodations," he said, smiling slightly before he padded back down the hallway, out of sight. A moment later, I heard the front door creak open and then shut again.

I was alone. Without food. Without water. Not that I had an appetite for anything.

Something furry scuttled across my feet. I cried out in surprise and backed up until I hit a stone wall. I curled my knees up to my chest, as if making myself into a small ball would somehow protect me.

I inhaled a deep breath, instantly gagging on the stench in the air. I stood up, suddenly aware of how filthy my surroundings were and not wanting to touch anything on the floor. The sound of flies buzzing caught my attention and drew my eyes to an old rickety bucket in the far corner. I walked to it to see what was inside. I peered into the bucket and almost lost the meager contents in my belly. The excrement of the person that had come before me was still there.

My eyes ping-ponged around the jail cell. I realized how dire my situation truly was. There were details I would never be able to unsee. Streaks of brown marred the walls near the bucket, clearly from someone defecating and having to use their hand to clean themselves. The floor was made of crude stone but was stained with various brown splotches.

Dried blood.

Death thrived here. Misery flourished, and despair prospered.

*Palacio de Sangre, indeed.*

I wondered how I was going to die. Because there was no doubt in my mind that I *was* going to die. How long would he string this along? What violations would I endure before the pain and suffering ended?

I went to the iron gate of the jail cell. I gripped the bars and with my limited energy, gave them a hearty tug. They steadfastly refused to budge. I clawed at the pins in the hinges that connected the gate to the walls to remove them, but they were rusted through, and the task would be impossible without tools.

The walls were tall and smooth, and the only window in the room was above the reach of my hands. There was no way to climb up to it and look out. Even if I turned over the metal bucket and used it as a stepping block, I wouldn't be able to see. No doubt the iron bars were secure there too.

I was trapped. And no one was going to save me.

It had been hours since I'd had anything to eat or drink. I was terrified, injured, and exhausted—but the idea of closing my eyes in this place meant that I'd wake up far too soon in another nightmare.

Reality.

The afternoon sun sank into oblivion and night came. I

resisted sleep, but I was no match for fatigue and finally succumbed, staring at the meager moonlight shining through the jail cell window before drifting off.

When I awoke, it was still dark, and I had no idea the time. But my bladder was full, screaming to be emptied. I squirmed in discomfort that eventually turned to pain. There was still enough moonlight for me to be able to see the floor of the jail cell. Woozily, I stood, grasping for the wall to steady myself before hastily removing my hand, hoping I hadn't touched anything disgusting. I padded over to the bucket, unbuttoned my pants, and crouched. It took a few moments for my body to let go, but when it did, I sighed in relief, even as the flies I had disturbed buzzed around me. I bounced a few times, drip drying, and then quickly pulled up my pants. As I plunked down onto the hard ground, I heard the scraping of tiny claws. I shivered, knowing I was sharing my cell with some hungry critter looking for its next meal.

My mind zinged with thoughts. The dull headache pounding at the lower base of my skull and dry mouth from lack of water were enough to make me check out again. I fell back asleep just as the pink rays of day came through the iron bars of the window.

A blast of cold water hit me in the face, causing me to choke and gasp for breath. In a panic, my eyes whipped open. Dante was standing outside my cell, holding a green garden hose with a high-pressure nozzle. A nasty smirk spread across his face. "Good morning, Princess. Sleep well?"

Today, he wore a pair of black trousers and a white silk button-down shirt. He looked freshly shaved, relaxed, like he'd gotten a good night's rest.

Dante blasted the hose again, blurring my vision, and ability to reply. Not that I would have. I scrambled back into the corner of the room, attempting to get away from the powerful stream of water. My back met stone as I hit the corner of the jail cell and dried feces that had been sprayed loose, rubbed off on my clothes.

Dante tossed the hose aside and came forward, reaching into his pocket for the skeleton key. The squeaking of the lock was like the ringing of a gong, symbolizing the beginning of my worst nightmare.

"Bruno! Juan! I'm ready," Dante called.

A moment later, two burly men with dark hair and hands that looked like they could rip grown men into pieces appeared behind Dante. One of them carried a small, wooden folding table. The other an old wooden chair. Dante stepped aside so Bruno and Juan could enter the cell.

Without a look in my direction, the men set up the table. It had two iron cuffs drilled into the top side at one end. A brute stayed, and the other left for a quick minute, only to return carrying a rusted metal toolbox.

Dante chuckled.

He was amused, eager. He gestured with his chin in my direction. A beefy crony came to me, reached down, and grasped my arm to haul me up. He thrust me toward the chair and forced me to sit. Before I could get my bearings, he was encasing my wrists in the iron shackles, which forced my hands to lay flat against the table.

Like a presentation.

An offering.

"You look tired, Princess," Dante teased. "Didn't you sleep well?" He looked around the room like he was seriously studying it. "Did you know this jail has been around since 1862? Oh, if these walls could talk about what they've seen over the years."

He flashed a grin, like we were at a party, and he'd told a humorous joke.

"The rats are fond of this cell in particular. It doesn't flood like the others when it rains, and sometimes I leave treats for them…"

Bruno and Juan moved to stand behind their boss, their eyes staring straight ahead. They didn't look directly at me, either because they didn't want to or because they chose to. Whatever I was to them didn't matter—I knew they would enforce Dante's will.

Dante began to whistle a happy sounding tune as he pulled the metal box toward him. He opened the top, but my view was marred, and I couldn't see what was inside.

And then he slowly began to remove tools from the box and set them down on the table.

A screwdriver, a hammer, a mallet, a hand saw.

I whimpered.

Dante looked up, a feral light entering his dark eyes. This man enjoyed the pain of others. He feasted on their terror.

He looked down, and with one finger, he traced the fingers of my right hand, skimming his thumb across my knuckles.

I curled my hand into a fist, which only made him laugh.

"Such lovely hands," he murmured. "You're a doctor, yes?"

My heart became a band of galloping broncos racing across the desert. My pulse drummed like hoofbeats on sand and stone.

"Bruno," he snapped.

Bruno moved from his spot by the cell gate and came to the table. With thick, sausage-like fingers, he pried my fist open, so my palm lay flat against the table.

Naked, unprotected.

Dante picked up a wooden mallet and stroked it lovingly, like a musician would caress a cherished instrument.

"Lovely tools," he explained as he looked me directly in the eyes.

And then he slammed the mallet down onto my middle three fingers, crushing the bones in an instant.

Pain, unlike anything I'd ever known before in my entire life assaulted me. It was so fast, so effectual, all I could do was inhale a sharp breath.

But before I could even muster a cry, I passed out.

I came to.

Red-hot pain in my right hand blew through me like a tsunami over land, obliterating everything in its path.

I turned my head and vomited.

The sour stench of fear and bile wafted to my nose. After a few more dry heaves, my insides stopped lurching. There was nothing left to purge.

I slowly swiveled my head. Dante sat across from me in another chair that Bruno or Juan must have brought for him while I was passed out. He looked bored and unhappy.

"I'm not a fan of your reaction." He sighed like a schoolteacher disappointed in one of his students.

I looked down at my hand. The bones of my right fingers were shattered and swollen. Constant pain throbbed through the nerves and shot up my entire arm. Tears welled from deep within me. They came of their own volition, and I could do nothing to stop them.

The irony of a surgeon's hand, a tool used to help heal

other people being so badly broken wasn't lost on me. The fingers looked mangled, nothing more than bone and fleshy pulp, now devoid of structure and beauty. Even if I lived, even if I had surgery, I doubted it would be reparable beyond being usable for routine, daily tasks.

Dante had broken more than my fingers.

He'd destroyed my ability to perform surgery in one fell swoop. He'd taken a vital piece of who I was and flushed a dozen years of schooling down the toilet in an instant.

Dante picked up a screwdriver that sat on the table and lightly dragged it across the knuckles on my shattered hand, causing me to whimper.

"No," I begged. "Please. God, no."

"I'm not God." Dante's voice was cold. "I'm the devil, and I'm going to make you pay for what your boyfriend has done."

He raised the screwdriver, and with a maniacal look, he rammed the screwdriver into the top part of my hand, sending it deep into my flesh.

I screamed.

And then he took the hammer and slammed it down onto the handle of the screwdriver, driving the metal deeper, straight through to the table.

My bloodcurdling shriek echoed off the stone walls.

"She pissed herself," Juan commented.

"Excellent," Dante said. "Unlock her shackles. Let her lie in it."

I passed out again, and the next time I awoke someone was holding a cup of water to my lips and cradling my head. The liquid was lukewarm and tasted brackish, but my lips were cracked, and I was dying for it. I tried to gulp it down greedily, but whoever held me wouldn't let me. "Easy," he said quietly in heavily accented English.

My eyes were caked with dried tears and dust from the floor, but I managed to flip them open. I stared into the face of a man with battered skin and grooves around his mouth that reminded me of dried riverbeds.

I glanced down. The fingers of my right hand were splinted, and gauze was wrapped around the palm to stop the bleeding. I couldn't feel anything. I frowned up at him wanting to ask questions.

"I've given you enough morphine to dull the pain," he explained, as if sensing my unasked query. "I'm a doctor."

"Why?" I croaked.

"Because Dante wants you awake and alert."

My eyes quickly scanned the area. It was just the two of us. Dante wasn't here. But I felt him. Like a malevolent ooze that stifled the air, threatening to appear at any moment.

"He wants me awake and alert…for what comes next?"

The man nodded, his brown eyes somber.

"Help me," I whispered.

He shook his head.

"He'll break me. Until there's nothing left. And then he'll kill me," I said.

"There are some things worse than death, no?"

*Like your last moments on this earth, filled with agony and torture.*

I'd diagnosed several patients whose last few months were nothing but pain. Death had been a relief, a blessing for them.

I closed my eyes briefly. This would eventually end for me. He'd take my life, and I'd be released.

The faint buzzing sound of a machine turned my attention. I heard the wooden door of the building slam open and then a moment later the noise grew louder. Dante loomed in the doorway of the jail cell holding an idling chainsaw that dripped blood onto the stone floor.

I gulped.

The doctor removed the cup from my lips and slowly released me. He stood up and hastened to the corner behind Dante.

This was it. The moment I was going to die.

Sawn in half like a magician's assistant, only there would be no magic to put me back together. My organs ripped through with metal teeth. Jagged suffering as my bones cracked and my muscles tore. My insides sprayed on the walls, so the next victim to come after me could wonder about her own fate.

"Bruno angered me," Dante explained with a casual grin. He turned off the chainsaw and set it on the floor. "You didn't think I was really going to use it on you, did you, Princess? No. That would have ended our fun *far* too soon."

He turned his head to address the doctor. "Well? How is she?"

The doctor's face was ashen. "I've tended to her wounds as best I can. And she's heavily medicated as well as sedated."

I looked at the sunlight coming in through the iron bars of the window. I had no idea how long I'd been passed out.

I briefly closed my eyes, willing myself to endure, willing myself to hold on to whatever remained of my sanity by the time this was over.

When I died, I still wanted there to be something of myself that Dante never managed to break.

"Help her up," Dante commanded.

When the doctor was sure I could stand on my own, he released me.

"You can go now," Dante told him. "Wait outside. I'll call you again when I need you."

The doctor didn't even look at me as he left.

At some point while I had been passed out, the table and chair had been removed from the jail cell. Placed up against the wall was a six-foot-tall St. Andrew's cross. Four leather cuffs were nailed to the wooden planks.

Dante approached me, and I shrank in fear. He took my elbow and walked me to the cross. I tried to fight, to resist, but my limbs refused to obey my edicts.

*The sedative.*

He cinched the leather pieces around my wrists and ankles.

I was tied to a massive wooden torture device.

He reached into his trouser pocket to remove a butterfly knife. His white silk shirt was stained with gore. I wasn't sure if it was mine or the recently deceased Bruno. The coppery tang of blood stung my nose and the back of my throat. It was a familiar scent from the operating room.

This was different.

Dante took the knife and slit my shirt, cutting it off me completely. My breasts were bare to him, but he didn't even spare them a glance. With a few flicks of his wrist, he then sliced off my jeans, leaving me in my underwear and boots.

"You're not just a smart doctor, are you?" Dante asked, grinning. "I know what he feels when he looks at you..."

His finger danced across my collar bone before sliding down my sternum.

"I'm a collector," he said. "A collector of hearts. I enjoy looking at the physical organs of people I've tortured. It's such a lovely reminder of the fact that no matter how much they want to die, their hearts betray them and beat on, pumping life through their veins against their will in the worst moments of their existence. Is there anything more beautiful than betrayal? I don't think so. I have several hearts in jars on my mantle. But *your* heart…is better left inside your chest."

I was nearly naked, strapped to a torture device incapable of escape. I'd been vulnerable before with my wrists strapped to a table, but this was different.

This would be another violation. A different sort of sick pleasure he was about to partake in.

I wasn't strong enough to look him in the eyes while he raped me.

I closed my eyes and waited for the sound of his zipper.

It never came.

When I heard his footsteps retreat, I cracked my eye lids open. He'd walked to the iron gate and was holding out his hand.

Someone handed him a branding iron, the end it of it angry and red, sizzling and popping as dust from the air lit on fire upon meeting the metal.

Dante turned to look at me.

His steps were slow, like the steady beat of a war drum.

"I'm not going to kill you, Princess," he said softly. "Alejandro doesn't want that. No. I'm going to send you back to your boyfriend broken and branded. Tell them, Princess. Tell them all that you're only the beginning if they ever cross Alejandro Garcia again."

He pressed the branding iron to the skin above my left hipbone.

I smelled my own burning flesh.

My screams mingled with his laughter.

In the distance, I heard the caw of a crow.

I wasn't dead.

I just wished I was.

Time ceased to have all meaning.

The burning of my flesh accomplished what the breaking of my hand hadn't. It fractured a piece inside my mind. It split my psyche apart, searing Dante's image within me forever.

Dante had infected my mind. He'd taken up residence there. The smell of sandalwood cologne on his skin mixed with the scent of my charred flesh would stay with me.

I screamed until my throat was raw.

I hung on the massive wooden frame like a scarecrow in a cornfield.

My lips were cracked and dry. The corners oozed blood.

Sometimes, I'd open my eyes and see the doctor. He would slather salve onto my wounds, patch me up, and give me just enough morphine to dull my pain. He mended me so Dante could torture me again and again.

Dante chopped my hair with pruning shears. My wheat blonde locks fell to the floor in a rippling cascade of beauty and femininity.

And when I soiled myself because Dante wouldn't untie me, he sprayed me down with the hose again like a rabid animal.

My head hung with exhaustion. My soul wept. My eyes were devoid of tears. I had nothing left inside of me to give.

Only then did Dante command the doctor to untie me. I fell to the floor as my weak muscles quivered.

"Women," Dante spat. "Useless. You almost take the fun out of breaking you. *Almost*."

I opened my eyelids. Night had fallen while I'd been tied to the wooden beams.

The doctor cradled me in his arms.

Dante crouched down on the ground next to the metal toolbox and extracted a scalpel.

Like the ones I used during surgery.

"You want her alive, don't you?" the doctor asked Dante in Spanish.

I feigned ignorance about my understanding of the language, hoping one of them would say something of true value. I remained limp, inactive.

"*Sí*," Dante snapped. "I want her alive."

"If you want her to make it back to Waco, then forget the knife play. You've heard of the saying *don't kill the messenger*, right? You've had your fun. Send her on her way."

"Fine," Dante snapped, throwing the scalpel back into the metal toolbox and shutting the lid. He rose from his crouched position on the ground and pulled out his cell phone. "Bandage her up as best you can. I'm calling Juan to come with the van."

Dante stalked from the jail cell and a moment later, I heard the creak of the rickety wooden door, followed by a loud bang as it slammed shut.

The doctor looked down at me, his brown eyes softening. "Valley of Hearts," he whispered in English. "That's where we are."

I moved my lips, but no sound came out. *Why?* I mouthed.

"You remind me of my daughter," he replied. "The one Dante took from me."

He lowered me to the soiled ground, but only so that he could administer a syringe into the meaty part of my thigh.

"You'll sleep the whole way home. Good luck to you."

# Chapter 30

"Oh my fucking God!"

I opened my eyes and winced at the bright morning sunlight beating down on me to stare up into Mia Weston's concerned gaze.

She crouched down as her gaze raked over me. "Linden? Is that you?"

What did she see?

Shorn hair.

Almost nude.

The bloody bandages.

A face covered in dirt, and skin soaked in urine and filth.

"Help me," I whispered.

The effort to speak stretched the dry, tender skin of my lips. The copper penny taste of blood filled my mouth.

She awkwardly squatted on the ground next to me and removed her brown leather jacket and gently covered my upper half with it.

There was a chill in the air, and her blue dress was

sleeveless. Goosebumps broke out all along her upper arms.

She pulled her phone out of her purse. A few moments later, she was barking orders at the 911 operator.

There was a giant black hole of time in my memory. Whatever the doctor had given me had rendered me unconscious for the entire drive from Valley of Hearts to Waco.

I didn't even remember Juan picking me up.

I was glad I couldn't remember the drive across the border. I wasn't sure I would've been able to endure being trapped again.

My wrists were unbound, but I didn't have the strength to lift myself off the asphalt even though it was digging into my exposed flesh.

If I thought too much about it, I might've been embarrassed at my state of undress. But the old Linden, the modest Linden, the Linden who cared how she presented herself to the world, didn't care about the fact that her breasts were on display.

Now I was raw, abandoned, left out in the sun like decomposing garbage.

The pavement scraped my bare skin.

Mia's voice was strong and sure as she gave the operator the address to Shelly's.

*Of course*, I thought. Why not dump me right in front of the place where I'd been kidnapped? It was Dante's way of letting the club know he was in complete control and could do as he pleased, right under their noses. What a perfect, sinister message to send.

Mia hung up and reached out to stroke my head.

I recoiled instantly and she pulled her hand back like a feral animal had bitten her.

"Ambulance should be here soon," she said, keeping her voice flat and devoid of emotion.

I didn't bother trying to reply.

With her eyes trained on me, she pressed a button on her phone and then put it to her ear. "Colt."

Her voice broke on his name, and then she bent her head. I wondered if it was to hide her tears. I closed my eyes and tuned out the sound of her anguish as she relayed the state she'd found me in.

Why did *she* have anything to cry about?

She wasn't the one who'd been tortured. Her life hadn't gone up in smoke like mine had the moment Dante smashed my hand with a mallet.

I was the shallow husk of what I used to be, not her.

A kernel of anger blistered hot within me, but only for a moment. And then it died out, hissing, like water thrown onto a heated coal.

In the distance, I heard the wail of the ambulance siren.

Her eyes searched mine. "What the fuck happened to you?" she asked softly, her phone still clenched in her fist.

"You can't figure it out?" I asked, my tone cold.

I was trapped in the prison of my mind, and even though my body was on the parking lot in front of Shelly's, my psyche was still on the floor of that rat-infested shithole of a jail cell.

Mia fell silent and didn't speak to me again.

The ambulance arrived, and two strong EMTs climbed out. Their eyes were somber as they looked at me. Then they glanced at one another. And like any two people that had worked together long enough, they had a conversation without speaking that said they knew what had happened to me.

The dark-haired EMT pulled open the back doors of

the ambulance and with the help of his partner, extracted the stretcher. They set it on the ground next to me and then eased me onto it.

Even though their touch was professional and gentle, it felt like a thousand insects crawled along my skin, making me want to burrow deeper inside my body for protection.

They pressed a button and the machine raised me up, and they wheeled me to the ambulance doors, and then slid me inside.

It wasn't until they tried to strap me in for safety that I balked.

"No," I croaked, attempting to summon whatever strength I had left. "Don't tie me down."

"We have to," the blond said, his blue eyes flashing with concern. "It's for your own safety."

"No! Don't tie me down!" I yelled. My throat was raw, and my voice cracked.

I screamed even as they ignored my pleas. I flailed and thrashed, knowing I could do more damage to myself, but I didn't care.

Mia climbed aboard the ambulance. "Linden," she soothed. "It's going to be okay."

"No," I cried, tears leaking from the corners of my eyes. "It'll never be okay. Never again."

I was trapped on a gurney, trapped in my own body when all I wanted to do was flee. Leave this broken, bag of bones behind and start fresh.

But there was no escape from my own mind, no escape from the pain, no escape from the life I was now living.

"John," the dark haired EMT said.

"I got it," John replied.

I looked at Mia and whispered, "Don't leave me."

And then I passed out.

My eyes flipped open, and I stared at a white ceiling. I detected no pain, nor any sort of feeling in my limbs. I was living in a general state of numbness, for which I was grateful.

Numb was better than fear.

Numb was better than pain.

And it was certainly better than wanting to rake dirty broken fingernails against my skin in an ineffectual attempt of trying to depart my own body.

I looked away from the ceiling down at my right hand. It was in a cast because it had been mutilated, demolished.

My left was intact.

It didn't matter though. I was a surgeon.

*Was.*

*Oh my God.*

"Linden," he said.

His voice was low and rumbly. Once upon a time, it would've made shivers of pleasure dance up and down my spine.

Now…

Boxer sat in the chair next to my bedside. His eyes were bloodshot and red rimmed. He was leaning over, elbows on his jeans, his hands linked. He looked horrible.

"Get out," I whispered. My voice was choked. I cleared my throat, which only made it hurt worse, but I said it again. "Get out."

"Linden, I—"

"Get the fuck out of here, Boxer!" I screamed. My anger obliterated the morphine-induced state of fog. "I don't want to see you. I don't want to see you *ever* again. *Get out!*" I looked around for something to throw at him. I reached over to the bedside table with my left hand, grimacing as the rolling movement of my body pulled the bandage flush against the brand on my skin.

"Linden, don't—"

Ignoring him, I chucked the plastic cup and sent it flying.

He didn't even bother trying to move out of the way, and the cup bounced off his arm. When he still didn't budge, I snatched the call button, pressing it like my life depended on it.

Boxer's expression was resigned. And then he rose swiftly from the chair and strode from the room, all but ripping the door off its hinges on his way out.

I leaned back against the less than stellar hospital pillow, my breath coming in rapid pants. I closed my eyes in an attempt to ward off the panic attack.

Fuck him.

Fuck him for all of this.

How dare he be here when I woke up? He was the cause of all of this. I'd suffered at the hands of a madman because of Boxer and the club.

The door to my hospital room opened, and Peyton rushed in. She wore a pair of light blue scrubs, her red hair pulled up into a high ponytail.

"Linden," her voice cracked. "What is it? Are you in pain?"

I shook my head, but it only made it throb.

Peyton went to the bedside table and picked up the pitcher of water, only to stop and look around for the missing cup.

"Floor," I said, gesturing with my chin in the direction.

"Why is the cup on the floor?" she asked as she went to retrieve it.

"I threw it at Boxer."

"You shouldn't have done that."

"Probably not," I agreed, grimacing. Morphine dulled most of my pain, but not all of it.

"Let me get you a clean cup."

"It's fine." If only she'd known that I'd been drinking brown Mexican water for days.

"You sure? It's no trouble."

"Peyton," I said with a sigh. "I've got bigger problems than a cup that's hit a sanitized hospital floor. Okay?"

"Okay," she whispered, nodding.

She poured water into the cup and then brought it to me. She stuck a straw in it and held it while I drank.

I was greedy for it, my throat parched even though I was on an IV to restore my fluid levels to normal. It reminded me of the last time someone had held water to my lips.

The water had been lukewarm and brackish.

Memories assaulted me, flashing before my eyes like pinwheels of light.

I choked on the cool water, and it ran down my chin. Peyton hastily put the cup aside and then helped me clean up once I was no longer coughing.

I leaned my head back against the pillow, exhausted.

Peyton's eyes scanned me. Not just as a nurse but as my friend. She wouldn't ask what had happened to me. She would keep it professional because I was in a hospital bed, but she was curious. It was written all over her face.

She could speculate. She *would* speculate. But I wasn't going to talk about it.

My neck was cool, and I remembered that Dante had chopped off my hair. I wanted to see the butchering.

"Will you bring me a mirror?" I asked her.

She blanched. "I don't think that's a good idea."

"Why not?"

"Because you look…"

I raised my brows. "How do I look?"

"Like someone assaulted you," she blurted out.

"Do I have black eyes?" I asked in curiosity. The areas around my eyes weren't swollen or tender. No. He hadn't used fists to beat me into submission. He'd chosen other ways to break me.

"No. No black eyes." Her somber gaze dropped to my injured hand.

I recognized the look as pity.

I didn't want pity.

"What happened, Peyton? Why am I not at a hospital in Waco?"

"Mia demanded the EMTs bring you here. You were stable enough for that, thankfully."

*Thankfully.*

"Chief Nelson took you into surgery."

Even though Chief Nelson was one of the best orthopedic surgeons in the country, I refused to bank on hope that my hand would ever be restored.

"It might be time to consider a change in profession," I said.

Her eyes filled with tears.

"Why are you crying?" I demanded.

"Because you're talking about no longer being able to be a surgeon—and I know how much that matters to you."

"*C'est la vie*, Peyton. *C'est la vie.*"

I'd once understood the empathy gene. I'd been born with it. Most doctors I knew found a way to either ignore it or compartmentalize it. Not me. My empathy had leaked out whenever I'd dealt with patients.

Their pain had become mine.

But this—Peyton crying over *me* and my trauma…I found it annoying. Compassion was one thing. Pity was another.

She hastily turned her head and wiped away her tears. "I saw Boxer leaving your room. He hasn't left your bedside in hours. We tried to kick him out; he wouldn't go."

"Don't talk to me about Boxer." I glanced away from her to stare out the window. The blinds were shut, but sunlight peeked through them.

"I keep saying all the wrong things, don't I?" she asked quietly.

I sighed and looked at the ceiling. I didn't know how to alleviate her concerns. I wasn't sure it was my job to do that. I was the patient. I was the one that was supposed to receive care. I wasn't supposed to be comforting my friends because *I'd* been the one to live through hell.

"Mia is in the waiting room," she said after a long moment of silence. "So are the other Old Ladies. Do you want to see them? Do you want one of them to come sit with you?"

I shrugged. I would be alone whether someone was in the room with me or not.

Safety was nothing more than an illusion, I realized. Because all it took was one moment, one wrong turn, one accident, or one attack and everything in your life could change.

Life wasn't safe, no matter how you tried to convince yourself it was. Dangers lurked around every corner. Shadows oozed in the night.

Some nightmares were real.

What I'd endured...I would never be the same again. Like clay shoved into a kiln, forever altered.

"I don't mind visitors," I said. "As long as it's not Boxer. He's not allowed in here. Do you hear me, Peyton? He's not allowed in here."

"Yeah, I hear you. Loud and clear. He's not welcome."

Her gaze was somber again, but she didn't try to dissuade me.

For the moment, I had my emotions under control. The anger was at bay, as was the hysteria. But seeing Boxer…talking to him…it would send me off the deep end.

Peyton examined my IV bag and made a few quick notes on her tablet about my vitals. And then she left the room.

What more was there for her to say?

I stared at the TV with the blank screen, watching nothing. A few minutes later, the door opened.

"Can I come in?" Mia asked.

"Sure."

She stepped inside the room, carrying her shoulder bag. Her brown leather coat was slung over an arm as she waddled her very pregnant body toward my bedside.

"I'm sorry," she said, as she plopped down in the chair.

"What do you have to be sorry for?"

She bowed her head. "I didn't think you'd react that way. When you saw him."

"How do you know how I reacted?"

"He told me. He told all of us. Everyone's in the waiting room."

"Why? Did you all drop everything and drive here only to camp out indefinitely?"

"That's exactly what we've done. And we've booked some rooms at The Rex so we don't have to drive back home tonight."

"Why? Why would you do that?"

She stared at me. "You really don't understand, do you? You're family, Linden."

Her words were shards of glass eviscerating my heart.

"That's not the only reason I'm sorry," she went on,

completely unaware of what her casual declaration did to me.

"I'm sorry I didn't hold it together when I found you in the parking lot. You didn't need me to fall apart or hear me panic when I spoke to Colt. I let my emotions get in the way of what you truly needed. You don't have to talk to me, Linden. But if you do, I'll listen."

"Why do people keep apologizing to me?" I asked after her impassioned speech. "Do you feel better saying everything you just said? Because it doesn't make me feel any better. It's not like it erases the past. An apology is just empty words."

The color leached from her face. I realized how I sounded but being tortured at Dante's hands had opened up something inside of me, and it was leaking vitriol. It wasn't just that he had broken my hand and no doubt taken away my surgical career.

No. He'd found the place deep inside me—my soul, my psyche, my very essence—and he'd peeled away the layers to reveal it. And then he'd bathed in the blood of its gruesome end, relishing in the destruction of who I used to be.

I wasn't the same person who'd fallen in love with Boxer. I would never be her again.

There was nothing left of me.

My feelings didn't belong to me. They belonged to the other. They belonged to the stripped-down version of me that no longer cared about platitudes or niceties.

If I had any hope of surviving this, I had to become something else. Something ruthless, feral, and angry.

Something powerful.

Someone in control.

Anger would be my fuel, like coal powering a steam engine. Anger would keep me going. Without it, I would just be a pathetic, broken toy to be discarded when others were done with me. If I stayed pathetic and broken, then what the hell was the point of living?

My eyes strayed to the dark TV.

"Do you want to watch something?" she asked.

"Sure."

She grabbed the remote off the bedside table and pointed it at the television. Cartoons. Game show. Animal kingdom.

She flipped through the stations, one by one.

"Go back," I commanded. "I want to watch that."

A lion ripping into the meaty flesh of an antelope filled the screen.

"You sure you want to watch this?"

"Why not?" The lion's golden muzzle was stained red as it gorged on the organs of the still living antelope as it was pinned down by massive paws, struggling to escape. "Nature is cruel. Especially if you're weak."

The morphine was wearing off, and lucidity was returning. I hit the call button, and Peyton came almost immediately. She greeted Mia with a smile and then turned her attention to me. "Can I get you something?"

"Morphine's crapping out on me," I said. "I'd like more."

"Linden, you're on as much as we can give you right now…"

We stared at each other, and then she sighed. "Let me get Chief Nelson, and I'll see what I can do."

I turned my head back to the TV, dismissing her. She caught her breath, like I'd hurt her feelings. I didn't have it in me to apologize.

If I didn't get another dose of morphine soon, the numbness would fade completely. And I wanted to stay there as long as I could. There would be plenty of time for rage. I'd embrace it when the time was right.

And when I embraced it, I'd unleash it on the person who deserved it the most.

Myself.

This was my fault.

Sure, I could blame Boxer. I thought he'd been strong enough to protect me. I thought the club was, too. But this was all on me, because I'd not only left Shelly's by myself, but I hadn't even thought to pull out my can of mace. I hadn't even considered the possibility that I wasn't safe because I'd been at a biker bar.

Never again. Never again would I put my safety into other people's hands. Never again would I be so damn foolish.

Mia's phone chimed softly. She reached into her bag and extracted her cell, reading the text. "Colt's asking if he can come talk to you."

"If he must," I said with a sigh.

I leaned my head back against the pillow, my eyes slowly drifting shut. The animal kingdom show had switched focus to a pack of lions killing one of their own. I appreciated the gruesome picture. I even felt a kinship with it.

The door to my room opened. "Hey, Doc," Colt said softly.

I looked at him, but I was unable to read his expression. He placed a huge paw on Mia's shoulder and gave it a squeeze, and then he helped her out of the chair. He leaned down and brushed a kiss along the apple of her cheek and then with a glance that seemed to say farewell, Mia left the room, leaving me alone with the president of the Tarnished Angels.

"How are you feeling?" he asked gruffly.

"Doped up on morphine. How are *you* feeling?"

He rubbed the back of his neck. "Fuck, Linden. I don't even know what to say."

"Then don't say anything," I suggested.

Colt sighed. "I'm not gonna bug you now and ask what happened. But I need to know how deep this goes."

"What do you mean?"

"I mean, do you know who kidnapped you?"

"Yes, I know who was behind it."

"Cartel?" he asked, pitching his voice low.

I hesitated and then nodded.

"Yeah. Thought so. Fuck." He shook his head. "Goddamn it all to hell; it wasn't supposed to be like this. You weren't supposed to—fuck, I have to let Boxer explain."

"I don't want to see Boxer," I protested.

Colt's brown eyes were hard. "You'll have to. At some point, you have to hear what he has to say."

I clamped my jaw shut and looked away from him.

"When you're ready, okay? Whenever that is. Listen, I hate to put the pressure on you, but there's something more pressing going on right now. There are two detectives here. They've been chomping at the bit to talk to you, but I got the chief to get in their shit and tell them you needed to rest. They won't wait anymore. Be evasive, Linden. Be vague. I need you to lead them to a dead end."

"Why? So I can protect the club?" I hissed. "It's all about the club, isn't it? I'm just a fucking casualty, aren't I?"

Before Colt was able to reply, the door to my room opened again, and Chief Nelson strode inside.

I'd once thought him formidable and imposing. Especially when he'd interviewed me for a job. But he didn't intimidate me now. Not after Dante.

Chief Nelson turned to look at Colt. "Mr. Weston," he greeted.

"Chief," Colt said, rising and holding out his hand.

They shook hands, and then Colt dropped his. "Mia will be back later, if you want."

"Fine," I said, my tone clipped.

Colt inclined his head and then strode from the room, leaving me alone with Chief Nelson.

"Nice guy," Chief Nelson said.

I raised my brows but didn't reply. I shouldn't have been surprised that Colt had gotten on the good side of Chief Nelson. The Tarnished Angels had ways, apparently. No wonder the detectives had waited to speak to me.

"You've made some very good friends," Chief Nelson said. "There are a lot of them in the waiting room."

"So I've heard." My eyes skated back to the television. Chief Nelson went to the TV and pressed the off button. The screen went dark.

He moved to stand at the end of my bed, drawing my attention to him.

"Peyton said you're asking for more morphine. Are you in a great deal of pain?"

"If I say yes, will you give me another dose?"

He didn't smile at my dry tone.

"The brand on your hip will scar and even with a laser, I don't think it will ever be able to be completely removed. The wound in your arm was paltry, all things considered, and you don't have any nerve damage, thank God. But your hand... Your hand is in a very bad state, Linden."

"I'm aware."

"We won't know the extent of the damage until you're healed and in physical therapy. What I'm saying is, don't think the worst—"

"Don't give me the party line," I said. "I'm a doctor. I know about party lines. Give it to me straight."

"I don't think you're ready for straight." He cocked his

head to the side and studied me. "The EMTs said you were hysterical when they tried to strap you to the gurney."

"And?" I prodded. "Did they tell you the state they found me in?"

"Yes. And that's exactly why I want you to talk to someone. A psychiatrist."

"Which one? Dr. Meddlesome or Dr. Happy Pills? I'm not a fan of either."

"You have to talk to someone." He leaned forward. "I've been practicing medicine for the better part of thirty-five years. I've seen a lot of shit. I know what was done to you. This is serious. The cops are here."

"I know."

"They want to talk to you."

"I'm sure they do."

"Tell them what happened. The truth."

"Here's the truth, Chief Nelson. I was kidnapped off the streets. I was tortured, maimed, and released. I don't know who did it or why. Wrong place, wrong time, I guess."

He stared at me for a long moment. "The blond biker. Boxer... He's your boyfriend?"

"He was. For a bit. He's not anymore."

"Doesn't seem that way to me," he said. "He hasn't left your side since you came back from surgery."

"You're my boss," I reminded him. "This isn't any of your business. Now, where do we stand on more morphine?"

"Of course, we'll modify your pain meds and take care of you, but I also want your word that you'll talk to a professional about what happened to you. Even if they don't work here."

I turned my head so I didn't have to look at him. "Please turn on the television on your way out."

# Chapter 31

"I ALREADY TOLD YOU," I said, trying to keep my tone from rising with anger. "I don't know where I was or who kidnapped me. I just know I was somewhere in the desert of Mexico."

The female detective looked at me like she didn't believe me. Her partner, Detective Buckingham, was clearly playing good cop in this situation.

"I'm very sorry we had to ask you these questions, Ms. Ward. But we——"

"Doctor," I interrupted.

His brow furrowed. "Excuse me?"

"It's Dr. Ward. I'm a doctor."

"Right, sorry. I meant Dr. Ward. Yes."

"I can't help you, Detective," I said. "I can't tell you what I don't know. This is a dead end. We've been at this for an hour, and I'm tired." I leaned my head back against the pillow and feigned exhaustion.

The two detectives exchanged a look and then rose from their chairs. Detective Buckingham reached into his pocket and pulled out a business card and set it down on the bedside table next to me.

"If you think of anything that might be useful, please let me know. A lot of women and children have been reported missing in the area. We just want to put a stop to it."

Guilt rested heavily on my shoulders. But what were the cops going to do about the missing women and children? If a biker club was trying to put a stop to it and were clearly failing even though they were willing to play outside the law, what good was the local police force going to be? If they got involved, it would just put them in the middle of a bloody war where only their enemies were able to play dirty, and they'd be bound by laws and search warrants, court orders, and schedules.

"I wish you a speedy recovery," Detective Buckingham stated.

"Thank you."

They both left, leaving me alone again. The female detective had offered me zero sympathy and platitudes. She was abrasive and hardened. The world had gotten to her, and she was as cold as anyone I had ever met.

At least they'd waited to speak to me until the following morning, so I'd finally had a good night sleep. It had been restful, and I remembered nothing of my dreams.

*Thank God for morphine.*

I didn't need to sleep to live my nightmares.

I reached for the remote on the bedside table and clicked on the television. It was mindless entertainment, something I stared at without actually seeing. The hospital room door opened, but I didn't bother looking to see who was there. It had been a revolving door of visitors. Nurses, Chief Nelson, the Tarnished Angels, the police. It was suffocating. And I wished for peace and a reprieve.

It was Mia who'd come in, followed by Joni, Rachel, Darcy, and Allison.

*No reprieve then.*

Joni and Rachel carted in two wicker picnic baskets, and Darcy had a leather bag slung over her shoulder, which she put at the foot of my hospital bed.

"Boy, they told me you looked like hell," Darcy said, her eyes raking over me. "Nothing like seeing it for myself, though."

"Jesus, Darcy," Joni muttered.

"What?" Darcy asked with a shrug. "The woman needs honesty. From the looks of it, she doesn't need any more coddling or tiptoeing. Do you, sugar?"

A slow smile involuntarily crossed my lips. "Darcy, I think you get me."

"We brought you lunch," Joni said. "Fried chicken, mac and cheese, potato salad, coleslaw, biscuits, mashed potatoes, and dessert from Pinky's."

"I'm sure you're dying for something other than hospital food," Rachel added. "I would be. I can't stand Jell-O."

My stomach rumbled at the thought of fried chicken. "And the guys? The kids?"

"Hanging out at The Rex," Mia explained. "Well, except for Boxer."

"And Zip," Joni added. "He stayed to make sure Boxer didn't…"

"Didn't what?" I prodded.

"Didn't march down the hallway and come in here, demanding you speak to him," Joni finished.

"Look," Rachel began. "We're your family now. All of us. You want to talk about what happened to you, we'll listen. You don't? We'll eat our food and shut up. We're not here to get your story, okay?"

Joni lifted the flap of a picnic basket and pulled out a container of fried chicken. "We love people through food. We bring comfort. We bring friendship and acceptance."

Darcy unzipped the leather bag. "I brought the works." She pulled out a pair of hair scissors. "I used to do this for a living. I thought you might let me clean things up a bit…"

"I still haven't seen how bad it is," I admitted.

"You haven't?" Darcy asked.

I shook my head. "Peyton wouldn't bring me a mirror. I didn't really have the energy to fight her about it."

"Don't look," Allison suggested. "Just let Darcy work her magic so the next time you look in a mirror, you see a version of yourself that you love."

Tears pricked my eyes. "See a version of myself that I love," I repeated. "I don't know if I've ever loved myself."

I hadn't meant to be so honest. But there was something about the Old Ladies. Their mere presence pried the feelings out of me, whether I wanted it to happen or not.

"I'm really good," Darcy said, her tone gentle. "And I think you have the perfect bone structure to pull off a pixie cut. What do you say?"

"Go for it," I said.

*Dive into the unknown.*

An hour later, Darcy held up a mirror for me to peer into. Before I faced myself, I took a deep breath. I didn't look like me at all. My blonde hair was cropped short. It highlighted my cheekbones and made my eyes appear bluer and bigger. I turned my head to the side to study myself.

"You have the daintiest ears," Joni commented.

"Like a little elf." Rachel smiled.

"I think you look amazing," Mia added. "Short hair really suits you."

I ran my hand down the column of my neck.

"You hate it." Darcy groaned, shaking her head. "I'm sorry, I just thought—"

"No," I interrupted. "I don't hate it. I don't hate it at all."

And then I began to cry.

"Shit," Rachel muttered, tossing her chicken leg onto a paper plate and setting it aside.

The Old Ladies crowded around me. Their arms embraced me as I cried out the storm that was swirling inside me.

"It's just hair," Darcy said. "It'll grow."

"No, you don't understand." Tears streamed down my cheeks. "I *love* it. I love it so much, and I never would've cut my hair. You were trying to fix a mess—and you did. You fixed it, and now it's beautiful again. I just wish someone could fix what's inside of me. What's the version of a haircut for your soul?" I asked on a sob.

I felt their tears on my skin as they held me, and we cried as one.

Rachel was the first to gain control of her emotions. She leaned away and swiped a hand across her eyes. "Fuck this shit," she snapped. "I've cried so much since I've gotten knocked up, and it just keeps getting worse."

I let out a soft, watery laugh. "Are there any more mashed potatoes?"

"Yeah. They're cold though," Joni said.

"Doesn't matter."

Joni riffled through the picnic basket and pulled out a plastic container. She removed the lid, stuck a spork into it, and then gave it to me.

"Any word?" Allison asked, her tone soft. "About the extent of damage to your hand?"

I inhaled a sharp breath, unprepared for the honest

question. "I don't know," I admitted. "I don't know if I'll ever be able to perform surgery again. And that, in and of itself, is the reason I'm contemplating a morphine addiction."

My joke fell flat, and no one laughed.

Joni looked at Mia. "You should tell her."

"Tell me what?" I asked.

"Did Boxer ever tell you about me?" Mia queried. "I mean, how I came to be an Old Lady?"

Hearing his name out loud had my insides stuttering like a flooded engine. I was still so angry at him, and I wasn't sure the anger was going to go away.

But I missed him.

That wasn't going away, either.

"He told me you were involved in some bad shit last year," I admitted, meeting Mia's pensive gaze. "But he didn't give me details."

"My boss got into trouble, and I got dragged into it," she explained. "And I brought it to the Tarnished Angels' front door. And instead of turning me away and making it someone else's problem, they took me in. Not just Colt, but *all* of them. And when my world fell apart, and trust me, it sure as hell did"—her smile wobbled—"they were there to help me pick up the pieces. My new family helped me keep moving forward in life. And that's exactly what we're going to do for you."

She stole a hand across her expanded belly. "I'm an Old Lady, but I didn't grow up in this world. I didn't even know what being an Old Lady really meant. But it wasn't until the chips were down and the club was there that I realized the loyalty they spout on about isn't bullshit. I know there are things you can't tell us, things you know that we aren't supposed to know, and it's okay. We're still here for you."

"How do you know that?" I inquired.

"They told us," Allison voiced. "They said you got involved fast and hard because you're a doctor, and you got pulled into something they normally don't include us in."

"It's why we're not pressing you to talk," Darcy said. "We respect the club's boundaries."

"Screw the boundaries," I said. "You guys deserve to know what's going on. For your own safety."

"That's not what's important right now," Mia interjected. "We can discuss that with the men later. This, right now, is about you. We love you. We love who you were before this happened, and we love who you'll become because of this. You don't have to hide, Linden. If you want to fall apart, go ahead. We can help you put yourself back together."

Mia was close enough to touch me, and she stroked her finger down my left pinky.

"You should throw more shit at Boxer," Rachel suggested. "It might help."

"Next time, use something with a bit more heft to it. A plastic cup ain't gonna cut it," Joni said.

"I should've known you guys would find out about that," I said in amusement. "There are no secrets in this family, are there?"

"Not when one of us is hurting," Darcy said. "And darlin', you're hurting bad."

I bowed my head.

"Do you want to talk about it?" Allison asked. "Has anyone actually asked you that? Has anyone asked you if you want to open up?"

I hadn't spoken of anything specific. I was tired of the secrecy, though. Were they strong enough to handle the truth? I believed they were. But as angry as I was at Boxer, it felt like a betrayal telling the Old Ladies before telling him. And since this was club business and connected to a cartel, I really did need to speak to him first.

"I think I have to talk to Boxer," I said slowly.

Part of me envied them. They were left in the dark. They were left not knowing about everything going on around them. But was ignorance truly bliss? Was it fair to make them sitting ducks? Waiting for someone to pluck out their feathers and roast them until they were charred? How could they protect their families and children if they didn't know what was going on right in their own backyard?

This was truly a matter of life and death.

The Old Ladies cleaned up, chucking plasticware and paper plates into the garbage. Darcy put all her haircutting instruments back into her bag and then hoisted it to her shoulder.

"I think you really rock the short hair, babe." Darcy smiled. "And I think it'll match your new affinity for leather pants."

I smiled. "Yeah. I'm calling it Biker Chic."

"Have you met Laura yet?" Rachel asked.

"No. Freddy's mentioned her a few times."

"When you're up to it, we'll all go shopping at Leather and Ink," Rachel promised. "You'll love her store."

"Can't wait," I said.

"There's strawberry rhubarb pie for dessert." Joni left the picnic basket next to my bedside. "There's also banana and chocolate cream pie in there. And chocolate chip cookies."

"Calorie dense foods. I appreciate it. Thank you."

"You're welcome," Joni said.

"Has anyone seen or talked to Freddy?" I inquired.

Mia looked at Joni and then me. "I've spoken with her. She feels like this is her fault. If she hadn't jumped behind the bar, she would've been hanging out with you. You wouldn't have gotten abduct—" She flinched. "Sorry."

"Do me a favor, okay?" I asked.

Her eyes were wary. "What?"

"None of this is your fault or Freddy's fault, or even my fault. Okay? So, let's stop talking around what happened or apologizing for things that can't be changed. I'll talk to Boxer and when I can, I'll level with all of you."

"If that's what you want," Darcy said. "Because again, we're not pressuring you to—"

"I know. Jeez, I know. You guys have been…" I searched for the right word. "Wonderful. There's just a lot of moving parts to all this. Okay?"

They nodded, and one by one, they left the room until it was just me and Mia.

"You want to talk to Boxer?" Mia asked me.

"Want?" I sighed. "No. Should? Yes."

"It's my turn to ask something from you," Mia said.

"Go on."

"Boxer. He loves you. He'd kill for you. Remember that when you talk to him."

The food and the company restored me on a level I didn't expect. The Old Ladies had helped lift my spirits. It would be a long time before I felt any semblance of normalcy, but they were there for me.

My hand began to throb. I was due for another morphine drip, but I wasn't sure I wanted it anymore. I didn't like the physical pain of my injuries—but I was slowly beginning to realize that I didn't like the idea of falling through the cracks that Dante had created inside me either.

It would be far too easy to escape into an addiction.

For the first time ever, I understood the appeal.

But I also recognized the danger.

I'd no longer judge those that had fallen because they'd been cut off at the knees instead of living fortunate lives.

It began to rain. A light drizzle rapped against the glass of the hospital window, but the afternoon sun steadfastly attempted to batter its way through the dark clouds. There was something so incredibly soothing about the weather. The angry rumble of thunder in the distance. The flash of lightning that lit up the sky. I wasn't one for symbolism or poetry, but I couldn't help but smile at the irony of it.

The opening of the door alerted me that he was here.

I felt him.

He was everywhere. Overwhelming with his presence.

Just for an instant, I closed my eyes and pretended I was in his arms again. Safe. Protected. Sheltered.

*Loved.*

My heart had belonged to him long before I'd been ready to admit it. And he had never once made me think that he would discard it. No, he was a protector by nature, and I knew what he would do for me.

I mustered the bravery to finally look at him.

He blinked tired, blood shot eyes and then scratched a thumb along his raspy, whiskered cheek. It sounded like sandpaper stroking a plank of wood.

"Have you slept at all?" I blurted out.

"I dozed for a bit in the waiting room," he said. "No more than a few minutes at a time."

His gaze was hungry as it raked over me, lingering on my hair. "It looks good," he said gruffly.

"But I don't look good. Right?"

He clenched his jaw and didn't reply.

"You can come in, you know." I gestured with my chin to the chair. "Have a seat."

"You're not gonna throw me out again?"

"I'm not going to apologize for that."

"God, Linden, don't apologize. Don't apologize for anything."

He shuffled over to the chair and plopped down. He stretched his legs out and rested his clenched fists on his thighs.

"Why did this happen to me, Boxer? Why was I kidnapped? Dante told me it was about you. That this was personal. I just don't know why."

"It's time to tell you everything. You deserve to know all of it." He sighed and leaned forward. "There have been two cartels competing for business in Waco. The Garcia cartel and the Sanchez cartel. The Tarnished Angels are drug mules for the Sanchez cartel, and up until recently, the Garcia cartel was only running drugs and only where we let them. They have a different part of the city. They kept to their side. We kept to ours. But something changed in the past few months, and when we found out they were peddling flesh, we went to Mateo Sanchez, and he ordered us to stop it. Mateo is all about making money, but he's not into trafficking humans."

"A cartel kingpin not wanting to sell humans? That doesn't make any sense," I said.

"Sanchez has no problem with drugs, guns, gambling. That's just part of the world he comes from. But just like the Tarnished Angels, he doesn't stand for human trafficking. We can do business with him, Linden, but that other shit doesn't fly with any of us. Get it?"

I nodded.

"We intercepted a few of the Garcia cartel's shipments," Boxer went on. "I told you about the children and the women we found. It was a clear message from us to the Garcia cartel to cut that shit out. That we didn't want that in Waco. It wasn't supposed to escalate, but the Garcia cartel didn't like being put in their place. They saw it as a challenge. They made it personal by coming after you. By kidnapping you, they sent a message of their own: women and children are fair game. Families are fair game. It's a declaration of war, Linden. And if they want war, they're gonna fucking get it. Because they don't get to do this. They don't get to—Christ, Linden. *Look* at what they did to you!"

He fell silent, and he struggled to take a few deep breaths, obviously trying to get himself under control.

"Do you want to know?" I asked quietly. "About what happened to me?"

"Do I want to know? No. But I have to. I'll listen and stomach it. Because this never should've happened to you, and I'll have to live with it for the rest of my life." He met my gaze. "I see it in your eyes. You'll blame me forever."

"You should've protected me."

"I know."

"But I should've protected myself," I said. "This isn't all on you."

"Don't absolve me."

"I'm not. I'm not at all. But you did try and tell me what I was getting into with the Tarnished Angels. I just didn't think…" I shook my head. "I was stupid. Stupid and too in love with you to see straight." I looked at him to gauge his reaction at the admittance of my feelings.

His gaze was tender, soft.

I sighed. "There was no listening to reason. I didn't have to stick around, but I did. And here we are."

"Here we are," he agreed, his tone dark. "Tell me what happened to you, Linden. Don't leave anything out."

I didn't.

I talked for so long without interruption that my throat went dry. As I recounted everything that had occurred, everything I remembered, Boxer remained silent and unmoving. A muscle in his jaw began to tick. Only when I got to the part of Dante branding me did Boxer get up and start pacing around the room, clenching his fists. He prowled like the lion on the animal kingdom show, only the lion had had an outlet for his energy.

"There was a doctor," I said. "He patched me up and kept me alive so Dante could continue his...torture. But he also whispered the name of the town where I was."

Boxer's eyes met mine. "Town? You know where you were taken?"

"Yes."

"Tell me," he commanded.

"What are you going to do?"

"Seriously?"

"Yeah, seriously. What are you going to do? Run down there and storm the town? Are you going to go on a killing rampage and murder everyone who lives there, including the peasants living in abject poverty and fear because Dante rules over them?"

"I don't kill innocents," he said tightly. "And I'm pissed as fuck that you'd even say that. But what if they're not innocent?"

"What does that even mean?"

"It means, that any one of them could've gotten word to—"

"Dante saws people in half with chainsaws when they piss him off. Do you really expect these people to go out on a limb for a stranger?"

"The doctor gave you the name of the town," he

pointed out. "So clearly courage isn't absent in all of them."

I clamped my mouth shut.

"I want the name of that town," he went on. "So the boys and I can go down there and fucking end him."

"And then what?" I demanded. "What happens after you kill him? Play this forward for me, because I have a pretty good idea of how this goes. Garcia retaliates. And they bring it here. To our streets. Think of the casualties."

"Are you asking me not to?" His gaze turned dark. "Shit's been set in motion, and we can't back down. If we don't end him, he'll just do this to someone else. Go after someone else's woman or kid."

"I know." I looked up at the ceiling. "He doesn't deserve mercy. He may be human, but not all human lives have value. That's what I've learned."

"Doc," he began.

"Don't call me that. Don't," I said softly. "I don't know if I'm a doctor anymore."

"Fuck, that's my fault too."

"I'm not the same person that I was. He took so much from me, Boxer."

"Are you afraid I won't love you?"

I flinched.

"I love you. Any and all parts of you. I love who you were, and I love who you are now."

"I don't know who that is."

He came over to the bed and sat down next to me. His gaze scanned my body, as if he was looking for a place where he could touch me that wasn't injured. His nearness made my heart jump, but not in fear. Boxer's hand reached out to gently cradle my cheek.

I leaned into his touch, and it made me feel weak and strong at the same time. Even though I was angry, I wanted to forgive him. I wanted to forgive myself. Hopefully, in time...

"I told you once I'm not going anywhere," he reminded me. "I'm the one who should be asking if you still love me. If we still have a shot at this. Have I lost you? I'm the one that brought you into this world. I'm the one that didn't let you go. I'm the one that hoped you'd stay."

I took a deep breath and leaned back. "I don't know what life looks like on the other side, Boxer. I can't promise what it'll look like. It's all murky. It'll be murky for a long, long time. Even after physical therapy. Even after counseling. Even after I find my new normal, I still won't be who I used to be. When you look at me, will you be able to forgive yourself for not protecting me?"

"Jesus, Linden. I wish I could go back in time and undo everything that's happened."

"Well, you can't. Life doesn't work that way and wishing for a different outcome is stupid. It prevents you from moving forward."

"Can we? Move forward?" he asked. "We were just about to get there. We were just about to figure out our lives together, and then this happened. Can we ever be happy again?"

"Yeah. I think we can still be happy."

"You do?"

I nodded slowly. "I think so. I really do. Because I know one thing for certain: It was hard enough to find you when I thought I was normal. It was hard enough finding someone who loved me, quirks and all. Now I'm not normal."

"Hold on a second," he began, "I don't want you staying with me for that reason. You don't have to be *stuck* with me or the club."

I lowered the blanket of the bed that was covering me.

I inched up my hospital gown and pointed to the bandage on my hip. "I have a giant D branded onto my body, like I'm a piece of livestock. Even after it heals, even after plastic surgery to remove the scar, even after I decide to turn it into a tattooed piece of art, to make something ugly and gruesome into something beautiful, it will always be there as a reminder of what I've been through. I'll never forget. Neither will you."

"Linden…"

"I'll tell you the name of the town," I stated. "But you have to promise me something."

"Anything."

"I want you to bring him to me."

"What?"

"I'm in, Boxer. I'm all in. I'll be part of this world. Not just because I was pulled into it, but because I choose this. I choose *you* and the club. But you have to do this for me. You have to bring him to me, and you have to let me be the one to kill him."

He didn't say anything for a long moment. He stared at me and then looked at the ground and then back to me. "I have to take this to the club. I have to take this to the brothers, and we have to vote on it. But I'll go to bat for you with them if I have to, to sway them."

I raised my eyebrows in surprise. "I wasn't expecting that to be your answer."

"You expected me to try and talk you out of it?"

"Yes," I said. "Why aren't you?"

"You know your own mind, and I won't disrespect you by choosing for you."

"Thank you," I said, my throat thick with emotion. "You *have* to tell the Old Ladies. Maybe not specifics, but they need to know to be on their guard. They have to know they're in danger."

"They know," he said. "They've been in lockdown at the clubhouse since you were kidnapped."

"Seriously? None of them said anything."

He shrugged.

"But Mia was the one who found me," I said. "What was she doing out of the clubhouse?"

"Crow was with her," he said. "Anytime any of the Old Ladies have to leave for whatever reason, they have a prospect or a brother with them for protection."

I swallowed and looked down at my broken hand.

"What? What do you want to ask?"

"Did you try and find me?" I blurted out.

"We knew Dante had you, but we didn't know where."

"And if you'd known where I was?" I prodded. "Would you have come for me?"

"Damn right I would've come for you. That's not even a question you should be asking."

"No?" My blood boiled with rage. "I almost died. I *should've* died. So forgive the fuck out of me for wondering if I was important enough for you to save."

"Damn right you're important enough to save," he said, anger coating his tone.

We glared at one another.

Boxer was the first to break the silence of our standoff. "I'm so fucking sorry, Linden. I'm sorry this shit happened to you."

"I can't hear it anymore. I can't hear another apology. Don't look at me with pity. Don't stay with me because you pity me."

"God, woman. It kills me that you think pity has anything to do with this. If I have to, I'll spend the rest of my life proving to you that pity's got nothing to do with it."

"Regrets are a waste of time, aren't they?"

"Damn right they are," he agreed.

I exhaled slowly and then nodded. "Would you kill him for me? If I asked?"

"Without hesitation. Say the word and I'll be the one to put a bullet in his head."

"Mia said you'd kill for me because you love me."

"I would kill for you. And I do love you."

"I don't know if that's enough," I admitted quietly.

His expression was bleak. "It's all I've got."

# Chapter 32

I YAWNED, my mouth stretching far enough that the bones of my jaw popped. When I opened my eyes, I tried not to startle when I saw Amanda checking on my IV bag.

"Hey there, sleepy head," she greeted with a soft smile. "I thought about waking you, so you weren't jumpy when you saw me, but you looked so peaceful, I didn't have the heart to do it."

"Thanks."

"But I do feel it's my duty as your friend to tell you that you sleep with your mouth open." She grinned.

"I do not."

"You do. You might want to work on that. It's not very attractive."

"Like I'm worried about being attractive right now." I wrinkled my nose. "What time is it?"

"A little before six. I haven't seen Boxer for a while."

"I sent him away. He was in desperate need of a shower. Like desperate, desperate."

"How are you feeling?"

"My hand is about a seven on the pain scale."

"Okay. We can work on that, but that's not what I was asking about."

"I knew that's not what you were asking about. I don't really want to talk about it. All I do is talk about my feelings—it's all I've done for the past many hours. I'm exhausted. Please don't take it personally."

She paused for a moment and then said, "Your hair looks good."

"One of the Old Ladies used to cut hair."

The door to the hospital room opened and Freddy came in, carting a plant in a clay pot. It was tall and thin, but very leafy. She wasn't in her usual 1950s garb. She was dressed way down in a pair of skinny jeans, slouchy sweater, and subdued makeup. Her platinum blonde hair was pulled up into a messy top knot, the too short tendrils pushed behind her ears.

"Hey," she greeted, looking from me to Amanda. "I know visiting hours are almost over, so I won't stay long."

Amanda glanced at me for confirmation, and I nodded.

"Holler if you need anything, Linden," Amanda said. "And by holler, I mean use the call button, it's easier." She shot Freddy a smile on her way out. And then Freddy and I were alone.

"Nice plant," I said, breaking the ice.

"Yeah, I heard plants really liven things up." Her mouth quirked up into a grin as she set the leafy plant on the bedside table.

"Yeah, I heard that once too," I said.

Her eyes landed on the cardboard to-go container with a Pinky's sticker on the top.

"Strawberry rhubarb pie," I explained. "I'm saving it for a midnight snack. The Old Ladies brought it to me earlier."

"Oh. Oh, I see." Her eyes surveyed me from my head to toe. "I'm digging the hair."

"It wasn't my first choice, but it was either this or leaving it the way it was. And leaving it wasn't an option."

"Mia told me," she said softly. "About the state she found you in."

"You're not here to apologize, are you? Because I'm done with the apology side of my life."

"Why would you think I was going to apologize?" She finally took a seat next to the bed, realizing we were about to dive into it.

"Because that's what people do when they don't know what else to say, or they have some sort of misplaced guilt. Mia doesn't feel guilty, and it happened right outside her bar. So, you shouldn't feel guilty about helping her out that night and leaving me alone."

"Okay," she whispered.

"I really mean it, Freddy. Don't waste any time feeling guilty. There's too much other stuff to worry about, okay?"

"This was because of the club, wasn't it," she asked after a long moment of silence. "What happened to you, I mean."

"Yes."

"Yeah." She sighed. "I thought so."

"How attached are you to your life?" I asked her suddenly.

"How attached am I to my life? What a weird question."

"Freddy," I began.

"I like it here. I like it here a lot. I enjoy my job, I finally feel like I have a good group of friends, and I've got the casual thing with Bishop."

"Damn it," I muttered.

"Why?"

"Bad shit is about to go down," I said bluntly. "And if I were you, I would leave. I would go somewhere else and start over."

Her eyes widened.

"Trust me. Stay as far away from the club as you can. Things are going to be very different soon. And I don't want you getting caught up in it because you have ties to the club."

"Fuck," she muttered. "What's coming down the pipeline? You know what, never mind. It doesn't matter, does it?"

"No. It doesn't matter."

She nodded slowly. "If you could go back and do it all over it again, knowing what you know now about the club, would you choose differently?"

"Yeah. If I could do it all over again, I would walk away. I never would have gotten involved. I love Boxer. I really love him. I love the Old Ladies. I even love the loyalty and the family aspect of the club." I pointed to my injured hand. "But this—this is who I am. Who I *was*. And I don't know if I'm ever going to be able to perform surgery again. The love of my life cost me the other love of my life. And I don't know yet how to reconcile that. I don't know if I'm ever going to be able to forgive him or forgive myself fully. But I do know I have to find a way to live in this new reality because this is what I've got." I shrugged. "Being a doctor was always more than just a job. It's what got inside my soul and lit me up. It was my purpose—and now, I might have to find a new purpose."

She stared at me, her eyes filling with tears. "I've never had that kind of passion for anything in my life. It was easy to walk away from college and my degree in engineering. I envy you for that, Linden." She blew out a breath of air.

"Sometimes I wonder, if I'd loved engineering, would it have been enough to get me through the darkness?"

"Did you ever get counseling?"

"Yeah. For a little while. It felt weird to talk about it. Because even though it was bad, and even though it affected me, I still wasn't *hurt*, you know? My physical body hadn't been violated."

"No, maybe not, but it's still a form of rape, Freddy. Someone drugged your drink and took your memory for a while. They took it without permission. That's rape. And until you deal with it, you're not going to move on. You're not going to connect or fall in love or have a beautiful life, and I want that for you. I want that for you so much."

"What about you? What are you going to do? Are you going to leave Boxer and the Tarnished Angels behind and start over fresh?"

"No. For better or for worse, I'm here. I've made my play. I've chosen Boxer and the club."

"Would it be different? Would you leave if it wasn't your hand that had been injured?"

"I don't know. That's one of those questions I can't answer because I'll never know. It's the *what if* game, it's the *if only I'd turned right instead of left game.*"

"What happened to you?"

"I was kidnapped," I said baldly. "Kidnapped and tortured and sent back broken as a warning to the club."

"What kind of warning?"

"That none of us are safe. Even the women and children."

"My God," Freddy muttered.

"You're special. There's something inside you that you haven't figured out yet. I just want you to be alive so you can discover it. If you can't do it for yourself, then do it for me. I couldn't bear to see you get caught up in this shit. Leave, while you still can."

"Okay," she whispered. "I'll go. My parents have been asking me to visit. I've been putting them off because I just can't seem to…"

"You've got parents who love you? Stay with them. Don't hide from their love. Let your mother dote on you. Watch TV with your dad. Talk. Make some meals. And figure out what it is you really want. You're young. You have your whole life ahead of you. Don't waste it."

"You're talking like your life is already over."

"No. My life isn't over. But it has taken a detour." I smiled slightly.

The door to my room opened, and Amanda stepped inside. "Hate to break up the party, but visiting hours are officially over."

"All right, I'll go." Freddy rose. "Don't want you to have to throw me out."

"Oh yeah, you look like just the type who needs to be wrangled by security." Amanda winked.

Freddy leaned down toward me. "Can I hug you?"

"Yeah, you can hug me."

She gently wrapped her arms around me and gave me a light squeeze. "I'll keep in touch."

"You better."

Freddy shot Amanda a smile on her way out.

"Do you need anything? Are you good?" Amanda asked me.

I thought for a moment, smiling at her. "I'm good."

It was the middle of the night, and I couldn't sleep. The TV was on low in the background, and I was watching a

1980s romantic comedy. The antics of the heroine who had gotten herself into a case of mistaken identity had me chuckling every now and again.

I didn't used to enjoy romantic comedies, but now I realized how much the world needed them. The lightness, the laughter, the happily ever after. Life so rarely looked the way you thought it was going to. But in cinema, in the world of love, everything always worked out. It was a beautiful lesson to remember—that sometimes, some dreams really did come true.

The door to the hospital room opened. I frowned in confusion, wondering if it was Babs peeking her head in to check on me. She was the nurse on duty for the night.

It was Boxer.

"What are you doing here?" I asked. "And how did you get past Babs?"

"Woman, please," he said. "You're still doubting my charms?"

"No, I'm not doubting your charms, but it is the middle of the night, and there are such things as visiting hours."

He shrugged and looked at the TV. "What are you watching?"

"Something fun."

"Can I watch with you?"

"Sure." He came around to the side of the bed and gently lowered himself next to me. He put an arm around me, tentatively, like he wasn't sure if it would be accepted.

I leaned my head against his shoulder, my eyes drooping shut. Boxer's comfort in the moment was a natural sedative.

"I couldn't bear the thought of you sleeping here alone," he said finally. "I just wanted to be with you."

Emotion rolled through me, and I blinked back tears.

"I'm surprised you're awake," he said.

"It's harder to sleep without the morphine."

"You're not taking morphine?"

"I am, but my dosage is way down. Enough to dull the pain, but not enough to really knock me unconscious." I paused. "I'm afraid of what waits for me in my sleep." I turned my head and sniffed him. "You showered."

"Glad you noticed."

I breathed in the scent of his cologne on his skin and tried to hold it in my mind. Every now and again, I'd take a deep breath and remember the scent of sandalwood and the acrid stench of my fear. I didn't need to physically be in that jail cell to still *be* there. I exhaled slowly, letting go of the memory for now. Knowing there would never be a day that I could forget it completely, but maybe it didn't have to poison everything good for the rest of my life.

"We had church," he said.

"Yeah?"

He reached for the remote that rested on my lap and then muted the television. "They've agreed that you can be the one to end Dante."

"Thank you," I whispered. "Thank you for giving me that."

"You sure about this?"

"No." I let out a long exhale. "But there will be nights that I lay my head down on a pillow, and a few hours later I'll wake up screaming from what he's done to me. And when I wake up, I need to know beyond a shadow of a doubt that he's gone, and that *I* did it."

He didn't say anything for a long time and then he asked, "What's the name of the town?"

"Valley of Hearts. That's where I was kept. Valley of Hearts." I turned my head to look up at him. "When do you leave?"

"Couple of days," he said. "It's gonna take some time to plan. Gotta talk to Mateo Sanchez and the Idaho boys. What we're about to do will be insane."

"The Idaho boys? You're going to involve them?"

"Yeah. A lot of them are ex-military. We need that."

"This is so much bigger than Waco, isn't it?"

"Yeah, darlin'. Way bigger than Waco."

The next few days crawled by. Even with visits from the Old Ladies, I still found myself with a lot of downtime. And the problem with downtime was that you had time to think. Thinking led to self-examination.

It took you down a rabbit hole that was dark and deep. Into places long forgotten, some even previously undiscovered.

I thought a lot about my parents. I wasn't sure how I was going to deal with them moving forward. I was already estranged from my father. And my mother had blown our chilly relationship to smithereens when she'd invaded my privacy. But now, if I reached out to them, how was I supposed to have a relationship with them? How was I supposed to explain my substantial injuries? How was I supposed to justify any of this?

And it wasn't even as though I missed them—more like I mourned the loss of what never had been. Perhaps it was better this way. Perhaps this was how it was supposed to be. Maybe it was easier.

I wasn't even sure I was still able to practice medicine —and becoming a doctor had been such a sore point with my mother. I couldn't tell her *anything* about my life. Not without revealing far more than I was comfortable with.

The truth of the matter was I didn't want a relationship with either of them. Even when I hadn't been involved with Boxer and the Tarnished Angels, I didn't particularly care for them to be in my life. I didn't see the purpose of trying to reconstruct a bridge that had been blown up with emotional grenades. I was trying to rebuild a life; I was trying to rebuild a life that made sense to me, and my parents had no place in it.

I didn't see much of Boxer during the days. He checked in with me via text on the burner phone he had given me, but I knew he was dealing with club business and coordinating with Mateo Sanchez and the Idaho boys about what was about to go down in Mexico.

Every night, he slipped into my hospital room, and we fell asleep watching television, his arm around me. And in the morning, the nurse on duty would find us in bed together, though she never put a stop to it.

Late one morning, I said to Boxer, "I have a newfound respect for you."

"What do you mean?" he asked as we shared a piece of banana cream pie. I was pretty sure Boxer was keeping Pinky's in business by bringing me and the entire floor food.

"I mean, it's hell lying in a hospital bed watching nothing but bad TV and not being able to move around and live your life."

"You're ready to live your life?" he asked.

"I wouldn't go that far," I said, "but I think I'm ready for what comes next. By the way, what *is* coming next?"

"The boys and I are leaving tomorrow morning. Early."

I nodded, my heart in my throat.

"We have cabins," he said. "In the Kisatchie National Forest in Louisiana. It's about a six-hour drive. They're off the grid, and you won't find them on any map. It's private land run through an LLC by our attorney, so there's no link to anyone from the club. While we're gone, you, the other Old Ladies and the kids are gonna stay there."

"Are we?"

"Yes."

"Why can't we stay at the clubhouse?"

"We want you all out of Waco. Peace of mind, since only the club knows about the cabins."

"Okay," I said.

"No fight?"

"About safety? Never."

"The cabins have everything. Food, water, all the medical supplies you'll ever need. We've had the cabins for years, and they're always stocked and ready to go. You can never have too many escape plans. You can never have too many backups."

"When you say off the grid…"

"Generators and solar for power and a pump for the well. It just means we're completely independent of the system. We don't need anything from the outside world. Lots of bugs if you're outside, but AC and running water inside. Comfortable beds, all of it. They're quaint, but clean and in good condition."

"What about you?" I asked him. "Will you be safe? I know you like to take risks, Boxer. And I know this is about so much more than just the women and children. Because it's about me now. It's personal for you. Please, please, keep your head. Keep your cool. Keep calm and for the love of God, come home to me. Because I swear to God, if you die—"

His lips covered mine before I could even get the next words out. His tongue slipped into my mouth, effectively obliterating any words or thoughts or feelings I had. That was one thing that was always the same between us. Lust came roaring back. Blazing through my veins. But my body was in no shape to enjoy him. Not the way I wanted. Not with the violence that I was ready to unleash inside me. That would have to wait until I was healed.

He pulled back and cradled my cheeks in his hands. "I'll come back to you."

"I won't survive your death. I'm not being dramatic I —" His mouth covered mine again effectively shutting me up. A few moments later, he lifted his lips from mine.

"One thing that hasn't changed," he grinned, "your inability to stop thinking."

"I won't survive you dying. I won't," I vowed again, as though I could ward off his death by admitting I was too emotionally fragile at the moment to live through it.

"You won't have to survive that," he promised. "I'll be careful. More careful than I've ever been in my entire life because, damn Linden, I have to come home to you. There is no other option. And I'll bring him to you. I'll bring you Dante."

The hospital door opened, but Boxer didn't move away from me even though we'd been caught in an intimate position.

"Sorry to intrude," Peyton said. "But I have your discharge papers."

"Finally," I muttered.

"Chief Nelson wasn't taking any chances. So he kept you here a little longer than normal."

Thirty minutes later, Boxer was helping me into a dress. Nothing fancy. Black and cotton that barely touched my skin and allowed me to move comfortably.

"I'm not letting you push me out of here in a wheel-chair," I protested. "I'm not an invalid. My legs aren't broken. Just my hand."

"You've been supine for days," he reminded me. "I don't want you to get lightheaded."

"Boxer," I warned. "Did I give you grief about your limitations when you were my patient?"

"Actually, yeah. You did. You gave me a lot of shit about my limitations."

I glared at him. "Well, stop giving me shit about mine."

He smiled. "Alright, woman, alright. Let's just take it slow, okay?"

Boxer grabbed the plant Freddy had brought me, and then we left the room.

I smiled in surprise when I saw Acid sitting in a chair in the hallway. He rose when we came out.

"Hey," I greeted. "I didn't know you were here. I thought you went back to Waco when the Old Ladies did."

"Nah. A few of us stayed behind and traded shift watch," he said.

"Shift watch?" I looked at Boxer. "Have I been guarded this whole time?"

"Damn right," he said gruffly.

"Oh. I didn't realize. Thanks. Both of you."

With his free hand, Boxer grasped my elbow and gently guided me to the elevator. I lifted my right hand and wiggled a finger at Peyton and Amanda. They had been working almost around the clock, checking in on me. I was grateful for them. Not just for their friendship, but for the caliber of their characters. They were both truly special people, and the hospital was lucky to have them. They made their patients' lives better, and they made my life better too.

The day was chilly, but the sun was bright.

"You're cold," Boxer noted as I shivered next to him.

"A little bit," I admitted. "I'm not used to having a bare neck."

"I love your bare neck." He dragged a finger across my skin, making me shiver for an entirely different reason.

Boxer helped me into the truck and then handed me the leafy plant, which I placed in my lap.

"I hope you don't mind," he said as he climbed into the driver's side, "but I had Joni and Mia go to your condo and pack you some clothes before they headed back to Waco."

"How did they get in without a key?" I asked.

"Ramsey."

"Ah. Well, thanks for taking care of that for me."

"No problem." He gripped the steering wheel so hard that I heard the squeak of the material under his fingers. "He called."

"Who?"

"Dante. He said he had you and then he hung up. I had no idea where you were and it drove me bat shit."

Boxer turned on the engine and got the heater cranking.

"I can't imagine what it must've been like for you," I said.

"You're the one who had to live through it, Linden. I've got nothing on you."

We drove in pensive silence as I looked out the window. There were discount signs and people in parking lots. Everything seemed so normal. The world still turned. People still went out to eat. People still laughed.

I was the one that was different.

An hour and half later, he turned down his street and then drove the car into the driveway. He cut the engine, and I unlatched my seatbelt.

"Wait. Let me help you."

It was a slow-moving process. He took the plant from me and then helped me out of the truck.

"Don't freak out when you see the place," he said,

dropping my elbow so he could use his keys to unlock the door.

"Why would I freak out?"

He sighed. "Just promise me."

"Okay, I promise." He pushed open the door and flipped on the light, and then he moved to the side so I could enter.

My breath caught.

There were holes in the walls like someone had gone berserk. The furniture had been split open, stuffing coming out of the seams. Broken picture frames were haphazardly strewn about and an old sledgehammer rested in the corner.

"What happened," I asked, mouth agape. "Did Dante order this? Is this cartel retaliation?"

Boxer shook his head. "No. This is how I took out my anger after he called."

"You destroyed your home," I said. "Why would you do such a thing?"

"Says the woman who smashed an entire kitchen's worth of dishes."

"Touché."

He set down the plant in the hallway and then went to the bedroom. I followed at a slower pace. The linens and comforter had been torn to shreds, like he'd taken a blade to them.

"This house was just a house before you came into my life," he said. "But now, every room in this place has a memory of you. Fucking on the living room floor. Cooking breakfast in the kitchen. I had thoughts about our future and what our life would look like together. I was so fucking angry that Dante took that from me. From me. From us." He shook his head. "The idea of coming home to this place every single day, knowing you'd slept in my bed, knowing that your perfume would eventually disappear from my pillow had me going ballistic."

I sat down on the edge of the mattress. "So, you took a sledgehammer to the walls, and battered your furniture? The Boxer equivalent of setting things on fire. Starting over, huh?"

He nodded. "I haven't slept here since you've been gone. I've been at the clubhouse. It was easier that way."

"Why did you bring me here? Why did you show me this?"

"Because there are ugly parts of me too. Because Dante taking you, changed me, too. This is no longer my haven. Now this is just the place that reminds me of everything I almost lost. And I don't want to live here anymore."

"Okay," I said quietly. "Then we'll move somewhere else."

He paused. "We?"

I looked at him. "Yeah, Boxer. We." My smile was sad. "It's too bad. I really loved your house. It felt...homey. I didn't have that growing up. This was going to be..."

He walked to me and placed his hand on my shoulder, urging me to stand before gently pulling me into the wall of his chest. "We'll make the new place just as homey. I'll even let you pick out the couch."

I grinned against the side of his neck. "What if I like floral patterns?"

He laughed. "You don't. But if you did, I'd suffer through it. No lace curtains, though. That's where I draw the line."

"That's my line too," I assured him. "I'm also not someone who likes doilies and useless knickknacks."

"So, I'm not in danger of living with a cat-figurine-obsessed lady?"

"Definitely no cat figurines. Maybe frog figurines. I could do frogs."

He paused for a moment. "A lot of changes have been happening in your life. You sure you're ready to live with me fulltime?"

I nodded.

"I'm a bit of a handful," he warned.

"Pot, meet kettle." I pulled away from him, frowning.

"What?"

"I'm concerned."

"Sit, I don't want you tiring yourself." When I sat on the bed, he went on, "What are you concerned about?"

"Are you sure moving in together is a good idea?" I asked, worry marring my expression.

"You afraid you're gonna get sick of me."

"No."

"You afraid I'm gonna get sick of you?"

"No."

"Then what's the problem?"

"Me. I'm the problem." I raised my injured hand. "This is going to take time to sort through. I might never have it fully sorted."

"All right. So what?"

"So what?" I asked in exasperation. "That's a lot to take on."

"I thought that's what people did in relationships. For better or for worse, richer and poorer, and all that mumbo jumbo."

I paused. "You think marriage is mumbo jumbo?"

"Yeah, I do."

"And yet you want to live together?"

He sighed and began to pace. "Marriage is a piece of paper. It's an institution created by lawyers. A business arrangement."

"Wow. That's cold."

"I'm not wrong," he pointed out. "But choosing you, day in, day out, choosing a life with you, there's nothing cold about that. And that's what I'm saying, Linden. I don't believe in marriage. You want to get married? Fine we'll get married, but I don't have to do it to feel secure in this. What about you?"

"What about me?" I evaded.

"How do you feel about marriage?"

"If you get married, there's a possibility of divorce," I said.

"So, by not getting married you don't have to worry about that?"

"Contracts can be dissolved, rings can be removed, even ink can be lasered off. What's the guarantee that any of it will last?"

He walked toward me and leaned down to cradle my cheek for a moment before letting go. "There's no guarantee about any of it, Linden. You just have to live each day as it comes. Live in the present. The future will take care of itself."

"I don't like the idea of marriage in the general sense," I said slowly, looking up to meet his eyes. "But I kind of like the idea of marriage to you."

He smiled. "Is that a proposal?"

I snorted and pulled away. "No."

"I accept."

I stilled. "You accept?"

Boxer nodded. "Yeah. I accept."

"I didn't ask," I said in exasperation.

"You didn't? Sure sounded like you were asking."

"Boxer," I began.

"Marry me."

"What?"

"Marry me," he repeated.

"But I don't—and you—"

"Linden," he said quietly. "We're not your parents, darlin'. So, marry me and we'll figure it all out."

"Shut up," I said.

"Hey," he protested.

"Not you. My brain. I was telling my brain to shut up because it still thinks it calls the shots." I shook my head and then smiled. "Yeah, Boxer. I'll marry you."

He leaned down to gently kiss my lips, and then he pulled back, a big goofy grin on his face. "We better get going or we'll be late."

# Chapter 33

WE DROVE through the gates of the clubhouse, and I waved to the prospects on duty. "Are they going with you tomorrow?" I asked Boxer.

"No. They'll head with you to the cabins. Even though you guys will be off the grid, we're not sending you into the wilderness unprotected."

"Get the women and children to the lifeboats," I quipped.

"Something like that."

There were more motorcycles than just those that belonged to the Waco Tarnished Angels.

"The Idaho boys are here," Boxer explained.

I nodded thoughtfully. Tomorrow was the beginning of something new. It would change all of us, whatever happened.

"If you'd told me even three months ago that I was going to get engaged to a biker, I would've told you to get your head examined."

He cut the engine and grinned. "Life's pretty insane, isn't it?"

"That's putting it mildly."

He came around to help me out of the truck, and then we walked slowly up the porch steps. Boxer opened the door, and I was immediately greeted by a loud chorus of "SURPRISE!" The entire living room was full of Tarnished Angels.

"What is this?" I asked in confusion, stepping back and nearly plowing into Boxer.

Rachel was sitting on the couch, but she stood up and then pointed to the balloons and the banner. "It's a welcome home party."

"A welcome home…" I blinked back tears.

Boxer came and wrapped his arm around me, and then I attempted to burrow into him so I could hide my feelings.

"Not just a welcome home party," Boxer announced, "but our engagement party. Linden asked me to marry her, and I said yes."

I elbowed him in the ribs, causing him to grin. "I didn't ask you."

"Darlin', you all but *begged* me to marry you."

"Shut up, Boxer," Mia stated, getting up from her seat and ambling toward me. "And get out of my way so I can hug Linden."

Boxer stepped back, and then the Old Ladies were all hugging me and jabbering like magpies.

"You didn't get the poor girl a ring?" Darcy asked with a frown at Boxer. "A proposal includes a ring."

"And candles," Joni added.

"And sex," Rachel added. "Lots of sweaty sex. Linden's hair doesn't look at all messed up. Shame on you, Boxer. Shame. On. You."

I looked at Boxer and grinned. "You can have a do

over of the proposal, if you want. I wouldn't be upset about it."

He sighed and rubbed the back of his neck. "Yeah, I might need a do over. Otherwise, the Old Ladies will never let me live it down."

"My boy's all grown up," Colt teased, slapping Boxer on the back.

"We have a lot to celebrate," Zip said. "This is good. All good."

"Should we wait to celebrate until you guys get back?" I asked softly.

An ominous hush fell over the room; no one quite knew what to say.

"Never know when shit's gonna go south," Darcy said. "Let's celebrate now, but then have a huge party when the guys get back."

Mia went to the kitchen counter and grabbed a red Solo Cup, added some ice, and a hefty splash of coconut rum.

"Oh, I don't like coconut rum," I protested.

"Trust me," she said with a wink.

"Mia has yet to make me a cocktail I've hated," Darcy assured me.

Mia added orange soda to the cup, took another one, and poured it into it to mix the drink. She handed it to me. "Go ahead. I'll wait."

I took a sip, my eyes bugging out. "Holy cow, that tastes like an orange creamsicle."

"You're welcome," she said with a laugh. "Now, can we steal you away for a bit?"

"Sounds good," I said with a look in Boxer's direction. He was already drinking a beer and talking to Bishop, the vice president from the Coeur d'Alene chapter.

"It's going to be a full house tonight," I noted.

"But not one of our usual parties," Mia said. "Come on, let's head outside."

"Where are the kids?" I asked. "Usually there are a few of them running around."

"They're in the basement watching movies and playing video games," Darcy said, as we made our way to the backyard. They took the camp chairs and dragged them into a circle. I wanted to help, but they waved me away.

I did not like the idea of the next many days being reliant on them.

"Okay," Mia said, easing her bulk into one of the chairs. "Now that we're out of ear shot of the men, we need the full scoop on this proposal situation. Because while you do look radiant, you seem far too calm."

"I'm not allowed to be calm?" I asked.

"You just agreed to marry Boxer," Joni said with a teasing grin. "I expected more of a freak out."

"Oh, there was a freak out, trust me." I took a sip of my drink. "He brought me to his house. I saw the carnage."

"Ah," Rachel said with a nod.

"He told me why he went nuts." I looked each and every one of them in the eye, one by one. "Do you guys know why?"

"Because you were kidnapped," Darcy admitted baldly.

"Do you guys know *why* I was kidnapped? Did they level with you?"

"A bit," Mia said. "Colt and the boys sat us down and told us that we had to head to the cabins with the kids. He didn't give us details, but he said it's bad."

"And you got caught up in it," Rachel added. "We don't know particulars. We don't need to know particulars, only that things are about to go down and we need to be out of the city to ensure our safety."

I blew out a puff of air and nodded.

"All the Coeur d'Alene boys are here," Darcy went on. "We know whatever's going on is some dark stuff because the prospects have been our living shadows, and the whole crew being down from Idaho is very rare."

"How do you explain all this to the kids?" I asked.

"It's a normal existence for them," Darcy said. "They don't know anything else. They just know there are times we go to the woods, and then we go back home and it's all okay again."

I nodded slowly.

"So, this proposal," Joni said. "I want more details."

"There aren't that many details," I said with a chuckle. "I was standing in his house with sledgehammered holes in the walls and ruined furniture, and he said he didn't want to live there anymore. So, I told him we'd move. That turned into a conversation about living together, which brought up the marriage thing."

"He brought it up, or you brought it up?" Allison demanded as she put baby Tank to her shoulder.

"I don't even really remember."

"It doesn't sound very romantic," Rachel said.

"Do bikers and romance usually go together?" I asked.

"Well, maybe not romance per se," Rachel relented. "But my proposal definitely included food and sex."

"Mine too," Mia said.

"Yep," Joni said with a nod. "There was a lot of sex and a lot of food with Zip."

"You guys are making her sad," Allison said. "Look at her face."

"I'm not sad," I protested.

"Yeah, you are," Darcy insisted. "It's okay to admit you wanted something different in a proposal."

"Everything has been happening so fast anyway. There wasn't really time for him to—it's not like we'd discussed a life together." I frowned and then sighed. "Darn it."

"You wanted a good proposal story, didn't you?" Mia said gently.

I nodded. "Now that I've had time to think about it, yeah. A real proposal would've been nice."

"Ask him for a do-over," Joni said.

"*Demand* a do-over," Rachel said. "You're worth it."

I smiled at her. "Thanks. It feels stupid, though. You know? Because there are so many other more important things going on now."

"Matters of the heart are important too," Allison said.

"Even when the world is falling apart?" I asked quietly.

"Even then," she assured me.

"It feels selfish. They're about to go to Mexico and…" I shook my head and fell silent.

The Old Ladies looked at one another and then Rachel asked, "They're going to Mexico?"

*Shit.*

I exhaled slowly and then nodded.

"Cartel stuff," Joni said. "Right?"

I paused and then nodded again.

"Fuck," Darcy muttered.

"This is bad," Rachel said.

"Very bad." Darcy sighed. "I knew it was bad, but not cartel bad."

"Is that where you were taken?" Allison asked quietly. "Mexico?"

"Yes."

"Holy fuck," Rachel stated, letting out a long breath. "I had—*we*—had no idea. They didn't tell us that part."

"This feels like my fault," I said, bowing my head.

"Hey," Mia said. "Look at me."

I took a deep breath and lifted my head to peer at her.

"The Coeur d'Alene boys are here, which means this is first and foremost club business. You got caught up in some shit. This shouldn't have happened to you, Linden. And their message has been received. Could have been any one of us. We don't need the guys to point that out. So don't you dare apologize for any of this. What they're about to do needs to get done. Okay?"

"Okay," I said with a shaky breath. I took a long drink of the cocktail Mia had made me and then glanced around at the Old Ladies who were smiling at me in compassion—not pity. Never pity with them.

"So," I began, wanting to change the subject, "how rustic are these cabins?"

I screamed. My throat was raw with terror. Arms encompassed me and I fought against them, thrashing to escape their confinement.

Someone cursed.

Male.

My hand throbbed.

Why was it throbbing?

*Oh, right.*

Because someone had taken a mallet and a screwdriver to it.

I wept tears of fear and pain.

"Linden. Linden, wake up."

My hand collided with flesh.

"Shit!"

Something crashed to the floor—it sounded like glass.

I turned my head and opened my eyes to darkness. Tears cascaded down my cheeks, and my neck was hot and feverish.

A light came on, banishing the cobwebs of my dream. The memory of blood cloyed at the back of my throat, and I desperately wanted to gulp water to rid myself of the pain and horror.

Boxer stood at the edge of the bed wearing nothing but a pair of navy briefs. His eyes were wide with concern.

"What happened?" I croaked, attempting to sit up.

"You were having a nightmare," he said flatly. "I tried to wake you up, but all that did was make you fight me more."

He turned his head, and I noticed an angry red welt along his cheekbone. "Did I do that?" I asked in horror.

"Yup. Should have a pretty good shiner in a few days." He moved to the edge of bed and took a seat. "Don't worry about me, Linden. How's your hand?"

"Hurts." I'd only had one of Mia's cocktails, knowing I was going to need some painkillers if I had any hopes of sleeping through the night. "What time is it?"

He got up off the mattress and went to the bedside table to grab his cell phone. "A little after four. We might as well get up."

I nodded but didn't make a move.

"What?" Boxer asked. "What is it?"

I bit my lip. "You can back out, you know?"

"Back out of what?"

"Marrying me."

"Ah, shit, woman," he muttered. He wrapped me in his embrace and gently pulled me into him. He brushed his lips across my forehead. "If you think a punch to the face or a nightmare is enough to scare me off, then you don't know me at all."

"It's more than that, and you know it," I murmured.

"I'm not going anywhere, darlin'. I don't know if you'll ever believe me. But if my ring is on your finger and my last name is yours, then maybe you'll start to trust it. Trust us."

I sighed and lifted my mouth to his. He gently covered my lips, and I sank into the feel of him. In the feel of us.

I trusted this aspect of our relationship. Why couldn't I trust the emotional aspect of it too?

I got dressed in a sundress and matching cardigan that Joni and Mia had packed for me, and then Boxer and I went downstairs.

Darcy was already awake, and the coffee maker was on, gurgling and wafting the bold aroma of coffee through the kitchen and living room.

"I didn't know you were an early riser," I said to her.

Every time I'd seen her, her hair had been done and her makeup had been in place. But this morning, she was dressed casually in a pair of jeans, a black T-shirt, her face scrubbed clean.

"She's not," Gray said, coming up behind his Old Lady and wrapping her in his arms. Darcy leaned back against him and tilted her face up to his for a kiss. He obliged her. "She takes forever to wake up, usually."

"Then why—oh," I said in realization, heat coloring my cheeks. "You heard me."

"Yeah," Darcy said without any hesitation. "We heard you."

"Sorry," I mumbled.

"Hey, don't do that," Gray said. "Don't apologize. You're dealing with your shit. It's okay."

Boxer pulled me into his side. I buried my face against him, wishing my trauma wasn't so vocal. Wishing everyone didn't know about it, even though hiding away from it wouldn't do me any good, anyway.

By five thirty in the morning, everyone was awake except for the children. People kept shooting me loaded looks, and it became too much. I took my cup of coffee out back, ducking my head and refusing to meet penetrating gazes.

I sat in a camp chair near the bonfire that had long since burned out.

The screen door opened and then creaked shut. I didn't turn, expecting it to be Boxer or Mia. I couldn't contain my surprise when I saw it was Reap. He plopped down in the chair next to me, a mug of coffee in his hand.

"Mind if I smoke?" he asked.

"Yes."

He grinned. "Then I won't." He reached into his inner breast pocket of his leather cut and extracted a flask.

"A little early for that, isn't it?" I asked.

"I haven't gone to bed yet," he said. "And it's not for me. It's for you."

"What is it?"

"Bailey's."

I handed him my mug, and he poured a hefty shot into it. He gave it back to me. I took a sip and nearly purred in delight.

"Thanks," I said.

"Just what the doctor ordered."

"I might not be a doctor anymore," I said.

"You'll always be a doctor. You just might not be a surgeon."

I stared into my coffee. "Ouch. Rip off that Band-Aid, Reap."

"I'm sorry as fuck it happened to you, Linden. If any of us could undo it, we would."

I nodded.

"Did Rach ever tell you how we met?"

"No."

"Her friend dragged her to a party at the clubhouse. Wasn't really her scene. Her friend ditched her, and she was kinda stranded. She went into a room, hoping to escape the party. Shit was getting rowdy. Real rowdy." He grinned. "I was sitting in the dark, nursing a bottle of liquor. It was supposed to be a one-night stand."

"Clearly it wasn't."

"Clearly," he agreed.

"Why are you telling me this, Reap?"

"Because life doesn't always go according to plan. And sometimes, even the shittiest situations bring something good. I was drinking alone in the dark because it was the anniversary of my first wife's death."

"Oh," I said quietly.

"Yeah."

"I'm sorry, Reap."

"Thanks, but that's not why I told you."

"Why did you tell me?"

"To remind you that sometimes life is shit, but shit is just manure, and beautiful things can grow in manure."

It wasn't poetry and it wouldn't heal my wounds, but it was comfort. And I took it.

After the adults were fed and caffeinated, the Tarnished Angels began loading luggage into the cars of their Old Ladies.

I was going to ride with Joni since I couldn't drive myself. Colt put a sleepy Silas in the passenger seat of Mia's truck and then had a not-so-private goodbye with his wife.

Rachel flung herself into Reap's arms, and I could tell by the shaking of her shoulders that emotion was getting the better of her. After Reap had shared the story of how he and Rachel met, watching them saying goodbye made me a bit teary myself.

Torque leaned down and gently cradled his infant son's head, and then he stared deeply into Allison's eyes and whispered something I couldn't hear. She nodded and kissed him. When she pulled back, her expression was resolute and strong.

"Hey," Boxer said, drawing my attention to him.

He pressed his body against mine, forcing me against the passenger door of Joni's car.

"I'm coming home to you," he said. "I promise."

My eyes were misty when they met his. "There are some promises you can't keep, Boxer."

"I don't know if you're the praying type, but if you are, send us your prayers, darlin'. We're gonna to need it." He pressed his forehead to mine. "When I get home, I'm gonna do right by you, Linden. I'm gonna propose the way I should have proposed." He flashed a smile. "And I'm gonna convince you that I'm the man you always wanted. I'm gonna convince you that us meeting wasn't a mistake, that I'm not something else that you have to regret. Do you hear me?"

"I hear you."

I touched my lips to his, breathing in his scent, praying in that moment that he came home safely, praying they all came home safely.

# Chapter 34

We arrived at the cabins early in the afternoon.

"I'm so glad to be here," Joni said, cutting the engine after pulling onto the gravel driveway of the first cabin. "I'm ready for a nap."

"Sorry I couldn't share the driving burden with you."

"Don't sweat it," she said with a grin.

There were six cabins, and even though they looked rustic, they had all the modern amenities, including air conditioning and heat. Winter in Louisiana wasn't like winter up north, so I knew I'd be fine wearing jeans, sweaters, and a light jacket.

The prospects were going to bunk in one of the cabins, the Old Ladies with kids would stay in another, and then Joni, Rachel, and I would take a third.

While the prospects unloaded the grocery bags, the Old Ladies and I got settled. The kids were grouchy and hungry. Darcy fed them while the pregnant women took naps. I sat idly by, feeling useless.

After the kids had been fed and plopped in front of the

TV to watch a movie, Darcy popped open a beer and handed it to me.

"Come on," she said. "We're going to the lake."

"We are?" I asked in amusement.

She grinned. "Yeah. Hey, Cam…"

"Yeah, Mom?"

"I'm going to the lake with Linden. Watch your sister, okay?"

"K," he said with an impish grin and then turned his attention back to the TV.

Darcy and I headed out the back door and took the path down to the lake. It was quiet and pristine, and if we weren't there for the reason we were, I might've enjoyed it more.

"Cop a squat," she said, sitting down at the bank.

I sank down next to her.

"How are you holding up?" she asked.

"I guess because you're asking that question, then you already know the answer." I flashed her a grin and took a sip of beer.

"Waiting for news is bad enough. The fact that we're in a dead zone of cell service doesn't help. Sure, we have a satellite phone, so if we need something in an emergency, we have access, but out here, we're basically cut off from it all."

"Might be nice for a while, though," I pointed out. "I don't feel unsafe here. I just—the last thing I needed was more time to think, you know?"

"Have you tried meditation?"

I chuckled. "Good one."

"It sounds like a crazy thing, but I'm serious. I meditate. When I started, I could only do it five or six minutes at a time. Now I can knock out an hour or more before bed. It helps."

"Do you meditate before or after the cannabis oil?" I asked with a raise of my brows.

She grinned. "Depends on how hard the day has been."

I laughed and shook my head, but then I sobered. "How do you do this?"

"How do I do what?"

"Be an Old Lady? How do you sit around waiting for news? How do you not go completely crazy wondering if your husband is going to come home alive?"

She paused as she played with the label on her beer. "You're really not going to like my answer, Linden. But I'm going to tell it to you straight anyway. I just do it. You become a part of the community. You find your hobbies; you find your passions. You find your friends. You have children." She smiled. And you just…deal with it."

"You're right. I don't like your answer."

She chuckled.

"My career means everything to me," I said. "My career is my passion. I don't know what I'm going to do if I can't do that anymore."

Darcy took a sip of her beer. "There was never anything else you wanted to do?"

I shook my head. "Never thought I was going to have to entertain the idea that I'd have to do something else. I'm afraid it'll make me bitter. If I can't practice medicine, everything I've ever worked for is gone."

"Only if you let it be that way." She paused. "Do you like kids?"

"In theory. Why?"

She shrugged. "Just wondering if you were thinking about going down that path."

"I haven't given it much thought," I admitted. "Are you glad you had kids?"

"Mostly."

I snorted. "Mostly?"

"I'm not going to sit here and tell you I was destined to be a mom. They're challenging at the best of times. But they light up my soul in a way nothing else does. I'm not saying you should have kids or that they need to be your reason for living. And I'm not saying they can replace what you've worked for. I'm just saying, when one door closes, sometimes another opens. Life is odd that way."

"Thanks," I said. I took a long drink of my beer. "I don't even know if Boxer wants a family. His dad was a real jerk."

"I think he'd make a great father," she said with a smile.

I sighed. "Yeah, I think he'd make a great one, too."

"Are you worried about having kids because of the biker thing?" she asked pointedly.

I shook my head.

"Really?"

"Really," I insisted. "I'm worried about having kids because I'm afraid I'm going to be no good at it."

"Oh, you'll fail for sure," she said.

"Hey!"

She laughed. "No, I didn't mean it that way. I meant, as a mother, you're constantly worried that you're screwing up your kids. But so long as they're healthy and happy, you're doing fine."

"It's not that simple, is it?"

"Why does it have to be complex?"

"I guess it doesn't," I allowed. "My parents screwed me up royally."

"Have you forgiven them for it?"

I sighed. "I'm trying. I don't know if it's working."

"Drink more beer. It helps."

"But I don't like chili!" Lily whined.

"Yeah, and beans make me fart," Cam added.

I coughed into my napkin as Darcy glared at her children.

"I told you not to talk that way at the dinner table," Darcy admonished.

"Can I have another bowl?" Silas asked.

"Kiss up," Cam said to him.

"*Hey*," Darcy warned. "Thin ice, buddy."

"Hard pass," I muttered.

"What was that?" Joni asked.

"She said *hard pass*," Rachel said with a raise of her brows.

"Er—I'll explain later." I looked at Lily, who was scooping chili out of her bowl and not too discreetly feeding it to Captain, Silas's rag-tail mutt.

"Fine. Today, the heathens win," Darcy said. "Peanut butter and jelly it is."

"Yippee!" Lily yelled.

The rest of us ate our chili, which by all accounts was delicious.

"Crow missed his calling," I said. "Forget being a biker. He should open his own restaurant. He's a stellar cook." The prospect hadn't just made us chili, but homemade bread to go with it.

"Some woman is going to be really lucky when she nabs him," Mia said, rising from her chair at the kitchen table. She went to the sink and leaned over, placing her hand on her belly.

"Mia?" I asked. "You okay?"

My question drew everyone's attention, except for Lily

who was badgering Darcy for creamy peanut butter instead of crunchy.

"Yeah, I'm fine." Her face was pinched, and her cheeks were white with pain.

Joni and I exchanged a look before both of us rose from the table.

"How long," I demanded.

"How long what?" Mia repeated.

"How long have you been having contractions?" Joni asked.

"They're not contractions," Mia negated. "Just Braxton Hicks."

"Are you sure?" I asked. "Are *you* a medical professional?"

She glared at me.

"Tell the truth," Joni said.

"I wasn't feeling them when we were driving here," she promised. "But after I woke up from my nap, they started."

"Where's the nearest hospital?" I asked.

"About an hour away," Rachel said. "We're in the middle of nowhere."

"I'm not due for another few weeks," Mia complained.

"Baby has other plans," I said, snapping into doctor mode. I looked at Joni. "I'll go with her to the hospital."

"Ah, fuck a duck. I think my water just broke," Mia said.

"You said a bad word!" Silas said, eyes widening.

"Don't panic," I said.

"South Paw can take you two in my car," Joni said, handing me the keys.

Mia bent over and struggled through the pain. When a contraction cleared, I took her by the elbow and helped her to the door.

"Are you going to be okay?" Silas asked, fear coating his voice as he ran to Mia.

She placed a hand on his head and forced a smile. "I'm going to be fine. Your sister is just as stubborn as her father it seems, and clearly wants to meet you early."

Silas grinned and gently wrapped his arms around Mia.

Crow and South Paw were sitting on the porch, and they both jumped up when they heard the front door to the cabin crash open.

"What's going on?" Crow asked.

"Mia's in labor," I said. "South Paw is going to drive us to the nearest hospital."

"Fuck, Colt is gonna kill me," South Paw muttered as he took the car keys from me.

"Why is Colt going to kill you?" Mia asked. Crow went to her other side and helped her down the stairs.

"Because he told me he'd kill me if you went into labor early."

"That's not your fault. That's his daughter's fault. He can take it up with her when he gets back. You're not to contact him on the satellite phone," she commanded. "Promise me."

"I promise," South Paw said.

"You too, Crow. Promise me."

"I promise," Crow relented.

South Paw got Mia settled in the front seat, and then I quickly got into the back. South Paw and I attempted to keep up a steady stream of mindless chatter, but it was always interrupted by Mia's heavy breathing and groans of pain from her contractions. I began to time them. They went quickly from five minutes apart to three.

As we pulled up to the hospital, her contractions were only ninety seconds apart.

"You sure hit the labor ground running," I said with a smile.

"I was born early and fast. This is all genetic," Mia explained. "Now that we're back in cell service, I need to call my doctor and let her know."

Mia was admitted quickly. South Paw remained in the waiting area, but I sat with her in the exam room.

"Thanks for coming with me," she said softly.

"Oh. Yeah, of course. I didn't even think that maybe you'd want one of the other Old Ladies. I'm sorry if I—"

She shook her head. "I like your bedside manner. And you're a doctor. I'm glad you're here."

I looked down at my hand that was in a cast.

"You're coming in with me, right?" Mia asked. "To the delivery room?"

"You're sure?"

She nodded.

"I'd be honored to be in the delivery room with you," I assured her.

"I'm scared," she admitted.

"I know."

"I think you should procreate with Boxer."

"What is it with you guys? You want everyone knocked up?"

"The next generation," she said. "I love the idea of a huge family with tons of kids running around laughing and playing." She paused and shook her head. "I keep seeing Lily as a young woman, and I keep imagining that moment she brings home a guy for the first time. And all her tattooed uncles give him hell and send him running."

I laughed. "That's such a clear visual."

"Don't you want to be around to see that?"

I paused for a moment, and then I nodded. "Yeah. I do."

She braced for pain, breathing through it. When it was over, she leaned back, exhausted.

An hour later, they wheeled Mia into the delivery room. She was ready to give birth to her daughter. I donned a pair of scrubs and took my place next to Mia.

"Okay," the doctor said, smiling behind her mask. "During this next contraction, give me a *big* push."

Mia nodded. The dark hair at her temples was damp with sweat, and her face was wreathed in exertion. When the next contraction hit, she clamped down and gripped the nurse's hand.

The contraction passed, and Mia collapsed against the bed.

"You're doing great," I told her with a smile. I looked at the doctor, and even though half her face was concealed, I'd spent the better part of a decade reading facial expressions behind masks. And I knew the doctor was worried.

Mia shrieked.

She was feeling everything, because by the time we'd gotten to the hospital, it had been too late for an epidural.

After another push that failed to yield any results, Mia wised up and looked at the doctor. "What's going on? What's wrong?"

"The baby is breech," the doctor said. "We need to deliver her as quickly as possible."

"Okay…" Mia said weakly, appearing afraid of what was coming next.

"When I say push, you push as hard as you can. With all your might. Do it for your baby, Mia, push *hard* when I tell you."

Mia nodded and shot me a look of fear.

"We got this," I told her. "I'm not going anywhere. You can do this. Do what the doctor says."

"Okay, Mia," the doctor said. "Now!"

Mia pushed and then let out a scream that chilled my blood.

"Give me one more good push, and she'll be here. Come on, push!"

Mia clamped down and gave it her all, and moments later, her daughter was born. With a cry of relief, Mia fell back against the bed, her eyes on the doctor as she placed the newborn child against Mia's chest so they could bond for a few moments before the umbilical cord was cut.

"How do you feel?" I asked her when the nurse took the baby to be cleaned and swaddled.

"Exhausted," Mia said with a tired laugh. "And elated."

"What's her name, Mom?" the doctor asked, removing her gloves and tossing them in the trash and then pulling down her surgical mask to smile at Mia.

"Scarlett," Mia said immediately. "Scarlett O'Banion Weston."

"Beautiful," the doctor said.

When we were back in Mia's recovery room, she said, "I miss her. Is that weird? She was just inside me, and I actually miss her already." She began to cry, so I did the only thing I could do. I crawled into her hospital bed and hugged her.

Mia fell asleep, and I quietly padded from the hospital room, in desperate need of caffeine. I went to the waiting room and told South Paw all was well and that there was a new Tarnished Angel baby.

He swept me into his arms and spun me around. The pressure on my bandage made my brand twinge, but I couldn't stop the gurgle of laughter from escaping my lips.

And just like that, a new life had begun.

# Chapter 35

I FELL asleep in the chair next to Mia's hospital bed, only to be awakened by the opening of the door. The nurse wheeled in the baby to be fed.

"I'll leave," I said, rising. "To give you some privacy."

"Stay," Mia insisted. "I don't mind. Really."

I sat back down, a tender smile creeping across my face when I saw Mia's enraptured gaze peering at her newborn daughter.

After a few moments of quiet while Scarlett nursed, Mia said, "I know what you're going through."

"What are you talking about?" I asked in confusion.

"Aftermath. From your trauma."

"How can you know about aftermath? Were you tortured? Did all your dreams go up in smoke?"

She looked up to meet my gaze. "No. Nothing like that. But I *do* know what it's like to lose something important. And I know what it's like to want revenge. Like you do."

My blood ran cold as she stared at me, seeing below the surface.

"How do you—"

"Boxer."

"He told you? After all that crap about Old Ladies not allowed to know anything about club business?"

"Boxer was losing his shit over what happened to you. I nagged him into confiding in me. Colt doesn't even know that I know."

I paused, digesting her words. "So you wanted revenge," I repeated. "Did you get it?"

"No."

"Why not?"

"Because it didn't happen that way for me."

"Do you regret the outcome?"

"Every damn day," she admitted quietly. "But I've learned to live with it."

"How?"

"I didn't have a choice." She bit her lip, her brow furrowed in thought. "Boxer told me what you asked the club."

"Are you going to try and talk me out of it?"

She shook her head. "No. I was going to tell you to look that fucker in the eye when you end him."

My gaze widened.

"Boxer loves you, but you already know that. You wanting to carry this out...well, it proves to him you're Old Lady material, through and through."

"Should I feel guilty? About wanting to kill a man? Being what I am—a doctor who's supposed to save lives?"

"Eye for an eye or turn the other cheek," she said. "But if you ride with the Tarnished Angels, you know which one to choose. So no, Linden. Don't feel guilty. Don't feel guilty at all. And when you kill Dante, it won't just be your revenge, but revenge for all his victims."

A weight lifted off my heart. "Thanks, Mia."

She smiled softly. "Grab yourself a cup of coffee. You're dragging."

I did as she suggested and then went to check in on South Paw who hadn't left the hospital. He wouldn't until he was driving us back to the cabins to wait for the Tarnished Angels to wrap up their business in Mexico.

My heart ached to hold Boxer, to touch him, to ensure he was alive. I missed his teasing presence, his masculine assurance that he would give me the moon if I asked for it. And then my mind began to turn over so many things.

Could a man be both a storm and a lighthouse? A danger and a safe haven?

Seeing Mia cradling her newborn daughter had changed me. It was the first birth I'd witnessed that was personal. Mia hadn't been a patient. She was a friend, and she'd brought new life into this world.

I wanted that, I realized. I wanted a family. I wanted it all. The happiness, the devastation, the milestones, the ups and downs, and everything in between.

Something inside of me settled, a clarity that I'd been sorely lacking.

If I could never practice medicine again, a piece of me would die. But I'd find a way to be reborn. I'd find a way to give back, to contribute, to love something enough that would light up my soul and make life worth living again.

For the first time since being kidnapped, I felt hope.

Two days later, Mia and the baby were discharged from the hospital. Mia sat in the back seat next to Scarlett, who'd been strapped into a carrier that South Paw had run out to buy. And when we returned to the cabins, it was to tears and cheers. The kids clambered around Mia, wanting to get a peek at the new baby.

Darcy unscrewed a bottle of water and handed it to Mia. "Linden? Do you want a beer?"

"I'm good. I just want a shower." I wrinkled my nose.

"I'll wrap your hand," Rachel offered.

After I showered, I towel dried my hair, marveling at how little I had to do with it. Though I liked what Darcy had done, I couldn't wait to grow it out again. For me, long hair symbolized luxury. Decadence. Feminine beauty.

I wouldn't let Dante take that from me.

The Old Ladies were waiting on Mia hand and foot, and she was protesting and laughing at their antics. "I'm fine, guys, really."

"You've got an ice pack between your legs," Rachel pointed out. "We're more than happy to help you."

Darcy grabbed me a beer before raising her own. "To Scarlett, the newest member of the pack."

"To Scarlett," the Old Ladies chimed and then downed their drinks—most of which were nonalcoholic.

Mia raised her bottle of water toward me. "To Linden. For being there every step of the way."

"To Linden, the newest Old Lady," Joni added.

"To Linden," Rachel said with a smile, "who is now one of us."

My throat constricted with emotion, and I raised my beer. "To you guys. My tribe."

Crow had made a pulled pork with homemade coleslaw and potato salad for dinner. Even Lily, who was a picky eater, ate it with gusto.

"Where did you learn to cook this way?" I asked him.

"My mom owns a restaurant in New Orleans."

The way he said New Orleans came out *Nawlins*, and it made me smile.

Rain began to fall, and we all bedded down with sleeping bags and air mattresses instead of returning to our separate cabins, all of us wanting to stay close to one another. Even the prospects came in. The infants woke up several times, needing to be fed and changed, but it wasn't a disturbance. Most of us weren't falling into a deep sleep; there was a collective emotion floating through the cabin, as if we were all tapped into the same consciousness, waiting for the news about our family.

We got it in the middle of the night with the rumble of several motorcycles.

"They're here," Joni whispered.

I lifted myself off the couch. Crow and South Paw were already awake. One of them turned the lights on.

Darcy groaned and shielded her eyes. "A little warning next time."

"The guys are home," I said to her.

She instantly snapped to attention and got up, extracting herself from between her two kids that were sharing her queen-sized air mattress. She looked at her watch. "It's four in the morning."

"Better put on the coffee," Allison said, wiping a hand across her tired face.

I went out onto the porch, wrapping my arms around myself to stay warm. The rumble of bikes became a roar. Even in the dark of the night, the cabin porch lights were bright enough to illuminate the Tarnished Angels' faces.

I searched for Boxer and found him in the middle of the pack. He parked, cut off the engine to his motorcycle, and climbed off. I ran to him, my flip flops sinking into mud. I threw myself at him, and he caught me in the air. I breathed in the smell of him. The leather and oil, the scent of his skin from days on the road.

"You came back," I whispered.

"Damn right I did," he said, his mouth searching for

mine. His tongue plunged between my lips, and we fused together like two souls reuniting.

When he pulled away, he stared into my eyes. "Not all of us came back, Linden."

I stepped back and looked around. I saw Colt, Gray, Zip, Torque, and several of the Coeur d'Alene boys.

"Reap!" Rachel yelled, coming down off the porch. "Where's Reap?" She ran a hand through her hair pushing it from her eyes as she searched for her husband.

"He was shot, Rach," Colt began as he approached her. "He didn't make it."

"No," she whispered. "No!"

She would've fallen to the ground if Colt's strong arms hadn't come around her. I immediately ran to her, but she pulled out of Colt's embrace to face me.

"Get the hell away from me!" she screamed.

I halted.

She turned and sprinted up the porch steps, pushing between Darcy and Joni, and disappearing inside.

My heart broke for her.

The brothers' faces were somber, and tears began to cascade down the cheeks of the Old Ladies. I looked to Boxer. "Who else," I asked, my voice barely above a whisper. Rachel's heartache tore at me, splitting open the guilt I'd attempted to contain.

"Bishop, too." Boxer said, tone bleak, and then he pitched his voice lower. "We got Dante. He's out cold right now." He gestured to the van that was parked behind the brigade of motorcycles.

"He came at a price," I said quietly. "A terrible price."

I flung myself into his arms again, wanting him to take away the pain, but I also wanted to take away his.

"Where's my wife?" Colt asked gruffly.

"Inside with your newborn daughter," Joni said. She'd

moved from the porch to Zip and was now nestled in his side.

Colt looked shell-shocked. "My what?"

"Mia went into labor a few days ago," I said. "I went with her to the hospital. Both mother and baby are doing fine."

Colt paused and then dashed up the steps into the cabin.

"Fuck, I need a drink," Zip muttered.

"Same," Knight said. The president of the Coeur d'Alene chapter looked beaten and sad. He'd been close with his VP and their chapter suffered a great loss.

The men with children went inside to see them, leaving the rest of us to fend for ourselves.

Boxer and I headed to the pit where he lit a fire.

"She's going to blame me," I said when Boxer took a seat next to me.

Boxer drank from the bottle of bourbon and then handed it to me. "It had to be this way, Linden. We couldn't let the cartel get away with kidnapping women and children, let alone going after one of our own. We knew there was a possibility of losing a brother. Losing several. But that was the risk we had to take."

I took a sip from the bourbon bottle and then handed it back to him. "I know. I just—Christ. Reap didn't deserve this. Neither did Rach. She's pregnant, Boxer. How is she going to get through this?"

"She has us. And we'll be there for her." He paused for a moment. "He died in my arms."

I closed my eyes.

"I held him as he took his last breath. The blood at his lips. The light leaving his eyes. He knew he was dying, and his last word was his wife's name." He lifted the bottle and took a hearty swig.

"Bishop?"

"Knife to the ribs by one of Dante's men. Knight went apeshit. Like full-on apeshit. I've never seen him that way."

I didn't know what to say, so I said nothing.

"So, Mia had her kid."

"Yeah."

"Of course she did." He shook his head and downed more bourbon.

"Her name is Scarlett."

"After Mia's mother," Boxer explained. "Thank God for a little bit of happiness in this shit storm called life."

I hated that my friend was hurting. I hated that Reap and Bishop had died—even though it had been for a cause. I hated that it never seemed like things were going to get better.

"What happens now?" I asked. "With Dante?"

"First we drink. And then," his expression was grim, "execution."

One by one, the brothers joined us. Some of them sat on logs, others in camp chairs. We all drank as though booze could banish ghosts.

The prospects remained out front to guard the van that held Dante captive. The Old Ladies remained inside with the children, so at least there were no questions being asked.

We watched the flames flicker and dance in melancholic silence.

Even though Colt was a new father, he didn't have the elation one would expect. Under the circumstances, I didn't blame him. He paced back and forth, looking up at the clear sky every now and again. Finally, he took the empty chair next to me.

"Should I go inside?" I asked Boxer. "Leave you guys to talk?"

He shook his head and grasped my thigh. "Stay."

I was glad. I didn't feel comfortable going into the cabin and lending my support to Rachel. Not when I felt responsible for what had happened. I was sure the other Old Ladies would blame me, too.

"Thank you," Colt said to me.

"For what?" I asked in surprise.

"Staying with Mia while she was in the hospital. And being there while she delivered. Fuck, I can't believe I missed Scarlett's birth." He shook his head and hung his neck in shame.

"Stop," Zip said. "All of you fuckers need to stop. That includes you, Linden."

"Did you just call me a fucker?" I demanded.

"Yes," he said. "You're a fucker."

"Brother," Boxer began. "Do not make me fight you. I'm in no mood."

"None of us are," Zip said. "That's the point. This shit with the cartel isn't Linden's fault. She's a victim caught up in this bullshit. Reap and Bishop dying isn't Linden's fault." He looked at me. "Do you hear me?"

I nodded slowly.

"Those bastards were taking women and children," Knight seethed. "We did what needed to be done. We knew the risks. Reap and Bishop died for something real. So, we need to honor them the way they are meant to be honored." He rose from his seat. "I was already a brother when Bishop was nothing more than a prospect hoping to patch in. He gave it his all. In everything he did. Some thought he was too young to be my vice president, but he proved them wrong. He carried the weight of responsibility with ease."

Colt stood, a bottle in his hands. "Reap was a tough son of a bitch and as ruthless as they come. But he laughed from the belly and said fuck you to death. He lived free, loved hard, and there will be a piece of him left in this world with the birth of his child. I'm honored to call both Bishop and Reap my brothers."

The president of the Coeur d'Alene chapter raised his bottle of bourbon in the air. "To our fallen brothers. Fucking heroes."

"Fucking heroes," the brothers chimed in unison.

And then we drank to the memory of good men.

After the informal eulogies, we left the cabins. The prospects stayed behind with the Old Ladies and children.

The sun was just creeping up when I hopped on the back of Boxer's bike, a small bag slung across my shoulder. I wrapped my arms around him, and he drove us through the woods on a dirt road that no motorcycle belonged on.

A while later we came to a clearing. The brothers parked their bikes at the edge of the glade, and Acid cut the engine of the van. Colt and Knight ripped open the back doors of the vehicle and hauled Dante out by his arms, which were bound behind his back. A hood covered his head.

My torturer fell to the ground.

He'd once been formidable and terrifying. Now, his white silk shirt was stained with blood, the sleeves torn, and he was the one at our mercy.

Boxer walked toward Dante's hooded form and gave

him a boot to the ribs. Dante let out an enraged, surprised bellow.

Zip and Acid dragged Dante to his knees and ripped off his hood so Dante could finally see. Dante's face was battered and bruised, his nose a jagged remnant of something that had once been handsome. It was shattered now.

But despite his situation, he smiled when he saw me.

"*Princesa*," he greeted.

My heart drummed in my ears, and I was frozen to the spot.

*Princess*.

My blood stewed. Any fear or hesitation about what I was planning to do vanished with that single word.

The Tarnished Angels stood in a circle around Dante, but their eyes were on me. Their bodies were taut with tension, their fists clenched. I knew they wanted to mete out their own justice before ending Dante's life, but they'd voted.

This was mine to do.

I set my shoulder bag onto the ground so I could pull out a small black pouch. I unzipped it to remove a syringe and a vial of clear liquid. Boxer came to my aid when he saw my struggle. He held the needle for me so I could pop off the cap before stabbing it in the rubber top on the glass vial. The syringe filled when I pulled back the plunger. I flipped the syringe over.

"Flick out the air bubbles," I said quietly to Boxer.

Dante began to laugh. "What do you have there? Morphine?"

"Yes," I lied.

"My little angel of mercy," he crooned.

"Turnabout is fair play, don't you think? You tortured me. They're going to torture you."

He began to fight against his ties, even though it was futile.

Boxer handed me the syringe and then marched forward to pummel a fist into Dante's jaw. Dante's face snapped to the side, and he groaned in pain.

"We can do this with or without the morphine," I said to Dante. "They'll rip you apart either way. Your choice."

Dante spit blood onto the ground. No doubt Boxer had broken a few teeth with the force of his punch.

"Morphine," Dante gritted out. "I'll take the morphine."

"So weak," I tittered. "You almost take the fun out of breaking you."

I looked down at the bag on the ground. Boxer immediately returned to me and leaned down to remove the band. He stalked back over to Dante and wrapped it around the upper part of his arm. A meaty vein popped from his flesh almost immediately.

My heart drummed in my chest as I stalked forward and stabbed the syringe into him, plunging the liquid into his vein. It took nearly thirty seconds for the potassium chloride injection to hit his system. His body seized and he gasped for air, but his heart wasn't getting enough oxygen.

I wanted him to see me before he died, so I came around to face him. I smiled and said in Spanish, "Angel of mercy? Fuck you, I'm the Angel of Death. Enjoy hell, Dante."

I stood at the edge of the lake and stared across its silvery, glittering surface. The afternoon sun rays bounced off the placid water, but I knew things lurked in the cool murky shadows beneath.

Everyone had left the cabins. Everyone except Boxer and me.

We were taking a few days for ourselves.

"Linden?" Boxer asked from somewhere behind me.

I took a deep breath. "He ruined so many lives," I said after a long while of silence. "Rachel's included."

"Yeah, he did."

"I don't have any regrets." I turned around and looked him in the eye. "But I'm feeling something. Something I'm not sure I have the words for."

Boxer nodded, his expression full of understanding. "I know."

"Can I even call myself a doctor now?" It was a rhetorical question that no one could answer except me.

I looked up at the sky. It was a clear day. Not a cloud in sight. Perfect.

I shook my head. "Is life just about losing more and more pieces of yourself?"

"You find new ones, Linden."

"Yeah, I guess you do." I frowned. "I thought I'd feel different."

"Different how?"

"Vindicated. I don't feel that. Not right now, anyway. Maybe I will later, but for now…"

"Now, you're just kind of living it, yeah?"

I nodded. "Processing. Making peace with who I am. Who I've become, I guess." My brow furrowed. "I thought I'd be able to take a deep breath about it. I thought I'd feel a twinge of guilt. I'm not feeling either of those things. If I had to name what I'm feeling, I'd say it was grief. But I'm not mourning him or the loss of his life. Or even that I was the one to end it. I think, I'm just mourning everything I used to be…because I'm not that anymore."

"No, you're not," he said slowly. "You're something different. That's okay, too."

"Thank you," I said to him.

"For what?"

"For loving me through all of this. For still wanting me."

He came to me and cradled my cheek in his hand to stare deep into my eyes. "You're my ride or die. I know that in my bones. I know you have the strength to be part of this life. Forever."

Boxer leaned down and kissed me. "Ride or die with me through life, Linden."

# Epilogue

*Several months later…*

I STUCK my key into the lock of the home I shared with Boxer and opened the front door. "What the hell?"

The hallway was lit with dozens of white candles, and the floor was scattered with linden flowers.

I set my keys on the foyer table, shut the door, and dropped my purse.

"Boxer?" I called out.

When there wasn't a reply, I followed the trail of flowers through the house and up the stairs to the bedroom.

"You've got to be kidding me," I said with a laugh.

Boxer stood completely naked, except for the leather bowtie around his neck.

He flashed a sexy grin. "I asked Joni and Mia's help with your proposal. They told me candles, flowers, and sex."

"What about food?" I inquired. "I heard food is part of a proposal."

"We're ordering pizza after I ravish you."

With a laugh, I ran to him and jumped into his arms. He caught me and then we fell to the bed.

"Damn, woman, I really love you," he said softly.

"Shut up and fuck me, Boxer."

"It'll be my pleasure."

His hands slowly peeled away my clothes, and then his lips covered every inch of my skin, lingering on the wounds that were healing. I'd gotten a Tarnished Angels logo tattoo on my upper left arm. I'd become addicted to ink. As soon as my brand was completely healed, I had plans to tattoo over it and make something beautiful from my pain.

I slid my fingers across the ink Roman had tattooed on his pectoral, right above his heart.

*Linden* in a big, bold font.

I couldn't wait to take him into my body. I rolled over onto my back, opened my legs, and welcomed him home.

Our mingled cries of pleasure echoed off our bedroom walls, our bodies slickened with sweat and pleasure, and when I tightened around him, I clasped him to me, not wanting to let him go.

After he came, he slid off me, and collapsed onto the mattress.

"So, you're gonna marry me, right? And make an honest man out of me?" Boxer asked. "I'm tired of giving away the milk for free."

I sat up and grinned. "I don't know. I kind of like living in sin."

"What will we tell our dog?"

"What dog?"

"The dog we're gonna adopt together. I want him to know his parents are in a loving, committed relationship."

I snorted. "Yeah, okay, I'll marry you. For the dog's sake."

"We're not very good at this romance thing, are we?"

I tucked a strand of hair that was growing out behind an ear. "Romance is overrated."

"You really are my perfect woman. You were born without a stitch of sentiment."

"Toss me your phone, I'll even order the pizza."

"A woman who can dial takeout. Sexy."

The last few months hadn't been easy. I was in counseling twice a week, still plagued by nightmares. And on the days I didn't have counseling, I was in physical therapy for my hand. It was slow going and extremely painful.

It was getting better, little by little. I didn't dare hope that I would get my full dexterity back, but Boxer reminded me to take it day by day, win by win.

The Old Ladies came by a few times a week to stock our fridge and catch up, but they never stayed long enough to exhaust me. I was lucky to have them in my life.

I'd spoken to Freddy a couple of times; she was still hanging out with her parents. I'd been the one to tell of her of Bishop's passing, and though she put on a brave face, I knew his death rattled her despite the casualness of their relationship.

Rachel had gone to stay with her mother in Wyoming, and she checked in with Mia every now and again. My voicemails to her were never returned. I hoped that changed soon. I'd be here when she was ready.

After I called the pizza in, I tossed his phone aside. "So, with a proposal, aside from sex and food, I was kind of hoping for a ring?"

"Right, a ring." Boxer got out of bed and pulled on a pair of briefs.

I frowned. "Where are you going?"

"Do you want your ring or not?" he asked.

"I might not be sentimental, but I do like sparkly things."

He opened the top drawer of the dresser and tossed me a T-shirt of his. I pulled it over my head and then found my underwear in my discarded jeans.

Boxer took my hand and linked his fingers through mine. We went down the stairs, and then we stopped in front of the half bath on the first floor. I heard something scratching at the wall.

He opened the door and a wiggly puppy shot out of the bathroom.

"A puppy!" I yelled in excitement, plopping my bottom down and reaching for the animal. "How did you know I wanted a yellow lab?"

"Just a lucky coincidence." He grinned. "I told you we were adopting a dog together."

"Yeah, you did. Nice surprise." I looked up at him and smiled.

A red bow fell off from around the dog's neck.

Boxer leaned down and picked it up. "Uh oh."

"Uh oh what?" I asked as the puppy collapsed into my lap and showed me its belly, which I happily gave a good rubbing.

"The ring was tied to the bow around his neck. And there's no ring."

I let out a laugh and then buried my nose in the puppy's belly. "Did you eat my ring?" He bathed my face with his tongue. "I think that was a yes."

Boxer sighed. "This is what I get for trying to be romantic."

I lifted the puppy into my arms and then stood. I kissed Boxer on the lips, and the puppy licked Boxer's cheek.

"This is the stuff of life, Boxer." I smiled up at him.

"And in case you didn't know? My answer is yes. Ride or die."

He grinned. "Ride or die."

**Thank you so much for reading Boxer and Linden's story. This isn't the end of the Tarnished Angels!**

**Slash and Brooklyn's story is next in *Madness & Mayhem!***

**Scan the QR code for more information.**

# Additional Works

The Tarnished Angels Motorcycle Club Series:

*Wreck & Ruin (Tarnished Angels Book 1)*
*Crash & Carnage (Tarnished Angels Book 2)*
*Madness & Mayhem (Tarnished Angels Book 3)*
*Thrust & Throttle (Tarnished Angels Book 4)*
*Venom & Vengeance (Tarnished Angels Book 5)*
*Fire & Frenzy (Tarnished Angels Book 6)*
*Leather & Lies (Tarnished Angels Book 7)*
*Heartbeats & Highways (Tarnished Angels Book 8 -
pre-order)*

## SINS Series:

*Sins of a King (Book 1)*
*Birth of a Queen (Book 2)*
*Rise of a Dynasty (Book 3)*
*Dawn of an Empire (Book 4)*
*Ember (Book 5)*

*Burn (Book 6)*
*Ashes (Book 7)*
*Fall of a Kingdom (Book 8)*

Others:

*Peasants and Kings*

# About the Author

*Wall Street Journal & USA Today* bestselling author Emma Slate writes romance with heart and heat.

Called "the dialogue queen" by her college playwriting professor, Emma writes love stories that range from romance-for-your-pants to action-flicks-for-chicks.

When she isn't writing, she's usually curled up under a heating blanket with a steamy romance novel and her two beagles—unless her outdoorsy husband can convince her to go on a hike.

Made in the USA
Coppell, TX
03 September 2024

36754222R00256